MW00341623

Modulus

RTRomero

Copyright © 2013 Richard T. Romero
No part of this document or the related files may be reproduced or transmitted in any form, by any means (electronic, photocopying, recording, or otherwise) without the prior written permission of the publisher.

Revision: April 2014

ISBN: 978-0-9898689-0-7

Dedication:
To Laura my sweetheart,
to my children Eva, Jessica, and Logan.

With heartfelt thanks to my editors
Jessica Koch, Laura Kassoy,
and Senior Editor Warren Weiner,
and to my alma mater,
Saint Mary's College of California.

Contents

Chapter 1: Atrocity

A wholly unwelcome howl of sirens broke through the morning chill outside the Alliance Reserve Hall at Porter's Field, surprising everyone.

The families already gathered in the hall's gymnasium for the annual Midwinter Holiday breakfast were dismayed, and braced themselves for the worst. They recognized the loud, wavering warble as an alert. A rising wail would have sent them to shelter underground, in the hardened bunker.

The base moved to high alert, sending pilots to the ready room while their ground crews rolled out to prepare the ships. With a sprinkling of hasty hugs and stolen kisses, the pilots hustled to the briefing room. The families left behind busied themselves straightening the hall and packing up the food for the pilots' return. Hopefully they could resume their holiday festivities after the drill.

It was the wrong weekend for a drill, and Steve felt uneasy as he double-timed with the rest of the pilots. As senior NCO he would have heard about any scheduled drill, and would have tried to get it rescheduled until after the holiday. To his knowledge there had been nothing of the sort planned.

In the ready room the pilots were informed this was indeed not a drill.

The duty officer told them "A heavy cruiser, using an unrecognized identification transponder, is approaching our planet. According to our system registry log she didn't transit the modulus."

The officer watched the pilots sternly while they digested that information. He didn't blame them for being agitated, but he had to lay out the few facts he had quickly. The questions raised were too many. How had this warship entered the system? It could have come from nowhere except through the modulus. The sentry boats reported no recent military traffic, and the patrols at the modulus maintain continuous monitoring. The cruiser must have come from out-system, but arriving without a transit of the Al Najid modulus was impossible.

The duty officer continued: "However it got here, the meteorologists aboard the northern orbital weather station have reported that the cruiser is deploying a picket of interceptors. The ship has failed to respond to emergency communications on any channel. The cruiser will be presumed hostile until it provides identification with an explanation of intent."

The thought that any great power capable of deploying a capital ship would attack their planet seemed absurd, yet there was no responsible alternative other than accept the unexplainable and prepare for the worst. Perry, the third planet in the Al Najid planetary system, was a simple, under-populated, agrarian world in the middle of nowhere. Mining and light manufacturing were almost all conducted off the planet in the asteroid belt. The planet had no known enemies powerful and wealthy enough to field a capital ship.

Criminals might occasionally infiltrate the system, pretend to be traders or miners, and then lurk among the asteroids waiting to commit piracy on commercial traffic, but the system defense force could combat that.

Not a capital ship.

In his day job Steve served as the local sheriff. He kept himself trim and fit. He had been recruited while still in active duty status. After mustering out into the Reserves he came to Perry to work directly for the Grange. Landholders paid his salary and funded his operations to solve conflicts and to moderate disputes fairly. When successful his efforts permitted everyone else to focus on farming and all the infrastructure that industry required. Steve's deputy, Kyle, was also in the ready reserves, and flew as Steve's wingman.

Kyle was a little shorter and more wiry than Steve. Where Steve was normally thoughtful and soft spoken, Kyle was more spontaneous and outspoken. They each enjoyed making one another laugh.

Kyle's eyes met Steve's as they rose to grab flight kits from their lockers, gear up and head for the launch apron. "So much for a new Hollywood holo" said Kyle with a wry grin. Everything else about his mien showed him just as worried as Steve felt.

The planet's defenses didn't include any warships, let alone anything that could stand up to a cruiser. Perry couldn't afford more than a few scattered flights of small in-system fighters supplemented by a detachment of heavier attack craft assigned to the Al Najid system by ACM Joint Systems Command.

The ACM represents an alliance of Al Najid, Cygnus, and Mazzaroth, three solar systems linked together by moduli. Cygnus also provides a second modulus linked to Arcturus and the rest of explored space.

The ACM's four F/A Strikers would be joining them, able to launch credible anti-ship missiles. It was all the defense the frontier planet could afford. So far their firepower handled all challenges, but this new threat represented something completely abnormal. A heavy cruiser possessed far greater kill power than the system could reasonably hope to match, let alone defeat.

Not that the Reservists wouldn't try.

Traffic through the modulus was normally monitored by patrols charged with inspections, tariffs, and transit safety. They were tightly controlled to minimize the potential for corruption. Al Najid System Command sent one of the patrol craft through the modulus into Cygnus system to broadcast an official distress call. By law and custom such a distress signal required an immediate response, and would be relayed through connecting moduli. Any available military ship in nearby systems would respond to the distress call, and all civilian craft would steer clear.

The frontier worlds were universally careful to avoid false alarms because of the expense involved in an all-points response. Trade was too important to permit interruption.

As he hustled to get ready, Steve had to assume the worst. He mentally sorted through his pilots: who was quick thinking, who was more organized, who was more reliable, and who would bear watching when the pressure was on.

Perry's defending fighters were only intended to police their own system and keep the trade-routes between Perry, the Al Najid asteroid belt, and the modulus safe for commerce.

Unopposed a hostile cruiser could inflict serious damage to the planet, and it would take a miracle to hold off the cruiser until outside help arrived. Steve desperately hoped the intrusion represented some kind of misunderstanding, but didn't really believe it. Unopposed it could easily destroy everything Steve's adopted people had built.

Steve regulated his breathing as he dashed across the concrete apron, his web and harness flopping around him. He felt he was getting old. He hustled to catch an ordinance sled about to head out toward the spacecraft revetments, the bunker emplacements that sheltered the ships against a surface explosion. The sled would get him to his ship much faster, and deliver him in much better condition.

As he rode he thought about his ex-wife Sandy and his children Stevie and Kathlyn. He pushed away the frustration she caused him by failing to respond to his calls for the last two weeks. His scheduled time with the kids was fast approaching and they needed to coordinate the pickup. Security regulations prohibited him from contacting Sandy during an Alert.

Steve pressed his precious memories into a protected part of his heart as he arrived at his fighter's revetment. He dismounted the sled and settled into his well-trained routine; external inspection of his fighter craft.

Steve's maintenance specialist audibly reported systems status off her electronic checklist, raising her voice against the chill buffeting wind and the rising howl of engines nearby. She then recited the ordnance load, and Steve electronically signed off on it.

The Technical Sergeant for the boat opened the canopy and helped Steve into his acceleration couch. Steve fingered his neck seals and settled his helmet into place. The sound and feel of the wind vanished, replaced only by the sound of his breathing. The sergeant secured Steve's interfaces, and double-checked the seal of Steve's helmet. The receiver of Steve's comm-set muted the sound of his breathing with a faint hum of white noise. Steve requested a comm check and received an immediate response from control. Before closing, sealing, and checking the integrity of the cockpit canopy, he verified that his bio support, inertial dampening, and fail-safe lifepod systems were each enabled.

Steve glanced over at Kyle and saw his boat's linefeed disengage and fall away. Steve's status board was lit green. He spotted some brightly colored wrapping paper in the cubbyhole: a midwinter gift from his Blue team counterpart. It looked like a bottle. Steve raised his eyes to the heavens. If caught with alcohol aboard, a pilot would have a real problem. Mentally, Steve toasted his benefactor with a wry grin.

Steve increased thrust, released brakes and rolled his fighter onto the runway with the rest of his flight. All four accelerated to lift off in tight formation. Steve's Head's-Up Display (HUD) was nominal, all other systems still showed green, and his landing carriage retracted correctly. On conventional thrust the flight rapidly ascended through the thick winter cloud cover into high atmosphere. Control filled them in on the invader's location and the latest intelligence estimate on the cruiser's intentions. Four landing craft had separated from what Command already named the 'black cruiser', but otherwise intel had no meaningful explanation.

After visual confirmation of the weather station's initial report, the recon flight fell silent. Then an agitated and unintelligible transmission from the northern orbital weather station terminated abruptly. The cruiser was undeniably *hostile*.

Other flights of the squadron joined Steve's as they raced across the continent and north across the equator into the high stratosphere. In unison the squadron ignited their disposable chemical boosters to attain relative vacuum and orbital speed.

The four transports from the black cruiser descended to the surface on the other side of the planet. One settled onto an uninhabited wilderness area, well inland. None landed near a population center or military installation. The other three submerged into the ocean. The landing sites formed an equilateral square twelve hundred kilometers to the side. No one had a clue what their tactic meant, but it violated sovereign territory. On the planet surface a platoon of Perry Guardsmen boarded a hopship transport to surround the inland landing site, and the only Coast Guard cutter on that lonely coast raced to check the nearest ocean landing.

Command also directed a pair of atmospheric fighters toward each landing site with kill orders, while Steve, Kyle, and the rest raced weapons-free toward the cruiser and her pickets, far above the planet in the primary radiation belt.

Although Steve's squadron was now above the atmosphere and taking full advantage of its ability to safely fly faster than 6,500 meters per second, time still seemed to crawl. Their four flights were in relative vacuum, but still too deep in the planet's gravity well to really kick up their speed. Their annihilation drives were significantly more powerful than the expendable chemical drives, but safety requires hard vacuum in the anti-matter annihilation chamber. Regulating the hydrogen feed would be rendered meaningless by any residual atmosphere: the ship and its pilot would have vaporized.

To keep his mind off his children, and to ignore the flutter in his stomach, Steve kept a constant check of his instruments. He watched his sensor interface as the squadron crept all too slowly across the digital map toward that pulsing bright oval onscreen that represented the cruiser. It helped maintain calm to report status in a professionally dispassionate voice. Steve noted some small blips separating from the cruiser's image on his sensor display. Then more and more blips appeared. She was deploying fighters.

"See that, Steve? At least we'll have something we can actually fight." Kyle's voice came over the comm.

Flight Commander Evans cut in, "No chatter, Kyle. Transition thrust to antimatter and discard the boosters. Steve, You and Kyle take the top. Delaney, you and Graham take the bottom. Evans and Hastings wing right, and we'll take left. We'll have the flight from the ACM Attack Squadron with us, and we need to keep them alive for a launch. Three minutes to launch."

Four F/A Tactical Strikers from the Joint Command detail pulled into their midst from behind, their big STS missiles looking lean and hungry as sharks. All four of the Striker pilots were female and well-trained professionals.

Steve checked his ordnance and other status lights once more, and again saw green lights all across the board. He felt as if he needed to pee, but it was only nerves. He quickly checked his vent tubing, just in case it became a necessity.

"Vampire!" someone called, and Steve's stomach lurched. The black cruiser, still far away, had launched a missile. The missile was not aimed at the squadron at all, but instead the trajectory angled down toward Perry, the planet they were trying to protect.

The opposing fighters entered range, and Steve focused on staying alive and protecting the Tactical Strikers.

A great flash from below compelled his eyes to the planet against his will. He tried to maintain his focus on the maneuvering fighters but something he saw beneath the blinding flash and its expanding shockwave riveted him.

Moments after the Tacticals launched their ordnance they broke off, and that missile fired from the cruiser exploded in high atmosphere over the four transports that had touched down. It was a nuke, triggering an electromagnetic pulse that reached all four landed transports simultaneously.

The unthinkable happened.

The surface of the planet began to dimple around the landing sites into hollow, rapidly expanding hemispheres, and the rest of the planet seemed to flow around them. The four expanding hemispheres punctured the surface of the planet itself, staying in place while the rest of the planet kept moving in solar orbit. The ground around and beneath the hollowing hemispheres behaved unnaturally, liquifying under the stresses. Around the four deepening depressions the planet crust rippled, ripped, and broke apart while moving at the planet's orbit speed.

The planet was tearing itself apart, and somewhere down there was Steve's family. Mouth agape, his mind stopped functioning. Helpless, he felt disembodied, and watched as the universe appeared in slow motion.

Someone howled mindlessly on an open comm. The enemy fighters also seemed completely surprised by the unbelievable sight of the planet's destruction. They didn't fire, didn't maneuver for position. Had they not been so surprised and transfixed by the cataclysm below Steve and the others would have been quickly destroyed as they coasted, stunned and helpless. The planet's defenders were at once unbelieving, astonished and outraged. Each gave primal voice to their shock and pain, an elemental protest that was all the response they could muster to the catastrophe they couldn't stop. Stricken with disbelief, and sudden, unexpected grief for their families and homes, their minds strained to deny what their eyes told them... wives, parents, daughters and sons, so full of innocence and curiosity, gone with neither warning nor mercy.

Then there was no more time: it was past. Though the shattered planet continued to crumble massively along in its orbital path, the time for shock and disbelief ended.

"Head's up, people!" was the last command from Colonel Evans. Their training snapped them back into action, but Col. Evans' fighter exploded as he took concentrated enemy fire from most of the approaching aggressors. His warning broadcast, monitored by enemy electronic warfare suites, had identified his location and singled him out as a leader. The enemy reacted accordingly.

If the Perry defenders somehow survived there may someday be time for grief. For the moment, it was all they could do to stay alive. Steve struggled to keep up with his own reflexes and maintain awareness of literally everything in the whirling madness of mortal combat. He needed to respond to threats, exploit openings, keep slipping past certain death and deliver it instead. The pilots, to a soul, fought like madmen.

For a while they really were.

The enemy cruiser, mission accomplished, started to withdraw into deep space behind a screen of quick and wicked fighters.

Through it all, the question 'Why?' hung in the background like black space itself. "Why?" is the last meaningful question for survivors in the grip of an incomprehensible disaster. But these survivors fought back any way they could. It didn't matter now how futile the fight might be. They fought desperately against reality itself, denying despair, and refusing hopelessness. For a few, the question was not "Why?" but "How?"

Steve remained coldly mindful in his anger, though his defense was frantic. There was neither time nor attention to waste on the irrelevant. Attempting to perfect his economy of motion and reaction speed, he sought the quickest and most efficient use of time and space. Though his arms tired he fought to move them faster, to find a shorter distance between his controls than the natural arc of his hands. His legs ached from the foot controls, and his abdominals cramped with nitrogen from the exertion. His shields returned to thirty percent, but they covered armor now pocked with impact craters seared in desperate moments of vulnerability. Moments ago his shields had been beaten down faster than they could regenerate, and his armor was eroded by the ferocity of the attack. He had to focus wholly on evasion then, reducing his power to weapons and increasing it to shields and thrust. But now his shields had regenerated. He pulled back on the controls, twisted a bit to port, and juiced the annihilator to throw off his opponent. Then he twisted more to port and hit the burners again to change his vector. He increased the power to his offensive weaponry, spun in motion to catch the bastard and fired a burst from his hardball cannons. His opponent's shields dropped a bit as he slipped in behind. The enemy fighter was moving too fast to stay inside Steve's turn, even with inertials, but that didn't stop him from trying to spin back on Steve and fire again. Steve jammed his controls hard over and hit the annihilator to jerk the ship out of his enemy's arc of fire. Steve twisted his ship bringing his lasers to bear on the other pilot's flank, firing fully powered coherent beams all along his opponent's side.

Steve desperately tried to pivot exactly equal to his target's trajectory, keeping him under his reticule as the beams chewed through shields and into the armor plating, igniting puffs of glowing metal where he hit. Steve's beams vaporized little hemispheres into his enemy's armor as the coherent light pulses diffused momentarily into small glowing clouds of molten metal particles, until they cleared away with acceleration.

Bearing in from the other side Kyle laid heavily into the enemy fighter, hammering away at the armor, keeping the shields depleted as Steve again wrenched his controls to get in another good shot. The enemy's armor glowed bright orange from the heat of their onslaught, with molten metal vapor expanding from his depleted armor.

The enemy pilot tried hard to evade, but he had few choices. Steve picked the vector he thought the pilot would choose and set up for the kill, and the fighter pulled right into Steve's sights. Steve fired both cannons and beams. The enemy hull popped as it jettisoned the lifepod. Kyle cussed a blue streak at the pilot, but Steve only looked toward the pod as it streaked toward the murderous black ship as that world killer accelerated massively away.

"Kyle, let's finish them off before they get away" Steve commed. He started to call in their few remaining pilots, but Kyle interrupted.

"Who the hell are these guys?" Kyle asked. As Steve glanced at his wingman another pair of enemy fighters appeared inbound.

"Evade!" Steve ordered, and Kyle reacted instantly, changing his orientation and firing thrusters with practiced skill.

Steve vectored away and boosted a two-second burn, then pivoted to loop back and hopefully get below and behind them for a strike. There was faint chatter coming in on the comm from some surviving defenders at the far end of the system. The communications channel was unclear, but they said something about the modulus. They reported something coming through, and Steve thought he heard one of them say 'cruiser'. Another one? A dread sensation fluttered somewhere around Steve's liver as he focused once more on the immediate fight. Instead of engaging, the two enemy fighters swept past, clearly attempting to rendezvous with their main body. The black cruiser accelerated on a course that would take it into an unpopulated region of the system, out of normal scanning range. Yet to leave the system they should have been heading toward the heavily-traveled region near the modulus. Steve had no time to waste wondering, but was unavoidably puzzled.

"Let's get 'em!" came Kyle's voice. Steve accelerated in pursuit, aligning where he anticipated the two fighters would be in a few seconds. He disengaged his inertia dampening and hit the annihilator heavily, pressed back into his acceleration cushion. The boat responded, rocketing him forward. It was a dangerous move. The sudden acceleration reduced his maneuverability, but it was the only way to propel him back into range. Steve looked over and saw Kyle had reached the same conclusion at virtually the same time.

The sudden acceleration pushed them within range. Steve choked off the hydrogen feed to the annihilator. Inertia still carried him faster than his unboosted top speed as he opened up on the trailing pilot with cannons. His ammo telltale lit up as his remaining cannon ammunition dropped to a hundred rounds. Now finally within effective range for his beams, Steve let the guns fall silent to depend on his lasers. A glance at his meters told him his shield capacitors were above safe capacity and he needed to discharge energy anyway.

Kyle, also low on ammo, fired the rapid pulses of his light lasers. Between them they had the shields of the nearest fighter down to about ten percent before he finally turned to engage them. The other fighter raced ahead, trying to reach the black cruiser while his wingman bought him time.

As the enemy fighter pivoted back toward Kyle and Steve, the pilot burned some hydrogen, trying to get behind the pair. If Steve and Kyle countered by pivoting, the maneuver would let his wingman escape. Steve cut his thrust and pivoted, engaging inertia dampening and setting his maneuvering thrusters to seventy percent to optimize the available energy for both weapons fire and shield regeneration. Getting the enemy again into his sights he opened up with both beams and cannon, quickly depleting the enemy shields to zero. The enemy's armor plating lit up with hot puffs of vaporized metal. Down to seventy cannon rounds Steve let his cannons fall silent and struck the fighter with only his beams.

The enemy hadn't been just taking damage. He was laying into Steve's shields with everything he had. The dogfight continued, but Steve's fifteen percent shields and fifty percent armor certainly over-matched his opponent.

Then Kyle, who had continued pursuit of the other pilot, commed that he was about to pod. He also warned there were enemy fighters returning from the black ship.

Steve's target deployed his lifepod before the hull popped, and he spun around to get eyes on Kyle and the approaching swarm. He saw the strobe of Kyle's pod as it accelerated past him toward the wreckage of the planet. With the entire planet now a vast asteroid field of fragmented magma, Steve wondered where Kyle's lifepod would end up.

The returning enemy on sensors showed Steve he was hopelessly outnumbered, and they were too close to devote any more time to wondering about Kyle.

Chatter on the comm indicated the remnants of the Al Najid defense force were headed Steve's way, and with his shields nearly depleted Steve chose to try and regroup with them rather than flinging his rage at the enemy in a suicidal charge. So he oriented his ship toward his reinforcements and hit boost.

Unfortunately, the returning enemy fighters had replenished their fast and accurate missiles. Steve was already within their range. His HUD lit up with missile locks and the klaxon sounded the alarm. He launched the last of his decoys and began maneuvering in hope that he might be able shake a missile lock or two.

Then, with a deafening clang, the cratered shell of his ship cracked open to the final void.

Chapter 2: First Response

The Aldebari cruiser *Jade Temple* had been approaching Cygnus when the alert came through from Al Najid system, and immediately diverted to respond to the mayday as required by Interstellar Law. Passing commercial traffic turning back from their former course toward the Al Najid modulus, the *Jade Temple* prepared all-hands for an as-yet unknown emergency. All hands stood at their duty stations ready for either conflict or rescue. They loaded missile tubes and readied the ship's coherent energy and ballistic artillery batteries. Shields were up and their capacitors were warmed and waiting to absorb any hostile fire. A few ACM patrol craft formed up with her, but no other capital warships appeared within range to respond. Other than an appreciative electronic memo received from ACM Alliance Command on Cygnus, communications channels were clear of chatter. The *Jade Temple* passed through the modulus.

A stellar modulus is a very large and very ancient ring-like structure built long before humanity ever launched into space. Exactly how old they might be was unknown. Each modulus tames the violence of an anomaly in space. Anomalies occur where space has bent to overlap itself, merging distant points in space. Energy imbalances between these merged places surge and churn too violently to be safely traversed, but when asteroids pass through such an anomaly any iron in the stone is transmuted into an element with unique conductive properties. Humans have named this new element 'modulinium'. Modulinite can be refined into the metal modulinium, and modulinium is what the ancient 'moduli' are made of. Each of the fourteen discovered modulus rings moderates the energy in the anomaly it encircles and renders it safe for passage. Most known anomalies are not modulated and brood throughout deep space like great reddish-orange spheres.

Upon transit Tibs, the *Jade Temple*'s captain, could already see something wrong with the planet Al Najid III even before increasing magnification.

His second in command, Master Kinkaid, advised that energy weapon's fire had been detected near the planet.

"Increase our speed to flank, and set course for the fighting, Lu."

"As you say," Elder Lu, the master pilot acknowledged.

Magnification displayed the destroyed planet. The near side of the most intact hemisphere showed horrific devastation. The continents were obliterated by massive fragmentation. From their vantage point it was difficult to see, but the farther side of the planet appeared to consist of only planetoid-sized chunks and vast sprays of slowly moving stone and magma tumbling in space. The captain stared in awe and horror. He quickly looked up the former population and was appalled at what had to be the worst calamity in human history.

Sensors began picking up signs of wreckage from a significant number of small spacecraft. All weapons signatures had gone silent. "Scan for surviving lifepods." the captain ordered.

"Affirmative, One. Actively scanning," came the reply.

"Prepare recovery crews to retrieve flight records from these wrecks. I want to know what happened here."

"Affirmative, One"

"We also need to locate the planet's moons. I don't see them. When the planet broke up it lost it's center of gravity. Those moons could be anywhere, and I don't want to find either one of them the hard way."

Chapter 3: Awakening

Steve's consciousness roused to the curious sound of gurgling water. He laid on his back, unable to move. His face frowned in what felt like warm sunlight, and he tried to imagine where he could be. Had it all been only a nightmare? He listened intently and tried to remember.

"The ancient poet Li Po once observed that the sound of running water cleanses the mind," a quiet male voice said. It had a slight but unusual accent. Steve opened his eyes to see a blue sky and drifting clouds. The sound of water continued nearby. Steve decided it couldn't be a dream, but he was utterly confused.

"Welcome to the *Jade Temple*, pilot," the soft masculine voice said. Steve tried to turn his head to see who had spoken but could not move. The attempt to move made him wince.

"Please don't try to move quite yet, you are still under treatment for the injuries you sustained when your fighter was destroyed. The pod itself was damaged, and you with it. Reviewing your logs, you evidently tried to disable the safety triggers. Is it my imagination or were you attempting an impossible victory?"

The voiced paused and Steve remained silent. "Anyway, when I reviewed your flight recordings I decided I would like to meet such a pilot, and had you brought here to recover. The universe has been exceedingly gracious to allow us to find your pod, and you within it still alive."

"You cracked our flight record encryption?" Steve asked in alarm.

"We are the Aldebar, the Children of Science, descended from the first of those who rebelled against the plutocracy of Earth's Board of Corporations. Perhaps you have heard of us?"

This was surreal. "Alde...Where am I? You said this is some kind of temple?"

"You're aboard an Aldebari ship, the cruiser *Jade Temple*." Immediately Steve made the connection to the cruiser that destroyed his planet. It turned out a good thing he could not move, but as he lay there lashing out in his mind he realized the black cruiser had not had the lines of an Aldebari ship. Steve struggled to calm himself.

"We are still within Al Najid system, trying to discover the nature and cause of this cataclysm. The system's third planet, Perry, is completely destroyed. Its remnants are still orbiting the star, though the orbits of some large pieces have degraded and will eventually fall into Al Najid. We are convinced that it was not a natural disaster because of the wreckage we found, but I am at a loss to offer any explanation. Are you able at this time to submit to a debriefing? Your recollections might be of great aid in our efforts to solve this mystery."

Great: Steve thought. He had been rescued by Aldebari religious fanatics. He carefully remained poker faced, trying to hide his dismay. The Aldebar were human, of course, descended from the first scientific colonies of Earth following the discovery and transit of the first modulus. Those scientists rejected their allegiance to Earth when the Board of Corporations seized power and replaced the United Nations as the world's government.

Naturally, Earth didn't put it in quite those terms. A large mercenary expedition sent to retrieve the scientists eventually abandoned their contract and also rebelled. Earth had no immediate way to bring either group to heel. The Board of Corporations calculated the costs of forcing the Aldebari schism into line, and found it far exceeded projected trade benefits. Besides, they preferred to pursue more profitable options.

Earth's resources were strained to capacity just trying to build a new defensive fleet to ensure the rebellious forces would stay away. The Board of Corporations expected espionage could uncover those scientists' advances until such a time as Earth's population advantage rendered the value of the Aldebari scientists trivial. Yet over the years the Aldebar prospered, despite a horrific eviction from the Aldebaran system by the same mercenary force that later rebelled against corporate Earth. The Aldebari eventually developed a primarily space-borne lifestyle; developed an almost feudal system of governance; and became infamous for a religion based on the worship of the universe and the scientific method.

"Are there any other survivors?" Steve asked.

"There were twenty-seven other escape pods maintaining position near the remains of your planet, and all that we found have been recovered. Most of the pilots are already up and about, asking questions for which we don't have the answers, and requesting the use of our fighters. Sadly we do not have the specifications for your designs, and Aldebar spacecraft may prove... challenging for your pilots to master. Besides, whoever destroyed your planet appears to be gone, but not by way of the modulus."

Steve felt relief of a vague dread: he wasn't a man without a people. But who destroyed Perry, and why? "When I last saw the cruiser it was moving away from, not towards the modulus."

The gurgling in the background again piqued Steve's curiosity. He couldn't help but ask "What is that sound, like running water?"

"It's running water from the aerators, but why it gurgles here may take some explaining.

"Your injuries prevent you from looking around, but we built a garden in this ship. Some of it is holographic, such as the sky, but much of it is not.

"We Aldebar are a peculiar people, as I am sure you have heard." The voice chuckled musically. "To understand that sound you need to learn more of our history, and what we have learned. If I may introduce myself, my name is Tibs. I command the *Jade Temple*."

"I'm Steve Holbrook, Tibs."

"Ah: thank you, Steve. But to answer your question, long ago we realized that keeping our people trapped in the gravity well of a planet was tactically indefensible. We were and are confronted by space-traveling enemies. Any modest trawler could load a cargo net with asteroids and dive it, and its antimatter drive core, into the planet at great speed. The result would be devastation, though nothing so great as whatever destroyed Perry. But any weapon system that could counter even such a kinetic strike as I described would itself do great damage to a planetary ecosystem. There could be no effective protection. We learned thoroughly the hazards of living at the bottom of a gravity-well at the hands of a harsh teacher, now known as the Legion, when they bombarded our former home in Aldebaran system."

As the Aldebar spoke, the image of Perry's destruction welled up from memory. It felt to Steve like his throat had been tied in a knot.

Tibs continued: "But the Aldebari also found we had given up too much in leaving planetary life behind, even though it was best for our safety."

"We built our new habitats among the asteroids. The planet we first colonized gradually recovered from the Legion's bombardment, and has begun to flourish naturally once more, but our own minds began to wither in our unliving refuges among the stone fields of the void. Aberrant personality disorders grew too common. Almost all of us felt strangely alone, so completely outside any natural biosystem. So now, on every ship large enough to support modulated gravitation, and in every Aldebar outpost, we have created gardens like this. Even though they're partly holographic, we find it helps, even so. That water gurgles because we line this segment of the aeration system with river stone to create the sound of a brook running through the temple garden. Which reminds me, you'll soon hear the ship's bell sounding the hour. Don't be alarmed by it."

Steve reflected on Perry, his adopted planet's natural beauty, and as he remembered his lost family it re-awakened his grief. He wished he could move, to wipe away the damned tears leaking from his eyes. He had lost his children and his wife. He caught himself, and marveled that he no longer thought of her as his Ex. The knot in his throat grew more intense.

His heart brimmed with a rain of hopeless sorrow, and it overwhelmed his reserve. "I failed them!" he hoarsely whispered, shaking his head despite the pain. The memory of his bright and handsome son, his beautiful daughter so full of life, and especially his wife filled his mind. Steve's breath grew shallow and rapid. "Why am I alive?" He could not help shuddering, despite the searing pain of it.

The Aldebar's voice grew very still. "Son, my heart beats with yours." Steve felt a warm hand touch his arm and give it a small squeeze. "You did not fail, you were overwhelmed. The wreckage of your enemies tells a distinctly heroic story. You defended your home and loved ones with all the skill and bravery that any warrior could give. "

Tibs paused. His eyes were thoughtful. "It is little consolation I know, but I don't see what more anyone could have done. Remember: It's not your fault. It's the fault of whoever committed this monstrous crime. Not even the barbaric Legion stooped so low."

The Legion. Despite his distress, Steve's memory involuntarily referenced stories of the dreaded Legion, Earth's mercenary fleet that nearly annihilated the rebel scientists on Aldebaran before turning its back on Earth's Board of Corporations and aborting the mission to bring back the rogue scientists.

"Do you think the Legion might have done this?" Steve asked. "It doesn't make sense. What could they have possibly hoped to gain by destroying us?"

"I very much doubt it was the Legion." Tibs responded. "They are far away. The wreckage does not look right. The destroyed ships used the wrong alloys to be from Legion shipyards, and they used weaponry and engines no Legionnaire would use if he had a choice. Oh yes, we have not been idle waiting for you to awaken. No, the wreckage appears to be of Earth manufacture, but then Earth's corporations will sell anyone anything for the right price. If you have enough money you can buy their equipment and ordnance almost anywhere. We will know more soon, though, because not all of the ships were completely destroyed. We are recovering data cubes from the wreckage to decipher and examine."

The Aldebar continued, "As for 'why', I don't think we know enough to identify a motive. Whomever destroyed an inhabitable planet clearly wasn't bargaining for political favor. Possibly it was terrorism, but they haven't advertised their cause or made demands. I'd say it probably had some kind of an economic motive. Maybe they hoped to remove a competitor. The destruction of a habitable planet, primarily an agricultural resource, seems completely contrary to Earth's own best interests. The Corporations may be vicious, blood sucking predators, but no-one would accuse them of being so stupid as to destroy a food source they nearly had in the palms of their hands. Perhaps it was greed, but that would require something to still be available when the planet broke apart."

"But it may not be as simple as that. We cannot know, not until we have hunted them down and extracted the motivations from them, or something else unexpectedly turns up that will make it understandable."

Suddenly Steve thought of his dad, so long ago, and so far away. What would dad have said? The loss, the grief was too great, and threatened to drown him in depression. Steve pulled himself back from an emotional abyss with all the conscious force he could muster. His father would have advised him to "clear the decks", and focus on what is here and now.

"I will tell you what I remember. Maybe it will bring us closer to finding them." He savored his sad rage, like a tiger wounded in the brush: quiet for now, but murderous in intent.

The Aldebar named Tibs listened attentively as Steve related his memories to the best of his ability, leaving no detail to the imagination. He recalled the attackers engaging the defending fighters, and the single missile launched toward the planet. He had hardly caught more than a glimpse of the destruction, even though he could hardly tear his horrified eyes away once he saw it.

"Please, can you describe more closely what you saw as your planet broke apart? We need to understand the mechanics of the event better."

Calling it an 'event' seemed such a dry description of the planet's savage death and the instant annihilation of rugged and hearty people. The people of Perry had such high hopes... and it was all just starting to come to fruition, people finally beginning to prosper and have time for a little comfort... only to have it all brutally ripped asunder.

"It looked like something huge struck the planet, but invisible, something... almost as big as Perry itself. I saw the planet ripple all across the surface, almost like it was fluid instead of rock."

There was a moment of quiet, only the sound of running water punctuated what seemed like an interminable silence.

At long last the Aldebar broke the silence. "The attackers did not pass through your modulus when they left, since we came through and have had sentry ships posted there. We know they are now gone from the system, yet how can this be?"

Steve had no idea how it might have been done.

"I think the fact that the pilots who fought with you were apparently as surprised by the destruction of the planet as you were tells us something." Tibs continued. "I don't think we are seeking a whole organization as much as we are seeking a rogue individual, or a limited number of rogue leaders. Most likely the person or persons behind the attack didn't tell the rank and file what was intended, and not just to limit security exposure. I bet their leaders worried that those pilots you flew against might have become reluctant or even rebellious had they known what was about to happen."

Tibs consulted something outside Steve's view, surely some sort of terminal. The Aldebar remained silent, presumably intent on something he was reading. Then Tibs turned back to Steve to share what he had read.

"We think we may have an idea how your planet might have been destroyed, based on what you saw and what others have reported, but it seems to me very unlikely. There is still too much we must learn before we can know for sure. Meanwhile, understand that your sadness and grief will soon give way to anger. It is natural: It is how people respond to such trauma."

"We will speak again soon, but for now try to rest.

"Oh, and before I forget, there is a bottle in a colorful wrap that we found in your pod. I will leave it here beside you for when you are feeling better."

Chapter 4: Purpose

Steve took chow with Kyle and a few other pilots, eating a nutritious Aldebari interpretation of lunch, but they wished for real food. They were eating in the commons, a park-like gathering place in the central promenade of the cruiser. Several Aldebar were nearby, taking their meals as calmly and quietly as ever.

At least the bread was good, and Steve was starting to develop a taste for an Aldebar soup. He had no idea what might have been in what they called 'Drop Soup'. It was a light fragrant broth that simply smelled right, and in the broth were vegetable-filled dumplings.

"I'm going stir crazy," Kyle was saying, dropping his spoon noisily into his empty bowl. "It's been over a month. We are healed and ready, with nowhere to go and no way to get there."

Steve nodded. "We have to acquire some ships," he agreed. "Maybe we can find them in Cygnus. The Aldebar have been kind hosts, but we are no farther finding the enemy than we were in stasis in our pods. Perry had food products out on the market. There should be a way to get hold of that money."

The other pilots nodded as they ate. Steve decided he had to ask the Aldebar why they thought he couldn't fly their ships. He believed they couldn't be all that different.

He stood to clear his bowl. "I'll be back. I'm going to ask the captain about maybe getting some basic training in their ships. After all, we are all veteran pilots."

Kyle looked him in the eye and smiled. "Good luck with that. Funny, thing though. They don't call him Captain: If I know who you mean, they call him 'the One'. Anyway, I tried to bring the subject up to that officer Elder Lu and he just laughed at me. Well, he smiled, and he never smiles. Have you figured out who he is?"

Steve thought. "I don't know what ranks the Aldebar have. If he isn't the ship's captain then he is close enough for me. All the Aldebari are very deferential to him, and yet I have never seen anything that looked like a bridge on this ship. Have you?"

Kyle shook his head that he hadn't. Steve waved to the rest of the pilots as he left, heading up the promenade alone, back toward the garden area where he had awakened. Ahead he heard the deep intonation of the great temple bell sounding the hour.

Steve approached Tibs, the man Kyle said was called 'the One'. He waved to Steve, smiled, and patted the area beside him in invitation. He was seated on the grass, back erect and legs crossed. He seemed as comfortable in that position as Steve would have been reclining in his acceleration couch. Steve felt a little uneasy, since the Aldebari have a reputation for being religious fanatics. Steve's legs were a little stiff trying to sit flat on the grass, and his stomach muscles clenched to keep him upright. So Steve leaned back on his hands and stretched his legs out in front of him. The Aldebar didn't seem to notice that Steve wasn't used to sitting without a chair.

"How have you been, pilot? Is your body well recovered?" Steve nodded, recognizing the man's face and voice. Aldebari medical skill was famous, and justly so.

"Then what about your soul?"

Oh, here we go, Steve thought. "What do you mean, sir?"

"Please, there are no ranks between us: You are not in the network of command aboard this ship and you are my guest. You are offered my respect and friendship. Just call me Tibs, please."

"Well Tibs, I want to thank you for rescuing us and for your hospitality. My soul, if I know what that is, is the same as it has been since I first awoke here. But I wanted to ask you something else..."

"If I can answer, you may rely on me, Steven. Besides, I'm not really sure what a soul is supposed to be either: a sense of presence, perhaps, or maybe a 'life-force'."

Steve looked at Tibs askance. What an odd admission from a religious fanatic. Tibs might have been any mature age, and appeared quite fit and alert.

Avoiding the obvious invitation to discuss religion Steve amended his request: "Two questions really, Tibs. Our pilots are restless, no longer having any practical function. Our culture identifies the person with what they do, and feeling purposeless they are confronted with an identity crisis. So we need to go on with life and discover a way to do that. But we also need to find out what answers we can, to learn the identity of the criminals who attacked and destroyed our world. As far as we know, our people never gave anyone cause to hate us, especially not a nation able to deploy a capital warship.

"Tibs, when I awoke here in this garden you told me you didn't have the designs for our ships, and that we could probably not fly

Aldebari ships."

"Yes, that is so. What is your first question?"

Steve paused, trying to prioritize what he most wanted to know. Who it was that destroyed the planet would play heavily into what they would do. "Well, unless you've learned who did it, the first question is how do you think our planet was destroyed?"

"We may have an answer for that, but the hypothesis remains improbable in my view," Tibs replied. "After we discovered the first modulus, and after we studied the composition of the modulus' ring, humanity learned to manipulate forces in ways that were previously thought impossible. In this case, I think we are most concerned with inertia.

"We think the four transports that touched down on your planet's surface may have placed unusually powerful inertia dampeners, similar to what you had in your fighter but very much larger and more powerful. To generate inertia fields powerful enough to do unleash such force, they would have to transmit a massive electrical burst into tremendous amounts of modulinium. There are many more problems with this hypothesis than I like, but there aren't any alternatives we have been able to come up with. Those inertial field generators must have been powered by the electromagnetic pulse from that nuclear explosion you described. Unless heavily shielded, generation of electromagnetic fields emitting the right frequency could only have lasted brief moments before the generators were themselves destroyed. What I don't understand is how they could have deployed as much modulinium as it would have required. I can't imagine where they even found that much modulinium, or why they would have expended what it must have cost. I doubt that quantity of modulinium could have been acquired on the open market. So understand, Steven, that I have serious doubts about this hypothesis. The only reason I mention it is there is no other remotely plausible explanation."

Deep in thought, Steve's face reflected that odd sensation you get when the facts cannot adequately explain a result. Then Steve recalled a recent mining accident on Perry.

"What if there were large deposits of modulinite already in the planet itself?"

Tibs considered the idea briefly but saw a problem with it. "That would explain much, but it is very unlikely. What leads you to think there were modulinite deposits in the planet's crust?"

"Miners on Perry had serious problems mining deep. It limited our planet's development. The large mining companies don't like their information going public, but just last year my Search & Rescue team had to recover bodies from our first deep mine. The casualties looked like they were burned from the inside-out." Steve recalled, "It reminded me then of the safety training vids in the military about maintenance accidents involving modulinium." The fact that the bodies had been seized by the corporate owner of the mine before a local autopsy could be arranged already raised suspicion. Steve wanted a full autopsy, but a Perry government magistrate overruled him.

"It is very unlikely that was caused by modulinium exposure, Steve. Modulinite has only been found in vacuum, near anomalies and moduli. It deteriorates like a caustic when exposed to oxygen, and oxygen is common even in stone. We think that when nickel-iron asteroids pass through an unmodulated anomaly the elements are transformed somehow by the exposure." Tibs paused a moment in thought. "Still, it seems more plausible that the modulinite was somehow already on the planet rather than someone spent a fortune to acquire something so rare, transport it undetected, and then deploy it across thousands of square kilometers in mere minutes. To waste it all to destroy a perfectly habitable planet still in the early stages of development is completely irrational. Yet some kind of military or paramilitary organization, definitively rational, executed the mission."

Tibs was plainly reconsidering. "But if there actually were large deposits in Perry it would play neatly into a greed motivation hypothesis. No other commodity is as valuable." Tibs thought a moment more.

"I'll have our scouts specifically look for any sign of it among the planetary debris. The remaining atmosphere hasn't had enough time to dissipate completely, and residual oxygen should cause a visible reaction in any exposed ore."

Tibs looked down, plucked a blade of grass and smoothed it with thumb and fingers.

"We are, in the meantime, pursuing other avenues for investigation. There are a limited number of cruisers. While cruisers are powerful, they do not normally have the power to do anything like this. Yet this cruiser was the most significant agent involved, at least as far as we know. I'll see what I can learn from our Naval Intelligence, but please", Tibs looked up again at Steve, "understand that I might not be able to share everything with you."

Tibs again looked down at the blade of grass he was smoothing. He was clearly thinking about something else. With a mischievous look on his face he held the blade of grass between his thumbs and blew through the gap, making the blade of grass vibrate like a reed instrument to produce a wailing sound like a small animal in great fear. Then he looked back up at Steve and grinned. Steve shared his amusement, but felt intensely curious about Tibs.

"I'm not at all sure how it was actually done, Steve, but if we can substantiate that Perry had modulinite deposits, then we will have a motive. But if Perry turns out to not have large quantities of modulinite, then it would have required either a significant advance in technology, or a prohibitive investment in modulinium from elsewhere. We should easily be able to spot that kind of transaction in the commodities market. An advance in technology seems much more likely an answer."

"But, if your hypothesis is correct, let me imagine aloud what must have transpired, the moment the missile detonated above your planet. Your planet was moving along at her natural orbit velocity when a large part of it was slowed dramatically from electrifying a massive quantity of raw modulinite in the crust, triggering the famous 'inertia dampening' effect. In a manner of speaking, your planet impaled itself. The observations fit. On a planetary scale, stone subjected to stresses of this magnitude would behave very much like a liquid, and would appear to 'splash', as you put it. As an hypothesis this would account for every detail we know of. I see no contradictions... except that the presence of so much modulinite in the planet's crust is exceedingly unlikely."

"But even if this hypothesis is not true, the presence of the cruiser still tells us much about who did it. They were organized, very advanced, and have resources on the scale of at least an industrial nation-state. But without the hypothetical modulinite none of this reveals the motive, assuming it can be classed a motive and not madness.

Tibs paused again, clearly still in thought, and then with startling clarity met Steve's eyes.

"I think you should realize, Steve, that if you allow your desire for vengeance to guide you, your enemy will be better able to predict your reactions." He tapped his chest over his heart: "Let your heart tell you what will satisfy your vengeance," Tibs tapped his brow, saying "But let your mind alone guide you to the achievement of that satisfaction."

Steve realized Tibs knew full well what these questions were really about.

"What was your second question?"

After pausing to gather his thoughts Steve responded, "As I was saying, my men and I share one purpose. It may be all that is left of our world. But to move on with life, we need to at least have ships we can fly, good ships, hopefully like those we lost. I'm unsure where we could live. Possibly we might migrate to Cygnus, or maybe with time we could construct some sort of space habitat like your people did after Aldebaran. We might mine resources here for the market. I don't know how we can do it, but we have to try. I suspect our planet has accounts receivable somewhere that we can tap to help us purchase suitable spacecraft. We have to try something, and we are doing no good just sitting around aboard your ship. But more to the point, while I realize there will be differences between Aldebari systems and ours we are all skilled veteran pilots. Is there no way we can master the differences and return to space under our own power?"

Tibs pondered the question for a moment, and then carefully chose his words. "I have been thinking on this. Not long ago Elder Lu came to talk with me about what could be done.

"I also consulted with our other significant factions, the Elders of Draco and the Celestial Brotherhood, to gain their insights. The Celestials insist that you must convert before we can even consider offering our aid, but they do not yet have adequate strength in the Chair's council to dictate their conditions. I resist the idea of forcing our beliefs on anyone, and doubt it is a good idea to even try.

"Our conclusion is that we do not think you can adapt to fly Aldebari fighters. But in light of your tragedy it also would also be unfair to refuse you a chance to try. I warn you it will not be easy. You will have to have new circuitry implants for one thing, and some of that will have to replace what you already bear from your native technology. Our surgeons assure me it is possible to give you the technology that will enable you to train your neural net, but there is a strong chance that implanting our tech into you will fail. We would be basically overwriting your own neural implant technology. Failure could mean irreversible neural damage, and that could mean you will never pilot another ship again. It might lead to disability, or possibly to death. Please give this careful thought. After all, an uninformed decision could be permanently disabling."

Steve weighed the alternatives. They could wait and, if the planet had sizeable account receivables they might acquire some inexpensive but serviceable small craft and retrofit them with weapons at Oberon in Cygnus. Or they could try and fly Aldebari ships. What Tibs offered seemed the better deal because cheap ships would give them no advantage over pirates but the Aldebari fighters would. "I will talk with my people. For my part, I only want to know how and when we may begin."

"Steven, once the cyber-neurological implants are in place and have successfully tested, you will begin by learning to dance." Tibs said, his eyes twinkling.

Chapter 5: The Dance

The neural implants Tibs mentioned represented sophisticated bio-interfaces to various digital devices. The first such device, a powerful but compact Aldebari computer in a backpack, was equipped with sensors to measure the natural bio-electric signals generated by the pilot's neural synapses.

The 'dancing' that Tibs warned Steve about was an interesting and systematic method of Aldebari exercise, led by an attractive and fit Aldebar woman who instantly had Kyle acting like a lovesick pup. According to her, they needed to learn the complicated dance step sequence and gestures perfectly. Then she would initiate the learning sequence of the backpack computer programs and lead the dance for each pilot individually, with the computer linked by their new biological interfaces to the pilots' nervous systems. The idea was that the computer would begin learning their bodies' bio-electrical signals for the whole series of complex moves, including how each pilot signals their muscles to start, set amplitude, move and stop. The Aldebari were advanced far beyond Perry's rudimentary neural biotech.

The Aldebari ship systems would eventually be linked to each pilot neurologically.

Steve wondered if he were in combat while in the neural link to one of these ships, a stray wisp of rage or fear might send his ship crashing into an asteroid by accident, so he brought it up to Tibs, who promptly rolled over on the grass, laughing.

"No, Steven that is exactly why we do as we do.' Tibs sat up again and explained, "The dance is only the initial stage of programming the interface system. The link will eventually distinguish between what you really want to do and your primal reactions like fear or anger. The neural links are not only an interface to guide the navigation of the ship, but the weapons systems also will detect your focus and reactions and optimally adjust the intensity and power allocations for your weaponry and shields. The neural links can also provide interface to our powered combat armor systems. If you have to deploy for an infantry action, to ensure the completeness of your training, once Lian has finished her dance calibrations, then the next phase will feature open-hand combat. Depending on your progress either Elder Lu or Master Kinkaid will lead the course. You have been trained in some form of personal defense?"

Steve assured him that the surviving pilots were proficient in hand-to-hand combat, and Tibs seemed pleased.

Steve had one other topic on his mind. "Tibs... so... have you learned anything about those who destroyed our world?"

Tibs turned solemn. His brow furrowed with doubt. "I believe we have discovered where they went, but as to where that took them or how they managed to go there...". His voice trailed off and he looked toward the holographic sky. "It will be easier to just show you." He waved his hand to his left, away from Steve, and a view screen materialized as if by magic at his side. The Aldebar clearly enjoy their technological toys.

In the view screen was an unmodulated red anomaly. Formations of patrolling Aldebari fighters swept around the anomaly, giving an idea of the scale. It looked like an immense swirling sphere of chaotic reddish energy.

"You think it went in there?" Steve looked at Tibs in disbelief. "I thought raw anomalies were much too violent for our ships. If anyone got too close, the anomaly would rapidly wear down the ship's shields and armor and, if the ship didn't depart immediately it would destruct. No one who enters ever comes back."

"Within the limits of current technology that is true, but we believe the Ancients, who originally built the moduli, had a way to traverse them. We know a modulus is built of rings on both ends, and unless you pass through there is no way to determine where in the universe the other side of the anomaly might be. Otherwise we would have tried to find an unmodulated pair so we could send iron through one side and harvest modulinite on the other. In fact, if we refined the iron first it would probably save us most of the time and expense of refining the modulinite into modulinium. But the Ancients must have discovered a way to traverse an anomaly in order to know where to build the ring on the other side, and that confirms that it is possible."

Steve nodded reluctantly. He knew anomalies exist where distant points in space folded and overlap, even if it was hard to visualize. He had gone into a modulus in one star system and come out in a different star system without understanding *where* space bends. The calm blue fields of the moduli are attuned for transit by the technology of the ancients, a people of whom almost nothing is known. They built these systems long before humans walked on two legs.

Tibs continued, "Steven, I think someone has figured out enough about the anomalies, and the modulus technology, to build a portable modulus into their ship's hull and enable them to make transits that we, as yet, cannot."

"This idea is not something for which I can take credit. It was suggested as a possibility by one of our theoretical physicists. She ventured an hypothesis that the anomalies form conduits to more than just distant places in space, but also interface with other dimensions. That is why modulinium can affect so many types of energy. It acts as a conduit of conflicting energies to their respective home dimensions. We have the dimensions of space and time, but evidently gravity and inertia are also dimensionally dependent influences. Her hypothesis goes far to explain why manipulating and using these great forces eluded us for so many centuries. Until modulinite was discovered in Earth's solar system, we lacked any way to influence either gravity or inertia."

"And maybe magnetism?" Steve asked. "We can generate a magnetic field with electrical current just as we can influence gravity with specific frequencies of electrical current using modulinium."

"Consider, Steve, all three great powers, Earth, Legion, and Aldebar, have been trying to discover how modulus technology works for centuries. Now it looks like someone succeeded, but kept it a secret. We also know that the one who succeeded is inhumanly ruthless."

"For your immediate question, who did it and where they are, we have scouted and comprehensively scanned as far as we reasonably can in the Al Najid system. If the criminals who destroyed your planet are still anywhere in this system we would have found them by now. As I explained earlier, we know they did not leave via the system's only known modulus, because we have had pickets patrolling there ever since we entered the system. We arrived too late to save your home world, but soon enough to recover you." Tibs looked apologetic.

"You were in time to rescue some of us, Tibs. Thanks to your people we have a chance to start again. Maybe Cygnus will work out as a new home base, or maybe we will build a mining colony in the Perry debris field, or in the asteroid belt farther out."

Tibs nodded slowly to Steve. "You may find it is not such a bad life to live, Steven."

They both gazed at the image of the anomaly's swirling red mass as if it were a crystal ball, as if looking long enough they might find answers to unasked questions.

"Could there be an undiscovered modulus somewhere beyond the planets of our system in interstellar space?" asked Steve.

"We have looked, and will continue to look, but I think it very unlikely. Still, that is a tremendous expanse: anything could be out there."

Tibs continued, "Steven, there is one other thing I should tell you."

Steve looked at him quietly, waiting for more insight.

"I am convinced that the motive behind the destruction of your planet was economic in nature. We have been surveying the planetary remains in the debris field, in part to check out your idea that there may have been modulinite in the planetary crust."

Steve paused, looking intently at him. "Did you find it, Tibs?"

"Yes. Until now it had only been found in very limited quantities near unmodulated anomalies, in asteroids that transited those anomalies."

"Until now?"

"Steven, the remains of your planet bears very large deposits of this rare material. More than I have ever heard of before. If your people maintain control over it you will not have to worry about money for a very long time. Given human avarice, that is a very big 'if'."

Steve thought. With an Aldebari cruiser now in-system things appear calm, but once the *Jade Temple* leaves the Al Najid system the survivors would have to be able to defend themselves, and with wealth comes danger.

Unless the Aldebari decided to seize it. Steve glanced quickly at Tibs, but was reassured. Had they wanted to the Aldebari could have killed all the remaining survivors. "Do you think that the planet went through an anomaly?" Steve asked.

"The planet is much too large to fit through any anomaly we've ever discovered, and most of the planet is normal. It must have come into contact with either that anomaly," he pointed to the swirling maelstrom of red energy in his display, "or the one the modulus now tames, before the rings were built here and in Cygnus system. We don't know enough of the causal event to be sure which occurred. But this planetary system has two anomalies relatively close to one another. It may be that space is particularly bent here. More certain, however, is that system drift has moved your sun and the planets orbiting around it since that event. The planet would also have changed its orbit as a result, since the conversion of iron to modulinite would also change the planet's mass, and thus its orbit."

"On the surface of the planet the modulinite would have decayed rapidly long ago, due to the presence of water and atmospheric oxygen. This would explain why your people were unaware of it. Depending on how exposed it was, it would have decayed until it was indistinguishable from regular stone or soil. Deeper deposits of modulinite would decay more slowly than at the surface. Oxygen in stone doesn't migrate far, and our samples indicate the bulk of the material was quite deep in the planet."

Tibs continued, "Someone who believes they need large quantities of modulinite, somehow knew where it was, and valued it more highly than the lives of your people. That is our criminal. He or she chose to destroy an inhabited planet without warning, which suggests a monstrous personality is behind it all.

"By destroying the planet they exposed the modulinite to the vacuum of space, where it can be easily mined. The method they chose eliminated the need for heavy-lift assets to extract the ore from the planet's gravity well."

Immediately, Steve thought of Earth's ruling Board of Corporations. "Who do we know that would have such a need? Perhaps the one responsible wanted to build a fleet of these anomaly transit-capable ships, or even create new moduli. Modulus rings would require a huge investment in modulinium." Steve speculated, "But if he could transit an anomaly, and modulinite is created when iron passes through an anomaly, why didn't he just pull iron ore through the anomaly to make his own instead of destroying the planet?"

"I don't know, Steve. When we find the person responsible, we will ask."

Steve was not satisfied to wait for that day. He tried to imagine the mindset of someone who could do such a thing, and considered everything they had inferred about what he must have been thinking. Or *she*, Steve corrected himself. Tibs was silent in thought with him.

Steve and Tibs looked at each other at the same time, and saw realization in each others' eyes. Steve spoke his thoughts aloud. "Whoever it was didn't want anyone to find out that he had discovered how to transit an anomaly. He knew the technology would be even more valuable than the modulinite. Someone who is so extremely competitive and greedy that they have become maniacal. He also was worried someone would discover where the new modulinite was coming from, and that could mean the loss of his technological monopoly."

Tibs looked at Steve, eyebrows raised. "You've given voice to my own thoughts." Tibs looked into Steve's eyes, and reached out to grip his forearm: "Now, imagine the possibilities for your people. The remains of your planet hold large quantities of this exceedingly rare, valuable element, and you may be onto the trail of the most significant technological advance since the discovery of the first modulus."

Steve pondered a more alarming thought. "*We* may be, not just my people." Steve said, stressing the 'we'. "You have a stake in this too, Tibs. Let's not become as greedy as the person we're chasing. And imagine the danger we face when he returns. I doubt he will just say 'Oh well' and give up. We have no navy to defend our resources without your support, Tibs."

After a moment of consideration Tibs responded, "You will not be able to keep it a secret once people begin to mine the debris field, but for now let's try to limit this revelation. Every pirate and fortune hunter in the galaxy will be here once word gets out. There is no legal precedent that covers who owns the debris when a planet is destroyed and there are survivors."

Chapter 6: Charity

Aside from the aches left by the past month training under Elder Lu, Steve was feeling more fit than since graduation from basic training. Engaging in virtual-contact hand-to-hand combat in twice normal gravity was exhausting. Having to overcome the fatigue of even holding his hands up had been one of the most tiring challenges in his career. At last the Elder decided Steve and his team of survivors had reached an adequate level of proficiency to let the neural devices take and record their readings in normal gravity, and with Tibs' satisfied approval graduated them to their next phase of training.

Master Kinkaid, Executive Officer of the *Jade Temple*, led the twenty-eight surviving Al Najid pilots to look over their small fighter craft. Tomorrow they would fly again. The hanger bay was cylindrical, leading from the actual hanger where the small craft were maintained to a pair of armored bay doors at the cruiser's hull. Along either side were emplacements where other starcraft were kept fueled and armed, ready for the unexpected. In the hanger itself an Aldebari light fighter hung magnetically suspended, looking trim and deadly with blackish-green photo-ablative enamel and brilliant LED accents for navigation lights in normal flight, and line-of-sight signaling for stealthy missions. Arrayed in a semicircle around it were niches, like the cells of a giant honeycomb, holding other light fighters.

An access bridge spanned the bay aft of the readied spacecraft, allowing a pilot to reach the armored access hatch at the rear. Kinkaid opened its hatch and began pointing out details, underscoring basic information the pilots had already studied in the ship's centralized data center. He advised that the light fighter would be the only version that would be provided for manufacture.

It had been welcome news that the Aldebari decided to help re-establish Perry's surviving population in their home system, but it was also a little troubling. An even greater newsflash came when Master Kinkaid advised the Perry pilots that, with the help of delegates representing the Legion and Earth, a new artificial habitat was being built for them near the planet's remains. The survivors, including those who had been traveling or were stationed at diplomatic and trade posts elsewhere at the time of the attack, would be meeting with diplomatic representatives of the great powers after settling into the new housing. A couple of big names were already maneuvering for position in hope of controlling the nascent government of what was being called *Perry Station*.

Steve had been staggered with hope by this change in their prospects, but Master Kinkaid, as always, acted as if it were routine that the three major powers, ostensibly hostile to one another, cooperated for the sake of a minor power almost wiped out by catastrophe.

Steve was suddenly unsure whether he wanted more to hop into his new fighter or discuss the future with Tibs. Despite the eagerness to launch, they would have to wait overnight to do so.

Steve recognized it would be foolhardy for his people to presume anything about what seemed a too-good-to-be-true political scenario. Thinking the situation was already well above his pay grade, Steve realized that the Perry survivors needed to organize the right kind of government to handle these sorts of things.

"Master Kinkaid, I appreciate what is being done on our behalf. How did the three powers start working cooperatively for our benefit?" he asked, shoulder to shoulder with the other surviving defenders.

Master Kinkaid looked sad and amused at the same time. "Steven, politics are seldom altruistic. Each side has their own self-interest at heart. There has been considerable debate among the Legion's negotiators, the *Jade Temple* acting as the agent of several allied Aldebari factions and Earth's Board of Corporations. Various members of your planet's diplomatic corps and trade representatives have returned with their families from across the galaxy, and are forming a council to represent your people. The discussions superficially touched on what needs to be done, but more subtly it became a game of maneuver and advantage. You were fortunate Tibs was interested in furthering your people's recovery. He has been instrumental in safeguarding your sovereignty. Working in coordination with your diplomats, he has been instrumental in negotiating an outcome that I think will be to your best advantage as well as ours, assuming that you wish to remain our friends. Suffice it to say, each of the powers foresees future benefit from this investment in your people's resettlement. Each power wishes to see you, and your resources, added to their own list of 'assets', as the Board of Corporations' delegation put it."

Kinkaid's eyes surveyed the pilots one by one as he spoke. "Something else to consider is that were we to do any less than we have planned, the probable outcome would have been for your people to turn understandably resentful, and that would be more expensive for us in the long run than what we cooperatively plan.

"Furthermore, if you ably defend this planetary system from pirates and other undesirables we won't need to invest our already-thin forces to do so.

"Finally, while each power might wish you would formally join their respective faction, in my and Tibs' opinion you may ultimately be more valuable to the Aldebari as an independent state, a truly neutral power." His eyes rested coolly on Steve. "You may have a larger role in the future than you imagined.

"Related to this last point, Earth and the Legionnaires are envious that we Aldebari were first to respond to your planet's distress call and were able to rescue your pilots. We have enjoyed unequaled access to you as your benefactors, which gave us an opportunity to reveal our true selves to you, rather than the fanatical caricatures our competitors claim. This parlayed into an advantage for your people. The other two powers increased their financial outlay to try and balance our proposed investment package."

Kyle was the first to find his thoughts. "It seems too good to be true that the three powers are cooperating to make a new home for us. But, of course, it cannot replace our home planet."

Master Kinkaid pondered Kyle's words. "No, of course it can't replace your world, but it is a start. And as for the 'too good to be true' part, well, all I can say is we are lucky that the galaxy isn't a monopoly. So it is in each power's interest to appear generous."

Kinkaid consulted a text message and transitioned to address the near future.

"When you finally launch and resettle in your new home, and you make yourselves accessible to the diplomatic representatives of the other powers, they will present their interests in the best light possible. We Aldebar are convinced that it will be better for us if you to treat them from a position of independence, and develop your own opinions, and reach your own conclusions. You should make your decisions based on your values rather than upon present need or transitory gratitude. By your decisions, your choices, we will come to better understand you, and this should reinforce our future friendly relations."

"For now, after your long recovery, it is only natural if your people feel bonded to us in ways that may ultimately prove artificial: You may harbor feelings of allegiance that are inspired more out of relief from an evil and intolerable condition than out of any real merit you ultimately find in us."

"We Aldebar consider ourselves integral with the universe, and we are all about the ultimate ends of life. Our patience is, if I may compliment my people, legendary. So we believe what you will ultimately decide about our culture will be more significant to us into the future than the gratitude you feel now. We desire our friends to be *real* friends, and more than momentary sentiments can ever support."

The pilots had much to digest before departing the *Jade Temple* for their new home.

Chapter 7: Fanatics

Tibs was where Steve had left him, in the *Jade Temple*'s semi-holographic garden with the great temple bell, which set him to wondering whether Tibs ever went anywhere else. As he waved Steve in with a smile he gestured to two view screens that then visually dissolved into the scenery.

"Thank you for seeing me, Tibs. I wanted to take a moment to thank you personally for your hospitality, and for the wonderful things that I hear you are doing for us."

"It isn't just us, Steven. You surely will benefit from what all three powers are doing, but please understand that we are each doing it, ultimately, for ourselves. By providing you with a basis for rebuilding your own nation, with your own culture, we believe we have gained a good neighbor and hopefully a partner. The Board of Corporations believes they will gain an excellent trade partner, and the Legion hopes to gain a new foothold in the Al Najid system to balance the influence of the Board of Corporations and we Aldebari. The Legion sees your people as a potential future ally. Arrogant though they are, the Legion seemed quite impressed with the data we shared from your valiant defense against the enemy. You may find, if you play your hand well, that your people can rise on the fortunes of those with whom you trade and negotiate, playing each off the other in a way that may leave you independent, and beholden to no one.

"For me, I think we have made a sound initial political investment.

"And I have a keen interest in seeing this matter through to the end. The criminal power that destroyed your planet must be neutralized before he strikes again.

"And you would also like a crack at their tech, Tibs, wouldn't you?"

Tibs' eyes twinkled and his face crinkled into a grin. "Of course. Who wouldn't?"

A young Aldebar approached with a tray of cups and a bottle of brewed tea. Tibs poured a steaming cup, and offered it to the young man. The fellow politely declined with a slight bow, and left. Then Tibs offered the tea to Steve.

"Steven, before the *Jade Temple* departs, I wish your people's permission to sow a minefield around Al Najid's unmodulated anomaly. Your people will soon be able to defend themselves against pirates and 'normal' criminals using your new light fighters as well as any new hulls you manage to deploy, but I doubt you will be able to build a capital ship any time soon. If that black cruiser comes back using that raw anomaly as we suspect it can you would be hard-pressed to survive. This is why I want you to allow us to weave a tight net of anti-ship mines around that anomaly."

"What if they just send some fighters through to take out the mines? Maybe we need to keep patrols monitoring the anomaly for such things."

Tibs shook his head. "I don't think fighters are large enough to be able to house the technology that allows safe transit of an unmodulated anomaly. I think they have to transit in that cruiser, and then launch their birds when they are through. Unfortunately I don't know this with certainty, so it would be a good idea to also maintain a patrol outside the minefield anyway, assuming your people will permit our placing the mines there in the first place."

"I think our people would do just about anything for the Aldebari to express our gratitude, Tibs, but I cannot presume to speak for them. We'll have to ask."

"Please do, then, Steven, and let me know the answer as early as you can: The *Jade Temple* has been here too long now, and we should return to home space."

"Tibs, I would ask one more thing before I go, please."

"Well of course, Steven."

"I had always heard that the Aldebari are fanatics about their religion, yet you have never once preached at any of us, nor tried to convert anyone, nor even mentioned your beliefs in my presence. Had I just heard lies? Are these rumors without foundation?"

Tibs smiled a slow sad smile and shook his head. "No, we certainly are religious fanatics, although some of us are more so than others. I believe we are very poorly understood religious fanatics, but the stereotype is appropriate. If you really understood our culture, and our way of life in the universe, then you would be surprised were we not rather fanatic about it. In fact I think you would think us awfully stupid if we weren't a bit fanatical."

Steve raised an eyebrow. Tibs smiled as he explained "We Aldebari are the descendants of scientists. We examine what is presented to us, through our senses and through our instruments. We note but distrust belief, and continuously test what we think may be. We are never satisfied that we know much of anything. What we worship is the universe. Not our concepts of it. Not our impression of it. Belief for us is the most suspect of sentiments. Certainly we do not worship the mythological footprint of an otherwise wonderful people who attempted to understand it all many millenia ago, before we ever knew the little we know now."

"And yet we cannot avoid noticing that throughout human history, as far back as we have managed to delve, most people believed in something they conceive of as deity, whether pantheist or monotheist. It seems unavoidably part of the human universe. This *concept* of deity is, as far as we can tell, only a human concept. An image we always seem to have, as if imprinted on our DNA. Atheists deny it, yet even that denial appears to affect their world view. Even the patterns of classical reason that defend it appear to be hardly more than a consequence of how human beings think.

"All known cultures have traditions asserting that there is something that can be called 'deity'. So as scientists we are confronted with a choice: A deity exists, or a deity does not exist. Is deity a concept only, resulting from a self-awareness confronted with the reality of a universe that differs from the perceiver, or does this pervasive concept correlate to something that is sentient but not itself human? We do not know. We only know that historically almost every known culture thought deity was more than just a concept."

Tibs refilled both cups.

"So what characteristics do people universally attribute to a deity? Creation of the universe? A prime mover? I'm sure the list is long but these are the two most universal characteristics. If there is a deity, and that deity created the universe, then the universe provides us something by which we may better know that deity, just as we know the apple tree better when we eat an apple. The apple is very different from the tree, but we could not say we know apple trees without tasting the fruit.

"We Aldebar study and contemplate the universe. The universe is the object of our religion; our way of life. Others ask us for proof of our religion and we reply it is all around us, yet we are not understood."

Steve nodded, and sipped his tea. "It sounds pretty reasonable, at least the part I understood. You certainly don't seem fanatical. You never even spoke of your God until I asked."

"It is that 'reasonableness' that tends to get us in trouble with the organized religions of Earth. Most are heavily invested in whatever it is they call 'revelation', arguing that reasoning is inadequate. We consider the presence of the universe itself to be a revelation, and that we can reason our way to understanding it.

"I do not casually speak of God because I cannot comfortably use that noun in conversation. Too many people get too many different images in their heads when they hear it. I have my concept when I say it. You probably have a different concept when you hear it. That means the word we use is an inadequate vessel to carry clear and distinct meaning. Recognizing this, after many years of conversation, I do not commonly use it in public."

Steve saw an objection. "But you just said reason is sufficient. Reason uses words, but words are inadequate to some meanings: doesn't it follow that reason is inadequate?"

"Were we trying to assert the nature of the apple tree from the characteristics of its fruit, then yes: that reasoning would be inadequate. But we do not try and pretend the fruit is the tree. We are content to enjoy the apple. And if the deity is as bright as they say, then the apple we are given to bite into is probaby all we can handle."

Steve considered the argument. Then he observed "I am still puzzled that the Aldebari did not simply adopt one of the major Earth religions rather than making one up of your own. There are great traditions, rich in cultural heritage."

"Well first, Steven, we didn't *make* it up. Instead it was given to us," Tibs mused, a little distantly.

"Do you mean to tell me you had a revelation or dream?"

"No," he chuckled, looking again into Steve's eyes with a wry twinkle, "nothing like that." He looked at his hands in thought for a moment. "In the early days we had scientists from around the world. I think we had members from every major Earth religion as well as some very devout and outspoken atheists. From accounts I have read, personal journals some of our people left behind, great debates raged in the early days as we gradually melded into a confederation of moderately independent people. The common threads between religious traditions, even the social aesthetics of the atheists and social Darwinists, were too pervasive to ignore as coincidence. The differences between the factions also had profound similarities. Eventually, this too was observed and discussed. We noticed, for example, that in large measure the disagreements arose over issues that showed political fingerprints, so to speak.

"This is not to say everyone agreed with the general consensus. To this day we have devoted Jesuits, Hindi, Muslim, and other scholars among us. But all were in accord that each of us, as scientists, must be accepting and tolerant of each other.

"It was not difficult for any one religious faction to point out what in others was motivated by human values, desires, or political convenience. When each faction could so quickly and easily point out problems in the other, we dutifully noted that fact and studied it. We eventually reached a consensus that if we are willing to point such things out to others about their traditions, we should also be willing to listen to them when they point out our own. Many had difficulty with this, but it wasn't really reasonable or productive to allow schisms to dominate the conversation. Leave all evidently human prescriptions out of the mix, and what is left is remarkably uniform and homogenous. We took the essence from our cultural traditions, added the yeast of science, and over time fermented it all into the fine wine of conversation we have today. It is an evolving conversation still, because what exists is as it becomes. All we can do is share our observations.

"Some of the traditions we inherited seem clearly sourced in a need to be able to say something else, something humans really have no words to express. For example how to consistently explain the unknown. The origins of things, the creation stories, were some of the first to recede into the background context. We relegated creation stories to preservation, as wonderful teaching stories and examples of cultural and psychological archetypes."

"Like the forbidden fruit?"

"You picked up on that. I meant more practical things like cleanliness, things that help the members of a culture survive in the world, dietary restrictions that helped them avoid disease, behaviors that promote community and interpersonal cooperation, or other cultural instruments by which humans learn. These are things that aid governance, and represent human values couched in terms it would be hard to question since they promote survival."

"I think the story of the fruit of good and evil cautioned against trying forbidden things just to experience why they are evil, rather than forbidding knowledge itself. But anyone who is willing to admit the possibility of a creative deity will also recognize that we live in this universe, and it is both consistent and chaotic. If there is a deity, then the closest we can come to understanding that creative deity is to understand what has been, and is being, created."

Tibs paused. "The best we can do to show our appreciation of being in this universe is to deeply appreciate our lives.

"Anyway, we Aldebar came to a general consensus that just as each culture has its language appropriate to its people, so too does each culture differently pronounce wisdom. The wisdom that produces religion in humans also produces the human traditions that shape their distinct perceptions. If we can translate words of wisdom from Sanskrit, or Aramaic, or from a folk song, then we can translate the ideas enshrined in these expressions to find a common meaning that is fundamentally part of being human.

"Have I adequately responded to your question, Steven?"

"I think I will have to study more to know whether I have adequately heard your answer, Tibs."

Tibs sipped his tea, nodded, and then smiled as if pleased with Steven. "You see? You may be one of us after all."

"One more question, Tibs?" Steve asked.

"Of course, Steven."

"When you wave away the view screens, where do they go?"

Tibs paused a moment, then grinned and tapped the air to his left. It made a thunking sound. "Plexiclear cubes filled with a gel containing some ungodly number of nanotubes that emit various colors of light when charged with the appropriate frequency of electrical current. Other than the projected holographic field technology we use for instrumentation interfaces, Aldebari 3D viewing interfaces are invariably based on this technology."

Chapter 8: On Station

Steve was a bit clumsy, but passed Master Kinkaid's 'final exam' anyway, managing to launch the Aldebari light fighter, circle a small practice beacon, and dock, all without touching the controls or issuing voice commands to the computer. It turned a little dicey near the beacon when his mind momentarily wandered away from immediate tasks and the ship seemed to become a little confused trying to interpret his neural signals. He refocused, managed to get back on track, and gained confidence through the exercise. Tibs sent a personal text message that, besides congratulating Steve, gave him a digital address, a direct line of communication. It was an honor, but also an important personal compliment. It was the closest thing to a heartfelt handshake that is possible over digital media. Friendship is rare, and to be treasured. He left his ship and joined the others at the graduation reception.

It was finally time to leave the *Jade Temple*, wonderful though the big ship had been, and discover his new home. Steve joined the rest of the survivors, twenty-four men and four women. They looked forward to meeting the rest of Perry's surviving population already on the Station.

Many of the *Jade Temple*'s crew, including Tibs, and Master Kinkaid and Elder Lu, were in the launch bay ready room for the reception and to see them off. After a brief speech by Tibs, Steve tried to get off the hook with a simple statement of appreciation to the Aldebari, but Kyle dashed his hopes for a quick getaway by calling loudly for a speech. Tibs laughed and agreed, joining in the chant with the rest of the pilots.

"My friends," Steve began when they all quieted, "we were plucked from a cold sleep by these Aldebar. They took us in like family. They fed us and gave us clothes. We had nothing. We were worse than homeless, but they found us shelter. We had no way to travel, but now they have given us wings. Let us never forget the example they have shown us. This is how humanity is meant to be. If we ever find someone in need, let us be as they have been for us, and let us credit any good we do, any kindness we show, to their example. I believe that is the only way we can, as Tibs would say, 'adequately' thank them."

Kyle called "Hear, hear!"

"So Tibs," Steve finished, raising his glass, "Master Kinkaid, Elder Lu, Lian, and all the crew of the *Jade Temple*, we raise our cups to you now, we honor you and the Aldebari, and we will praise and defend you wherever we go, and whenever we get there."

The Perry pilots filed out to their new ships in pairs for tandem launch. Kyle and Lian seemed closer than they had ever appeared before in public. Everyone gave them some room and politely did not notice anything unusual. It was evident that everyone knew and approved of their budding romance.

Steve and Kyle were the last pair to leave. Steve waved farewell, and saw Tibs nodding back at him.

The fighter was a sweet little ship. She boasted enough cargo capacity to serve as a light mining vessel in a pinch. She was agile, well armored for her class and boasted decent shields. She could be fitted with energy, ballistic and guided weaponry.

Steve entered the cockpit and connected his augmentation umbilical from the flight suit to the console. While the hardwired connection was less cumbersome than the old ACM military issue, it was more secure than civilian wireless in combat conditions. The ship informed his readouts that it was fully prepared and ready for launch, once he powered up. The ship shuddered just a little when the magnetic launcher took hold.

He waited for the armored outer launch bay doors to slide open, got his green signal, and savored the anticipation of full control of this nimble spacecraft in the vast and star-filled freedom of space. It was an anticipation of having the full sense of ownership that he hadn't felt before in training. Always the ship belonged to his instructor and the Aldebari cruiser, but now it felt like it was about to be his own, and somehow that possession added to his sense of personal liberty.

He signaled to the *Jade Temple*'s launch officer and received a ready signal in reply. Steve keyed the comm channel to Kyle and said, "Let's go, buddy". Kyle replied "Roger, that". Steve initiated launch and rested back in his couch. The magnetic launch rail then snapped his small ship from within the *Jade Temple* and out into the glory of unending stars.

Not terribly far away Steve could see the skeletal framework of the *Perry Station* hub, centered around a heavily shielded power plant and a cluster of other buildings forming the beginnings of a sphere. Construction apparently was well underway. The first of the hydroponic farms formed the largest of the new sections and the waste treatment facility seemed nearly as large. The docks extended far out on one of the elevator pylons that showing the vast outlines of the station's planned building envelope. Six elevator pylons extended equidistantly from the core revealing the Station's rotation, designed to keep the interior temperatures in balance as water circulated through the honeycombed reservoirs in the concentric bulkhead shells. The compartmentalization afforded by the reservoir design provided increased damage control in the event of a breach or other malfunction. Near the Station, strobe beacons sparked in sequence to guide ships to the docks.

The Station's development plan called for mining asteroids for metals and other valuable materials. They could also use less valuable mining byproducts, such as schist, that could be collected and stored in compressed blocks. These blocks were gathered into large nets and held together with magnetic fastenings. The blocks were tethered together and stored, suspended in the vacuum of space in a specific area near *Perry Station*, rather than allowing them to drift as a navigation hazard. These blocks would ultimately be fed into a manufacturing plant of Aldebari design which blended the dust with a resin produced by the waste conversion plant with chemicals imported from Earth. The extruded mixture would form a useful and abundant construction material.

Behind him the *Jade Temple* prepared to leave the Al Najid system. He wished they could stay and help more, but they said they needed to return home. The Aldebar were largely migratory, holding vast regions of space. They had inhabited no specific worlds since the disaster at Aldebaran. Steve knew he would miss them, but he didn't expect to feel such melancholy here in the midst of stellar glory. Tibs with his sense of wry, knowing humor; Kinkaid with his dour looks and analytical grumpiness; Lu with his calm, above-it-all way of looking at Steve when he accidentally slurped his soup. Steve chuckled affectionately and then sighed as he nosed over toward the guiding strobes.

Fortunately not all of Perry's people had been on the planet when it was destroyed. The meteorologists aboard the northern orbital weather station had been caught by the destruction, but others survived. Besides those who, like Steve, had been scrambled in defense, there were a few miners who had been working among the asteroids. There were administrators and installation support personnel on Al Najid V, and a few more who had been manning the beacons, communications relay, and the trade offices at the Transit Duty Station near the modulus on the Cygnus 29 side. Finally, there were others who had been traveling or conducting trade outside the system, as well as several Perry diplomats and their staff. From Earth, the Legion, from the Aldebar home fleet, and from ACM Command on Cygnus these people were trickling back, their intermittent arrivals marked usually with displays of grief, which triggered echoes of emotion from the community of survivors gathered to meet them.

A small group of these people welcomed Steve and the other pilots as returning heroes. The welcoming committee's apparent leader, David Lyman, had been the senior Ambassador to Corporate Earth and so missed the planet's destruction. Lyman, a large, intelligent man with a well-modulated voice and impeccable diction, had clearly taken leadership of the provisional council.

Chapter 9: Growth

As the only lawmen among the Perry survivors, Steve and Kyle were assigned by the council to similar roles in Security for the new artificial habitat, which people were calling *Perry Station*.

Seen from the inside, *Perry Station* was mostly a lattice of girders extending between and beyond elevator towers that rose from the sealed core of the power plant. The hydrology plant and its atmosphere annex, the waste conversion plant, hydroponics, and mechanical engineering formed the primary extensions of the facility through hallways sealed and insulated from the cold vacuum and searing heat radiating from the star. Beyond mechanical engineering was the shipyard, and a machine shop was adjacent to an expansive docking area with planned warehousing. Only one warehouse was already built, and it was filled with all the myriad hardware needed to build a self-contained habitat in space. A commercial zone, including a shopping area and a small administration complex with a meeting hall were planned for construction near Steve's office, but not until the Station had reached sufficient population. Security remained in a small annex, just beyond hydro-engineering. A modular residential district was already growing beyond that, but was still sparsely populated. Steve had modest quarters but very little time to do more than sleep there.

Additionally, the Earth corporate interests expanded Al Najid's existing ore refinery in the old asteroid belt, and constructed a state-of-the-art, zero-gravity manufacturing installation nearby to make products other than the schist/resin construction material. Water and the gases needed for atmosphere were still being tanked in from Cygnus.

The Aldebari also provided grief counselors to help survivors recover psychologically, and from Earth came a pair of compassionate Franciscans to help develop coping mechanisms.

A joke became popular at the *Cog and Sprocket* bar, the first business to open its doors on the Station, about why the Legion had not also been approached to counsel the grieving. The joke presented a stereotype about how Legionnaires handle sentiment. Any laughter heard on the Station seemed to help heal the community, and the Legionnaires who heard the joke laughed just as hard as everyone else.

Legion engineers were constructing heavy structural defenses for *Perry Station*, including some artillery, a missile battery and a large defensive shield generator. The generator's capacitor banks and heat radiators would allow the shield to deflect meteoroids, fast projectiles, or focused radiant energy and still allow light from Al Najid to pass through. The remaining vulnerability to slower objects like slower meteoroids, fighter ships, torpedoes or boarding transports would have to rely on point defenses.

The Station's most immediate problem: insufficient population with the expertise to fill all the positions required. The manufacturing facility needed people to operate and maintain the machines. They needed personnel to change calibrations, set up functional templates, and attend to a vast array of storage, transport and administrative tasks for the various products. Hydrology, Atmospherics, and Waste required highly trained specialists, and *Perry Station* had precious few. There were no Human Resources people to recruit and train candidates who might wish to immigrate. The provisional council negotiated for specialists from the three powers to take care of things temporarily, but *Perry Station* needed to recruit permanent personnel.

Steve, with Kyle as deputy, filled most of their waking hours helping to set up the provisional government while maintaining the civil peace.

Steve scanned the budget request form for the balance of the current year. He tabbed over to the one intended to predict the needs for next year and then set his tablet down on his desk and rubbed his eyes, stifling a yawn. Budget estimates would be wild guesses at this point, but he had to give the budget committee some kind of guidance. He took all his meals in the administration's cafeteria, which still only offered the basic bland nourishment of military-packaged rations. His craving for a big juicy hamburger grilled over hardwood coals haunted him. Steve stood up from his desk and stretched, with his back and shoulders making a loud popping sound. He felt the need to get out of the office and patrol the expanding Station to get a sense of what could reasonably be expected in the coming year.

Steve found a few shops already opened for business, despite the scarcity of customers with time to shop. While making his rounds Steve drew satisfaction by stopping in to say 'hello' to the struggling shopkeepers. It was as if the promise of rebirth for his people as a culture found a symbol in every sign of retail growth. People were talking together, but they were still far too few in number.

More space for stores and shops was under construction in hope customers would come. Everyone shared ideas about how to attract new citizens.

Everywhere workers used the synthetic construction material made from mixing newly mined schist with chemicals and resins that were a byproduct of the waste treatment systems. The resin bound the schist into an impermeable solid that could be used like wood, or could be extruded like plastic into pipes and ducts or molded into other architecturally desirable shapes. The resulting material could then be bonded with an epoxy similar to plastic cement. If the Station ever ran out of space it could be extended using the tailings from the mining operations. The increased population could produce enough waste to make the resin needed.

Any schist not used for construction material would eventually have to be gathered together into large space-born rafts and sent star-ward. If these measures weren't taken, the area around the mining or manufacturing facilities would eventually become congested with mining waste until it became unnavigable.

Steve consulted his calendar on the wrist comm he wore on his left forearm. There was a new appointment scheduled tomorrow with the council, and he briefly wondered what it was about. But it was past the end of his shift, so he entered his time code instead of opening the appointment memo and made a few notes for tomorrow before remotely locking the office.

While standing in front of a shop between the office and his quarters, Steve looked through the plexiclear window and saw refrigeration units being stocked with food. He wondered whether they would offer real beef at a price he could afford. He was growing weary of the bland cafeteria food and decided to search for an infrared grill. He could buy it online and have it shipped, but decided he wanted to support local business. Keeping the money local would be a greater benefit to his community.

Thinking about grilling triggered a thought of how he would season his grilled burger, which in turn started his mouth watering. He noticed some strands of woven garlic bulbs hanging in the store, and decided to look more closely at the kitchen in his quarters to determine the storage capacity. He thought he might take up cooking as a hobby, since he dearly loved eating and did not care for the small portions in the prepared frozen meals on which most people lived. He would have to make sure he had everything that he would need. Maybe some wine. And glasses: He would need more glasses than the one he'd been using for everything.

A woman inside the store was preparing to open the shop. She looked athletic, and he wondered who she might be. He approached the door and it slid open for him. The surprised shopkeeper turned to see who had entered. Once she saw him, she flushed slightly and moved to straighten a wisp of auburn hair that had strayed as she cleaned. She turned away and set down the sonic cleaner she had been using to sanitize the trays of a refrigerated display unit. She then turned again toward him and smiled. He noticed she was misty with a light perspiration from her work, her hands immaculate and well groomed.

"The store isn't quite open I'm afraid, but we should have the shelves stocked later this week." she began.

"What will the store be selling? I was walking by just to see how things are progressing and saw the garlic in the window. My name is Steve..."

"Holbrook, yes I know. Everyone knows who you are Mr. Holbrook."

After the briefest of pauses he urged, "Call me Steve, please."

"Well okay, thank you. I'm Mary, Steve. Mary Stirling."

Mary turned away with an expression of slight distress. "I don't even have my net connection set up yet or I could offer you some garlic if you needed some. In fact if you give me a second...".

Steve realized she was about to offer him a bulb of garlic. "No, no: I was just thinking I need to supply my kitchen, and looking at your store I thought about trying to figure out what I can buy locally. Right now I'm not even sure of the size of my pantry, let alone what all I will need. If there is a local store offering fresh food, and maybe some appliances, well, I will be in the market pretty soon, I think. I mean, the cafeteria is okay as far as it goes, but..."

"Oh I know what you mean. Good food does make life a little better. Well, I'll have this place open soon and perhaps we'll be able to figure something out for you."

Steve found himself gazing into her eyes, and when he caught himself it startled him. "Well that sounds like it should work out nicely, Mary. I'll drop by again when I see you are open and we'll talk. I'll have some measurements and you can see what we can do."

"Okay, Steve. It was a pleasure meeting you and I'll look forward to doing business with you," she said with a warm smile.

"The pleasure has been mine, Mary. Have a good day."

"You, too."

Steve turned and left the store. Out in the Station commons corridor he resisted looking back at her again. He kept turning her name over in his mind, associating it with her face and eyes. Then he looked back despite his intent.

Mary watched him leave and saw him look back. She thought he was pretty cute.

Chapter 10: Escape

In Manhattan Martin Avery's limousine didn't arrive this morning and his driver did not answer Avery's comms. When Martin arrived at the hotel lobby downstairs to take a cab, the building shook and the windows collapsed from the force of an explosion, upstairs in his suite. That was warning enough. The cab didn't take him where he wanted to go, so when the cab paused for traffic he quickly opened the door and jumped out onto the street. The cabby, a big burly guy, left his cab there in the street and chased Avery while yelling into his wrist comm.

Martin no longer concerned himself with questions of paranoia. He did not care what people might think of him as he ran deeper into the poorer neighborhoods of New York city where people don't run for fitness only survival. The only reason to slow down was to take shelter in the vast crowds that walked the street. Crowds had changed for him, from a unthinking herd into a living, moving hideout where he could blend in and maybe catch his breath.

Moments ago Avery had learned the bank froze his accounts because of embezzlement charges. His company had been taken over by a holding company which filed the charge against him. He was without even a job. No better off than any other pauper on the street, except the expensive cut of his clothes made him far more conspicuous. People stared at him as he ran through the narrow streets. Okay, so he did care a little about what they thought.

Avery looked back over his shoulder for any sign of pursuit. Then he spotted them, two athletic young men in generic business suits were scanning the crowd with their eyes. He knew in his gut they were looking for him.

He saw nearby an entrance to the derelict subway system, and he stepped quickly into it and down the broad steps. Many of the old tunnels were now filled with water, but so far this one seemed dry. The subway was filled with a honeycomb of shacks made of cardboard layers stitched together with plastic strapping. The shelters on the bottom rows had walls and ceilings that were bolstered with old boards. The dim lighting from the few remaining bulbs made it challenging to try and pick his way through the people who lived in these dark human nests. Not long ago he might have feared these people in their darkness, but now anonymity would be his close friend. At least these nameless ones weren't his enemy. He knew his enemy. His enemy had everything except Martin, and Martin suddenly had nothing. Nothing but his brain, his experience, and a rapidly growing desire for vengeance. And, oh yeah, a growling empty belly.

His eyes adjusted to the sparse lighting underground and saw a circle of men whose clothing was mismatched and worn, but clean and even looked pressed. The people made room for him. They were not unfriendly, and were not all men. He decided to rest his legs. He took an open seat in the circle on an old plastic crate that had probably not been in sunlight for a century. There was a flickering holovid playing to one side with the sound turned low. The voices of the actors were distorted by antique diaphragm speakers instead of modern sonic emitters. The people watching it spoke together with voices too quiet to be distinct. A woman next to him in an old suit jacket and trousers asked where he was from. She had been pretty once, and still carried herself with confidence. An older fellow passed him a bottle of water, and Martin realized he was very thirsty. He consciously limited himself to one good sip and passed it back. He felt lucky to have found people who didn't look like they were about to murder him for his clothes. He did not want to appear as if he thought he was somehow better than them. The circle, of course, noticed how nicely he was dressed and one expressed his curiosity in a round about way. Martin began using his superb networking and socializing skills, earned through thirty years of negotiating business deals.

Martin felt again for the datacube in his jacket's inner pocket. It's contents would be the instrument of his revenge if he could find a way to deliver it intact to the right people. Martin knew it could destroy his enemy, but he could only hope it would also clear his name and return his former wealth and status. Preparing for the worst when he had the opportunity had been his hopeful defense, and so far he still lived. Avery surveyed his environment. He felt weary but determined. He had never been down this far before, but the sky had never been his limit.

Chapter 11: Politics

The provisional council, now setting up as *Perry Station*'s government, asked Steve to appear in person for his meeting rather than over comms. Steve mentioned some things that needed attention to Kyle and headed for Station Administration. He felt a little trepidation. If they wanted to cut his budget he was determined to meet the council head-on.

The Station Admin section was across from Engineering near the space dock. A nondescript door led into an unremarkable pale yellow corridor lined with uniform blank doors with numbers on them. A plaque on the wall provided a list of departments and their corresponding room number. Currently almost all departments indicated the same door.

Inside was a woman in her late fifties with a stack of data cubes in her 'Out' bin and just a few in her 'In' bin. A younger woman with a worried expression on her face very quietly removed the Out cubes and carried them away. On the older woman's desk was a digital nameplate which read Margaret Lodge. She was intently reading something on her holoscreen when Steve entered, and only looked up when the door slid shut behind him. She did not look amused and finished reading another paragraph. Promptly enough to not seem rude, she asked Steve how she might help him. He told her his name and position, and that he had been instructed to report to the council in person. She raised an inquiring eyebrow and checked the time. Steve was surprised to feel like he had won a battle just by being on time. She verified his appointment on her holoscreen and an inner door clicked open behind her. Steve walked to the door and entered.

David Lyman was clearly the chairman, and the rest of the council members sat arrayed to his left and right. When Steven entered they all stood and welcomed him with what seemed a genuine warmth. Lyman was the last to greet him and the council members gradually returned to their seats, leaving the 'hot seat' before them for Steve.

"Steven," Lyman began, "We want to send you to Earth for a couple of weeks to give eyewitness interviews with several competing news organizations as well as a holodocumentary producer and his team about the mysterious threat of the 'black cruiser', as it is being romanticized by the interstellar media."

Earth? Now? Steve immediately began to object that there was still far too much to do in Security for him to leave, but Lyman rolled right over Steve's words.

"Your mission in the interviews, aside from presenting our cause in the most favorable light, is to invite skilled workers to come bolster the Station's population. We'll need at least a thousand skilled émigrés to make the Station self-sufficient. Add a half dozen for every thousand miners that show up as soon as word spreads about the money to be made here."

Steve pointed out that immigration would complicate and increase their security risk but the council seemed unimpressed. Taking another tack, Steve asked "Why go all the way to Earth when we can conduct the interviews remotely?"

Lyman was playing with a data cube, rolling it over in his hands. "It's marketing, Steve. Your presence on Earth for these interviews will lend weight to our cause in the minds of Earth's viewers. It will show the people of Earth that they are important to us, so important that we would send the hero of Al Najid III there to ask for their help."

"I'm no hero, sir," objected Steve, growing concerned.

"You don't think of yourself that way, no. But the stories are already public, and being popularly embellished. The bare reports provided by your fellow pilots have already caught the public's imagination. In point of fact the myth, the Steve Holbrook they think you are, has grown into a hero.

"And frankly, Steven, your self-image is skewed by what I believe is a sense of guilt. I think it is because the planet was destroyed despite your best efforts. It was, but nobody could have tried harder, Steve. That is what your fellow pilots tell me, and I will take their word for it."

Steve had no response to that. He did blame himself for failing to save the planet and his family.

"To be honest, Steve, I need you to leave for political reasons."

Steve's brows furrowed and his eyes hardened.

"Your popularity is a problem. If I am to take the leadership role for this council, and an election were held today I could not win with your name on the ballot."

Steve's confusion was evident on his face. He truly had no interest in setting himself up as a politician. Yet, if the Counselor's information was true (which Steve didn't yet fully believe), then he might well be on an unwitting path for a role in a bureaucratic hell.

"If you did win such an election you would not do well, Steve. You are not devious enough. You would be torn to pieces in high-stakes politics. You might enjoy a game of political chess now and then, but I don't believe you are ready to sit down across from the top players of every system, every corporation, and every power-hungry professional in the galaxy. Every one of them is playing a cut-throat game with millions and even billions of lives on the line.

"Steven, you may not realize it yet, but you really want to get out of here for a couple of weeks while we get this government up and running. Let's use your strengths where they are most needed. Let's capitalize on the hunger for tales of adventure among the idle billions of smart, well-trained people of Earth to draw the best of them to *Perry Station*."

Steven's natural suspicion of the politician was disarmed by the man's honesty and adroit insight. He was right. Steve knew he wasn't politically adept. He hated politics. The stakes were at least as high as Lyman projected.

The room became completely silent as the council waited for Steve's response. They had clearly discussed how to proceed. Each of them was ambitious and smart, motivated by power, yet had thrown in with David Lyman's vision. That fact told Steve volumes in itself. The thought occurred to Steve that Lyman's open honesty was a very skillful, calculated tactic.

Still, it sounded like the council intended to implement a democratic form of government. A representative democracy, just like Perry had before the destruction, was exactly what Steven expected.

"The decision is above my pay grade, sir. But I'm going to need quite a bit of money for any trip to Earth."

Counselor Lyman beamed at Steven. "I knew you were the right man, Steve, and I wouldn't expect you to subsist on nibbles while you are there. You will arrive at New York, a Historical Reservation. Don't expect modern conveniences, but that is where all incoming travelers are required to land. Services are primitive in New York but the city offers everything you could possibly need. If you left New York the technology you are used to would be available, but don't go seeking adventure in other cities. Outside the Historical Preserve social unrest is common. Your business on Earth is all scheduled to happen either at the DisCom HoloMedia complex downtown or in Central Park, where the documentary producer hopes for a suitable wintery backdrop, even though it is more likely to rain than snow this time of year. As a matter of fact, you will want to take a warm coat to wear.

"The ACM Reserve has promoted you to Lieutenant, by the way, and I'm glad I was able to be the one to tell you," Lyman continued.

"As for the politics, I feel honored to have the opportunity to say that in an ideal world I would vote for your leadership, Steve. The sad fact is this isn't an ideal galaxy in which we live. If I am elected it will be my honor to serve you and the people of *Perry Station*.

"Marge already has your travel arrangements and expense account. She will need your digital signature. Before you go there is one other thing." The Councilor extended the data cube to Steve. "There are several scenic holovids of Perry as it used to look on this cube for the documentary team. You will be met at the spaceport by a security contractor of my acquaintance who will keep you safe, but beware of straying into the streets unescorted, Steve, seriously."

As Steve rose to leave, Councilor Lyman added, "Steve, one more thing. Please start training Kyle for your job as Security Chief. If you're willing, the council and I have bigger plans for you, plans that were suggested by our friend Tibs, captain of the *Jade Temple*, before it departed."

"Yes, sir" Steve replied, who opened the door to leave but then paused. "Any details on what role you and Tibs have for me beyond my immediate assignment?"

"When you return we want you to focus all your attention on locating and apprehending whomever is responsible for the destruction of our planet. Beyond that, we're still working out the details, Steve. I can tell you it will be vital to the future of *Perry Station*."

Steve nodded without turning and left.

In the outer office Marge Lodge stood and stepped toward him. She had a digital official notary pad in her left hand and reached out to shake his hand with her right. "Call me Marge, Lt. Holbrooks" she said with a brilliant smile.

"It's Holbrook, Marge. But please call me Steve."

"Oh, of course. I'm sorry, Steve," she said, blushing slightly while she corrected the spelling on the authorization. She looked back up to him. "I need your signature accepting this travel chit for your trip. Three factor authentication. No need to worry about the accounting details unless you pay cash for something. Everything digital will work automatically on this end. Your intersystem shuttle to Cygnus leaves the day after tomorrow. You'll have a three hour layover there before catching a Transys Intersystem Starliner to Earth. It'll take you about a week to get there. Your itinerary details will be sent to your net address. Once you arrive on Earth you will be met by your contact. She will use a passphrase so you will know she is the right person."

"She?" Steve asked.

"Yes, the contractor is female, and very reputable. Given name is 'Pat'. The passphrase will be 'temple bell'."

"Very well, Marge. Thank you."

What was Tibs up to now? 'Temple Bell' was an unmistakable message that the Aldebari were behind the whole deal.

Chapter 12: Outbound

The outbound shuttle to Cygnus was deserted, except for Steve. Service only recently resumed between Cygnus and the Al Najid system. The residents of *Perry Station* were just getting organized, too busy settling in to take trips for anything but necessary business, and business was still scarce. Steve remained confident that would change soon.

Steve checked his inbox and spotted a secure message from the *Jade Temple*. When opened, the message read 'use passphrase'. A password dialog popped up when he tried to open the compressed attachment, and he input 'temple bell'. The encryption did not accept the passphrase, so he tried it again, this time capitalizing the T in 'temple' and the attachment opened. The wrist display was not large enough to usefully present the graphic image, but the text indicated that Aldebari Naval Intelligence, using imagery retrieved from several flight recorders, made a positive ID of the black cruiser. The ship was a Fisher class heavy cruiser, the *Pyotr Velikiyer*, decommissioned from active duty with her squadron several years earlier in 3006. Intelligence reported the ship was supposedly maintained in decommissioned status near a large mining and research facility in the Trondheim system, deep in Corporate Earth's own star systems. When she had been on active duty her complement of 800 personnel had controlled 20 long range missile tubes and 14 smaller medium range launchers, complemented by impressive point defenses. She had been an escort to an even larger warship, the battleship *Ariel*. The decommissioned squadron also included another heavy cruiser, two frigates and three destroyers.

Steve closed the attachment and message and scanned the deserted shuttle. The flight approached the modulus and would soon transit into the Cygnus system. An automated vendor offered assorted snack foods and drinks but he didn't feel like eating. Looking out the viewport he saw the modulus patrol cruising in apparently aimless formation, lit on one side by the blue light of the modulated anomaly and on the other by Al Najid. Beyond them the vast array of countless stars dusted dark space and a bit toward aft, behind the ship, he could see part of his planet's remains. He looked back to his wrist set and started browsing the interweb for information on the Trondheim system, where the mothballed ship was supposed to be stored.

The holovid above the snack bar automatically switched from Al Najid communications to a Cygnus news station when the ship passed through the modulus. Steve looked up at it from his research and became aware that the news program discussion centered on the destruction of Perry and what the several well-dressed authorities around the holographic table thought the attack implied. As he watched, the image of the commentators dissolved into a two dimensional animated video of the planet's cataclysmic end. The full motion image stopped as the commentators spoke, and part of the image zoomed in on the hollowing of the planet's crust while the rest of the planet continued in orbit. A computer graphic of a circle appeared around the hollowing area for emphasis. The holovid 'expert witness' expounded his theory that the planet had been destroyed by four 'inertia bombs'.

Steve immediately thought of his kids. His heart ached to hold them.

Chapter 13: History

Over Earth, at the central transport terminal above the atmosphere among the orbital cities, Steve transferred from the non-aerodynamic starliner to a luxurious and aerodynamic landing shuttle that had been picking up passengers from High New York and myriad smaller, even more exclusive habitats in orbit for the commute to Old New York, on the planet surface below.

When he took his seat among business people and tourists from other frontier planets he dutifully strapped in and sat back, half-listening to an absurd assurance in half a dozen languages that if the landing shuttle 'went down' the seat cushions could be used as flotation devices. Curiously, people used all those languages here on Earth: there was only one language common outside Earth's solar system, an evolved form of English that borrowed heavily from the other languages, primarily German, Hindi, Russian and Chinese. On Earth, people used different languages in their everyday life, although most business people could also use English.

Below him was the Earth. In the Pacific the islands of Japan and the Korean peninsula were clearly dealing with a storm system that looked as bad as a typhoon.

When the corporations grew to dominate rather than merely influence world governance, and population growth mushroomed to levels that were always thought insupportable, orbital habitats became the most desired commodity on the real estate market. Enclaves built in remote and exclusive locations on Earth were no longer considered safe from unrest. Since most food was now imported from the frontier planets, the orbital cities had first pick of the imports. They became, therefore, the residences of the wealthiest people. The bulk of Earth's population was still planetside, and that is where the most mundane business operations were conducted. Although automation and robotics had replaced human workers in many industries, people were still employed servicing and operating the machinery. People tend to find ways to make money, but the fact is inescapable that today those who do not have paid employment outnumber those who have. Increasingly, especially among the young, the most common occupation was providing entertainment for one another in virtual reality games.

The shuttle disconnected from the liner and gently pulled away, descending into Earth's atmosphere. The costly blessing of a modulinium anti-gravity generator allowed the shuttle to descend directly, instead of having to slow through several orbits.

As the shuttle hovered at low altitude awaiting clearance to land, Steve gazed down between the clouds onto Old New York, teeming with buildings and filled with Earth's quaint wheeled vehicles in an oddly orderly procession on what they called *streets*. Because of the inadequate supply of modulinium, antigrav vehicles were relatively rare, and of the land-transit alternatives nothing was more efficient than the wheel. It was so different from the frontier worlds, where modulinium-enabled gravitics were the dominant influence on transportation. Still, Steve mused, with all the wheeled vehicles he could see down there the galaxy's stock of modulinium would have been exhausted years ago to meet Earth's demand alone. It would have been unimaginably difficult for frontier worlds to have constructed roadways like these to connect farms and ranches to remote transit and storage hubs.

Each frontier planet had at least one spaceport, but few had four and only the Legion's capital planet had five. Earth had more than a dozen, one for each orbiting city, and unlike other planets only a small portion of the planet Earth's business was centered on space travel and material supply.

Steve had never seen mankind's home planet before, at least not in person. Earth remained the center of inhabited space. Earth was narcissistic, powerful and predacious.

As the shuttle approached the port and descended beneath the cloud cover for landing, Steve could distinguish individual people walking on the concrete apron in bulky clothing to protect them against the weather.

All around him passengers began reaching for their bags, ignoring a bored attendant as she asked them to please keep their seats until the shuttle fully stopped and powered down in its berth.

He felt disappointed when he debarked to find no shops in the terminal, just a utilitarian hub of corridors leading to connecting aircraft and spacecraft with desks for airport personnel and rows of seats for waiting passengers. He felt a dull pang of hunger and resolved to find some food soon.

Armed security guards were alert, as if they were waiting for a military incursion. While he waited for his luggage Steve read a brass plaque explaining the thousand year-old technology. It was inconvenient to have to carry his luggage himself, but the regular system of delivery by automated courier was prohibited in New York. There were even gender-restricted restrooms to one side and a 'lost luggage' office on the other. Digital identification for baggage and automated delivery made 'lost luggage' obsolete, but here it was preserved as if a valuable part of human heritage. Perhaps the Corporations were trying to demonstrate how much more convenient modern technology is to show off Corporate accomplishments. The main exit was visible beyond a manual customs inspection station where passengers were already lining up. Steve sighed, slightly annoyed. Evidently people used to do everything manually, and for some reason Earth seemed obsessed with the memory of it.

He spotted his bag as it emerged onto the conveyor belt, grabbed it, and hauled it out of the way to retrieve his coat from inside. He was glad he had thought to check the weather before packing. Councilor Lyman, having been a diplomat in New York, still had and was willing to loan a heavy black coat and a set of nice luggage to Steve. With the councilor's coat on one arm he extended the luggage handle and attached his overnight bag atop the wheeled suitcase as Lyman recommended. Steve then moved into the line for manual customs inspection.

A crowd gathered beyond customs, and several people in the crowd held signs with passenger names on them.

Even though Steve was certain he had already been thoroughly scanned and identified, New York obstinately preserved the manual methods that had been completely replaced by automation everywhere else.

The customs agent opened Steve's bag and began rifling through the clothes. "Are you carrying any non-digital or printed political literature, fiction, poetry, prose, or any scholarly documents?" the agent asked.

"No." Steve responded. While the agent scanned Steve's biometric passport and uploaded his digital travel documents the agent asked the purpose of Steve's visit. Steve replied "business only". The agent nodded, looking curiously at Steven's face, comparing it to the virtual 3D image in the passport. He handed the passport along to the next agent, who recorded the digital visa, which showed up as a complicated icon on Steve's passport interface. The second agent immediately tried to give it back to

Steve, even though Steve was still trying to get all his ransacked clothes back into the carbon-resin luggage and get it closed. The customs agent insistently waved the passport back and forth at Steve to get him to move on while the next passenger in line huffed and shuffled in impatience. Finally getting the bag's clasps to close, and feeling somewhat humiliated, Steve took his passport from the disdainful agent and pulled up his luggage handle. Steve deliberately straightened his shirt and coat before moving out of the line. The huffy guy behind him could damn well wait.

Steve couldn't believe the whole procedure. Imagine, he thought, searching for political literature? Were they worried he might be smuggling printed political hardcopy?

Steve spotted his name 'HOLBROOK' on one of the signs held by the waiting chauffeurs and headed for the attractively dressed woman holding it. She was very pretty, lithe and athletic, and her eyes and smile were sweet with promise as he approached. Clearly most of the other men within 20 meters were very aware of her allure. When he came within range to smell her perfume his purely sexual desires awakened as they hadn't in months. Involuntarily his eyes went to the swell of her breasts beneath her halter. When he did look she tensed her shoulders, lifting them slightly, and he had to force himself to look back up into her laughing blue eyes.

Suddenly he felt a small arm slip into the crook of his elbow. He looked down to his right to see a young woman with her hair in a boyish cut and intelligent eyes that twinkled as she said, "If she rings your temple bells you had best come with me, Steve."

Temple bells: the pass phrase.

"Pat?" he asked.

She nodded and said loudly enough to carry to the woman with his name sign, "I'm so glad you made it: Mom has been sick for so long and she's asking for you."

It was not without regret that he let her turn him away from the femme fatale, and toward the parking garage.

As the sliding door at the exit opened Steve was hit by the low-pitched rumble of a city alive with millions of people on the go. The air felt cold and damp, though he was sheltered by tons of concrete above him. To the left and right eight lanes of wheeled vehicles moved slowly, some to switch lanes, others accelerating into any opening ahead of them. Pat stopped at the edge of a river of traffic waiting for something, and as Steve looked he saw a light turn from red to green. As if by magic the river came to a stop, opening a path across the eight lanes. That's when he also noticed a set of red lights on a metal cylinder that arched over the thoroughfare. When Pat and he were halfway across the open path their green sign turned to yellow, and began counting down the remaining seconds to get across. Steve picked up his pace trying to keep up with Pat. The light turned red before he reached the other side. One of the vehicles on his left blasted a loud sonic wave that startled him. He flinched involuntarily, while the driver laugh aloud. The driver hooted at him derisively but waited for him to finish crossing before accelerating.

Pat looked at him a little amused. "So who was that woman with my name on her card?" he asked.

"Bait." She answered. "I'd say someone found out when you were arriving and hoped to get something from you."

"What would they want from me?"

Pat cocked her head slightly to one side. "It's hard to say. Perhaps it was for information, or more likely to create scandal: Take your pick. You're already a celebrity here, the networks that will interview you have already seen to that. You are currently one of the most interesting people on the planet. At least, until the next interesting thing happens." Pat shrugged. "Someone wanted information they could sell, and it would be all the more valuable if it involved scandal, sex, violence, or all of the above.

"Steve you may not realize it yet but you are now a tasty fish swimming in a shark pool. Not only are you on Earth where the sharks are kings, but you are in New York, one of the biggest shark pools on the planet. You need to understand a few things if you are going to survive long enough to complete your mission. My initial task is to give you that understanding and get you back to your home. It would help to know what you plan to accomplish. As usual my contacts came up short on the details."

They had arrived at her wheeled vehicle. The top half was lined on four sides with what looked like transparent plexiclear windows. She opened a hatch in the back of the vehicle, revealing a small cargo space for his luggage. She closed the hatch gently but firmly. Steve saw another hatch with a handle on the vehicle's side. Pat opened her hatch said "Get in", nodding toward the opposite side. It only took a moment to figure out how to operate the latch, and he slid into a reasonably comfortable seat next to Pat.

She looked at him from the pilot's seat as he closed his hatch and shut out most of the city's rumble. "Never been in a car before?"

"Is that what you call these?"

She nodded. "Strap yourself in and we'll get going. The car won't start until you do."

Steve complied and admitted that he had never been to Earth before, so he was used to more advanced modes of transport. She pressed a button, and her vehicle's systems display lit up with diagnostics. There was no sound until the car started moving, and even then it was barely audible noise from the wheels rolling on asphalt. He couldn't see the source of her sensor data that enabled her to navigate. She adjusted a lever, backed out, readjusted the lever, and moved into traffic.

"Where are your sensors: Retinal?" he asked.

"My sensors?"

"Sensor displays: radar, thermal. How can you tell what is behind you when you move the car backward?"

She glanced over at him. "I just use my eyes. Check the mirror." she said, pointing. Sure enough there was, of all things, a simple, slightly convex mirror on the outside of the plexiclear pane angled so she could see what was behind them. The engineer in him appreciated the effective simplicity of the solution.

"I think it would make much more sense to fly. Rolling along on the ground like this gives you no room to maneuver. I think I would get claustrophobic here."

"There are too many cars to invest modulinium in them all. The only antigrav craft are used by vehicles used by the Corporations, such as the police." She pointed out a swift patrol craft above the flow of wheeled traffic.

Steve decided to shut up: there seemed little point in asking questions that revealed his ignorance. He had so much to learn just by paying attention to his surroundings.

She navigated out of the spaceport and guided the car into a stream of traffic, then engaged the autopilot. The car linked up with the city's traffic computer. Once Pat merged into the great river of vehicles it took over, querying her for a destination on a touch-screen. Ahead, huge skyscrapers towered over the Grand Central

Parkway. Snowflakes the size of rose petals floated lightly from the sky, reminding him of that last morning on Perry. He looked back over his shoulder toward the spaceport and saw the East River beyond a seawall that held it back, and beyond that a far shore also covered in high rise structures.

"Are you tired?" Pat asked, considering what destination to input into the traffic computer interface.

Steve responded "No, I'm fine." The starliner provided him a stateroom to sleep and he had been quite comfortable.

"I'm hungry though." he added.

"Are you hungry for anything in particular?"

He looked at her youthful profile. She was pretty, in a perky kind of way. She seemed to have a fun, but no-nonsense personality. She glanced over at him. He looked forward again through the front viewport.

"I've wanted a good charbroiled hamburger for months now. I don't suppose…"

"I know just the place." she replied with a grin. She zoomed in on an area on the digital navmap by touching the screen with two fingers and spreading them wide until she could touch a specific building. She keyed it as their destination and looked over at Steve. He looked uncomfortable. "You're going to be all right, Steve. Hang in there. Meat is expensive though, so be prepared. I know a place where we can get a good burger. It's out of the way, but popular among successful business people."

The hamburger shop appeared to be hundreds of years old, and the smell of flame-grilled beef filled the neighborhood of dark ancient buildings under the gray overcast. He could smell the wood smoke rising blue to linger before dissipating into a breeze that infiltrated the neighborhood a few dozen meters above, around the fourth floor windows of the surrounding buildings. The burgers smelled delicious as they were grilled over red hot wood coals. He went to a sliding window so old that it's glass thickness was irregularly distorted over time. He ordered a double, medium, with all the fixings. Pat ordered a single. The cost was astronomical, but his expense account covered it so he didn't really care. Beside the shop sprawled a run-down baseball diamond, now looking forlorn and wet under the cloudy November sky. The snow hadn't reached this neighborhood yet. The vehicles parked nearby were much more luxurious than he would have expected in such an old residential neighborhood.

They went into a small enclosed seating area to await their order. The decor radiated warmth. Broad glass windows over varnished pine walls looked out over the baseball diamond. Ancient wooden picnic tables, heavily stained, varnished, and deeply etched with generations of hand-carved graffiti populated the room. Scattered, well-to-do people sat alone or in couples. The windows clouded with steam near the kitchen. A few tough-looking teens were camped in the farthest corner ignoring everyone but themselves.

"When I was going through customs back at the spaceport they wanted to know if I was smuggling printed political material." Steve said as they were sitting down. "Not drugs, not weapons, but words. Is there a political problem here on Earth?"

Pat looked up at him, her head canted a little to the right. "We have many problems. Customs doesn't worry about digital material because their mainframes will automatically interdict and neutralize any problem ideas transmitted on the net, and trace them back to the sender. But they can't do that with printed books."

Steve thought about that for a minute. "So some ideas are problems. You mean the Corporations try to control what people can read?"

She nodded. "Yes. Well, they're trying to control what people talk about or even think. They've been trying for as long as I've been here. It's difficult to think clearly about things for which you don't have words. Look, try to understand." she continued, "Earth simply has too many people. It doesn't look so bad here because New York is Earth's showpiece, a closely controlled, low-population historical reservation. Other cities have much higher population density. The crowding is much worse and people are desperate. If everyone started thinking for themselves and talking about volatile ideas it could lead to serious unrest."

A woman called the number for their order and they went over to the little sliding window to pick up their burgers.

Two small sacks of freshly fried and lightly salted potato strips, French fries, accompanied the burgers.

"So it isn't just books that are being suppressed, but even ideas that might lead to unnecessary expense?" Steve remained skeptical, but kept it out of his voice.

Pat nodded again. She rolled back the recycled paper that

wrapped her burger and prepared for a big wolfish bite.

Steve looked down at his juicy steaming double burger with shredded lettuce, a thin slice of tomato, a thin slice of red onion, and a pinkish-orange sauce with bits of pickle in it spread on the upper bun. It smelled divine! The bread roll was fresh, fragrant, and warm to his fingers. The twin hamburgers in it were dark and slightly crisp, each one easily 10 millimeters thick and singed by flame. The sliced and toasted bun looked perfect, right down to the tiny golden sesame seeds. This looked simply great.

The first bite was memorable. It seemed like his teeth and gums had developed new taste buds, appreciating the textures and flavors. The aroma filled his nose and sinuses with luxury, and he closed his eyes to dedicate himself to the sheer pleasure of finally having his dream hamburger.

Pat continued, "I'm not going to say who, but I know someone who's hidden away some of the really old books. Parts of them I still don't understand, but it's clear that what we think some things mean is different from what they meant a few centuries ago."

"Pat, language changes with the people who use it. That's natural, it seems to me."

"Yes, Steve, but what people can think will change if the language they use is changed."

"You are suggesting that those aren't the same thing. One is the natural evolution of language and the other is artificial manipulation."

"Right," Pat replied. "So the Corporations don't want people spreading dangerous ideas they can't control because it could get expensive in more ways than one if the people grow more discontented.

"Anyway," she continued just before taking another big bite, "I had a question you didn't answer earlier. For me to do my job, I believe I need to know why you are here. I know you have an interview with the 'Skywatch' show tomorrow. I know you lost your planet and it's really big news here. I'm sure you will be talking about what happened in the Al Najid system, so of course all the networks want an interview. But they could have done that remotely. So why did you come all the way to Earth and what do you hope to achieve?"

"The idea is that my being here will lend credence, and supposedly appeal, to attract skilled people to move to *Perry Station*," Steve answered. Pat paused, mid-bite, and shook her head. Steve explained "We don't have enough people to operate the Station efficiently, mine our resources, and also service our population. We have to gain a critical mass of population and skill sets for the station to work. And if anyone has extra people, it is Earth."

Pat finished chewing her bite and swallowed. "That won't sit well with the powers-that-be, Steve." She dabbed her chin with a tissue-thin napkin. "They aren't going to like you skimming our best and brightest. The Corporations support overpopulation to increase the number of exactly the same exceptional people who will be most receptive to your recruiting. Your missionary efforts will make enemies for you here. The news networks will probably just have to edit out some of what you say in your interview."

"Wait a minute. I don't think I understand. Earth is overpopulated. I thought siphoning off some of your surplus would be welcomed."

Pat looked at him sternly. "If you pulled from the bottom of the gene pool that might be true, but you don't want people with weak minds. You need highly skilled people, and that will diminish the high-end, people they want to retain. The Corporations aren't struggling to support as large a population as they can out of the goodness of their hearts."

"I don't follow. What do you mean?"

"The larger the breeding gene pool, the more genius and near-genius people they expect to have. The Corporations certainly aren't going to be happy to learn that you came here to skim off the very people they have been trying to train up for their own plans."

Steve considered "So Earth's overpopulation," Steve replied, "Isn't just an accident of nature. You mean people are being bred."

"You could put it like that I suppose," she added.

Steve sat back and stared at her. The burger tasted great, but the thought of people being bred like livestock was alarming. Perhaps he was over-reacting; maybe the hormones in the beef were affecting his judgment.

"Do you mean to tell me that the current government of Earth is trying to breed more intelligent humans? What happens to the less-than-optimal humans?"

"It isn't as bad as you think, Steve, and nobody phrases it the way you did. They do try to improve our health and intelligence from generation to generation, but they don't cull the less viable individuals from the herd. If they did, it would still reduce the gene pool. Eugenics is an old idea, but it was always diverted from its objective when people thought they could increase the top end by reducing the low end, or what they believed was the low end. Genetics doesn't work like that. To increase the high intelligence end, you also have to increase the low end, and the median."

Steve held his tongue for a moment. Breeding for a desired outcome in livestock had been common practice for centuries. But not for people.

"Even before taking over the governance of the entire planet, the Board of Corporations realized they couldn't get away with stopping people from reproducing. When it was tried before, back when the world had many conflicting nation-states, the only people who would control their reproduction were the same people most needed. The rest just kept reproducing into starvation. Yet more people also meant more bright people to recruit into productive interests.

"The corollary is that supporting a larger population also means supporting more not-so-bright people. Robotics compounded the problem. Automation meant more and more work performed by machines. Earth could either absorb the expense of making a tremendous amount of completely unnecessary work, along with its attendant costs, or try to change the work ethic.

"When you want a really large gene pool it is less expensive to simply feed, clothe, and house the unemployed than it is to do all that and also create jobs to make product that nobody needs. Besides, people tend to find things to do that will make them money. With the pressure of providing for themselves lifted they can get pretty creative. Supporting them also reduces 'crimes of necessity'. All the Corporates have to do is keep people fed, sheltered and out of trouble. The most efficient way to keep them out of trouble is to entertain them and minimize the emergence of ideas and conditions that might otherwise breed discontent. The biggest trouble maker is hunger." She waved the remains of her burger at him, a little drop of juicy sauce dripping from the wrapper onto the table.

Steve used his thin paper napkin to wipe the drip where it hadn't sunk into the graffiti. Steve thought about what he was hearing as Pat continued telling him what she felt he needed to know.

"So the Corporations calculated that if the people's attention could be focused somewhere else, they wouldn't be overly interested in such realities as variety in their diet. They could feed everyone if people could be content with eating very little meat, for example. They developed '*Nibbles*', a primarily grain product impregnated with a nutritious supplement of freeze dried sauce. Just stir boiling water into it and it makes something like beef stew... except it doesn't contain much animal protein. The problem: getting everyone to live on it. For those who were starving, they were very glad to get any food, but the more privileged people had to be gradually priced out of a traditional meat-and-potato diet."

So that's what the Councilman meant when he said he didn't expect him to live on *Nibbles* while here on Earth. At the time Steve thought he had been talking about pet food.

"Steve, relatively few people can afford to buy a hamburger like those we just ate, let alone a sirloin steak. The money you paid for these burgers would support your average idle citizen for almost a week."

"What did you mean when you said 'more people mean more bright people'? Steve asked.

"For centuries people in power despaired when their children weren't any more gifted than other children. Most of the wealth made by exceptional people was inherited by generally unexceptional descendants, and power follows wealth. Now that has changed. Corporations hold the greatest wealth and they don't make babies. Therefore power, the leadership of the Corporations, can be selected according to measured ability rather than inherited wealth. Children still inherit from their parents, but only in monetary terms not power."

"So Corporate Earth should be a meritocracy. I heard democracy died out here long ago." His eyes scanned the ancient tenements outside as he chewed. There was a church out there, across the street.

"Well, I should hope so, Steve. Do you mean there are still democracies out there in the galaxy?"

Steve nodded in affirmation. She looked incredulous. "Steve, how can they possibly get anything done? Half the people in a large population will have an IQ of 100 or less. You mix that with democracy and you're asking the wrong people to make the decisions."

"Pat, smart people can be just as wrong as average people. Their mistakes may be more spectacular, but where the bright are foolish or short-sighted the common man may apply practical wisdom. But do you really believe Earth is a meritocracy?" he asked. "I would expect power still accrues to inherited money."

She shrugged. "Of course it does, but the ways inherited money can express that power has changed. Genius parents are as unlikely to produce genius offspring as anyone else. The children of wealth do tend to get superior training, but training only supplements talent. Talent isn't often overlooked anymore, not with the online game databases."

"What do games have to do with it?"

"It's another 'path of least resistance' solution the Corporations created. They couldn't get the kids away from their virtual reality games. Almost everyone but the players and game developers considered it a significant problem. Then an advanced research firm sold enough corporate human resource chiefs on the idea of using supercomputers to sample what the kids did in these games, in order to identify talent. For awhile the anarchists resisted re-purposing the virtual reality environments, but eventually the developers redesigned the most popular games to be useful for inexpensively identifying the best problem solvers, the wizards at hacking computers, and social dynamo. Those kids over there," she said, motioning toward the young people in the corner, "aren't playing hooky from school; they are playing hooky from their games. They are breaking the expected mold and will be targeted for closer study. They might be found dangerous, or they might be found creative, but they probably have no idea they are self-identifying as 'out of control' and that their uncommon behavior patterns will lead to consequences, positive or negative."

The kids looked dark, unkempt, and a little wild. "They look like trouble waiting to happen." Steve commented.

"If they continue to be wasted they would eventually make trouble. The Corporations pose many problems of conscience, but they aren't wasteful. Efficiency is not always defined by expedience. When it comes to people, sometimes efficiency itself is inefficient. Industry has grown more long sighted, Steve. They are paying attention to the consequences of what they do. It's more profitable to be far-sighted."

"I imagine", Steve thought, "they must have also by now had

second thoughts about their privatization of government."

Pat crumpled her wrapper and napkin with Steve's into the bag and crumpled it between her hands. They were finely boned hands, and the skin was faintly tanned. "Bottom line, Steve, the companies that invest heavily into identifying and training the best and the brightest will be very unhappy with your plan to siphon off the best talent from the gene pool. Be careful what you say in your interview."

"Why can't things ever be simple?"

"We're human beings. Every angle gets tried, but the House dislikes losing," Pat replied.

They stood. Steve looked around the room. Everyone was middle-aged or younger. "So what happens with the old people?" Steve asked.

"Old people? What do you mean?"

"Well, old people have already contributed their DNA to the gene pool, and when they age their competitive skill-sets atrophy. They lose some brain power, experience difficulty remembering things. They become physically weak. It doesn't seem likely that they would be useful in an overpopulated, corporate-run world. What do they do?"

Pat gave a nervous little laugh. "Steve, come on. Nobody talks about old people."

"Well, what about your parents?"

"Steve, my parents died, okay?" Her brow furrowed with discomfort. "Come on, we need to get you checked into your hotel. Let's go. Your first interview is at nine tomorrow morning. Once I drop you off I'll return the car, and see you in the lobby at the hotel tomorrow at eight. Just be careful, Steve. You are in a strange and very dangerous world. Please don't wander away from the hotel."

As they headed toward the car Steve noticed the old church again. He asked Pat to wait a minute and walked over to the ancient edifice.

He crossed the street to Our Lady of Sorrows, a twelve-hundred-year-old Catholic church built from brick and mortar in the nineteenth century. The shrubbery out front, behind a heavily enameled wrought-iron fence, appeared well manicured and the rough edged granite steps were worn from innumerable shoes climbing and descending them over the years. The steep slate roof sheltered hewn oak doors and a statue of the Blessed Mother, hands outstretched in the classic pose of either benediction or supplication. A disk of stained glass, darkened with city grime, was inset in the brick façade. Steve paused a moment, looking back toward Pat, still at the foot of the steps looking up at him.

"I'll be just a few minutes." he said, then turned back to pull open the heavy door. The vestibule inside felt cool but comfortable and the air bore a faint scent of frankincense. Two long folding tables looked as if they had rendered a lifetime of service flanking the entrance. They were clean and sturdy. Each held a short stack of pamphlets that provided parish news, schedules, and notices of marriages, baptisms, and funerals. One pamphlet was loose and on its reverse were small block advertisements for local merchants. Steve picked up the pamphlet and a bingo game card slipped to the floor. When he picked the card back up he saw flat round baskets under each table woven from some dried broad-leaf grass or reed. Before him were two more hardwood doors, possibly walnut. Smaller than the heavy oaken outer pair, each door was inset with a pane of patterned amber-colored glass. Two different flags, clean but frayed from age stood straight on either side. To the left and right were carpeted stairs.

Inside, the dim lighting came primarily from overcast daylight filtering through the magnificent stained-glass windows, although toward the front of the church a spotlight illuminated a large crucifix. The once rich carpeting hushed Steve's footsteps preserving the deep silence. On either side of the center aisle ranks of empty walnut pews seemed to wait.

To Steve's right a small white marble font still held cool water. Steve dampened the fingertips of his right hand. He felt he would be the last to claim faith, but his childhood had been regularly immersed in weekly visits to the local chapel. Memories rose in him unbidden. Listening to a baffling old man his mother adored and his father derided, and reciting special words he had come to know by heart. He remembered how he loved to sing there with his mother while his dad fitfully grumbled along in rhythm, if not quite in tune. Touching the cool moisture to his brow, heart, and both shoulders his heart ached for home and his parents, but they were deceased. And then unsought he thought of his children. As he did, Steve finally felt the lock on his grief releasing its bitter clutch from his emotions. He sagged wearily. Sadness filled him to the depth and breadth of his being. Steve staggered to the nearest pew like a man overcome and seeking safe haven, and sat there with bowed shoulders, eyes weeping freely. He caught himself and struggled to be quiet, fearing he might be heard by a priest be back there somewhere behind the altar, or in the sanctuary near it. He knew he had to leave.

Steve suddenly became aware of someone behind him. He turned and saw an older man in a black cassock with eyes of concern. "My son is there some way I can help you?" Steve's mind registered this was the oldest man he had yet seen on Earth.

Steve wiped the tears from his eyes in embarrassment. Wishing he had a way to discretely clear his sinuses, he stood and turned to the priest. "No, Father. Not unless you will pray for the souls of my children then no, I'm afraid it is too late."

The priest scrutinized Steve's face. "I will. How long has it been since your last confession?"

Steve took a deep breath, and tried to remember. "Too long, Father. Unfortunately there is someone waiting for me outside, and I have already stayed here too long. But thank you."

The priest placed a firm, gentle hand on Steve's shoulder. Looking deep into Steve's eyes the Padre said: "I think you should come back when you are ready. Right now your children may not be the ones most in need of prayer."

"Yes, Father. I will do what I can."

"That is all any man can do. I hope to see you soon, then. Mass is at 7:00 and at 9:00. Confessions, Saturday evening starting at 6:00."

Steve ducked his head in agreement and then, after turning toward the sanctuary to genuflect, walked back out of the church. He did not think he would have time to make confession.

Chapter 14: New York

The multicolored spotlights were harsh on the newsroom set. A technician was fully occupied adjusting the gain on the audio pickups as the show's hosts engaged Steve in light Q & A across a three cornered plexiclear desk enveloped by holography lenses. His stomach was nervous and fluttery, but he managed to stay focused on the conversation. He responded in normal tones to questions about Perry, his old job as a Sheriff, details about Perry's Midwinter Holidays, and how life was changed aboard *Perry Station*. It was an effective method to acclimatize him for the interview, keeping his mind off the thought that possibly billions of people would be looking at him that evening when the show aired. A young woman brushed his face with a very fine powder to prevent his face from sweating under the lights.

He and Pat had seen the woman from the spaceport on his way into the studio and she had sardonically asked after his mother. He and Pat just grinned back at her and she said nothing more. The femme fatale smiled good-naturedly and wished him well in his interview.

Donna Wainwright, a famous and well-compensated commentator hosted the interview. Across from her sat another interviewer: Daniel Briggs a handsome man with a precise and articulate British accent. Steve took the third seat at the table for an interview presented 'in the round'. The viewer at home would be able to shift perspectives at will in his holoprojection interface. When the interview was broadcast the studio computers would track the viewers' digital hits and respond with more face time for the person of greatest audience interest.

The show's director called for silence in the studio as timers out of holoview counted down from 30. Steve felt a sharp increase in his anxiety and focused on controlling his respiration and heart rate, mentally 'clearing the decks' for action.

The director spoke calmly into his communicator "Ready and five… four… three… two…"

Donna Wainwright had been studying her script and at just the right moment looked up into the cameras with her clear brown eyes and said "Good evening, and welcome to '*Skywatch*', for Corporate Holonet Three, on Thursday, November 8th, 3015.

"Tonight we are joined by Lt. Steven Holbrook of the joint ACM Defense Reserve who was present at the destruction of the primarily agrarian planet Perry, Al Najid III, as he and his squadron attempted to defend the planet against the vastly superior firepower of a star cruiser."

The holoview of the three at the interview table dissolved into a 2-D full-motion view taken by in-flight sensors of the cruiser firing a missile at the planet.

"The ACM is an alliance of three modulus-linked star systems: Al Najid, Cygnus, and Mazzaroth. Al Najid is one of the stars in our Orion constellation, also known as Bellatrix, or Gamma Orionis. The planet's main export partner was Earth. Together the three star systems provide about a quarter of our imported foods and mineral resources.

"If you look at the constellation Orion," she continued, "you'll see the three stars of the belt and two bright stars on opposite sides of that belt. The red one is Betelgeuse, and the bluish one is Rigel. Al Najid is another bluish star on the Betelgeuse side of the belt, about a quarter of the way between Orion's Belt and the constellation Taurus. It's a blue giant, much larger and hotter on its surface than our own. Accordingly, the habitable zone for planets is both much farther out from the star itself and more broad in its range. This wide orbit also makes the seasons longer than those of Earth."

"In case anyone is only now learning of this tragic event, on July 19th of last year, by our calendar, the third planet in the Al Najid star system was destroyed by unknown means. Humanity lost a rich agricultural resource that was just beginning to hit its stride as a food producer, killing all of the more than 400,000 people who were on the planet."

The holocast cut to some of the images Steve brought from the *Perry Station* council on the datacube, replacing the scene of destruction with beautiful, but brief, views of the planet as it looked before the attack. Steve felt more emotional than he would have liked looking at the panoramas, and mentally steeled himself to keep control.

"Steve, you were there. Can you describe what it was like trying to fight a battle while your planet broke into pieces below you? How did you ever handle it?" Ms. Wainwright asked.

"Donna, to tell the truth I really didn't handle it. I couldn't handle it. Just like the rest of our pilots, I was incapable of doing much of anything when I first saw it. Fortunately for us, the enemy appeared just as surprised."

"Do you mean you think they actually didn't know what was going to happen any more than you did?"

"Well, that's the way it seemed, at least at first, when the planet was breaking up. I mean, they seemed very focused and disciplined in the attack, but when the planet itself began to collapse in on itself and break apart they seemed almost as distracted as we were. After the nuclear missile burst in high altitude the planet shattered like a gigantic snowball hitting a tree. When that happened their fighters just coasted along for several seconds, not firing. I think everyone who saw it was in awe as the planet broke up below us. All I could think of were all the people down there, and especially my children. I'm sure our pilots temporarily froze with horror. I've never felt so helpless. But then, in just a heartbeat, we were fighting again. There wasn't time after that to think about anything except trying to stay alive. The enemy pilots would have eliminated us, except for our Commander, who had the presence of mind to warn us."

"Who was your Commander, Lieutenant?"

"Colonel Evans, Ma'am. Frank Evans was a good commanding officer. When the rest of us were focused in horror on our personal losses, he was thinking of us and our survival. He ordered us to snap out of it. He used our training to wrench us free from shock. Unfortunately for us his warning broadcast was intercepted by EW, their electronics warfare suites. That allowed the enemy to identify him as a leader. So they fired on him as a priority target, hoping that his loss would throw us into confusion. His ship took concentrated fire from more than a dozen ships, both energy and projectile. It was more than his shields, armor, and lifepod system could possibly compensate for. He never really had a chance, but he saved our lives, ma'am. Colonel Evans was a hero.

"I remember he used to raise some really good beefsteak tomatoes. He would share them with me on my rounds." Steve reminisced, "They made wonderful sliced tomato sandwiches, with just a touch of salt and pepper and mayo on fresh baked bread.' Steve smiled reminiscing, his eyes friendly and sad. Then his brow creased as he refocused.

"Do you have any idea who attacked your planet, or what

weapons they used to destroy it?"

"No ma'am. We've only begun to speculate how it might have been done. We have images of the ship, as you saw at the start of tonight's interview. It looked like one of your Fisher class cruisers, but Earth decommissioned the Fisher class years ago". There was some rustling among the computers around the stage and sure enough, in less time than he would have thought possible, an orthographic rendering of a Fisher class cruiser came onscreen. Steve recognized her lines and confirmed the ID.

The show director ordered "Cut!" and the studio erupted in uproar. Steve had identified the cruiser as an Earth ship. "Thank God we aren't broadcasting live" the director complained. Steve noticed one of the holovid pickups had not shut down as ordered: a tiny green light remained lit. Probably a direct feed to corporate intelligence, Steve thought.

Daniel Briggs reported, a hand to his ear: "Contact in Corporate Command confirms off record/anon that one of their mothballed naval squadrons has been misplaced, somehow. We will surely not be able to disclose that, but someone is going to get canned over this."

"Is this the real reason you have come, Lieutenant?" demanded Donna. "Do you think Earth committed this atrocity?"

"No ma'am we don't believe it was Earth that attacked us, but rather a predator using a ship built by Earth. We think it was probably the *Pyotr Velikiyer.*"

Donna Wainwright looked almost disappointed. It would have made a bigger story if he accused Earth. Briggs looked like he was seeking the ship name on the list of ships missing from the mothballed fleet. He looked over at Steve and briefly gave a slight nod.

Steve continued, "We think an unidentified force may have commandeered some retired Earth assets for their own purposes. It might be an Earth citizen behind the attack, but we don't know that. All we can say it was a very well-funded person, or perhaps a rogue corporation."

Ms. Wainwright looked at once vindicated but outraged. "Lieutenant we would never..."

"Of course you wouldn't, ma'am." Steve assured her. "My primary mission here isn't to make accusations, or even to conduct an investigation. Your own security is surely more than capable of handling that end of it. I would be very interested in any relevant information, but that's not my purpose in coming to Earth."

"It was probably agents of the Legion, or the Aldebari, trying to..." Donna was interrupted as her boss waded briskly into the studio, a large, heavy set man with the impeccable hair and looks of a former newscaster. He was immaculately dressed and seemed used to wielding decisions like an ax. His eyes were fierce as he approached.

"What is your purpose, then?" he demanded. "Why did your council so readily accept the expense of sending you all the way here? What do you want, Holbrook?"

It was a make or break moment. Steve didn't ask the man who he was; it was obvious that he was the man Steve needed to convince. He didn't look like an easy sell. To the side, Steve could see Pat frantically shaking her head and drawing her finger across her throat. She was as cute as a button and he couldn't help but smile at her.

The large man in charge followed Steve's gaze, and Pat spotted it. She suddenly changed her expression to appear more casual and nonplussed. He said, "Come with me to my office, Steve. You can bring your friend."

Steve motioned to her, and they followed the man off stage. The director told everyone to take a break, but return in ten minutes.

The office was expansive and expensive. The big man moved around the desk gracefully for his size, and sat in a high-backed leather swivel chair. He looked like he was calculating his options.

"To answer your question, sir..."

"Auguste, Steve. My name is Auguste Tardieu." His name sounded French, but his accent was central North American.

"This is my studio and I'm responsible for everything we broadcast. I need to know what you will say. It will serve nobody's interest to say anything that leads our viewers to think you are blaming Earth for the loss of your planet. My interest is in real journalism and any marketable conversations that result from that. I am not interested in losing my position just because you didn't know how to say something politically correct. I understand you were just trying to answer a direct question with a direct answer. We can rephrase the question so that it can be answered in a way that won't sound like an accusation you didn't intend."

"But what else do you need to say, Steve? I don't buy that you came all the way to Earth just to give me a sit-down, when we could have done the whole thing remotely and at much less expense to *Perry Station*. So why did your council lay out good money to send you all the way here? What are you after? I need to hear something that makes sense. Your story just doesn't wash otherwise. If you aren't going to be honest with me, then I'm not going to give you air time."

Pat started to protest but Tardieu silenced her with a stony look.

"We don't have a large enough population to run *Perry Station*, Mr. Tardieu. We need techs and admin staff. We're hoping to get some talented people to emigrate and pitch in" Steve explained.

Tardieu's eyebrows went up. He considered the implications. "I see. Thank you." He interwove his fingers and his thumbs started circling. Pat did not look happy. After a moment's thought he consulted his contact list and placed a call.

"Gephardt? Tardieu. I have Steve Holbrook here in my office with a young woman." He listened a moment. "Yes, the Al Najid Steve Holbrook. He says they need some skilled people to help run their space station and he wants to make a recruiting pitch. What is Intel's position on that?" He listened quietly a moment. "Look: I halted a studio recording over this." He looked at his console, probably for the time. "Yes, I'll wait but get back to me ASAP, please."

Tardieu looked over at Steve as he disconnected. "You might have a prayer, Steve. He thinks they might have reason to let you make your pitch, but he has to clear his idea up the food chain."

Steve figured that meant at least one of Earth's intelligence contractors was interested in planting more agents aboard the Station. He didn't know how many were already there, but apparently there weren't too many if they thought they might want more. Steve looked again at Pat, who was deep in thought and staring off into a wall.

"Steve, I believe we have enough assurance to go ahead and get you back on set to record the show. But understand that anything you think is in the show now might be cut when we broadcast, and what remains might be heavily edited. Go back to the studio. I'll have to talk things over with the people upstairs once I get my call-back."

Steve and Pat walked out toward the studio's double doors. "I can't believe they are going to let you do this," she whispered.

"As you warned me, Pat, it isn't out of the goodness of their heart. They have an idea; I think one that plants more of their agents on the Station. I wonder what they know."

Steve took his seat again at the three-cornered table across from Donna and Daniel. Daniel smiled congenially, but Donna was still a bit frosty. As the countdown reached one, she smoothed her apparent attitude. Then Donna asked: "You said the enemy fighter pilots seemed almost as stunned as you were. Do you have any idea why?"

"Most likely they were deliberately kept in the dark. In fact, I really doubt that anyone could have orchestrated this had regular people known the true intent."

Daniel asked "Do you think *regular* people would have refused to carry out the order to destroy Perry?"

"Every soldier bears the responsibility for his actions," Steve replied,"This is part of the training we all undergo. For as long as I can remember, field command requires that of every pilot. It's my bet that they acted surprised because they were surprised. Nobody in active combat is going to stop fighting to pretend anything. There are few things more brutally honest than direct combat, as terrible as that sounds."

"Did you ever actually see the ship that launched the weapon or weapons?" Donna asked.

"I saw it on my VD at high magnification."

"VD?" Donna asked.

"VD stands for Visual Display, ma'am."

Donna looked into the holovid lens opposite her seat. "Skywatch has obtained combat footage from one of the fighters that were destroyed." The image of the cruiser replaced the holography in low quality 2-D. Most likely the recording had been damaged.

Daniel reported his information: "The ship has been identified as a Fisher class cruiser *Pyotr Velikiyer,* retired from service and supposedly in storage at Trondheim system, seven moduli away from Al Najid system. We have confirmed with corporate intelligence that the *Pyotr Velikiyer* is indeed missing."

"How could anyone misplace a cruiser?" Donna asked.

"What I would like to know is how did a missing star cruiser simply vanish and then reappear all the way out at Al Najid without anyone noticing?" asked Daniel. He turned to Steve, "Lieutenant, do you have any idea how that could happen?"

"Not really, Daniel. We have only a few ideas, none of which are likely. One already proved false, and another which seems impossible."

"What are those ideas? After all, you've had time to think about it."

"Well, we didn't know how far they had come, but we did try and figure out where they came from and where they went. The most likely possibility we already know is untrue: We know that the *Pyotr Velikiyer* did not traverse the Al Najid modulus."

Steve ticked off his remaining points, finger by finger. "We can infer that an absence of any sightings was not due to widespread corruption among the people monitoring traffic at the moduli. Our own records show the ship did not transit the last modulus, so there is no reason to suppose it transited the other moduli. So the *Pyotr Velikiyer* neither entered nor left the Al Najid system using the modulus. No currently known technology would enable them to arrive or leave without using the modulus. We also know they aren't in Al Najid system any more. Yet nobody has ever been able to travel fast enough to get from Trondheim system to Al Najid system in a human lifetime without using a modulus."

"So where does that leave us?"

"Somebody has developed a technological breakthrough unknown to the rest of the galaxy."

Daniel and Donna looked at a complete loss. Donna even forgot to close her mouth.

"Somehow, someone able to destroy a world has faster-than-light technology?" Daniel asked in disbelief.

"We don't know. But that might be the answer, even though virtually every physicist says it cannot be done." Steve replied cautiously, afraid they might somehow read his mind and learn what he and Tibs considered might be the real answer. It helped to think that if this part of the interview were actually broadcast, it would make that black cruiser one of the most sought ships in space. No space-faring power could fail to want superior technology. Steve had a momentary qualm, realizing *he* wanted that technology. But he suppressed it.

Steve knew the protracted silence that reigned in the studio as this information was digested would be edited out, but wondered what would make the final edit.

"Do you have any idea why someone would deliberately destroy your planet?" Donna asked.

"I've asked that question repeatedly, and can't imagine anything that could have prompted it. It is very hard to ascribe a motive when I can't identify a suspect. Perry had no enemies that I know, other than maybe some low-life pirates we've kept neutralized in our system. And this attack is way out of their league. There really isn't even competition yet with other pioneer worlds. Earth buys everything we can produce and always wants more."

"What about stealth technology?" asked Daniel. "What if nobody saw them using the modulus because they couldn't be seen?"

Steve paused, eyebrows upraised. "I hadn't considered that possibility, Daniel. It seems more believable than FTL travel, but still far-fetched. Compared to the other ideas we've come up with, though…"

Donna interrupted, "Well what are your people going to do? And how many people survived that can do anything useful?"

"Donna we need more people."

Chapter 15: Revelation

Auguste Tardieu sounded genuinely ecstatic when Steve called him the next morning. Overnight viewership ratings had been very good. Steve had watched it that evening with great curiosity. Most of the interview made it into the final cut, other than that first hiccup over the *Pyotr Velikiyer.* He felt he had made a good case, and was pleased that he hadn't made any significant mistakes or disclosures. He didn't think it would be long before people began speculating about a mother load of modulinite, which he expected would then start a rush of independent miners and criminals that *Perry Station* was not ready to handle. He felt he needed to return home, but he still had to meet the documentary team.

Steve showered and dressed and headed down to the lobby restaurant for breakfast. He had the same waiter who served him yesterday, minus the condescending air of superiority. The waiter seemed positively courteous.

Steve noticed the email telltale blinking on his wrist pad. He ignored it as Pat approached his table. Her perfume brought a delicate scent somewhere between cinnamon and frankincense, and he half rose from his chair as she joined him at the table.

"The show last night broke the Holonet with traffic." Pat said with a smile, "The talking heads on the morning shows cannot shut up about it."

"Are you hungry. Pat?"

"No thank you: I ate already."

Steve nodded. "Well, if it was that widely seen I guess my work is done here, then, eh?" he asked her with a raised eyebrow and a small smile. The wonderful apple wood smoked bacon, potatoes O'Brien and scrambled eggs smelled divine, a rare treat only possible on Earth.

"Not quite, I'm afraid. You still have an appointment today with the documentary crew, and another interview tomorrow. You also have a number of other reporters requesting interviews after last night's show. But those are optional."

Steve was growing weary of Earth, but he wasn't weary of the food. "Are there any interviews I really shouldn't skip? I very much want to get back to the Station to try and prepare for a deluge of immigration from Earth. It'll be a major headache if we aren't fully prepared. My deputy, Kyle, is good, but he may not have thought of everything."

"Well, there aren't any that you couldn't skip, though several can boast a significant audience share. It's all up to you." Steve finished his breakfast while Pat downed a cup of coffee, signed the tab and tip with his room number, and they started off.

As they headed for the hotel entrance to hail a cab they suddenly stopped. A flock of reporters and onlookers jostled for position outside the plexiclear doors. Hotel security held them back. Steve and Pat exchanged concerned glances.

"I think they're waiting for you Steve," she said.

Steve set his jaw and continued toward the door. If he dallied inside the hotel he feared the crowd could become unruly. One of the reporters saw him through the sliding plexiclear doors and raised his recorder high, streaming a 2D video record and shouting questions.

"Good luck, Steve, I'll catch a cab on the corner and bring it around to rescue you."

"Just like the cavalry, Pat. I won't forget it."

"Just don't forget to pay your bill and we'll be fine, Steve." she said, veering off to the left.

With each passing crisis he found her more and more likeable. The council was paying her retainer. Steve set his shoulders, waited for the door to slide open, and stepped out to talk with the reporters.

"Lieutenant Holbrook, Professor Mavis Trent of City College says the only way the cruiser could have caused the destruction of Perry is if there were massive amounts of modulinite already in the crust."

Steve looked at the reporter's name tag on his lapel. Mike Thornton. "I'm sorry, Mike, but was that a question?"

Mike was flattered to be on a first name basis and rephrased his question. "Can you confirm or deny that large quantities of modulinite were exposed when the planet broke up?"

Steve realized he had trapped himself. If he admitted the case, Al Najid would be swarming with prospectors and miners far too soon. *Perry Station* needed time to prepare for the modulinite rush. He raised an eyebrow. "I can only confirm that the professor's hypothesis was also our best guess, but when I left we still hadn't received spectroscopy results from the samples we retrieved. I recommend you contact the council at *Perry Station* for any further information."

"Steve!" it was a young female reporter with freckles, an Irish pug nose, and startling blue eyes. "Is it true your wife and children are alive on Cygnus?"

The question puzzled him, and then realization dawned. "What?.". He immediately remembered the email blinking on his wrist. He looked eagerly and there it was: an email from Sandy mixed among the unsolicited commercial emails, money laundering scams and requests for more interviews. The world receded to a distant roar as he opened the email.

"*Steve,*

The kids and I are all right. I didn't know until your show last night that you survived. I took the kids because I didn't want to let them go and it was almost time for your visit. I'm so sorry. I'm glad you are alive and very proud of you, but I'm starting our lives over again. Please don't come looking for us: it will only open old wounds. The kids are just getting back to normal."

She hadn't even signed it. Steve's world grew palpably darker and his pulse was loud in his ears. He felt rage. Rage at her unfair decision to take his children away from him like some thief, without even telling him. He doubted the kids were 'getting normal' at all, they were just becoming quiet.

The uncaring world intruded loudly on his consciousness, and he felt overpoweringly hurt, swirling with resentment. He just couldn't think about it right now. But then, all at once, his heart sang with light. He realized what she had actually said.

"Oh! My children are alive!" he replied, looking back up into the pretty Irish girl's concerned eyes with a sudden broad smile. His heart exulted, and his smile grew as broad as the morning sky.

"Thank God!" she said. "I'm so glad for you!"

"Thank you for reminding me to look at my email." He impulsively gave her a heartfelt hug, and she happily returned it. It was all on Holo and broadcast immediately. Live. He had no clue who this reporter was, but she had given him his life back. A vague, almost unformed thought wondered how she had known. Then he wondered how Sandy would react if she saw a Holo of that hug.

A cab pulled up smoothly with Pat in the backseat. She opened the rear door for him and he pushed his way through the crowd and slipped inside, closing the door. The media began reporting the breaking news with summaries of his comments.

Pat looked in wonder at his beaming face. He had always seemed more alive than other people, but now he was practically radiant. "What happened?" she asked.

"My children survived," he explained.

"That is wonderful news, Steve, but how?"

"My Ex took them to Cygnus before the attack, according to that reporter. She didn't want them to stay with me for a few weeks as they were supposed to. She thought it would upset them." He felt the heat of his anger rising again, but he rejected the reaction with contempt. "They are alive and safe," he reasoned, "and that's all that counts.

"But I am worried how that reporter knew before I did."

"That wasn't nice of your Ex, Steve, but it sure turned out for the best anyway."

"Absolutely!"

"As for that reporter," she continued, "if you have been in the CorpNet for more than a few hours then you should figure you are already hacked. I wouldn't send, receive, or open sensitive material until you are back home. Wait until you are behind a strongly layered defense that doesn't depend on Earth-built InfoSec software. I'd recommend wiping the memory of your wrist-comm when you leave, or just getting a new one. Yours is by now hopelessly compromised."

The cab pulled into a busy flow of traffic as they headed for the meeting with the documentary crew and Steve wondered whether a new wrist comm-unit would be a covered expense. His face was still all smiles, and he couldn't help laughing at himself for worrying about the cost of a stupid wrist-comm.

Since Steve's time in New York was limited and the documentary, tentatively titled "*Death of a Planet*", would include references to Midwinter Holiday on Perry, the interviewer selected Central Park for the shoot. Councilman Lyman had mentioned the original concept called for a picturesque snowy background. The introductory sequence would explain how Midwinter Holiday fell on July 18 on Steve's planet.

Unfortunately instead of a snowy Central Park background, a dreary landscape wrapped in heavy wet fog greeted them. Nevertheless, Steve provided the director scenic images from the council's datacube.

Despite weather that had the holovid crew in heavy coats and caps, curious onlookers were gathered around the perimeter of the bright lights and holovid cameras. As Steve and Pat emerged from their cab a few seemed to recognize him. Some of them approached to within about ten meters and then paused, as if hesitant to intrude but curious to see the space hero in person. An elderly couple, with a small furry dog on a leash, started bickering about whether he was taller or shorter than they expected, making Steve feel a bit self-conscious. But a couple of the onlookers, inveterate New Yorkers, walked right up as if they were long-lost family. They introduced themselves and shook his hand. There was also a furtive man who looked as if he were homeless, with unshaven stubble and slightly soiled and rumpled clothing. He didn't approach Steve directly, but went to Pat.

Pat appeared startled when she recognized the man, and began quietly asking what looked like urgent questions. Then one of the men who had stayed back a bit from Steve touched his ear, and then looked at the homeless man more closely. The man with the earpiece called aloud "It's Avery," and started walking quickly toward the homeless man. Two others in the crowd, one a woman, broke their cover and headed directly toward the homeless man at a fast pace. When he spotted them and turned to escape they broke into a run. Pat seemed puzzled, as the chase disappeared into the park. Steve walked over to her. "Did you know that man?" he asked.

"Martin Avery, formerly Chief Operating Officer for Antarctic Continental, one of the largest manufacturing and mining conglomerates on Earth and an ex-client. Very wealthy. His company holds the patent on Goop."

'Goop' was the silica-based gelatin used in all spacecraft and hostile-environment habitat bulkheads. It would reliably seal micrometeorite damage before a spacecraft lost significant atmosphere. Holding the patent to that product alone implied immense wealth.

"But Steve," Pat continued," he wasn't the same Martin Avery I remember. Something has happened to him." She looked curiously at Steve. "What do you think is going on?"

"What do you mean?" Steve didn't know Avery from Adam. "Do you think I had something to do with his problem?"

"No... I don't know." She looked away, toward the ground, and then back up into his eyes. "A man that powerful doesn't scare easily, but Martin appeared terrified of something. He slipped this to me." She showed Steve a small datacube shielded in her palm. She passed it to Steve. "He said the password you need is '@Antietam1862'."

"The problem now is that he told me you shouldn't look at it where the Corporations might get a crack at it. We know your wrist-comm is compromised. Probably my systems are also under surveillance. All my safeguards were produced here on Earth and shouldn't be trusted with anything you want to keep truly secret."

"Should we believe him? He's a man on the run. What if that datacube contains contraband?"

"It might, but from what I know of him, it's more likely a clue for you. He was always too nice to hold his job. He has a conscience in a world where that's a liability. And he is, or was, in a position to know things few others could. Now it looks like he's in big trouble, and it apparently has some connection to you.

"Martin was always impeccably groomed, but now he looks like a fugitive on the run. Those agents mingling in your crowd spotted him and broke their cover to chase him. My recommendation: get this datacube immediately to the ACM Embassy and ship it home via diplomatic courier. Don't access it until you know you have a secure environment."

"Well we can't get to the Embassy until I finish this interview." Steve didn't really have anywhere to hide the cube. "I don't know how you can make a living in such an information-compromised environment. How do you keep track of things you don't want others to know?"

"Oh, memory. And I use these." Pat withdrew a bound paper book and ink pen from her traveler's satchel. Opening the book she showed Steve blank pages, then found her ribbon bookmark and opened to a page filled with lettering that looked like a cross between Russian Cyrillic and Greek. "The ink for this pen is made by an old man in the Bronx. He is the only man that I know of who makes ink and refills cartridges, as far as I know, and I only have the one cartridge that still works."

"What language is that? It almost looks Greek, but it isn't. Or is it?" Steve asked.

"It isn't Greek and it isn't Russian, even though there are symbols that look like their alphabet. It is a letter substitution code. I created a list of twenty-six distinct symbols, each of which represents a letter. I had to use a key at first, but now I can sight-read and write it. The symbols have never been scanned, so they aren't easily reducible with a computer... especially when you don't know whether or not I used a shift cipher. The book itself is really old. I picked up a carton of them in an antique shop."

"What an antique shop would be I cannot guess, but let's not complete my education just now. Here comes the director."

The director, a bald man with a short graying beard and a pot-belly wore advanced tech glasses. Looking into the director's eyes Steve could see faint digital imagery and variable light intensities. Steve thought it would have been fascinating to put them on to get a good look. The man extended his hand to Steve and winked at Pat.

"Call me Mike. We're going to set up over there on a park bench." He said in a thick Brooklyn accent. "I apologize for the weather, but apparently my requisition for snow didn't clear the chain of command. Story of my life."

"It's good to meet you, Mike. What will we be talking about today?"

"Well, I watched your interview last night, and I'd like to touch on some things that'll give you and your *Perry Station* survivors some personal context for my viewers."

"You may have noticed things are different here on Earth," he continued "and while you might feel a little claustrophobic here, most of my viewers will find it challenging to imagine what it's like to live out in the open, with few people nearby. They don't understand what it's like to grow your own vegetables. That reference to the tomato sandwich yesterday, for example, was puzzling to some. Many folks have never seen a tomato, let alone a 'beefsteak' tomato. We want them to understand life on Perry so they can better understand the magnitude of your terrible loss."

That is what the interview was like for the next eight hours. Steve talked about the salmon that were only beginning to make spawning runs up the rivers and the way fields of grain rippled in the wind. He felt he had never been asked so many utterly uninteresting questions in such minute detail before, but he wasn't the target audience. His job was just to answer the questions. He felt mildly surprised and pleased that he knew more than he realized. By the end of the day, he was more than ready to call his mission on Earth finished. He looked forward to climbing back into space and returning to the Station.

Steve was careful to avoid mixing up the datacube carrying footage of Perry with the datacube from Martin Avery. They looked identical to the eye. He took the one from Avery to the ACM embassy. After getting confirmation from the *Perry Station* council, the ACM ambassador sealed the datacube into a secure diplomatic pouch for immediate dispatch. Then Steve returned to the hotel. The only part of Earth he felt he didn't want to leave behind was Pat. As he lay in the hotel bed looking at the ceiling, trying to fall asleep, he argued with himself that he was probably old enough to be her father. Well, maybe not quite.

He finally dozed off thinking of his children, grateful that they were safe and alive.

Chapter 16: Surveillance

Representatives from the three major powers, a few other independent planet and system alliance delegates, as well as commercial trade representatives were already settling into the new residential and retail commerce section of *Perry Station* while the queue of immigrants seeking entry grew almost exponentially. The immigrants came primarily from Earth, but also from other systems. Notably, Earth's Vera & Rodriguez Bank had begun negotiations to establish a branch office on *Perry Station*.

Perry Station also began negotiations to lease the mineral-rich but largely uninhabited fifth planet to the Legion for a mining and research outpost. The lease would definitely help balance the budget. The Legion pilots could help police transit lanes between the modulus and their Al Najid V base, a route that would pass through the asteroid belt for the next decade or more until the planet moved beyond on its wider orbit. Perry's surviving population couldn't settle on the fifth planet any more easily than they could live in a space-born habitat. Any commerce based there would have had to overcome the planet's gravity well every time they wanted to ship product anywhere, so this agreement seemed to be a win-win situation.

The Aldebari also negotiated a concession and began building a research platform outside the new anti-ship minefield surrounding the unmodulated anomaly. The construction offered a rich market for any parts and prefabricated structures that Perry could produce using resources mined from the debris field.

It turned out there was an astonishing amount of modulinite ore to be mined in the debris from Perry. Until the local system had adequate means to protect and manage it, they dared not breathe a word about it. But rumors already abounded.

It would not sit well with the rest of the Al Najid population when the official word came out, but the provisional council agreed on the practical necessity of keeping this secret... even if it became a more and more open secret.

The most conservative estimated value of the ore underscored the Al Najid system's need to build up a naval force capable of defending the system from pirates and other opportunists. Until Perry was strong enough to defend the system, the Council didn't want anyone selling modulinite on the open market for fear it could be traced to Al Najid. In a major concession during negotiations within the ACM alliance, the existence of the modulinite was secretly revealed to a few trusted Alliance leaders. Al Najid would cover increased costs once modulinite went on the open market. In return the ACM would engage in shipbuilding and a pilot training program to provide skilled pilots, new patrol craft and required logistical support... all based at *Perry Station*. Increased trade for Alliance members could be assured. The Alliance immediately grasped that maintaining secrecy was imperative until a strong defensive force could be readied. Investment in *Perry Station* businesses by Cygnus and Mazzaroth insiders also increased noticeably.

Already there emerged much speculation about the restrictions on prospecting in the Al Najid III debris field, but for the moment the *official* story would be that navigation was simply too dangerous.

Meanwhile the pilots surveyed the remains of the planet, setting beacons to subdivide and number the volume into addressed cubic sections. The pilots also collected and cataloged assay samples to determine which claims should be sold to private mining interests and which held as strategic reserves.

Most pilots spent free days mining asteroids because the pay was so good. *Perry Station* needed building material badly enough to pay above market rates for schist and especially for element-rich ore.

The surviving native Perry miners were sworn to secrecy in exchange for a priority in claims. They were tasked with clearing navigation channels in the debris field in preparation for the resumption of mining operations. They had been using their converted trawlers to work the asteroid belt during the attack, and so escaped destruction. Now they turned their efforts to working for the provisional government and reaping a rich reward. Even the schist that might have been discarded in other times now found demand as building material for construction of the station. The economic reality of dwindling coffers would soon force *Perry Station*'s hand.

Competing industrial and national agents already appeared on the Station, some open commercial ventures and a few who seemed to do nothing but had money to burn. Some were surely covert agents for organizations interested in the Al Najid system. They all seemed careful to follow the letter of the law, but it was only a matter of time before the security of *Perry Station* would be tested.

~

Jack Graham waited patiently in line with his battered gray plastic suitcase on the floor next to him. He had a receding hairline and his thick glasses held heavy lenses. When he reached the seated bureaucrat to process his immigration to *Perry Station*, his resume revealed that he had training in accounting and was seeking a position with the Station administration. As Jack had hoped, the bureaucrat fast-tracked Jack's application to facilitate a prospective co-worker who might soon take some of the workload off his shoulders. Jack did not disillusion the man. By the time the red tape was finished the soft spoken, amiable emigrant had an address and legal access to a small apartment in a just-opened residential area of the Station. Once inside, he used the apartment terminal to log in first as Jack Graham to create a profile for one of his business aliases, a fictitious machine shop. Then on that account he ordered a top-of-the-line 3D printer and a quantity of metallic resin compounds to be delivered to his new apartment.

~

Steve put in for some leave almost as soon as he returned from Earth so that he could go find his kids, despite Sandy's request to not disturb them. The Council denied his request. He still could grab a day free here and there, but no extended leave would be possible in the near future. At one point Steve considered the idea of quitting the service to go find his family. Ultimately he rejected the notion because it would do the kids little good to have an unemployed dad.

Steve's 'bigger and better' job, now that Kyle was firmly in charge of Station Security, was to identify and bring to justice whomever was responsible for the destruction of Perry. Secure in his office, Steve disconnected his computer from the network, put Martin Avery's datacube into its interface, and successfully gained access with Avery's password. Steve's computer automatically scanned for malicious agents, then loaded the image indices into volatile memory. On the console a single recording appeared in one of the common holo formats, preceded by an icon signifying encryption. He set the computer to load up the holovid, providing Martin Avery's password again to decipher the encrypted data compression and dimensional keys. In a few moments the holovid interface showed the recording ready for playback.

There was a date and time in the file log: 3010.01.30:16:38, almost five years ago. The recording appeared to be from a surveillance microlens.

A tall, well groomed man was visible next to a sunny narrow window that stretched from floor to ceiling. Steve couldn't see anything outside the window to tell him the location of the video recording, but the room itself was furnished like a plush conference room. The man looked down through the window as if deep in thought. To the left of the holorecorder the highly-polished table reflected a pair of large, well-manicured hands. The empty chair visible across the conference table was upholstered in supple old leather.

"There is no feasible alternative," the man at the window said. The sound quality was sub-par. From either side of the holorecorder there came a rustling sound as if those in attendance moved or adjusted their clothing all at once. The man turned away from the window and scanned the people in the room but their faces remained out of Steve's view. The handsome man's eyes came to rest just to the left of the holorecorder's position, and a very slight frown flicked across his face and then vanished smoothly into a well-polished smile.

"If we are to continue growing exostructure in support of our critical genetic investment, humanity must quickly find significant new sources of modulinite. I say 'Quickly', because it will take time to refine the modulinite, construct our own moduli and expand our transport and colonization fleet. And if we are to continue colonizing any new worlds that we find, harvesting their resources and adequately providing for Earth's necessary genetic investment then we must begin mining a very large deposit of modulinite ore very soon."

"Until now," he continued, "modulinite has only been found near anomalies or moduli, and almost all of that has already been assayed and claimed. Most of it has already been refined and used. There are no other anomalies within our immediate reach."

Steve paused the recording and began to make some notes. Then he unpaused the holo, raptly attentive. He would try and first view the recording once for content and then go back through it in exhaustive detail.

"We may eventually be able to move large numbers of people to Mars," the handsome man was saying, "but the planet will not be productively habitable in our lifetime despite our success in planetary mass enhancement using asteroid waste material. The proposed Europa relocation project is maddeningly unlikely to succeed, and in itself would require more modulinium than we can access. Possibly we could seize the Legion and Aldebar holdings, but that might solve our overpopulation problem in the least desirable way."

"No, we have to keep expanding our reach for resources available right now, or our population will start to die off from starvation and rebellion. The only alternative is to do nothing at all, and doing nothing will eventually force us to even worse options. Gentlepersons: to do nothing is in fact unconscionable."

"May it please the Board: We know enough of the technology now to construct and place our own modulus. With the success of the Al Najid project we hope to finally have sufficient quantities of modulinium to actually construct our own modulus rings, and still have enough left over to build an armada of colony ships to capitalize on them. If we can open up undiscovered new planetary systems the political resistance of the frontier planets will become moot. All that is needed is enough modulinium. And the only place with that much modulinite is in the crust and mantle of the planet Al Najid III, called Perry."

"To summarize: We have conclusively established that the unfortunate deaths among miners in the Al Najid system was caused by exposure to the caustic oxidation of modulinite. We have further assayed the mineral composition of a few recovered ore samples. We have evaluated unusual geologic density distributions in the planet's crust. Our findings suggest that there are significant deposits of modulinite ore, but the most important deposits are too deep to effectively mine, at least by conventional methods. Once we have it the ore's market value would be, pardon the term, astronomical. If we chose to sell it, but I tell you now," he slapped the table with an open palm, "we will need it all to manufacture new moduli and fit our colony ships with gravitonics and inertial dampeners. Without that supply we face certain political and economic failure planet-wide." The man paused for effect. "We know all too well what the consequences of inadequate material supply would mean. We must expand our resource base in general, and the only practical way to do that is by opening more planetary systems."

The handsome man scanned faces and checked for expressions

of agreement. A couple of the board members appeared sharply doubtful.

"We have managed to contain news of the find, and of the miners' deaths. Our security has been air tight." He spread his hands in supplication. "We performed the autopsies and assayed the modulinite at our own mining facility in the Trondheim system."

One of the board members raised a finger and consulted his assistant for a moment. The assistant referenced the electronics on his bracer and everyone waited patiently.

"Paul, we have never before found modulinite on a planet, only in vacuum near either moduli or unmodulated anomalies. It is very unlikely that we would discover it now buried in the crust of a pastoral planet with a breathable nitrogen-oxygen atmosphere. The violent reaction between modulinium and oxygen is well documented. This leads me to consider that your proposal is in serious error. There is oxygen present in many deep stone formations, such as iron oxide. Subterranean oxides and groundwater should have ignited any modulinite in the crust long ago. All this suggests to me is that, despite your results, large deposits of modulinite in the crust of an oxygen-bearing planet are so unlikely that there must be some other explanation."

The board member continued. "It is unconscionable to sacrifice an entire agrarian planet because of speculation. We cannot permit you to do what you suggest to any inhabited planet. Even if we had concrete evidence that the value derived would far exceed the value of the required investment, we cannot sacrifice a world on the altar of profit."

The man named Paul was clearly displeased, but the unidentified board member, who Steve assumed was Martin Avery, continued.

"How do we know that those miners weren't exposed to an anti-inertia or grav field core that somehow broke open and exposed its modulinium to the air? It wouldn't be the first time that happened, and it won't be the last. The cause of death was an industrial accident. It's much more likely that the modulinium samples you assayed were recovered from machine cores exposed in the accident. It's much more likely that the cause of death resulted from shoddy safety procedures for which someone in middle management should be held liable. Frankly I think that the manager in charge fabricated this wild story to cover his own ass."

"There is no more credible explanation, Mr. Avery," the man named Paul responded. "We have sealed, unrefined modulinite samples, not refined modulinium. They were covertly obtained from deep within the mine by our investigating operative, and there are no gravitic or inertial open core accidents on record in Al Najid system. Those cores would only have had refined modulinium rather than modulinite ore. The corpses of the miners were pulled from the mine by the local sheriff and his search and rescue team, an event officially documented, and a matter of public record. Further, the levels we see from orbital geological sensors only make sense if the deposits are actually there. It would be an otherwise inexplicable geological puzzle without massive modulinite deposits."

"To the best of our knowledge, Mr. Avery, this deposit represents not only the largest ever found, but also the first discovery of modulinite outside of a neutral-gravity environment. According to my lead geologist, the deposit is so massive that at some point in the distant past there must have been an unparalleled stellar system event that created the modulinite."

"What kind of 'unparalleled stellar system event' do you mean?" Avery challenged.

The handsome man flushed slightly, but his eyes narrowed defiantly. "My experts hypothesize the planet's orbit once passed through one of the system's two local anomalies. The first anomaly is now modulated, the one used by commercial traffic linking the Al Najid System to the rest of explored space. The other is an unmodulated anomaly, outside the planetary orbits, but on the local ecliptic plane. We believe normal system migration, relative to local stellar drift, finally changed the planet's orbit, but it may well have struck one of the anomalies through many orbits, millions of years ago.

"The value of the find may be astronomical, but it is only a practical resource if we can devise a method of extraction that minimizes oxygen contamination while delivering it to a zero or near zero-gee environment. The nature of modulinite prohibits lifting the ore by normal bulk methods into orbit. The expense of chemical-based heavy lift rocketry to extract the ore out of the gravity well and into the vacuum of space, where it can be safely refined, makes even that alternative unfeasible. Every other method of achieving orbit also generates too great an energy field for the modulinite ore to be safe: inertia/mass fluctuations have proven too dangerous in even small unrefined quantities. The corollary requirement to shield the ore from electromagnetic fields would add tremendously to the risks, expense, and lift weight. Static electricity alone could cause the modulinite to irregularly resist motion, despite its impure and unrefined state.

"And by the way, Mr. Avery, if the modulinite isn't there, then the proposed extraction method would have no other real effect than a moderately expensive electromagnetic pulse. And incidentally, it would mean an untimely end to my own career with the company. That is a measure of how strongly I feel."

The man named Paul paused and stared at Avery, daring him to push the issue further.

After a moment Paul began to summarize. "So the only option for us to extract the modulinite is outlined in the secure dossiers I provided." All eyes turned to the electronic documents before them.

"Mind you, political considerations for this solution require complete secrecy and we already implemented extensive measures to prevent undesirable repercussions."

"I propose, therefore, to use our 'Drop' deployment technique to rapidly place specialized electromagnetic pulse amplifiers that could use the modulinite ore to extract itself for us, wholesale. To do so requires a significant energy source. We intend to use a high-atmosphere, high-yield nuclear burst to simultaneously empower and amplify the electromagnetic field amplifiers we will deploy. The amplifiers will trigger the anti-inertial properties of the modulinite ore beneath the planet surface to an estimated depth of 500 kilometers." Tapping the large map displayed on the main screen in the four proposed locations, Paul announced "We will drop the amplifiers into carefully chosen sites planet-side from orbit, roughly 1200 kilometers equidistant around the mine.

"Timing will be critical in order to achieve optimal yield while exposing as little modulinite to the atmosphere as possible. Placement must be precise to maximize optimal fragmentation, achieve precise trajectory, and ultimately realize maximum profit."

The Executive Board stirred in interest, with the single exception of Avery, who sat perfectly still, his eyes hard with resolve. The handsome man observed the reactions of each board member. When you control what power values, you control power itself. His eyes narrowed again at Avery. He did not know what the man valued and that made him unpredictable, a threat. Avery would eventually have to be eliminated to remove an excessively unpredictable political outcome, but all things must have their own time. Elegance is in the planning.

"For the sake of Earth's economic future, and our whole way of life, it must be done" Paul continued. "Without new moduli connecting us to new resources we will again experience serious shortfalls within the decade. The board of corporations has already determined that military options are inefficient and counter-productive. Therefore, in order to maintain our population's genetic advantage over our developing competitors, we must not allow our base population to stop growing. And if we cannot provide adequately for the projected growth, deprivation will eventually overcome the industrial psycho-social measures that maintain our control.

"This modulinite discovery couldn't be more opportune. I don't have to remind you of the dire consequences should these people down there," he pointed forcefully toward the streets below, "find themselves once more so hungry that they rise in revolt."

His presentation swayed the board and carried the motion. Only Avery dissented.

As the board filed out, surrounded by their stylishly professional staff, Paul gazed out once more on the great city. He looked like he was thinking he had so very far to fall.

He turned to his monitor and began re-aligning his investments. He heard Avery clear his throat in the doorway.

"Harden." So that was the handsome man's name: Paul Harden. "We can't do this and you know it. That planet is populated, and it's already supplying us with resources. You want to sacrifice a real asset for the sake of a potential that may not be realized. What if you destroy a world, build your new modulus and it opens onto interstellar vacuum?"

Paul Harden looked regretfully at the powerful manufacturer.

"Perry isn't supplying us with so much food that we cannot do without it in the short term, and modulating other anomalies will present us with many more opportunities for colonization and food production in the long term. We must accomplish this mission before things come to a head with the people. We must be ready to use them to colonize our new properties before the masses begin to starve and rise up to destroy the support system that their lives, and our lives, depend on. No morally acceptable solution will be possible unless we capitalize on this opportunity. Your dissenting vote today was ultimately a moral failure. Except that your dissent was overruled, we would have ended with unconscionable euthanasia on an epic scale.

"Martin, wherever an anomaly connects to an empty region we simply dismantle that modulus and tow the parts to build another elsewhere. We will not waste these assets."

Avery had the impression that Harden wasn't sharing something important and objected "But compensating the settlers, Paul, relocating them and their possessions, will cost many billions more than you requested!"

Paul Harden raised an eyebrow: Avery had done the math. "Some things just have to be done, Mr. Avery."

The holo came to its end, and Steve immediately made a backup copy. He put the original into his safe. He turned the copy over and over in his hands, thinking. Steve wondered what Paul Harden had done to ruin Martin Avery, and whether Avery still lived. Steve speculated that had Avery come forward with this recording earlier, a half-million lives might have been saved. But Avery had not come forward, not until he desired revenge and much too late to save Perry. Pat had described Avery as a nice guy. Steve stopped himself and considered the timing. He realized that Avery had stepped forward only after Harden didn't move and compensate the settlers. Then Steve's arrival on Earth provided him an opportunity to deliver the datacube.

With a sigh that expressed his frustration with civilians in general, Steve set himself to confront what he must do now with his information. He reconnected his workstation to the network and composed a secure email for the *Perry Station* council, summarizing the recording and requesting a meeting. He worried that one of the council members might be an agent of Harden, but he had to work with what he had. Duty trumps fear.

Chapter 17: Salvage

The Station Council took their time but developed a plan, not all of which was made available to Steve. From what he did learn it was evident that he hadn't overestimated Councilman Lyman's subtlety. Unfortunately, it turned out that Paul Harden no longer resided on Earth. His whereabouts were unknown. Steve's immediate mission was halted, but he must remain on-call and, to his consternation, the Council still would not give him extended leave.

The Station's pilot roster and duty schedule was posted on the local network forum. Steve felt a need to put in some hours piloting and had filed for temp duty surveying and mining asteroids near the modulus. The rest of the pilots, when not engaged with patrol duty, tried to survey the debris field still expanding from the hot planetary core remnant. Surveying the planet's remains was an emotionally draining and unpopular duty. Some pilots seemed able to handle it okay, but most did not. Despite the importance of obtaining an estimate of available natural resources, including the remains of the planet, the work felt ghoulish to most pilots. Steve was in no hurry to try his hand there.

Steve had his Aldebari light fighter's technical chief and her Perry Station team replace his beam weapons with mining lasers and install the Bussard scoop. It was configured to sort particles that the mining laser freed from an asteroid into the four-compartment cargo hold. When the holds were filled the material would be transported back to Perry Station and from there to the manufacturing and mining facility near the asteroid ring. Modulinite entailed a special case where the frequency of the laser pulses had to be metered to avoid the frequencies and harmonic multiples that could trigger trans-dimensional inertial and gravitic conduction.

Steve's boat also carried two 'Raptor' AI guided missiles and a rail gun for defense. The transport of valuable commodities within a planetary system always presents a risk of piracy.

System checks passed their diagnostics and Steve initiated the launch of his modified light fighter into the vast uncaring void outside Perry Station. Minds strain to comprehend so much nothingness. The immediate and naked presence of space isn't something the mind can argue with. The stars are so far away in their beauty that they accentuate and deepen the emptiness. They emphasize what it means for a man to be alone. And Steve's planet, once so abundant with precious life, was now broken into lifeless fragments, a harsh reality that seemed to confront him every day. Steve wondered if that loneliness that comes from looking outward on distant stars is why Perry Station seemed built to look inward on itself, and had so few vistas on space.

As Steve accelerated from the launching bay his eyes were drawn to the great crescent of debris from his planet. Large chunks still moved away from the fractured hemisphere, drawing with them, and gradually being slowed by, the vast aggregate of smaller fragments.

Someday in the very distant future it would all be a planet of some kind again. In the meantime, and until the survivors were ready to market modulinite and refined modulinium, it was only a gargantuan asteroid field waiting to be mined. Steve gloomily considered that even when reassembled, the inertia dampening that caused its destruction may have slowed the whole enough that it would eventually fall into its blue giant sun, Al Najid. Miners might as well harvest what they could. Intellectually Steve knew that was the only practical thing to do, but emotionally the sight of his lost home still packed an emotional wallop.

The pale blue star, Al Najid, lit the scattered crescent of drifting stone against the jeweled blackness of outer space, and in the distance Steve could just make out the fifth planet as a tiny point of reddish light.

Steve spun his ship away from the planetary remains and headed toward the modulus, which was the day's assigned area. He engaged thrust to seventy percent and began a slow arc toward his intended mining site.

The stars dazzled in their glory, and as he sped through the interplanetary void Steve reflected on what he grasped of Tibs' religion. The magnificence of space, with all her stars, lent considerable weight to his sense of the Aldebar's fanatical worship. He remembered his childhood, soaked in Catholicism, wondering about the concept of an omnipotent deity creating it all. It seemed to Steve there really wasn't a strong contradiction between the two ways of viewing it at all. He knew that what Tibs described looked like Deism, something the Vatican ages ago rejected as contrary to its teaching because it denied revelation and challenged authority. Steve wondered whether that was due more to theology or politics.

Tibs' view could be considered Naturalist rather than Deist because the existence of a deity was considered an unknown rather than a premise. He mentally shrugged his shoulders. "It's above my pay grade," he muttered.

The *Jade Temple* disappeared from the sector a long time ago, and he wondered where she was cruising now. He pictured Tibs still sitting on the grass with his holographic cloaked controls and view screens trying to be 'one' with the cosmos. Steve envisioned Master Kinkaid preoccupied with scheduling duty rosters, and Elder Lu was probably standing somewhere important. Steve knew there were others among them he would have loved to get to know, but his duty remained with his people and their efforts to survive and prosper.

Pat had emailed, and in his reply he requested she watch her information sources for anything unusual involving Cygnus, especially as it might concern his children. He explained his circumstance at work and how his orders prevented him from searching for them. He had worried about their safety ever since learned they were alive. A screenwriter on Earth wanted to make a Holodrama about Steve's personal life, and he fretted that his celebrity might make his children targets.

He came up fast on the target asteroid field near the modulus, and backed the controls to half-throttle. Steve fed some of the surplus power to the Bussard scoop to warm-up the fields, and triggered the mining lasers to see the indicators light up green. He saw a stable asteroid ahead that looked promising, and reduced his speed further to begin maneuvering into position. When he pulled close enough to see nodules and clusters of valuable ore, he engaged the inertia dampeners that act as frictionless brakes. If he didn't fire any thrusters they would eventually bring his ship to a relative standstill vis-à-vis objects in the environment.

Asteroids are naked stone and ore left from the formation of the universe, substance within an otherwise absolute vacuum.

Steve lined up the mining laser with what looked like a node of rich metallic ore and hit the trigger to fire the ultra-short range mining lasers to heat and liquify the node. The metal and rock expanded with heat and spattered into the Bussard scoop, which would convey the cooling product to the first cargo bay. The ship's computer would remember the contents of each bay. When he moved to another node that yielded something other than metal, such as water ice, or radioactive ore, or modulinite, the CPU would automatically move that into a different cargo bay.

If he gathered too much low grade material and later found something more valuable, he could jettison the contents of a bay to give priority to the resource-of-choice.

He moved to another node as the diminishing returns told him the first site was nearly depleted. He gently eased his ship up toward some greenish stone, possibly a radioactive ore. The sensors registered no signs of significant atomic decay.

Over the local comm channel he picked up some chatter between two pilots, Graham and Delaney, on patrol at the modulus and advised them of his presence. Graham and Delaney were good men and flew well together.

The greenish stone turned out to be magnesium silicate, so Steve scanned for something better to mine. He felt vaguely uneasy and wished Kyle was with him. With no one to watch his back Steve felt awfully naked and vulnerable with his nose up against a rock and his tail hanging out into the void. He stopped his train of thought, deciding he was just conjuring up bad juju.

He spotted an ore node about three meters away, cut his dampeners and gave the side thrusters the tiniest nudge to head toward it, then re-enabled the dampeners to anchor his ship over the new spot. With the center of the node in his reticule, he hit the power for the mining lasers. It struck high density nickel iron, always useful when feeding a construction site, even though not terribly valuable.

The problem with mining is that you have to stay focused on very boring work just to keep your reticule where it will extract valuable ore and avoid as much dross or schist as possible. He also started picking up some ice and kept it. Even though the Station could make water with oxygen and hydrogen it would kill anyone who drank it pure. Pure H_2O, he had been taught, would leach the minerals right out of a person's bones. Instead it must always be run through granulated minerals and aerated, the mix of which was something of an art form among astrohydrologists. Natural water ice from space always represented a special treat for them, so Steve never missed an opportunity to bring some home if it turned up. God knows what they did with the stuff, but Steve learned long ago that in space if you keep your water guys happy they will keep the bar ice tasty. Tainted bar ice gives everything an off taste, Steve's Dad used to say. After an idle moment remembering his father he refocused his attention on mining, nudging a little farther to the left as the node trailed off in that direction.

After a bit, he realized that Graham and Delaney should have come back on their patrol by now. The node was getting thin, so Steve cut his laser and elevated his ship's position so he could peer over the asteroid toward the modulus. His gut dropped into his flight boots as he saw them maneuvering tightly in combat with multiple unknown hostiles. Why hadn't they signaled for help?

Steve keyed the emergency channel to base and started to maneuver toward the dogfight. He advised Command of the situation, recommending they scramble their ready crews and a few off-duty pilots for reinforcements. Simultaneously he cut his navigation lights and dampeners and accelerated smoothly; trying to minimize his visible signature. He really wasn't equipped for this, but he wasn't going to let his buddies down if he could help it.

It looked like Graham and Delaney were tangling with about three bandits apiece and Steve knew damn well those were losing odds, even when he made it two to one.

Suddenly Steve realized his radio was being jammed. He looked through his canopy and spotted a big, matte-black Corporate-design gunship. It didn't show up as bigger than a breadbox on radar, so he was probably EW (Electronic Warfare) with a light offensive load out. His shields and armor would probably take every round of ammunition Steve had just to get a chance at taking him out. But it was either that or fight blind. He regretted taking only the minimum ammunition load out for his primary weapon. Steve gave his AI Raptor missile optics a peek at their designated target. They flashed green, so he kicked them off their pylons and jacked up his thrust to the max. A rail gun is easy on power consumption even if it uses up a lot of ammo in just a heartbeat. No need to balance power for ballistics, only the shields.

Like a big vulture the Corporate EW Gunboat had been floating outside of the fight. Steve did seem to get his attention pretty quickly.

The gunboat lit his afterburners just as the first Raptor hit him dead on, putting his shield down to twenty percent. Steve opened up with a sustained burst of fire, leading him by just a little. If the EW platform pilot didn't have a big bag of tricks, Steve would know in just a moment. The second Raptor hit the gunboat's fuselage, taking his shields all the way down and depleting a chunk of his heavy armor. The enemy pilot wasn't pulling anything fancy, so Steve tried to gauge where he would move, eased back on the throttle, and pulled up to rip off another burst from his rail gun. Steve watched the gunboat's armor shred as his first railgun burst chewed up the raider's flank, just behind the command deck. Steve altered course and slipped in behind him.

Steve noticed his shields were taking light laser fire from someone outside his visual arc. His defenses remained in good shape, but he needed to finish off the gunboat before he could try and evade his other attacker.

Steve's second burst ripped into the gunship along the fuselage, just forward of the first hit. The pilot didn't pop his pod, but nevertheless comms were suddenly live and Steve heard the desperation of his buddies calling out for help. He took another look at the gunboat but it seemed to be drifting dead and lifeless. Steve was down to under 200 rounds. He decided the EW pilot wasn't just playing possum since he let the jamming down, and he spun on whoever it was that had been shooting at him. It was a corporate-design light fighter called a '*Lynx*'. Steve shunted to port with his yaw thrusters and let the *Lynx* have a burst, reducing his shields. The *Lynx* pivoted and goosed his afterburners to evade an anticipated second burst but Steve, low on ammo, held his fire. He tracked the light fighter as he showed his flank. Steve hit his thrusters and pulled up behind the Lynx for a burst up his attacker's main thrust, dropping his shields and chewing into his armor. Steve had only 100 rounds left but the armor on the *Lynx* was easily down to thirty percent.

Something made Steve take his eyes off his target to glance at the gunship. The EW pilot had played him for a fool and was pivoting to bring the fight into his forward arc. Steve let off another burst into the light fighter, which popped its pod in a ring of pyrotechnics. Just then the gunboat fired into Steve's side, dropping his remaining shields in one hit. Steve goosed the throttle with hydrogen to escape the gunboat's firing arc. He glanced at the rest of the battle and saw one of his guys still in the fight, badly outnumbered and heavily damaged. On the comm Steve could hear the inbound cavalry, whooping it up like a bunch of drunks. The gunboat kept pivoting on Steve, trying to reacquire. It looked like the gunboat was without main thrusters, so Steve angled up, slowly changing his trajectory. The gunboat's next burst passed safely below, so Steve pivoted on him and laid the last of his hardball ammo directly into the cockpit.

The three remaining corporate fighters broke away and headed for the modulus as reinforcements appeared inbound on radar. On the comm Steve heard Delaney cussing at them to stand and fight, but his ship had been through the shredder and was barely holding together.

Nevertheless Delaney still took shots with his beams as he chased the intruders, leaving Steve with the inert EW gunboat wondering why the guy hadn't hit his pod and set the self-destruct. There it hung adrift in space, sparking a bit off the shattered fuselage. Steve nudged in closer as if it was an asteroid waiting to be mined.

"Whiskey Zulu Niner to Base: I'm claiming salvage rights on the gunboat," Steve registered to base.

"Acknowledged and recorded, Whiskey Zulu Niner. What's your situation? Over?"

"Delaney chased them into the modulus, Base. Graham's pod should be there shortly. Please update with his status when you can, over."

"Roger that, Steve. Will advise as soon as he gets here but his vitals are all green, even if he does have an elevated pulse"

Delaney came back through the modulus and radioed, "I'm calling you 'Miser' from now on, Steve: I don't think you wasted a single round that time."

"'Miser'? Why not something cool like 'Ghost' or something? I was pretty sneaky there, you have to admit."

"Think of it as cost cutting, Miser: We don't want to have to fit you with a bigger helmet."

The pilots in the reinforcing flight all laughed on comm and he could only shake his head. His heart felt some kind of fluttery feeling for these guys, and he was grinning. It had been a long time.

"Well, Delaney, I'm just going to call you 'Rotor', so you can sit on it and spin." and even Base laughed at that.

As Steve maneuvered closer to the wrecked gunship he could see electronics in the cabin still aglow in the cabin behind the soberingly gruesome wreckage of the controls. Not a wasted round indeed: Only a wasted life for the gunboat pilot and any crew he had aboard.

Steve flew as close as he dared. Using his maneuvering jets he spun his ship around to position the hatch near the gunship and set the controls to maintain position relative to the wreck. He unstrapped from the acceleration couch and swam back through the living quarters to the suit locker next to the airlock. With practiced ease Steve slid an arm into the environmental suit, turned to step into the feet and then powered on and sealed the suit before worming his other hand into the opposite sleeve and glove. He strapped on a tool belt, and clipped one end of a long tether to a ring in the tool belt. The helmet idiot lights showed green in his 'head's up' display (HUD) and he tested the suit radio with a comm check.

"Reading you five by five, 'Miser'" answered Base with a chuckle. "Graham's pod has docked safely at the station and he's going to be fine."

"Thanks, Base, I'm glad he's okay. Stand him a beer for me when you get off"

"Affirmative, Miser"

"Base I'm going to look around inside this gunboat for a few minutes."

"Understood, Miser. Be careful. We'll direct the reinforcement flight to stand by until we can get a pair of pilots reassigned there for regular sentry duty. Want me to ask around and see if there is a hauler willing to tow her in?"

"Affirmative Base: Try and get someone we know. That hauler we've been using for the Research Station runs would be a good choice if he is available. His name is Bill Hillman, I believe." Hillman was a trans-system hauler from Earth, and a good man. He had been running supplies back and forth between the manufacturing plant and the Aldebari research station at favorable rates, and Steve wanted to help compensate him with a nice little side job.

Steve opened the inside door of the airlock and stepped in, feeling the environment suit's temp capillaries cooling his skin. The inner door closed automatically, and he clipped the anchor end of his tether to the airlock's interior mooring ring. He hit the airlock cycle switch. The chamber evacuated its atmosphere to the ship's compression tanks before the light changed and the outer door slid open to the stars.

The destroyed cockpit was jaggedly open to the vacuum a few

meters away. The sharp metal frame had fragmented and bent inward under the impact of the rail gun's ammo. Getting inside would be easier than getting out. Steve pushed off gently into the opening, the inertial dampeners holding his ship stable for the hop.

The pilot's head was missing, though his corpse remained securely strapped in. Artificial gravity was inactive, and the man's gore, floating like a fog of pebbles and clods, bounced off Steve's suit as he moved in. The freeze-dried blood bounced around in the open cockpit, though some escaped through the cabin rupture. Steve saw where his second burst had breached the cabin, and in a lucky penetration broke the pilot's left arm. His throttle was on that side, but his right hand still gripped his control stick and weapons pickle. Steve checked the destruct/pod button and it still glowed ready, but had been clearly out of reach for the pilot if he wanted to stay in the fight to pivot and fire. Steve mentally toasted the pilot's courage and determination.

Farther back into the cabin the electronics array looked like it was in mixed condition. Steve found an unsuited female corpse there, surely an EW officer who clearly died a horrible death by sudden decompression. The main CPU array and memory core were still active and Steve felt his pulse and respiration quicken. He powered the unit down, flipped the quick release latches, and pulled the assembly out from the rack by its metal handle. It was very dark farther back, away from the starlit open cockpit, so Steve flicked on his suit lamps. The living quarters hatch was sealed so he looked through the inset porthole into a room in weightless disarray. The room was lit red by the telltale of the rear airlock. That lamp should have been glowing green unless it was sealed and occupied. Either there was someone inside, or it was malfunctioning.

"Base we might need a medical team out here: I think someone may be in the aft airlock."

The control officer at base sounded as surprised as Steve was: "Affirmative, Miser."

After a moment base advised, "I have notified the medics and they are scrambling".

Steve didn't want to unseal the door to the pressurized living area to see who might be there because the airlock might be damaged and the atmosphere in the living quarters might be all that was keeping them alive. Leave it to the pros. Memory core in hand, Steve carefully followed his tether back to the wrecked cockpit and cautiously launched himself back to his ship, avoiding the jagged metal struts that could have compromised his suit or snagged his line.

When Hillman, the hauler, arrived to pull the wreck back to base, Steve asked him to just stand by and keep an eye on things until the medic said it was okay to move.

Steve was focused on getting back to his quarters and into that memory core to find out for who these bandits had been working. It might be that word was out about the modulinite and they were pirates, or they might have been working for that Paul Harden who was in the holo. If it was Paul Harden, or whichever corporation employed him, then the station might be in more serious danger.

"I'll look forward to having a drink together at the *Cog and Sprocket* when you get there, Bill." Bill made an affirmative-sounding reply in his gravelly voice as Steve powered up and headed in.

Technically if someone were still alive in the airlock, they had prior claim over the wreck, but Steve felt he needn't worry about it. As far as *Perry Station* was concerned they were outlaws, and had forsaken their rights when they ambushed Graham and Delaney.

Besides, he had a feeling he would want to keep whatever was in memory and storage on the computer core he had recovered.

When Steve docked he turned the ship over to the techs. After they offloaded what little ore he had mined he watched the read-out as precious few credits were deposited to his account. He then carried the captured computer core to his quarters. He connected the core to his computer and started the diagnostic routines. The drive was encrypted, naturally, so it would be awhile before he gained entry. Steve locked up with the nibbler routine inexorably trying to crack the encryption unfettered by human impatience. Steve went up to the bar for a cold one.

Delaney and Graham already had a table at the *Cog and Sprocket* and bought him a drink. Shedding the stress of combat, they joked and laughed together a while. Then they received a message from Kyle's office: the survivor from the gunship airlock was a young man, a boy actually, apparently the son of the pilot and the EW officer. The boy said his mother had told him to get in the airlock when they realized they were in more trouble than expected. That explained why the pilot hadn't podded and triggered the self-destruct.

Steve immediately realized that the boy would have bona fide claim over the wreck because a minor couldn't be rightly held responsible for his parents' actions. He thought about the ethics of hacking into the gunboat's computer. It wasn't really his to crack after all. In fact, it belonged to someone who might very well hate him for ... It wasn't like he murdered the parents, was it? How is a boy supposed to figure out the fine points? Steve had an idea how unforgiving he would feel were the roles reversed, and began to try and come to grips with his predicament.

Steve decided he needed another drink, so he rose from the table and bellied up to the bar next to a guy who had to be the tallest Legionnaire he ever had seen. The man filled an immaculate Legion uniform and was drinking Gleneagles, a famous single malt whiskey. It's distinctive bouquet smelled great, so Steve ordered one neat. The barkeep had a twinkle in his eye when he slapped the empty jigger down and brought the bottle of Gleneagles from the highest shelf to fill it.

Steve's new wrist comm vibrated again: It was Bill, having just docked. Steve texted him to come up for a drink, and then transferred his fee into Bill's account. All of a sudden Steve's personal account was looking awfully skinny. If he couldn't legally sell off the wreck for salvage, he had better plan on mining in his spare time to build it up again.

By the time Bill arrived Steve was into his third ounce. He bought another for Bill, but the Legionnaire at the bar knocked over the jigger. "You better watch where you leave your drink, shorty," he said to Bill. Bill stood almost as tall as the Legionnaire, and from the look in his eye he was in no mood to be bullied. So Steve stepped between them feeling pretty small and tried to diffuse the situation. It was a big mistake. The Legionnaire just wasn't going to have a good night unless he could bust a knuckle on someone, and Steve had just made himself the nearest target.

Steve had an uncanny knack for seeing something coming later than he should. Unfortunately the block he set against the Legionnaire's uppercut was not stout enough to fully deflect the blow. The big bruiser's knuckles grazed Steve's forehead hard enough to give him a new perspective on the barroom ceiling. Bill stepped over Steve and waded in like a grizzly bear. Quickly the two big men started throwing each other all over the barroom, breaking furniture and having a grand old Donnybrook before Kyle showed up with his deputies to taze, tag and bag them both.

Then a news flash came across on the holo above the bar. Steve raised himself up, though still a bit wobbly. The newscaster reported "In a rare display of tripartite diplomacy the three Galactic powers have just issued a joint declaration making the destruction of a habitable planet the first pan-galactic capital crime. Anyone knowingly contributing to or aiding those who destroy a habitable planet can be tried as if they had committed the act themselves." A small cheer went up from the patrons at the bar.

With that news, Steve decided to head back to his quarters and see what he might discover on the gunship data core.

The array of measures he had set in motion to decrypt and copy the contents of the core system pulled from the gunboat were still percolating, although the log showed it had broken the encryption and handled a couple of tripwire defenses.

Steve also found a secure message from Tibs in his inbox advising that the Aldebar intelligence services had picked up word of a hit contract on Steve. The mercenary network chatter attributed the contract to an organization called the *Celine* corporation. They were offering a hefty reward to whomever managed to eliminate him.

He sat back, having trouble imagining what had triggered a contract on his life.

It was late, so Steve decided to try and get some sleep. He set the computer's interface to finish the cracking sequence with a chime, and laid down on his bunk for a nap.

Steve tossed and turned. He kept thinking about the boy on the gunship, and how he would have to meet him. Steve tried to imagine what he could say to him when, after all, he had killed the boy's parents. It would probably make a mortal enemy for life, and there might be hell to pay. But the honest thing to do would be to explain to the boy what had happened and who fired first.

He knew his wife would have had words of wisdom. He missed her, but wasn't able to divine what her advice would have been. She wasn't with him, and he had no way to reach her.

Steve knew he needed to sleep, but he was still thinking feverishly about everything that had happened when the hack array chimed completion.

Immediately Steve sat up, swung his feet to the warm floor and, bleary eyed and exhausted, went to see what he had found.

Everything that was safe to move had been ported to his computer system, so he launched a utility named *B-Cube* to look at the file structures. Up from the holoplate ascended imagery depicting the superficial logic of file dependencies and references. Using his finger Steve touched the image root of the new structure in the system and the computer listed a summary of topics. Steve chose 'route' first, and found the gunship had passed through several systems, but the most recent journey originated at Habersham, one of Earth's core systems.

He told the computer to open a new file named '*gunship research*' and remember the route, sector names, stopovers, and any cargo carried on the manifest. He also discovered the point of origin for the last mission's orders was Paradiso, in the Dante system.

He discovered that the gunship had actually been named '*Gryphon*'. He never ceased being amazed at the Corporates. They somehow see benefit in giving a sentimental name to a spaceship instead of simply using its registry, yet would cheat their own grandmother out of her false teeth. Capital ships, sure: they were bigger than a registry designation, but a little gunship? It made no sense.

The next logical branch was labeled '*Accounting*'. The ship had belonged to the Celine Interstellar Corporation, out of Paradiso, in Dante sector. Steve recalled that Paradiso had been one of the stopovers on his return flight from Earth. Steve commanded the computer "Computer, link this entry to the Paradiso stopover and the appropriate navigation chart subsystem". The computer bleeped acknowledgment. "Add reference to the link to file '*gunship research*'. It bleeped. This Celine Interstellar needed to be researched, so he flagged it in the system with a timed reminder that would pop up with any notations he linked.

The gunship pilot had been Gavin Morrison, and his EW Officer, Elaine Morrison. Their son was Robert Morrison. They had received two hundred thousand credits and been given command of the Gryphon by Celine Corporation the day after the destruction of Perry. They must have been a good team to pull down that many credits. Steve added the entries in his research file to provide any follow-on investigation a lead, in case something unexpected happened to him. Young Robert Morrison was going to be a man of respectable wealth for his age. Assuming he sold the Gryphon for scrap he would be rich enough to make life very uncomfortable for Steve.

The chime sounded at the entrance to Steve's quarters. He stood up, stretched and walked over to the slider. He pressed the switch for it to open. Staring him in the face was the odd, cross-like muzzle of a deadly fletchette pistol.

Like a miniature rail gun, a fletchette pistol throws low-mass razor blades at extremely high velocity. Steve knew they didn't have great range in atmosphere, and couldn't punch a hole in the hull of a spaceship, but it was accurate enough to be very deadly at short range.

Fortunately for Steve the boy holding it was unaware that he needed to hold down the safety for it to fire.

"You must be Bobby," Steve said more calmly than he felt. Bobby pulled the trigger, but suddenly looked confused and disappointed when nothing happened. He looked at the pistol in his hand. Steve reached out and wrested it smoothly away before the kid could figure out what went wrong.

In dismay, Bobby looked like he would run, but Steve kept his face calm, and slowly backed into the room. "Come on in, son." he invited cautiously. Down the corridor they could both hear security officers approaching. Bobby decided to enter, and the door slid shut behind him.

"You aren't a prisoner, Bobby. I'm glad you weren't wounded. I recently lost my family too, you know. I had a son a little younger than you."

Steve continued in a quiet voice "If you want to leave, the door isn't locked. But I'd like to talk with you first, if that's okay?" Steve said.

Bobby clearly wasn't sure about buying what Steve was selling. He looked around the quarters, checking to see if there were anyone else there.

"Where did you get this pistol?" Steve asked him, not knowing what else to say to try and get the boy to say something.

"My mom gave it to me when she had me get in the airlock. It was in my pack."

"She must have loved you very much." Steve ventured.

If looks could kill Steve would have dropped stone cold dead. "You killed her."

Steve winced like he had been slapped in the face. "Bobby, look..." he removed the fletchette clip and set Bobby's pistol on the desk. "I had no idea who was in your ship. I only saw your ship fighting my friends. I didn't mean to kill your mom and dad. I expected there to be only the pilot aboard. I thought he would pod."

"He couldn't, because of me." Bobby said before his tears came washing down his cheeks. The kid blamed himself. Steve knew how that felt, and his compassion wrenched at his heart.

So Steve moved forward and tried to comfort him. As Steve approached, the teenager's grief turned to anger. He punched Steve fiercely in the abdomen. When Steve didn't react he threw a left and a right and left, over and over again, venting his rage until he wore himself out. It stung more than Steve expected, but he tensed his abdominals and let Bobby do it. The boy had to get his demon out.

"I understand, Bobby." was all he could say. When the young man had exhausted himself he slowly looked up into Steven's eyes as his anger faded, and then his eyes fell away. Steve could sure empathize. After a tense bit the youth calmed down, regained his breath, and dried his eyes. He stood erect, looked Steve in the eye again with a level gaze, and left.

Steve went over to the cooler and grabbed a beer, his hands shaking. He sat down at his workstation and stared at the fletchette pistol, his abdomen sore and aching where the boy had pummeled him. He looked back at the holodisplay, thinking about Bobby and his parents. What were they thinking, to have their son aboard ship on a dangerous mission?

Setting the empty beer down, a wave of exhaustion swept over him, double what it had felt before Bobby arrived. He didn't know what that kid was going to do. Steve also realized that he didn't really know what to do. He needed to talk with the Station's makeshift government and explore what they could do for him. But for the moment Steve knew he needed to collapse into bed and get some sleep. He thought again about what Bobby must be going through, and weighed the threat of the hit contract. Steve locked the door, and then collapsed into the warm embrace of his bed.

He dreamt he was in the garden aboard the *Jade Temple*, listening to the Temple bell intoning its deep slow cadence when the sound resolved itself into the chime of an incoming signal on his comm. He opened his bleary eyes and shuffled to the holo terminal to answer. It was late: he should have been up hours ago.

It was Tibs calling in a live transmission. His face in the holo looked a little distracted.

"Steven, hello. I was afraid I had missed you and was about to leave a message. What happened to you? You look terrible!"

"Tibs I'm so glad to see you!" Steve replied. He tried to clear away the shreds of sleep, organized his thoughts and filled Tibs in on the skirmish at the modulus, the seizure of the gunship and its records, and its origin. He told Tibs about the encounter with Bobby and the anguish he felt for his role in the boy's predicament. He also related the details involving Celine Interstellar. Tibs' eyebrows raised just a touch at the mention of Celine.

"You should try and convince Bobby that he's not responsible for his mother and father's decisions, and that he should not blame himself."

"Tibs, I cannot for the life of me understand why they brought their son into such a dangerous situation. It was dangerous not only for him, but for themselves because they couldn't pod to safety. A gunship is not a cruise liner that has lifeboats for passengers. And yet from his reactions they had to have loved him as much as any parent."

Tibs looked seriously at Steve's holographic image and pointed out, "Just because a young man loves his parents does not mean that they also love him." Tibs asked Steve then whether he knew about Dante's *Hell's Gate*, in classical literature. "Over the lintel of the gate to Hell were inscribed the words 'Abandon All Hope, Ye Who Enter Here.' Steve, the Morrisons may not have had much of a choice. It may well have been the only way for them to stay out of a corporate debtor's prison where they would have worked for the rest of their lives, and for the lives of their children. They couldn't leave their boy behind."

"Things didn't look all that bad when I was on Earth." Steve protested.

"New York is a historical preserve, unlike other cities. And Earth has not always been as it is," Tibs assured Steve. "Once, before the rise of the Board, before either the Aldebari or the Legion had broken away, Earth's republic built the crowning achievements of human civilization. It is where we began, after all. In those days Earth was a champion of enlightenment and learning. Responsible liberty and independence were upheld as ideal.

"It was all lost to small, insidious changes in Earth's laws. Over many years, and for various pretexts, individual liberties and responsibilities were lost. Corporations became like feudal states where economic instead of military strength established rule," Tibs fervently continued.

"Lawmakers of the republic auctioned off their legislative powers to the highest bidder in order to retain power... and even that power proved illusory. They were like shadow puppets acting out entertaining dramas to distract the public, while the real decisions played out in secret. The powers of their elected positions became dedicated to protecting the moneyed interests who paid their bills and funded their elections. The votes of the people were a sham, decisions made based on deceptive information. Political power that they were no longer free to exercise was exchanged by legislators for personal gain. And in the name of security and convenience the people believed political rhetoric was fact, and allowed it all to happen.

"This may explain the contract placed on your head. Steven you're seen as a hero you know, and your recruiting interview carried a message of great hope to people who thought they had no real choices left. The deal you offered as representative of *Perry Station* has presented a great threat to corporate power. Now they will want to squash that hope, and I'm afraid you and *Perry Station* are both in jeopardy."

Tibs had a point, even if his bias was clear. History wasn't something he could change, it was something to learn from. Steve knew most of the new settlers at the Station were of corporate origin, arriving as highly skilled refugees; eyes alight with hope for a new beginning. They were happy to get even the most menial of jobs, if only because those jobs were better than a lifetime of Nibble and video games. Those jobs represented the equivalent of freedom, even though they might no longer have a word for that. It meant the ability to set goals of their own, and an opportunity to achieve something, rather than just waiting around for old age and death. Even the least glamorous job is an expression of hope, Steve concluded. He filed away the Aldebari's version of Earth history in his memory. Steve resolved to gain the Legion's perspective, and talk with Pat more directly about it when he had an opportunity.

"Knowing what you now know, are you certain you chose rightly, Steven?"

"Do you mean the recruitment effort on Earth? Yes Tibs: we need people. And if anything I would have tried harder to give them hope."

Tibs had a twinkle in his eye again. "I am glad for you my friend. If we count ourselves wise enough to hear wisdom, then we should also count ourselves wise enough to speak it. As the old saying goes. 'Actions speak louder than words'. Let me see what we can dig up on this Celine Interstellar. I will send you anything interesting that we find if I can. Tibs and the *Jade Temple*: Out"

Steve cut his end of the transmission in deep thought, his eyes resting on the file structure of the gunship's databanks. It would be a very different galaxy if everyone who thought himself able to recognize wisdom would integrate that wisdom into their decisions.

There were still large structures of data depicted that he had not explored. He put a finger at the base of one of the larger structures and read the pop-up: *Schematics*. His eyes widened and his pulse quickened as he explored further. He had blueprints for the gunship!

Chapter 18: Assassin

Steve was in the Office of the Master Shipwright, with Chief Armorer Mackenzie and a gaggle of other engineers going over the gunboat blueprints. Each was making calculations, conferring, and sending queries to the naval architecture team for subsystems that could be adapted from the existing Aldebari stock or customized for parts that would otherwise have to be made from scratch. Out in the weightless vacuum of the space dock the robotic construction units were laying out the hull's framework. The shipyard workers at their sheltered workstations guided the construction machinery using remote operator gloves, and viewed their handiwork on 3D displays at graduated levels of magnification.

Modifications would be required to replace the design's heavier and very expensive corporate thrusters with a comparable aggregate of light fighter engines, capacitors, and containment field generators. It was evident that the engineers could achieve comparable performance with their hybrid Aldebar and Corporate designs. But there would be limitations everyone would have to live with such as increased mass aft, hopefully to be compensated by the lighter alloys standard in Aldebar hulls, and balanced by an under-slung heavy forward cannon and ammo locker they acquired from their Legion colleagues.

Steve was clearly out of his depth, and although the engineers were polite, he was unmistakably distracting them with his uninformed questions. Even though they were very tolerant, even enthusiastic about trying to help Steve understand why tensile strength is so important for some applications and shear strength is more important in others. Steve eventually retreated when the engineers began to dive into the relative merits of composite ceramics.

The schematics he found had great intrinsic value for ACM Command. Fortunately the provisional government treated him fairly and provided reasonably handsome compensation. Command also assured him that if he signed a committment to fly whatever tests the Naval Yard needed, the first gunship produced would be his.

Steve decided to take a walk around the Station's new construction to see how things were coming along, and maybe stop by that shop and see Mary. A new deck had just opened across from the *Cog and Sprocket* bar. Perhaps forty new immigrants were lined up at a temporary government office to register. Most of these folks would be miners, but some intended to open a few new shops.

Bobby sat at a table in the *Cog and Sprocket*, looking at a glass half full of water. The bar was convenient and very busy, the most popular meeting point on the Station. Many residents met there for business as often as they did for pleasure. After a moment's hesitation, Steve walked quietly to the bar and asked for two bowls of soup and a small loaf of fresh bread to be brought to Bobby's table. He sat down across from Bobby while the other customers maintained a steady din of conversations around them. The boy looked miserable. "Hungry?" asked Steve.

Bobby paused before answering. "Yes, but I haven't found a Nibble vending machine or anything. I saw someone here eating so I sat down too. All the lady brought me was this glass of water. It is good water, but I'm still hungry."

"Well we don't have Nibble here, Bobby. We have many kinds of food, but no Nibble. Would you like some?" Steve asked, seeing the waitress approach with her serving tray carrying two steaming bowls, large spoons, and a small loaf of freshly baked bread still warm from the oven. She placed one of the bowls in front of Bobby and one in front of Steve, and set the loaf of bread on a plate between them. The soup smelled delicious, a mélange of vegetables in a tasty tomato-based broth. Bobby clearly liked the aroma as he inhaled the gently rising vapors from both the soup and the bread. Steve reached for the bread and broke the loaf in half to share with Bobby.

Bobby was all eyes as Steve picked up his spoon in his right hand, but dipped the broken end of his loaf in the soup before taking a bite of the bread. Bobby picked up his spoon, took his loaf in his left hand, and after dipping a corner into the broth, took a bite. Like magic, Bobby transformed from a sad and lonely little boy into a happier, animated, and ravenously hungry eating machine.

"So Bobby, where are you staying? Do you have anyone helping you figure things out?"

After a moment Bobby was able to answer "Your friend, Mister Kyle, is letting me stay with him. He's with his girlfriend right now, so I thought I would look around."

Steve dipped his bread again, and with his other hand, stirred the vegetable-laden soup, to let it cool a bit more.

"Any idea what you will do next?" Steve asked casually.

Bobby thought for a few seconds before answering. "I think there's too much left for me to learn for any real decisions. I would like to learn who sent mom and dad out here to do something wrong."

Steve's eyebrow rose. Abstract thinking wasn't something he expected from a fourteen year old. "Who's been talking to you about this?"

"After I left you last night, Mister Kyle found me. I had been hiding, but fell asleep." Bobby looked disappointed in himself for being caught. 'Mister Kyle and I talked at his place and he told me how sometimes good people do bad things. My mom and dad were good people, Mister Steve. I want to know why they were doing a bad thing. I want to know who made them do it."

Steve was impressed. "Well, I'd like to figure that out too, Bobby. Let me know what you find, okay?" Steve reflected on his own conclusions about vengeance. "But Bobby, when we do find whomever it was, let the Law decide what to do with them no matter what we might believe, and no matter what we might feel like doing to them, okay?"

"Why?" Bobby asked.

"Because if we act on our feelings counting only on what we know, we might do something very wrong ourselves. If we got the wrong person, or there was something else we didn't know, we might make an even worse mistake."

"What if the Law makes a mistake?"

Steve nodded sadly."Sometimes the Law makes mistakes too, but it's the best we can do, Bobby."

Bobby looked questioningly at Steve, then picked up his bowl to drink the last of the broth. "If the Law can make mistakes, how is the Law any better than a person? A Law is just an idea that can't really think."

"Our laws are guidelines that use the experience and wisdom of people who have had to decide hard questions all through history. The Law requires us to consider all the evidence and is careful that there is enough certainty to pass judgment. It is better to take a chance and let a suspect go than to punish the innocent by mistake."

Lunch finished, Steve told Bobby to be careful, shook his hand, and said goodbye. Steve resumed his walk, but now with an unconscious smile on his face. People he passed tended to smile back at him. The Station suddenly had more people than places to put them. What had been nearly a ghost town was now becoming crowded, and available living quarters were scarce. More immigrants arrived with every transport. The system's manufacturing plants now operated around the clock to fill orders placed by construction firms, pushing up the market price for raw and refined ore, as well as for generic schist. Production was limited more by the scarcity of ready materials than by demand. There was plenty of demand and plenty of work, but the rapid population growth presented greater and greater challenges. The hydroponics systems needed to expand quickly to avoid a food shortage. If too many people took too much time off, the Station would be soon overwhelmed, and if any department dropped the ball the whole integrated system threatened to careen into chaos.

As he walked, fewer and fewer people smiled back and more and more seemed to grow distant. Steve felt the strange sensation of becoming lost in the changes. The surviving handful of original pilots were being swallowed up by the rising tide of immigrants. At times it seemed like the people of *Perry Station* were no longer *his* people. The Station had become an outpost of humanity; pioneers overtaken by civilization. Steve wondered what would become of them. He wished dearly that his son and daughter could be with him, but the threat of unknown mercenaries hunting him down meant that if he actually did go to them he could be putting them in serious danger. They should be safer with their mother. He worried that he should get word to her of the danger, but questioned if even trying to send an email might give away their location. Perhaps Pat...

As Steve approached the shops where Mary's little store had recently opened for business, a curly-haired tow-head boy ran into Steve's leg and caromed off, spinning, then scurried on, chased by a slightly larger girl, also with that same curly blond hair. The little boy shrieked happily as she almost caught him, but he got away by making a quick turn she could not match, running into a matronly woman who first scowled down in surprise but then her face transformed at the sight of the child and she chuckled with good nature. The two children sped over to a small island of curly-haired blond people huddled with their possessions around a tall older man with gray curly hair. The man appeared intent on serious conversation with a harried junior grade bureaucrat about available

Station housing. Steve noticed a sense of awakening hope in the immigrants that things would be okay, that life would go on despite the loneliness that temporarily enveloped them, and Steve felt kinship with them. He longed for his kids and his wife, but seeing another family still together, still caring and looking out for each other... well, it did Steve some good just to witness the scene.

Overhearing the man's name, Steve quietly checked his wrist interface with the station mainframe. The computer identified the tall man with the curly headed family as Liam Green, newly arrived immigrant from Earth. He had apparently sold his small industrial parts service to a larger competitor because, as he explained in his immigration application, he felt he was getting too old. Looking back at Mr. Green and his family, Steve felt it was more likely that Mr. Green as a boy had a dream of reaching for the stars. That dream, perhaps once forgotten, may have driven him to build a successful small business in Earth's extremely competitive market.

Steve turned his eyes from the scene, thought about dropping by to see Mary, and then stopped in his tracks to check another incoming message on his wrist. Suddenly there was a loud crack, as a projectile struck a column near his head, spattering resin chips and putting a web of cracks where the bullet hit. Immediately the sound the shot reached him from somewhere behind him, unmistakably the report of a ballistic weapon.

Steve hit the floor, drew his sidearm, and rolled but there was no second shot. He scanned visually for the shooter. The crowd was panicking. He noticed the tall man, Liam, was crouched protectively over his family but also looking for the shooter. Liam had no weapon visible, but he was looking up toward a balcony gallery above the main floor. Steve thought he saw a haze in the air up there, so he quickly checked the local Station floorplan on his wrist interface. That elevated gallery led to a residential area still under construction. There was an elevator behind his position that would give him access. He rolled up from his prone position and sprinted for the elevator. He kept his weapon out as he waited for the door to open, keeping a watchful eye on the area. Most people had reached cover and were hiding on every side of any solid object, unsure where the threat might be. Liam was gathering his family quickly to move, but looked calm and in control. Steve commed Security about what was going on and what he intended to do. It did not look like there were any casualties yet, and he requested backup. The dispatcher said she was routing two officers to each exit from the new construction. The elevator door slid open and Steve quickly entered and hit the button.

Approaching the hitman's original location on the balcony, Steve slowed, scanning for the slightest clue, sound, or movement. He walked carefully, committing to memory where he stepped. Crime scene forensics could work miracles, but disturbing the scene might alter a clue or destroy evidence. There was no carpeting in the hall leading to the new residential area. Loose construction debris littered the floor. The best Steve could do for now would be to cover the escape route without disturbing the scene any more. He trusted security personnel were already in motion to close the other exits, but many in security were untested new immigrants from Earth. Steve had to accept that he could control only so much. He couldn't cover all the bases. With his eyes steady on the corridor, he exhaled slowly and took a deep breath to clear his mind and focus. He carefully surveyed his environment, seeking anything out-of-place. He thought about what he would have done had he been the assassin. He would have tried to reach a pre-planned hiding spot to wait and pick his time to move to safety. Steve checked a ventilation duct and found it too narrow for an alternate escape route.

Two security deputies arrived and Steve briefed them on what they needed to know. Then the officers told him a detective would catch up with him later. For now Councilman Lyman needed to talk with Steve and was waiting in his office. A message on Steve's com confirmed the request from the Councilman. The visit to Mary would just have to wait.

Steve, still feeling shaken, headed up to the administration section and the Councilman's office. Marge was at the desk with a look of concern on her face, effectively forecasting what was on the Councilor's mind.

"Steven, come in," said Councilor Lyman. "I'm glad you weren't hurt. Listen, I think we need to minimize your exposure. I'm trying to figure out how we can best do that. Do you have any ideas?"

"I could leave the station and try to find my kids on Cygnus. The only problem is I'm afraid that might expose them to the same problem."

"True. It wouldn't really reduce your exposure, would it?"

"Well, it would until they found me again."

"That probably wouldn't take very long. Look, I can have someone check on them for you; maybe let your Ex know what's going on if you like. But for you, what if we use you to patrol and survey the Al Najid system? That would keep you in space and away from predictable routines among the general Station population until a new lead turns up on Harden."

"Lyman, how long do you really think that will last? The assassin would just take a ship and try and nail me out there."

"You would at least see him coming, there won't be civilians in your way, and I think you can hold your own in ship-to-ship combat, Steve."

So Al Najid Command drafted Steve for a tedious survey detail of several relatively unexplored volumes of space in the system. Kyle, preoccupied by Station security, would not be available to fly with him. Steve wished him luck with Lian and Bobby, but even more he wished Kyle were available to fly on his wing and help relieve the tedium a survey task invariably meant.

Chapter 19: Investigation

Shortly after lunch Kyle saw a text message on his wrist communicator from Gabriella, the Station's security dispatcher. Her message advised him of the assassination attempt on Steve moments before. He was off duty but immediately took leave of Lian at his apartment and headed for the Station Security office. There he found Gabriella coordinating his officers competently. Kyle armed himself with a heavy hand laser and headed for the construction zone. Gabriella let him know that the Station's new forensics expert, one Jack Graham from Earth, would meet him there.

Jack Graham was carefully extracting the projectile that had narrowly missed Steve from the structural resin column across from the balcony. While awaiting the elevator Kyle watched his new forensic specialist and wondered how bad the investigator's eyesight must be to need those thick eyeglasses. The door slid open and Kyle took the elevator up to where his two deputies were controlling access to the new residential construction area at the gallery entrance. He asked the deputies if they had seen anyone and they reported only Steve and the investigator from forensics had been there. Kyle drew his sidearm and entered the silent construction zone.

The air was still. The lighting was utilitarian, bright and harsh in work areas but dark everywhere else. The floor was littered with construction debris. Kyle switched on his flashlight, keeping his sidearm at the ready. The beam of his hand-torch lit an oval on the floor ahead of him and dust suspended in the still air near the flooring. He could see many footprints in the resin dust that had settled onto the floor but could not tell whether they had all been left by workers. He could tell which prints were new where they covered older prints. With perseverance he spotted an unusual pair of tracks that showed no elevated heel, as if someone had been wearing slippers of some kind. No construction worker would have worn shoes like that on the job site. On a hunch Kyle followed those footprints, to see where they led. In some places the dust had been disturbed, and they and other footprints vanished, but nowhere were the slipper prints beneath work boot footprints. In many places they showed up superimposed over the rest. It required patience but he followed the slipper prints to a spot sheltered from casual view by unfinished walls and large cartons. There Kyle found a single-shot resin-composite sniper rifle. Nearby was a bundle of dull black clothing. The bundle was on top of a pair of crepe-soled ballet slippers. Careful to avoid disturbing the scene Kyle notified Gabriella of his discovery and asked her to get his position on the Station from his wrist comm. This information would reach forensics right away.

Meanwhile Kyle examined the marks on the floor closely. He could see a smudged area where the shooter must have stood when he or she removed the black suit and ballet slippers. There was a battered gray plastic suitcase laying open and empty on a box. Or mostly empty. Kyle's eyes focused on something laying inside the suitcase: it was made of translucent clear plastic, a thin, rigid plastic sleeve intended to hold an identification card or badge. Careful to not disturb any evidence, Kyle took a step closer to get a better look. The plastic sleeve was empty. Kyle began an unhurried, methodical search of the room which contained many cartons, some open and some closed. The shooter wouldn't have left the card sleeve unless they didn't have the card for it. He found the card at last between two of the cartons. It had somehow slipped out of its sleeve. The shooter had to have been pressed for time if he left before finding it.

Kyle examined the card closely under his flashlight. It was a *Perry Station* residential pass key. He should probably have left the card where it was for forensics, but Kyle decided he had to identify the door it would open for himself. Any fingerprints on it would most likely be all over the plastic sleeve in the suitcase. If there were no prints on the sleeve or on the suitcase, then there would probably be no prints on the card. Kyle holstered his sidearm and pulled a slim metal ruler from his belt. With the blade of the ruler he lifted the side of the card and with his other hand picked it up by two edges and slipped it into his shirt pocket.

Kyle resumed his search of the floor, looking for the prints from the shooter's second set of shoes. The most likely prints appeared to be regular street shoes, with a low heel, maybe size ten or eleven. The prints appeared only where the construction and cutting of resin materials had left dust on the floor, but eventually led Kyle to a section of flooring that had been removed, revealing a ladder that descended into a utility closet on the lower deck. It was unguarded, since it did not appear on the Station plans. There Kyle lost the trail.

Returning to his office Kyle cross-referenced the numbers on the residential card key against the Station residential database, and what he found puzzled him. The card was registered to Jack Graham, the new forensic specialist. Kyle made a note of the address to the apartment, then checked the address of record in his personnel file. He took a look at the forensic lab, became worried, and checked the log for the evidence vault. Something was very very wrong. He returned to his desk to look more closely at Graham's personnel folder. He saw the man's background check had not been completed.

He walked the file over to Gabriella's desk. As short-handed as they were the day shift dispatcher also performed much of Security's clerical work.

"Gabby, what is the hold up on Jack Graham's background check?" he asked her.

Gabriella was a small, fierce woman who was extremely well organized. The security office would have been lost without her, and Kyle relied on her to keep his operations firmly anchored in reality.

"My contact in London sent a note that there was some confusion on their end. They were unaware that Mr. Graham had emigrated and were going to look into it." she said.

"I am beginning to wonder about our Mr. Graham." mused Kyle. Gabriella's eyebrows raised. "Where is he? The lab looks like it hasn't been used."

"He hasn't checked in." she told him. Gabriella could put two and two together. "I take it Graham is a person of interest?"

Graham had just been out there, digging a bullet out of a column.

"Indeed. Graham is a suspect. I need to check on a few things. I'll try to get Steve to help me. I'm not sure about trusting the rest of our new people until those background checks are complete. Try to expedite them, and don't cut any corners."

"You can count on me, Kyle."

"I know I can, Gabby." Kyle reassured her, then commed Steve. "Hey buddy: do you have some time this afternoon?"

After a minute Steve commed back: "Sure thing, Kyle. Just finishing a late lunch at the Cog. What's up?"

"Stay there, I'll be just a few minutes. Keep your eyes open."

Steve paused. Something in Kyle's voice said he had information he didn't want to transmit over an open comm channel. "Okay, Kyle. I'll see you when you get here."

As Steve ate the final few bites of his grilled ham and cheese sandwich he watched for any unusual behavior. Since he identified his location over the com the assassin or assassins might have learned where he was. Everything and everyone looked normal. Steve had a good seat among the tables outside, with his back to a wall next to the entrance. He still had his glass of water and he was nursing it, swirling the diminishing ice and taking an occasional sip. He wished for a good dill pickle.

Then he spotted Kyle's head over those of two women who were walking very slowly and casually ahead of him, blocking his progress. Steve stood from his place. He turned to catch the eye of the barkeep and made motions to tell her he was leaving. She would put it on his tab. Then Steve turned to join with Kyle, who had finally maneuvered politely around the amblers.

"So what's up, Kyle?" He asked once they were walking briskly side by side. "Where are we headed?"

"Steve, we may have found our assassin, but I don't know for sure." Kyle then told Steve what he and his team had found: the weapon, the ballet slippers, the residential card key, the footprints, and that London believed Jack Graham was still working for them on Earth.

"Do you mean London in England, or the one in orbit?" asked Steve.

"You know, I didn't even ask. But I was thinking maybe we would go look in on Mr. Graham. I saw him on the crime scene recovering the projectile from the column."

"The Cygnus shuttle doesn't leave for a few hours, so he must still be here on the Station somewhere. Did you check to see if he contacted Housing for a new pass key to his apartment?"

Kyle nodded. "He picked one up a little while ago. I checked the lab and saw no sign of the round he was recovering or any of the stuff I found in the construction site. There was no record of deposit in the evidence vault. Plus his comm signal has dropped off the grid. We can't locate him by comm positioning."

The two men kept walking toward the residential section where the man who called himself Jack Graham had rented an apartment.

"So he probably knows we know who he is." Steve observed. "Or was. You realize, of course, that we might be walking into a set-up, right?" Steve asked. "We might be under his sights right now."

"Maybe. There isn't anyone else I could trust this with, Steve. I can call for back-up if we need it but we haven't received half of the background checks on our new hires. If I am right, and Graham is your shooter, he might not be working his contract solo."

Kyle continued apologetically "Look, Steve, I tried to requisition a personal shield for you to use but the Corporates have priced them too high. We don't have anything for that in the budget."

Steve nodded in understanding as they turned the last corner. A personal shield would most likely only limit him to a slow ugly death rather than a fast clean one. Ahead was a corridor lined with residential doors. Steve looked over his shoulder to see identical doors in the corridor behind them. Then Kyle said "There it is." The door looked like every other. They paused. "Like you said, this might be a trap. It is unimaginable that he would have failed to take the time to recover his key when he dropped it. He actually picked up a replacement knowing that in all likelihood we were onto him. That suggests he had something in the apartment that he wanted."

"He may have thought he could recover it later. It's possible he doesn't realize we're onto him," Steve mused "but I wouldn't count on it."

"Planned or not, we must assume he knows we would come here. Let's check to see if his neighbors are home and make sure they get to a safety. He may have rigged explosives."

"We don't want to alarm them unnecessarily. Can you think of a story we could use to get them to move, other than a 'mad assassin with explosives' might be next door?" Steve suggested. 'What if we alert a neighbor who happens to be on his team?"

Kyle stopped in his tracks looking sideways at Steve. "You're getting almost as complicated as Lyman, Steve. How about, Let's see..." Kyle's eyebrows drew together in concentration. "I dunno. If we don't get his neighbors to safety we would be negligent. They are the people we are putting our lives on the line for, after all."

"And here I was flattering myself that it was me we were trying to protect."

"Stop pulling my leg, Steve. You've been a lawman longer than I have. Just go up and knock on the neighbor's door. They'll know who you are, but you can go through the motions to identify yourself..."

"Hold on: *Me* go knock on the door? How about *you* go knock on the door?" Steve objected.

"They won't know me. I'd have to flash a badge, and that could attract unnecessary attention." Kyle countered.

"Call Gabrielle and have her call the neighbors. Meanwhile lets just continue walking casually past." Steve suggested.

"Good thinking." Kyle agreed.

"Chicken."

They walked far enough to ensure that they wouldn't be easily noticed by the suspect if he looked, but close enough to keep an eye on his door. These residences abutted the station hull on the back, so they had no rear exit. Kyle called Gabby to ask her to call the neighbors. After a reasonably brief wait the neighbor nearest to them left his apartment and walked quickly away toward the central area. Gabrielle sent Kyle a text message that the other neighbor wasn't answering.

Graham should not have had time to have acquire and rig enough explosives to endanger the deck above or below, so the two quietly approached his door. There was no apparent reaction from the residence. Steve detected no signs of movement in the window blinds. He felt sure that they had missed their quarry and Graham was already gone. Kyle asked Gabrielle to access the residential security controls and unlock the door, and after a moment the door hummed and slid open. It was dark inside.

Kyle said aloud 'Lights!', and the domestic artificial intelligence obediently closed the circuit for the apartment's illumination. The main LED circuitry and ground wire, however, had been bypassed with a low-resistance conductor and set to create a tiny electrical arc inside a container filled with highly flammable liquid, which ignited. With a deep concussion the explosion knocked Steve and Kyle flat on their backs outside the front door and set the apartment afire. Immediately the smoke alarm began shrieking and fire extinguishers sprayed fire suppressant onto everything, surely destroying evidence.

The two men got up, checked themselves for damage, and straightened their clothing. "The next time we walk into the darkened rooms of a dangerous man, let's just use our flashlights." said Kyle.

"You think?" Steve rolled his eyes. "If I were in his place I wouldn't even try to board the next shuttle. I'd lay low and change my appearance to try again later. Graham might have no intention of leaving until his job is finished."

"Thank you, sunshine. We're still going to have to keep a close eye on every shuttle, and we don't know whether he arranged for a private carrier anyway. Almost any of the miners would see only the profit to be made smuggling somebody out-system." Kyle's brow creased. "It looks like the flames are out. Let's check inside, but be careful: that might not have been the only thing he left for us."

Graham had left confirmation for them in the apartment's small utilitarian bathroom. The thick-lensed glasses were on the sink with a pair of countering brown iris contact lenses floating in solution. A full set of skin-colored fingertips with false fingerprints. In the trash receptacle were empty containers of hair dye in several different shades. In the bedroom closet were both male and female articles of clothing. The assassin successfully planted seeds of doubt in the lawmen that they would be able to easily identify him. Or her. Or them.

Chapter 20: Unknown

Councilman Lyman was convinced that Steve was not safe on the Station, and consequently the Station was not safe when he was there. So he ordered Steve to get into his ship to survey his assigned volume of space and let Kyle do his job.

Steve sent an apologetic email to Mary and then went to his dock. He inspected and boarded his light fighter, and brought up the official system charts on his astrogation computer. It was a fresh download from the Station mainframe.

The best analytic mining sensors available could only determine the general elemental composition of unshielded material in a vacuum at a range of about three kilometers, and that depended on how active the star Al Najid was. Not only was the range limited for a reasonably good assay scan, but it would take time for Steve's systems to analyze each object while it was being plotted.

To the best of his knowledge, there weren't many objects in Steve's assigned area, but he would need to factor for significantly reduced speed for his scanning runs. He wouldn't have to be as slow and meticulous as he would have were he formally assaying the densely clustered planetary debris, true, but it was still shaping up to be a very long day. Steve calculated his plotted way-points in twelve hour runs so he could finish in four days rather than six. Steve uploaded his intended flight plan for the first run, performed his communications checks with Command, and requested clearance for launch.

Steve shunted from the base and sped out about halfway to his first plotted waypoint, off the normal transit route toward the fifth planet's habitable installation. He synchronized his data feed with Command, and started the survey. It was slow, methodical, mind numbing work but it was something *Perry Station* needed. Besides, Steve had plenty to think about, and while out there he didn't need to worry about assassination.

Despite the need to mull over the most important questions, he kept thinking of his family at the most inopportune times. Steve vividly recalled playtime with his son. The memories brought a pang to Steve's loneliness among the far stars. He had to wrestle his attention back to his survey.

His wife used to call him a natural mind reader, but Steve always explained away those little coincidences with sensitivity to details and noticing patterns. But indications of prescience seemed too frequent to be completely coincidental. On reflection, Steve admitted that he had premonitions, as if part of him beneath his superficial consciousness somehow knew what was coming.

He remembered his mother saying he always seemed to bump into 'interesting' events more often than anyone she knew.

So he reacted with a roll of the eyes when he flew his spacecraft into something big that wasn't there. "Not again," he thought. This could throw his whole schedule out the airlock.

Steve had been scanning, analyzing, and cataloging a sparse scattering of debris as his shipboard computer logged the coordinates of every object on its sensors along with composition and events. He was actively trying to stay alert when his ship shuddered and bumped into something, triggering collision alarms. He quickly keyed up some diagnostics and scanned his status board looking for damage, and then turned to his sensors. There was no sign of anything out there he could have hit, yet he had definitely rammed into something. Visually there was no indication of any close object, let alone something as big as it had to have been. He checked the log for a location at the time of impact, and calculated roughly where whatever it was had to be, yet when he looked nothing was there.

"Steve: status?" Flight Control was checked, and wanted to know what happened. They had noticed his collision alarms on their telemetric displays. What Steve's ship sensed and recorded was simultaneously transmitted to Base. A creature of habit, and by now quite used to inexplicable things happening, Steve hesitated, trying to think of a way to word a credible reply. Simply saying he ran into 'nothing'" wouldn't sound right. He toggled over to a scrambled channel and told them his ship came into physical contact with an unidentified stealth object. He reported no apparent damage, and provided the coordinates. He suggested getting Chief Mackenzie and a couple of his engineers out there for a recovery attempt, "since something that looks like nothing is worth looking into." Naturally, it didn't come out quite right when he said it, but Control let it pass.

Steve held his position quietly for a while, impatient but curious, waiting for the duty officer to run the news up the chain of command.

Then he decided to make sure whatever it was hadn't left the area. Officially this was for verification, and he so advised Control. Actually, Steve didn't want to face embarrassment if the engineers arrived to recover whatever it was and there was nothing at all there. He gently nudged up to his previous location and lightly bumped it, again setting off the collision alarms. He again rolled his eyes at the harsh noise. He waited and quietly searched through his ship's system interface documentation seeking a way to tone down the alarms. While he did so, his mind sought to determine a logical path of consequences that might play out from this event.

Steve didn't know of any existing human technology that could completely cloak an object with invisibility to his sensors at such close range. It might not be of human origin. In all of humanity's travels we had never found any conclusive sign of non-human, truly intelligent life, other than the moduli. Humanity didn't even know the moduli's age. There was almost universal belief in the existence of other sentient beings, somewhere, but nobody had found any sign of them. As far as Steve knew, none had found us either. Steve didn't think the intelligence of dolphins and chimpanzees were really on the same scale. Perhaps, he thought, alien technology is simply far, far superior. That humans did not see them did not mean they couldn't see us.

It was notable to Steve that when his ship hit whatever it was, the object failed to react in any detectable way.

"Steve," Base advised over the scrambled frequency, "the watch commander concurs with your assessment. We're scrambling an engineering team with what we hope can be a recovery vehicle. Can you give us an idea of the dimensions of the object?"

"Give me a couple minutes, Command". Steve should have anticipated that. He nudged his way around trying to form a metric idea of the shape and size of this thing, all the while mulling over another rather obvious idea. He tried to recall the plumbing of his jet feeds, but after consulting his schematics realized he couldn't reroute his maneuvering jets to try and blow atmosphere onto the object. He thought the vented atmosphere might turn to ice crystals and reveal what the object looked like. It couldn't be done, and Steve supposed that was a good thing, since with his luck he might have screwed it up and ended getting his tail caught in the door.

"Base, it is roughly cylindrical, about forty meters by ten or twelve.

If the engineers haven't left yet, recommend they bring some kind of micro-particle dispenser to coat it with, so we can see it."

"Steven: this is Chief Mackenzie. We are en route. ETA fifteen. Good idea on the sprayer: I'll see what I can rig up on our way there. From your description I would guess it's some kind of spacecraft. In any case, we do have sufficient room to haul her in, assuming she isn't active, over."

"Chief, she didn't seem to respond when I bumped into her, over."

"Understood, Steve. Mackenzie out."

Steve clicked an acknowledgment. He didn't know Chief Mackenzie's full capabilities, but he knew the engineer was sharp and not one to take chances. If the object were an alien artifact, maybe left by the same beings that built the Moduli, Steve recognized that a science team might be needed more than an engineering team. Sad to say, *Perry Station* didn't have enough scientists among their survivors. He had no idea whether the immigrants included any scientists.

He sighed to himself. He could recommend bringing in the Aldebari and know that it would be heard, but he didn't think the idea would be well received. He hoped the brass would think things all the way through. He snorted at the thought. How likely was that?

Besides, he knew and respected what he knew of Mack. The Chief would most likely make the same recommendation, and invite some scientists to study it. They would probably be rather interested.

By the time the engineering team arrived with their salvage platform, Steve had marked out the object with small strobe buoys. Mack had no better success scanning the object than Steve had, but he did spray some light hydraulic oil on it. The oil didn't stick, but for a few moments it showed them what it looked like, or at least what the force field around it looked like. The droplets hit the surface, and then slid around it to the opposite side, where the oil pooled and drifted off into space. When Chief Mackenzie saw that, he wasted no more time. He guided the barge to envelop and secure the object. There was nothing to moor to on it. Since the object was ovoid, he had his men rig some stays around it to keep the it in place for the return trip to the Station.

Station Command ordered Steve to complete his survey mission after losing almost a whole shift to the discovery, so it was late and he was exhausted when he returned home.

The next day Steve stopped by the shipyard and looked up Chief Mackenzie, but he wasn't in his office. Checking with a few of the people he knew, his quest led him to an enclosed gantry he had never before noticed. A security sentry checked his credentials before Steve got halfway. At the end of the gantry a locked door blocked his path. The sensor had surely identified him by now, Steve thought, but the door remained locked. Through the door he could hear a stridently angry, deep male voice, unmistakable in tone but indistinct in content. He had half a mind to turn back, but it was a long hike and Steve remained decidedly curious. He pressed the keypad to request admission. The keypad verified his fingerprint and announced his name to the room occupants beyond the door.

The angry voice on the other side suddenly fell quiet, and after a moment the door clicked. Steve opened it and entered.

The door opened onto a small enclosed hanger and dry dock. A red-faced Chief Engineer Mackenzie threatened "I'm going to get me a bigger hammer, Steven". An assortment of tools, power and manual, and an array of modular electronic devices ringed the dock, all facing the middle. The chief glared. It was clearly not going well. "We can't even secure the damned thing in place. Magnetics don't affect it. There's nowhere to attach mooring cables. Ropes slip off, completely useless. I can't disable the shield no matter what I try. Steve: I'm at my wits' end."

"Maybe we should ask for an Aldebari science team?" Steve suggested.

At first, Steve thought Mackenzie would be indignant. Instead Mackenzie looked him in the eye and said calmly, "I'm not sure what else we can do." Mack conceded. "An engineer works with answers. Scientists are more suited to questions, and questions are all we really have. On the other hand, I haven't tried quite everything yet. I'd rather we had more information before we start bringing in anyone from the outside."

Steve nodded, and walked over to where the unseen object had to be. He reached up with his hand to try and touch it, but found it was several steps further in, toward two vertical and two horizontal stanchions. Another set of framing stanchions stood about fifty feet away. The surface of the object or field felt slick, and the temperature was neutral to the touch. Frustrated, Steve shrugged his shoulders and walked toward the door. Mackenzie headed for his computer terminal.

Then a thought suddenly occurred to Steve: "Chief have you tried securing it with a cargo net? There must be a thousand of them over in mining supply warehouse." Cargo nets were used to haul schist and dross left over from mining ore. They were fired from a missile tube, and small thrusters with magnetic housings wrapped the net around the clustered objects and held around the cluster magnetically.

Mack's eyes sparkled and his face broke into a wide grin. "You'll be an engineer yet, Stevie-boy!"

Chapter 21: Incursion

When the alarms went off, Steve woke out of a dream and reached over to reassure his wife. She wasn't there, and he wasn't at home. He felt shaken and mystified because the dream seemed so real.

He shouted 'lights' and the room's illumination winked into existence and flooded his quarters. The alarm that blared out in the corridor was insistent. Then he was up. He headed for the bathroom for a quick comb and face wash, then slid into his flight suit and boots. His wrist communicator told him he had slept only a few hours.

He reached the Station ready room to learn that their patrol at the modulus had gone silent after alerting Command of multiple hostiles entering Al Najid system. The Station alarms bellowed deep and rhythmic off the bulkheads, and the spinning amber lights in every hallway underscored the imperative to prepare for an emergency. The intrastation communications advised civilians to remain in their residences under pressure seals. The main station compartments began sealing off sections, leaving only single individual airlocks as passage ways.

Command assumed word of the modulinite ore had reached organized crime outside the system, and that they had begun an initial foray. Command inferred the largest and best organized of the pirate clans may head for the planet's scattered remains, hoping to seize the miners' laden holdings.

The pirates would have realized that the Station's defenses would make it difficult and dangerous to assault directly, so they intended to pick off and loot the miners and traders piecemeal. After a quick hit the pirates would try to exit the system back through the modulus and disperse back to hidden bases.

The Station broadcasted a general alarm over emergency channels to alert shipping and give the scattered miners a chance to get to their holdings and batten down, reduce their energy signatures and silence their beacons to make themselves harder to find.

Steve knew how vulnerable the miners were. Asteroid mining uses powerful short-range lasers to turn ore into a hot liquid that expands quickly. In a practically weightless vacuum the boiling material spatters into the void. The miner then uses powerful short range electrical fields to give particles a charge so that the cooling material can be drawn into the hold. Mechanical conveyers then funnel the cooling particles into a mechanism where it is sorted and shunted into the appropriate hold partition.

After a miner fills his cargo holds, he offloads at a *minehold*, a combined remote habitat and ore refinery. A miner is paid by cargo mass and type. Sorted and compacted ore dust is pulled into minehold kilns and smelted into ingots to reduce its volume. External cargo nets are then used by mineholds to contain the ingots until they had sufficient holdings to warrant the expense of a hauler, normally third party traders. The cargo nets, as well as the mineholds themselves are normally lit by navigation lamps and emitter beacons, but can appear and behave like regular asteroids to normal sensor suites if the lights and radio beacons aren't active. So their best passive defense is to power-down the beacons and hide, or become 'One with the Stone,' as the mining culture phrases it.

On deck at the Station, the flight techs prepped all ACM and Perry fighter-class patrol craft and loaded ordnance. Steve wished his new gunboat were ready for a real test but it wasn't, so he headed for his trusty old Whiskey Foxtrot Zulu Niner Aldebar Light Fighter, or WFZ-9 ALF. He patted her fresh photo-ablative enamel affectionately and swung into the cabin. His crew chief strapped him in, slapped his helmet for luck, and sealed him in. Then she armed the explosive bolts of his lifepod.

Steve momentarily felt renewed pangs of loss as he remembered his flight crew at Porter's Field that terrible morning when he failed to protect them and his planet. He had lost that day, and his people paid for it with their lives. He vowed that he must never fail his crew again. This handsome young woman winking at him with such courage and assurance must not be allowed to perish, at any cost. Not on his watch.

The techs scrambled into the airlocks and vanished, and the airlock status lamps changed to green as they gained seal. A big amber light strobed over the bay door as the atmosphere was pumped back into the pressure tanks. The lights glared bright red for a few seconds as the massive armored bay door pulled out and slid aside to reveal the stars. Steve heard his heart pumping like a hammer, just as it always did when he again saw the sudden glory of stars everywhere. The stars shone bright and steady, in every color of the rainbow. Most were like motes of bright dust, but even the nearer incandescent jewels were uncountable. The spaces between those nearer stars were filled with seas of much farther stars, a bright treasure far beyond any man's reach. Yet here, at least, humanity was among them.

Steve's flight of six fighters launched, accelerating toward the crescent of debris around the leading edge of his planet's core remains. Two more flights would follow to complete first squadron. Second watch, with another eighteen fighters, was readying and would hold for launch while the pilots of the third watch, whose squadron included the Station's tactical warcraft, were being roused from their beds as backup. Two escape pods from the modulus patrol arrived safely back at base. It seemed likely there were no casualties, other than the lost patrol craft. Hardware can be replaced, but not pilots. Thankfully, immigration and renewed commitments by the ACM alliance had greatly increased the number of available pilots and spacecraft.

Flying out near the mineholds closest to the planet's fragmented remains, Steve actively scanned for intruders. Then the duty officer at Command on the Station recalled the squadron because the invaders were heading the other way, toward the anomaly. The pilots spun 180 and kicked in their antimatter annihilators, quickly slowing and then reversing their momentum, back toward the raw anomaly, the Aldebari facility, and the anti-ship minefield.

Command also advised that a flight of four Legionnaire fighters intended to assist, and had already launched from their small outpost on the fifth planet. Command updated the flight's IFF (identify friend or foe) systems to recognize the Legion flight as friendlies. Command reported the Aldebari research Station would delay launching their fighters to act as ready reserve if needed. They would also launch if their research station came under attack. Diplomatic status made it incumbent on *Perry Station* to protect them and the Al Najid V outpost, though it was understood they could defend themselves if attacked.

Perry Station was now much closer to the intruders than Steve's flight, so Second Squadron launched to intercept. Third Squadron would now ready up, since their boats would have room to be prepped.

In a few minutes Second Squadron flew close enough to obtain a long range visual. Judging from what signals intelligence gleaned from encrypted comm intercepts, a C&C (command and control) corvette near the modulus was coordinating the pirates as they approached the anomaly minefield. After listening to the reports Steve concluded the intruders weren't pirates. He suggested to Kyle they might try to take out the Aldebari mines, and once those were cleared, major trouble might emerge from the anomaly. A hostile corvette was bad enough already. Steve believed there wasn't anything else out there anyone would throw fighters at. The intruders were not likely to start a war with the Aldebar. But if they planned to take out the anti-ship minefield, it meant that the Black Cruiser was going to come through again. It was a frightening thought, but Steve found himself intensely curious to see the transit of a wild anomaly. Noone had been able to accomplish that since spatial anomalies were first discovered.

The intruders ignored all demands to stand down. Then Command reported another flight of intruders incoming from the modulus. That made a baker's dozen, and it meant Steve's flight would be in the fight after all.

First flight, Second Squadron, reported multiple missile launches from the group they pursued: they were still too far out for the missiles to be anything but standoff ordnance intended for a fixed target, which meant they were going for either the Aldebar research station or the mines.

The Aldebar research installation confirmed their point defense system and shields were online and their fighters, if needed, were standing by for launch. On Steve's screen he was just starting to pick up signals from the second flight of incoming intruders as his flight raced to intercept them.

Second Squadron gave their pilots the green light to engage. First Squadron was still out of range of the second incoming group.

The Aldebari reported multiple explosions in the minefield circling the anomaly. The enemy's second group quickly approached the point where the first group had fired their stand-off missiles. They flew almost as fast as Steve's flight chasing them, preventing the pursuers from closing the range. The first group of aggressors had not turned back to engage second squadron. Instead they continued to bore in toward the minefield. This kept them far enough ahead of pursuit to render most of Second Squadron's fire ineffectual. That would change drastically if the raiders spent any time at the minefield. Until then they basically had a free ride. The enemy kept clear of the Aldebar installation.

As the enemy's first group reached direct fire range of the minefield they opened up with short range weaponry, detonating a few mines, and then swung around the anomaly in a wide turn. It looked like they were going to head back to the modulus to transit out of the system into Cygnus space. The Aldebar sent a coded transmission to *Perry Station*, and the Station quickly ordered second squadron to turn and engage the second incoming flight, while Steve's squadron vectored to catch the first enemy group head-on as they headed back toward the modulus.

Third squadron, Gold team, launched from *Perry Station*.

"Targets incoming," Steve said quietly into his open mike as the leading enemy fighters began to enter range. His sensors couldn't detect them directly yet, but the Aldebar were providing their data stream to the alliance fighters.

The incoming hostiles appeared focused solely on getting the hell out of Dodge with their mismatched collection of light fighters and attack boats. First squadron endured the enemy's first salvo without a scratch. They never paused to engage, they just ran full bore for the modulus. If they were mercenaries they were awfully green. The squadron had orders to take them out, and take them out they did. Slowing to pivot on them as they passed, Steve's squadron fired on them the whole way. By then Third Squadron, approaching from *Perry Station*, achieved their targeting solutions and took out the last of the first group of hostiles. The defenders pivoted once more to take out the remnants of the enemy second group.

But as it turned out, the raiders had already done their job. Their escape pods were all speeding toward their Corvette at the modulus.

Chapter 22: An Unusual Tactic

Just as the squadrons were mopped up strays and prepared to head for that unidentified C&C corvette near the modulus, they received a comm from the Aldebari advising that something unusual was happening in the anomaly. Steve checked his ALF's rail gun ammunition: 1100 rounds. He still retained his two AI Raptors, and the new Legionnaire pulse lasers seemed to be holding up well. His armor was only down a bit, at a little over 90%. All other systems looked good. "Systems check: good here, Kyle: How are you?"

"Systems are nominal. Still got my two Raptors, Steve."

Viewed on a VD feed streamed from the research station the seething anomaly bulged unnaturally. Then that wicked black prow emerged majestically from the violent sphere of churning energy. As it thrust through the anomaly into clear space Steve thought he saw the cruiser folding some sort of fins or wings back into its hull while it emerged. The ship's shields looked palpable, even though they weren't yet being fired upon: surely it was an effect of the transit. Aldebar station and First Squadron both reported to Perry base that the *Pyotr Velikiyer,* the black cruiser that destroyed Perry, was emerging from the anomaly. Base acknowledged and scrambled all remaining fighters that had been held in reserve.

Almost before her fantail had cleared the anomaly the black ship began launching a cloud of fighters that appeared on the defenders' sensor displays marked with little black triangles. The black ship itself was depicted as a small black lozenge on the screen.

"Engage," Steve called, quietly echoed by every other allied pilot except Kyle, who spoke their hearts: '*Come on, you sons of bitches*'.

Delaney, Graham, Kyle and Steve took up a square formation and headed in at seventy percent thrust. The flight had a short way to go before the nearest fighters would come into range. Some pilots who had been closer were already tangling with the cruiser's fighters in a fur ball, missed shots streaking through the starry backdrop, beams piercing, and all remote and distant, silent in the hiss and hum of Steve's cockpit. Occasionally a distant ship would explode and a pod would race back, either to the *Pyotr Velikiyer* or back to Perry base so much farther away. Having the ability to pod right back into their cruiser, take a new ship and launch would work to the black ship's advantage in the near term, until their losses depleted their necessarily limited supply of reserve hulls. It would take Perry pilots much longer to get back into the fight.

One thing was sure: They were in for a fight.

Suddenly Steve's sensor display went blank. The *Pyotr Velikiyer* was using electronic counter measures to blind them. Then just as suddenly the screen came up again filled with green triangles: The Aldebar had launched! And red! Four Legion fighters in tight formation were screaming in with them from the direction of their base on the red fifth planet.

The research station was wrestling with the great black ship for control of digital communications in the electromagnetic spectra. Sensors would one moment be a blank gray slate, and the next a confusion of color as first one and then the other gained ascendency.

Then Steve's flight swept in among them, dodging and twisting, firing and hitting afterburners. Beyond one black fighter he saw a standing diamond formation of Aldebari heavy and light fighters elegantly sweep in, with multiple black hulls bursting into fiery explosions before them. Then Steve dived, following his quarry as the enemy fighter tried to evade. Steve lost track of all but the immediate battle. All organization with Delaney and Graham evaporated in the imperative to survive. Through it all Kyle guarded Steve's six, kicking tail, and cussing with every breath.

Steve looked over toward Kyle, their latest kill just a pod streaking away toward the black cruiser. He saw Kyle flash a thumbs up. Suddenly, just beyond Kyle came a black medium fighter setting up for the kill. Steve barked a warning, spun port and got missile tone. He gave his AI Raptor a peek and saw the green telltale. He launched. Kyle juiced his afterburner: Steve's Raptor slid neatly behind Kyle and hit the medium black fighter dead-on the prow. Kyle pivoted and hit the medium in the flank, dislodging some glowing metal. Steve triggered a burst from the rail gun, chewing through the black fighter's armor. Kyle gave him another burst from his cannons and the foe's hull crumpled, popped the lifepod, and exploded.

The *Pyotr Velikiyer* had the range now on the research station, and a lance of brilliant white light lanced into the station's strong shields. The station countered with a salvo of heavy missiles that streaked into the cruiser's shields in a series of rippling explosions, but the cruiser's shields held.

Another lance of sun-hot white light speared out into the station's shield while the Aldebari return salvo slammed into the black ship's shields, attempting to overload them.

"*Jade Temple* clearing the modulus," came from a voice over the comm, and Steve smiled. He could see Gold Team incoming on his screen. The Research Station seemed to have won the EW battle for now, but her shields weren't very stable. The *Pyotr Velikiyer* still seemed strong. Steve's smile vanished. He didn't think the *Jade Temple* would arrive in time to save the research station.

"Kyle," Steve urged, "we need to get in close to the black ship and try to take her defenses apart. I don't think the Research Station is strong enough to take her out."

"Try and get Delaney and Graham with us," Kyle responded. "Maybe we can take out those defensive turrets. I wouldn't try to blow her shield array in the crossfire of those batteries."

"We heard you, Kyle, and affirmative," Delaney cut in, "we're heading for the cruiser with you." Delaney answered.

Kyle signaled he was starting to make his run. Steve pulled in tightly aft of Kyle's port side. Steve targetted a cannon emplacement that had acquired them and was starting to fire. Both Steve and Kyle fired beams but barely brought down the gun emplacement's local shield before they were past him. They looped out and back for another run. The defensive fire from the turret was heavy as it tracked their course. Delaney pulled in aft of Kyle starboard, and Graham took position on his outer wing when they swung back in for another run. This time the focused barrage of all four popped the gun to smoking ruins. They swept high and around the cruiser, looking for the next target. They spotted a dorsal emplacement behind the bridge tower and raced in. This one had protective armored cowling. As they brought down its shield Steve let him have a burst of steel, punching through the armor and silencing the gun as they swept down below the gigantic black ship before looping back. The Legionnaires were streaking along the length of the ship at maximum thrust, firing at something out of Steve's view. Behind the Legion fighters Steve saw four black mediums racing in on the Legion's undefended six. Steve's flight screamed down behind that enemy flight just as they began to fire on the Legionnaires. Steve opened up with his railgun and grabbed the enemy pilots' attention. They pulled up slightly, spun, and returned fire, kicking their afterburners to try and get behind Steve's flight. Steve and the others pivoted in turn, and kicked up their burners to deny them. But then the enemy was reinforced by another flight of four. Eight were too many.

"Evade! Star Pattern! Go!" Kyle commanded and the flight turned their bellies toward the black fighters and punched it, each pilot heading up and spreading out away from one another, trying to divide the enemy's focus. If the enemy all formed up on one, the rest of the team would converge behind them, and if the enemy split after each then the whole flight would turn to focus their fire on one pursuer at a time. But as Steve pivoted back to take them on he saw four heavy Aldebari fighters lay into the enemy fighters' flank, striking like a pride of muscular lions into a herd of hapless antelope, devastating those they caught before sweeping powerfully toward their next prey.

Steve's flight turned in an arc to seek out the next emplacement, when suddenly the great black ship's pale shield flickered out. A Legionnaire gave an ear shattering, very irritating war whoop over general comms. Steve would have known that voice anywhere. It was that deep voiced, tall Legionnaire from the bar. "Better run boys:" the Legionnaire called "Missiles incoming, and you don't want to be there when she blows!"

Steve's flight promptly turned away from the cruiser and hit afterburners, trying to gain distance. He looked back and saw the sparks of Aldebar heavy antiship missile thrusters rocketing away from the research station, seeming to grow larger as they accelerated into the bow of the *Pyotr Velikiyer*, striking her heavily. The explosions were immense. He could see shock waves ripple through the great ship's armor plating after each explosion, so powerful that the dense armor plates sprung and rippled like fat meat. "Can I have salvage rights?" the Legionnaire joked over the comm.

The *Pyotr Velikiyer* exploded catastrophically, and Steve felt a grim satisfaction. That damned ship had destroyed Perry and made his people orphans. This was payback, and something to savor.

Then every Aldebari spacecraft did an immediate about-face without any sign of celebration. They hit their afterburners, and sped away from the action, as if all on cue. Steve's jubilation at their victory trailed off when he saw it: It seemed very strange, and he wondered what was happening.

About ten seconds later all the cheering pilot voices were suddenly cut off. A priority communication from the Base Commander advised "Aldebari cruiser *Jade Temple* reports they are under heavy fire near the modulus."

No wonder the Aldebari all hit their boosters, Steve realized. Even with several bogies still flying the *Jade Temple* was calling for help.

Steve immediately turned his fighter and headed after the Aldebari, saying 'Let's move out, people!' to the rest of his squadron. Command openly confirmed his judgment without hesitation to First and Third squadrons.

Now Steve understood why the *Pyotr Velikiyer* had remained so belligerent, even after *Jade Temple* was reported inbound: They knew she would be delayed by whatever was attacking her. A lone corvette would be no match for a cruiser, which meant something more powerful threatened the *Jade Temple*. While boosting he had ample opportunity to send a private text, flagged low priority, to Tibs requesting information. Steve didn't want to distract him, but needed to know what they would be facing.

Base Command provided some insight. "Reports indicate a hostile EW platform, of unknown type, imposed jamming on our patrol at the modulus while their forces penetrated our space, just prior to the *Jade Temple*'s arrival. Hostiles then reported *Jade Temple* arriving on an open mike. We thought they were our guys breaking patrol comm protocols to reassure nearby civilians, but then our lifepods started arriving. Remote sensors now indicate multiple large spacecraft exchanging heavy fire in the modulus region. All combat ready craft are hereby ordered to engage at best possible speed to relieve the *Jade Temple*. Base out."

Steven knew 'multiple large spacecraft' might mean anything from a couple of corvettes to an assault fleet. A cruiser of *Jade Temple*'s class could handle the former, but certainly not the latter.

Anxiously Steve felt like their ships were standing still in space instead of moving along at maximum sustainable speed. The whine and hiss of the oxygen mix he was breathing became almost hypnotic.

Finally Tibs texted back:" Engaged 1 hvy cruiser 3 corvettes; outnumbered taking losses: make haste."

Steve texted his reply "On my way w/friends"

He relayed his information to Base per regulations. Base informed the rest of the pilots. Their ships made all the haste they could.

Three corvettes posed something of a problem. They tend to have weapons effective against single seaters, are about as maneuverable as a hauler, but big enough to pack a powerful wallop. As a rule they had shields and armor even a cruiser would respect. One of them would have been no match for the *Jade Temple*, but the heavy cruiser alone already over-matched the defenses Tibs could bring to bear. They might not go home happy, but unless the allies could get there in time they would likely go home victorious. Unless Steve's reinforcements arrived in time, the *Jade Temple*'s fate was sealed.

Base command advised "Legionnaire corvettes routing to this system but ETA is several hours away." Naturally, Al Najid command tried to get more reinforcements, but distances in space are long.

Steve finally reached a range that enabled him to see a few black fighters on his sensors. The leading Aldebari fighters from the research station engaged them, and the nearest black triangles began disappearing. Beyond them were plenty more. Steve realized he was straining to see the *Jade Temple* and tried to get himself to relax his neck and shoulders. He looked over at Kyle and saw him look back. "I think you're psychic, Kyle. How did you know I was looking over at you?"

"Don't start getting all warm and fuzzy on me now, Miser, but of course you would look at what it means to be a truly good pilot. I don't mind if you try and imitate these moves."

"No, no I was just trying to see if that sign is still on your fuselage, Kyle."

"What sign?" Kyle asked.

Steve tried to coax a little more speed from his fighter through an act of sheer willpower. It didn't help.

"What sign, Steve?"

One of the other guys snickered and the joke was past, with several people including Kyle laughing. It helped Steve's neck and shoulders to relax a little. Besides, they nailed the black ship.

Ahead he could see intense light as heavy ship weapons lashed out at each other, and gradually he began to see the cruisers ponderously maneuvering, lighting up each others shields. All around them there were intermittent bursts of light as fighters blew each other up, attacking or defending. Most of them seemed to ignite near the *Jade Temple*.

"Kyle, Delaney, Graham: Let's start trying to take apart the cruisers' defenses. Legion: are your pilots with us?"

"There are Legionnaire's in the fight," was the response, "That means *you* are with *us*."

"Whatever." Steve replied, ruefully. He wished he could think the legionnaire was overcompensating.

The corvettes had a different idea, turning temporarily from devastating the *Jade Temple*'s fighters and heading toward the arriving reinforcements. "Sir, the Corvettes have spotted us and are turning to engage, base." Steve recommended to the watch commander at C&C (Command and Control) center on the Station. "We need to dispatch some pilots onto the hostile cruiser's defenses if the *Temple* is going to see another day, over."

After a moment Base issued their orders on priority comms. "Second and Third Squadron you are now Gold. First Squadron and the Legion are Blue. Gold team: Interdict the corvettes. Blue team: Attack the cruiser defenses: Bring down its shields!"

Steve's flight started jinking, using brief spurts of movement using their lateral thrusters irregularly, attempting to confuse visual tracking. Enemy pilots started taking pot shots at them as they sped past on afterburners all the way to the heavy cruiser. By the time enemy pilots reacted, Steve's flight was out of effective range. If the enemy pilots gave chase they would be picked off by the rest of Blue team following them in.

Delaney and Graham had the lead and Kyle and Steve were just after them. The cruiser's flak was pretty heavy already as they angled in to pummel their first target. Checking ammo Steve had 900 rounds left for the rail gun, but both missiles had been expended.

Suddenly Steve had a bizarre impression that Tibs was speaking conversationally on open comm, and it threw Steve off because it was radically out of place in combat. Then Steve realized Tibs' face was in fact on the visual display, and he was talking to Harden over an open channel.

"Harden, we must parlay," Tibs transmitted again, insistent.

Delaney and Graham and then Kyle and Steve opened fire on the first point defense emplacement. They had slowed to half throttle to give themselves time to take the defense turret down in one attack run.

Steve's cockpit glared too brightly for a moment as the Heavy cruiser fired a massive coherent beam at the *Jade Temple*. To Steve it felt as the photo ablative paint on his hull should be blistering from it. Steve's vision cleared and he fired his rail gun as they were about to pass the emplacement. Fortunately the flak cannon crumpled like paper, and Steve enabled his helmet's polarizing visor.

"Harden, respond," Tibs repeated on the comm.

Steve wondered what Tibs was up to. The cruiser's shield flared from the *Jade Temple*'s heavy counter fire.

Steve's Blue team was sweeping in a broad arc toward their second objective behind the conning tower, on the back of the great ship.

"Why should I parlay with you, old man?" Asked a cultured and resonant voice. Steve recognized the voice from Avery's surveillance holo. Then Harden's face appeared onscreen.

Tibs replied "Because I have information you need that may save lives. Cease fire, Harden, and we will. We can always resume, but the galaxy is changed. There are things you need to know that may change your intentions."

"I'm dubious, but very well." Harden replied. "Pilots: Cease fire and hold your positions. But be ready for treachery."

Steve was amazed. Delaney said "What? We're supposed to just stop?"

Tibs ordered "Pilots hold your fire, but remain ready."

Against all instinct the pilots stopped firing when they saw the enemy abort. Nonetheless they maneuvered to make targeting difficult.

Steve would never have believed it possible, but then again, that's Tibs.

"What is it, Aldebar? Why are you broadcasting this conversation?"

"Everyone needs to hear this, Harden, especially your mercenaries. They need to know something that you might not know yourself."

"No, old man, they need to know only what I pay them to do. But

I'll tell you what, yield now. Stand down and withdraw. I might then allow you to leave Al Najid alive. Otherwise, I will not stop until I have destroyed you, your ship and your pathetic little space stations. That modulinite is *mine*, I need it, and that bastard sheriff friend of yours is going to die. He will be put down like a common rat for interfering with my plans."

"Harden: Take a moment and check your accounts."

The unexpected response caught Harden off balance. "What? What about my accounts? What..." his eyes diverted as he pressed some keys. His eyes narrowed. "What have you done!?"

"Your assets on Earth have been seized, Harden. Your have been recognized as the criminal you are. Even Earth's Board finds it inexcusable, for any reason, to destroy an inhabited planet. True enough, they look upon it more as criminal waste, whereas the Legion and Aldebar look upon it as a heinous act of mass murder, but you are now considered an interstellar criminal by all three of the major powers. Almost all minor powers are also signatories to the law, including, of course, the ACM alliance in whose space you are now located. In consequence of destroying Perry, all of your assets have been frozen. They will be seized, essentially by your own competitors. You will not be able to pay these mercenaries unless you act quickly instead of wasting the few assets you still control."

Harden' face scowled in angry confusion. "How did you...?

"We know how you wished to eliminate the inhabitants of this sector and create a vast and rich asteroid field of its planet. We have the evidence. We provided the proof to Earth's Board of Corporations and to the other powers, and Earth has verified it. Your attempts to eliminate Martin Avery backfired and you will pay for your crimes.

Harden, for once, remained speechless in his fury.

"You have many fewer allies, Harden. Consider well your next move. We will destroy each other here. Legion and Aldebari warships are inbound, and I need only survive long enough to win completely. But if you lose here, Harden, you'll have nothing left. You have already lost the *Pyotr Velikiyer,* and with her your monopoly on the anomaly transit technology." Harden's face grew hard as stone. It looked like he might reject reason and give in to his urge for immediate vengeance.

"Or, to my disappointment, you can still withdraw," Tibs continued in a subdued, resigned voice. "We haven't the strength yet to prevent your escape, but I do not want to waste more lives trying to stop you. I will have to console myself with the knowledge that you will find your destiny all by yourself."

Harden's face darkened in the holodisplay. "You know nothing, you pitiful man. I have assets about which neither you nor the Board know anything." He hissed, "You should learn to keep your nose in your own affairs before someone cuts it off." His eyes glared with hatred as he scowled in thought. There is no uglier face than a handsome one contorted in anger. "Nevertheless, you have given me an idea, Aldebar. I know exactly where and when I shall perfect my thought. You will regret your interference."

"Pilots: Regroup," commanded Harden. Some of his pilots advanced toward the heavy cruiser and corvettes, but several black fighters turned toward the modulus to begin solo journeys toward home.

The *Jade Temple* waited until the heavy cruiser accelerated toward the modulus, then majestically turned her prow toward Perry base.

Steve felt relieved, but at the same time deeply troubled. He had a dreadful feeling: The cost of fame is being targeted.

Chapter 23: Tech Recovery

Near the anomaly and the Aldebar research facility, Aldebari and Perry engineers swarmed all over and through the remains of the *Pyotr Velikiyer,* even before the Aldebari damage control crews had completely extinguished all the fires. At the same time security and medical teams roamed the ship, removing the dead and recovering any survivors from sealed compartments. Initially the engineers and the scientists focused on removing the wings Steve and other pilots reported in debriefing. The original hypothesis centered on the wings as an integral part of the technology that allowed the ship to transit an anomaly.

The *Jade Temple* had moored in an air dock at Perry Station to repair damage suffered in combat with Harden's heavy cruiser. The air dock functioned like a regular starship dock except it was pressurized with atmosphere and shielded from radiation to give shipwrights and engineers greater mobility, unencumbered by pressure suits and breathing apparatus. All the heavy machinery necessary to do extensive structural work was in place, but extra security ringed the perimeter because of the sensitivity of the intended refit. Tibs wanted to retro-engineer the technology from the *Pyotr Velikiyer* to enable the *Jade Temple* to transit unmodulated anomalies.

The technology didn't prove very difficult to decipher once they had their hands on it. The hardest part about copying it would have been refining modulinite and machining the modulinium to rebuild it for the *Jade Temple*, but Al Najid now had an abundance of modulinite for the project.

Refined modulinium is as conductive as solid metal can be. With wing structures inlaid with modulinium extending beyond the ship's shield they could conduct the energy of the anomaly itself to bolster her shields almost as fast as the anomaly reduced them. The process required a greatly increased shield capacitor array, and that would have to be built at an Aldebari facility and shipped in while the *Jade Temple* was retro fitted with modulinium-inlaid wings. A grateful Perry Station council supplied the modulinium needed for the project *pro bono*.

With the Aldebar re-establishing the network of anti-ship mines around the anomaly, and the Perry and Aldebari engineers and shipwrights extracting technology from the wreck of the *Pyotr*

Velikiyer, they put the work on Steve's new gunship on hold. Frustratingly, he found himself once again surveying the asteroid field and the remains of the planet. This left him with much more time to think than he wanted. His major mission was to bring Harden to justice, but until the madman surfaced somewhere Steve's mission remained a tangle of loose ends.

Most recently Steve's duty involved gathering up and netting the mining schist in the asteroid field for processing or, if there was an overabundance already held for the factories, sending it into a degrading orbit. However, with all the construction at *Perry Station*, the Aldebari research facility and Al Najid V, the need for schist as building material remained greater than the supply.

In mining from an asteroid Steve needed to separate the valuable ore and eject the waste as a compressed brick. To gather that mining waste his spacecraft's prow was fitted with a heavily structured set of bumpers, like steel prongs, and a corral net tube fed by a magazine that fired a large circular cable net.

Steve used the prongs to maneuver waste debris into a compact ball. The biggest challenge was in keeping all the pieces together. Like a rack of billiard balls struck by a cue ball, when a compacted brick hit the mass of other bricks it either stopped or ricocheted off. But if it was moving too fast part of its impetus would communicate to the other bricks and one or more could pop away on the other side. In a way it was entertaining, but after a few hours it invariably became extremely boring.

One evening after a hard day Steve learned at the *Cog and Sprocket* that to relieve the monotony some miners turned the schist gathering process into informal games that generally escaped the notice of people outside the close-knit mining community. The games include a variation of skeet shooting, while another resembled basketball. Rather significant amounts of money is won and lost in bets among the miners during these games.

Despite the games, Steve grew weary of mining and surveying and yearned for something more interesting to do, but he kept at it nevertheless.

Meanwhile the refit of the Jade Temple was being completed at the *Perry Station* shipyard in record time, and after a mere three months she was setting out on a trial run, heading first for the Aldebari research station.

Steve looked forward to messages from Pat back on Earth. She kept him posted on anything and everything she could learn about Sandy and the kids on Cygnus. Apparently Sandy had relocated and changed her email address, but Pat had found a reference to Kathlyn, Steve's daughter, and little Stevie in the academic records of a Cygnus public school. If he really made a concerted effort to find her Cygnus wasn't so densely populated that she could hide from him. But he worried that his search might be noticed by hit men contracted by Celine Corporation. Steve resented the circumstances that kept him away, but his family would be safer if he did not draw attention to them. He did not want to give the assassins a link to his ex and the kids. That would put them in jeopardy, and leave him with no way to protect them. Steve believed in his gut that Paul Harden was behind the Celine Corporation hit contract, but that didn't help if he couldn't neutralize Harden.

Steve had to assume that communications on Cygnus were compromised. Any attempt to communicate with his family might increase their danger. Counselor Lyman's plan to have Pat investigate seemed the best course, so Steve approved the plan in a personal email.

The identification transponder used by Harden's heavy cruiser, the *Black King*, was supposedly that of a large freighter, according to the interstellar ships registry. As the ship passed through the modulus to Cygnus she apparently disappeared. Steve could find no record of her docking at Cygnus, nor any record of her exiting the Cygnus modulus, so either the ship remained in Cygnus system but had not docked, Steve reasoned, or she emitted different identification signals in violation of interstellar naval law. Unfortunately the automated logs at each modulus only record the transponder identification and laden mass of each ship passing through. The only way he could track an alternate identification would be to cross tabulate the recorded mass of every ship leaving Cygnus system with the recorded mass of the ships leaving Al Najid. Since the ship's mass could change depending on the number of fighters she had on board or the cargo load there were too many possible matches to trace Harden. Harden had too many ways to game the system.

Steve resolved to see Tibs once more before mission priorities took him and the *Jade Temple* off on one of their voyages.

Chapter 24: The Ex

Pat debarked the shuttle from Oberon Interstellar Orbital Terminal with her satchel and communicator. The city of Oberon, bustling with business, enjoyed a good public transportation system.

Her employer, Councilman Lyman, wanted to know the reason Steve and Sandy separated. Steve was becoming an increasingly influential public figure, and any scandal that surfaced from his past could have far-reaching consequences. So Lyman sent Pat to interview Sandy to try and learn what had been the problem.

Pat had grown to like Steve, despite the brief time he spent on Earth. But she knew she could not tell what might lie beneath the surface of anyone, and neither she nor her employer were willing to rely on intuition.

Once Pat applied her formidable research skills to the task it wasn't difficult to locate Sandy. But talking with her and the kids without setting off Sandy's emotional alarms created a significant challenge.

Pat failed to notice the two men who had shadowed her all the way from Earth. They observed her unobtrusively aboard the liner, and, dressed as businessmen, boarded the shuttle with her. After leaving the shuttle in the terminal they found a private spot and one at a time changed appearance again to try and blend in with Oberon. Each changed clothing, hair color and grooming to look more like the locals, while his partner kept an eye on Pat's movements.

Pat found Sandy and the kids living in public housing in a poorer suburb, south of the small city. The home looked identical to every other house nearby.

Pat double-checked the house number against her notes, and stepped up the short concrete walkway to the front door. She used the home intercom, leaving a fingerprint. There was no answer. After waiting a minute, she tried again.

Just as she resigned herself to return later, she heard the entry terminal buzz. The face of a woman appeared on the 2D screen. The pretty woman looked like she hadn't been sleeping well.

"Mrs. Holbrook?" she asked the woman.

"What do you want?"

" My name is Patricia Williams. I just arrived from Earth. May I have a few minutes of your time?"

"What do you want?" Sandy insisted. "I'm not in the market for anything you might be selling." Sandy said in an exasperated, short-tempered tone.

"I'm not trying to sell anything Mrs. Holbrook. My employer is interested in Steve and has a few questions," Pat responded.

"Who is your employer? And who are those men?"

Pat's stomach lurched as she suddenly sensed someone behind her. She knew what this meant. She looked into the viewscreen and shouted "Run Sandy!"

Pat felt a sudden blow on the back of her head that turned half her world dark. The world her other eye saw tilted wildly out of control. Her face struck the smooth wall, unable to raise her hands to cushion her impact. Bleeding from mouth and ear, Pat fell unconscious.

The partner of the man who had struck Pat kicked in the flimsy door. As he entered Sandy screamed something he didn't quite catch. Meanwhile his partner secured Pat's hands behind her back with plastic cinches. He then crossed her ankles, looped another cinch around them and drew the binding snug.

Pushing into the entryway the first intruder pulled his sidearm, a powerful Craven Arms handlaser. He pivoted to check the short hallway to the right, but caught peripheral sight of Sandy on his left as she turned the corner of the kitchen. She gripped a large carving knife in her right hand, but held it inexpertly. She was taller than the gunman expected, and looked like she might be crazy. With misgivings he held his fire, hoping to disarm and subdue her to fulfill his secondary objective.

"Get out of my house!" she commanded. Sandy was filled with a terrible fear, but an even greater outrage. When he made no move to leave she lunged and thrust with the knife. "Get OUT!"

The gunman calmly moved his sidearm to his left hand, and with his right tried to sweep the knife away. Sandy drove her arm forward again. She saw his arm moving and twisted the blade instinctively, piercing deeply into his forearm. She screamed at him "Get OUT!" She pulled the knife out, and blood spurted from the wound. His weapon fell to the floor. He gripped his wound trying to staunch the bleeding, but set his foot on his weapon to keep it from her.

The second intruder saw the whole thing and dropped an unconscious Pat casually in the entryway and then calmly forced the front door closed, though broken it would not latch. With two hands gripping his heavy hand laser, he pivoted from the door and, weight evenly balanced, he took aim. His hand laser made a heavy bumping noise three times in rapid succession. Each pulse of coherent light penetrated Sandy as she moved, lancing into the side of her chest.

A laser does not have the stopping power of a projectile weapon. Each pulse of focused light burned a narrow hole in her flesh that she hardly felt at first. Three quick pulses made three narrow holes that sizzled. One was not stopped by a rib, and that lung began to fill with blood.

Sandy winced in pain, and turned her eyes terribly on him. She took an angry step forward. He fired again as she drew her arm back, this time hitting her forehead. The pulses did not penetrate her skull, but a crude pyramid of dots above one eye began bleeding profusely.

The man calmly fired a third burst of laser pulses.

Sandy wondered where the knife was, and lost vision as her blood obscured the room. She began to lose track of what was happening. She thought of Steve. Something was not finished, and she felt regret. Then she dropped heavily to the carpet, limp and irrevocably lifeless.

The man she had stabbed silently and efficiently applied pressure to his wound and walked into the kitchen for a clean cloth to bind it.

The other man holstered his weapon and secured communications with the ship waiting in orbit, advising they would need a corpsman with their pickup and a sanitation team immediately to clean up the evidence. He thought a moment, then draped Sandy's corpse with a large brown cloth that had covered a cheap table. Then he stepped deeper into the residence, seeking his primary objectives.

Chapter 25: Refit

With his dampeners off Steve reduced throttle and checked his vector toward the *Jade Temple's* docking bay. The great ship had been modified extensively in the refit, which was finally nearing completion. Steve looked forward to talking with Tibs, but he suddenly felt his curiosity more piqued by the changes he could see on the *Jade Temple*. Heavier armor plating at the bow and much heavier forward beam weaponry had been salvaged from the wreck of the *Pyotr Velikiyer*. Increased point defense batteries had been installed near a significantly larger shield generator from the Aldebari shipyards. More intriguing were what appeared to be odd disks, pale in color and slightly convex, mounted flush to the hull along the ship's length. Steve dragged his focus back toward the looming ship's docking bay and prepared to board the Aldebari cruiser.

Since the perilous battle with the *Pyotr Velikiyer*, Bobby had elected to leave *Perry Station* to live with Tibs aboard the *Jade Temple*. Steve was curious to learn how well Bobby was adjusting.

After docking Steve looked around for any familiar faces, but he recognized none. He stowed his flight kit and helmet in a locker and thumbed the docking log, read the rules and news, and thumbed his assent to acknowledge the forever evolving disclaimers and provisos. About that time a door hissed open and there stood Bobby. He looked like himself, but he had grown at least an inch and his jaw looked a little heavier. Steve smiled at him and the boy's stiff resolve melted away as he shook Steve's hand warmly.

"Hi Mister Holbrook." Bobby said, clearly happy to see him.

"Hi Bobby. Or should I call you Bob?"

"Either is fine from you, but around the ship my friends usually call me Robert."

"You're too young to worry about showing maturity, Bobby."

"I have to keep in mind that everyone has a different idea for what I should be like. Elder Kinkaid insists I behave maturely to begin to learn to pilot a scouting mission soon. I don't want him to think I'm too young."

"Please, I'm called Steve by my friends. So you are going out among the stars with Elder Kinkaid? That is a big step. Are you sure you want to be a scout?"

"Sure! I want to be able to fly in space, and discover everything.

Now that we know how to cross anomalies we'll have new places to explore, and I really want to be part of that."

"You know it might turn out that the other anomalies only open on emptiness."

Bobby thought about that. "But the black cruiser came from the anomaly, not the modulus. I bet there is something on the other side of that anomaly."

He had a point, Steve thought. This kid was pretty smart. "Point taken, Bobby."

Bobby smiled a secret smile of victory, and Steve felt good to have maybe enhanced the boy's self-confidence even a little bit. The kid earned it.

"Well, Bob, I need to find Tibs. Do you know where he is?"

"I don't know, Mister ... I mean, Steve. I thought he was going to the Station to see you."

Steve was slightly taken aback. He only thought of Tibs in his virtual garden. "Then I guess I better turn my head around and find him over there." He clamped his hand softly on Bobby's shoulder. "See you around, Bob."

Bobby nodded and grinned at Steve. He seemed happy aboard the *Jade Temple.*

Chapter 26: Cog and Sprocket

Steve found Tibs back at the Station in the *Cog and Sprocket*. He hadn't yet spotted Steve, and was sipping what looked like a martini. Tibs drew the glass away from his lips and smiled at his drink. He looked up as Steve approached and stood, offering his hand in welcome. Tibs was wearing casual civilian clothing and apparently had visited the Station barber as his hair was precisely trimmed and he bore a distinctive scent of bay rum. "I just looked up cogs and sprockets on the net. Do you know what they are?" He asked.

"No, I hadn't thought about it, Tibs. What did you find out?"

"Well a *sprocket* is a gear that works with a chain, while a *cog* is one of the teeth on a gear."

"One more piece of information that now I will never get out of my brain, Tibs. Thanks a bunch."

Tibs grinned, making his eyes twinkle. "Always ready to serve, Steve."

"I noticed you upgraded your shields and forward armor and added some heavy energy platforms," Steve commented. "But what were those odd disks I saw along the beam of your hull?"

"Naturally I cannot give you all the details, but those disks serve a dual purpose. The disks are modulinium caps for our new extendable fins. Your shipwright, Chief Mackenzie is a marvel. You folks are fortunate to have him. The wings they cap are steel with insulated conductive inlays of modulinium that connect to our shield array system. It is what worked on the *Pyotr Velikiyer,* so it should work for us. I was worried that they might drain our shields into other dimensions instead, but my engineers assure me that won't be a problem as long as I don't sneeze."

"What?"

He held up his hands, "I joke, I joke." Tibs chuckled and lifted his martini for a sip. "Your barkeep here really knows how to build a good martini. Come sit down and have a drink with me, and I will share a little secret." Tibs signaled the waitress, and then turned his eyes back to Steve as they sat down at a table. "In the battle with Harden, toward the end, our defenses were very nearly overwhelmed. If he had hit us a few more times with his incredible energy weapon, we might have been destroyed by the overload on our shield capacitors, and we would have been destroyed."

The waitress arrived. Steve settled on a cold local draft beer.

Cataclysmic amounts of energy were fired into the *Jade Temple's* shields. But energy doesn't simply vanish, it behaves in accord with the first law of thermodynamics. Tibs confided that his shield array had approached melt-down, something unlikely unless you flew too close to a star, or otherwise exceeded the capacity of the shield system to store, convert, or otherwise manage the energy.

"In order to prevent something like that happening again, we had to find a way to store all that energy, and if necessary let it bleed out through the modulinium. So those 'caps' you saw are actually part of our answer to overloaded shields."

"But Steven, there is another use for those energy sinks. Our tests revealed their potential for duplicating the *Pyotr Velikiyer* ability to transit an unmodulated anomaly. When we transit an anomaly the fins will extend until their modulinium caps are just beyond the shield envelope. Once fully extended they can draw on the violence of the anomaly itself to channel it's power to reinforce our shields. That will protect the ship as we pass through the danger."

Steve's eyebrows rose. "Have you tested this?"

Tibs set his empty martini down and cocked his head a bit. "Steven, I'd like to propose that we go hunting."

The waitress arrived with their drinks and Tibs thanked her with a moderate tip. Steve weighed the fact that Tibs hadn't directly answered his question about testing the *Jade Temple's* new wings. When the waitress left, Steve asked: "Hunting for Harden?"

"Exactly. If we go through the anomaly I think we will find the base from which he launched the attack on your home world. If I don't miss my guess, we might even be able to trace the whereabouts of his and Celine Interstellar's clandestine assets, or his scientific team. Perhaps we can find both. Since the *Pyotr Velikiyer* disappeared without a trace from the Trondheim system, and then withdrew from the destruction of Perry into the anomaly, and then again emerged from that anomaly three months ago, my bet is this anomaly directly or indirectly connects to the anomaly at Trondheim system."

Steve silently noted that Tibs had just confirmed that there was a significant link between Harden and Celine Interstellar.

"That would mean Bobby was absolutely right about where that anomaly leads."

"Really?" Tibs took a small sip of his drink. "He's a bright and interesting young man. His parents must have been remarkable."

Steve took a drink of his station-brewed cold beer and judged it was actually pretty good. Slightly nutty with just the right edge to the taste.

"It was difficult to understand how the transit was made, even once we acknowledged that it could be done," Tibs continued. "We had to deconstruct *Pyotr Velikiyer*'s modulinium-inlaid wings and the supporting technology before we could put it all together. Harden's scientific team must be profoundly brilliant to have made the discovery. I cannot adequately underscore the importance of retrieving those people, not just for the benefit of science itself, but to weaken the twisted organization Harden used to subvert science for his own benefit."

"Tibs, they might have had alien tech to copy." Steve was impatient with the council for the obstinacy that prevented Mack and Steve from inviting Aldebar scientists to help gain the secrets of the alien craft, still locked away in its stealth field.

Tibs looked closely at Steve with clear eyes. "They might, as remote as that now seems. But through the anomaly we may also find out where Harden has gone, and maybe even where he is getting his tech, if your hypothesis is right."

Steve still felt rage against Harden. Though the discovery that his children were safe had relieved much of his personal sorrow, it had not resolved the outrage over Harden's crime.

Tibs stirred the olive around in his glass, then ate it from the small red plastic spear. He looked at Steve. "It would be best if we could bring Harden back to stand trial for his crimes and shut down Celine's operations. Harden's trial and conviction would go far toward bringing closure to your people, every one of whom surely feels as you do. Plus," Tibs continued "if Celine Corp can't make good on their assassination contract, then that should resolve your personal danger. Your people may never be able to get past their sense of injustice as long as Harden remains at liberty. I believe it will be better for everyone to ensure that we serve justice, rather than revenge."

Steve needed resolution, but he recognized that simply killing Harden would give him only personal satisfaction. He knew Tibs was right: Through the public process he could help ensure justice for all his people, and allow them the satisfaction of deciding the man's fate. It seemed healthier for his people, and, he admitted, better for himself. He didn't want the foundation of the society they were rebuilding tainted with vengeance and retribution.

"I agree it would be best as you say, Tibs. I don't know if I'll be able to hold revenge back, but I will try."

Tibs nodded, acknowledging Steve's commitment.

Steve changed the subject. "So... what of young Bobby? Is he already old enough to learn to pilot a spacecraft? He mentioned Kinkaid was thinking to take him out."

"Well, Steve, we Aldebar differ culturally from your people. We do not believe that the age of a person defines him or her. Neither age nor gender really expresses who a person is, or their capabilities. The sum of his experience, genetic makeup, intelligence, passion, and self-control are more important than chronological age." Tibs looked into Steve's eyes. "Has Bobby ever shared with you his life before the battle that killed his mother and father?"

"No, Tibs, I never brought myself to ask him. I suppose it was because I haven't managed to shake guilt feelings for the part I played in their deaths."

"Then your sense of guilt denied you a most interesting conversation, Steven."

"Exceptional individuals still arise from Earth's masses by sheer talent to become outstanding technicians, pilots, entertainers, doctors, and industrial psychologists. I suppose it's an artificial form of evolution. Only the most able of all people can prosper there. But those who do prosper enjoy unparalleled luxury and reward."

"Bobby's parents were among a relatively privileged underclass. They were permitted to serve together as pilot and electronic intelligence specialist because of their exceptional skills."

"The contractor who assisted me on Earth told me about what they do with online games." Steve offered.

"Pat is very bright, Steve." Tibs looked at him meaningfully, then checked his wrist comm. A frown momentarily creased his brow. "I've been waiting for a message from her and she is uncharacteristically late."

"But yes." he continued. "Earth's networked interactive media system forms an amazing database that identifies any individual using it. Computer games most commonly identify a player's skill sets and aptitudes. Earth invests heavily in such entertainment systems in return for comprehensive, personally identifiable information about viewer and player aptitudes, skills and behavior. It gives the Corporations advantages in applying training as an informed investment, only for the most capable, instead of investing in universal education."

"That sounds a little spooky, Tibs. It seems to me everyone should have a chance at success."

"I think so too, but as long as they don't run into the unexpected, the system might prove very efficient."

"What are you suggesting?" Steve asked.

"Well, I think they may underestimate the capacity for creativity and inventiveness. If the unexpected arises, and everyone is only trained to handle expected situations, then they may be unable to cope. I think this is the real weakness of the Corporations' method. So long as they only encounter situations they have prepared for, it should work fine, but otherwise maybe not."

Steve thought a moment. "What do the corporations do for people without aptitudes for the skills they seek?"

"Hard to say," Tibs responded. "The players together produce such a prodigious amount of data that, unless your data displays characteristics the Corporations seek, your information is probably never accessed. There are billions of players being tracked. As far as I can tell, the Corporates don't do anything to those who don't match a targeted profile, but neither do they invest in them."

"That sounds wasteful in itself." Steve offered.

"Maybe. But it might be an accidental fail-safe that will only become appreciated when something goes significantly wrong with their planning. If you find a problem you cannot solve, a solution can come from the unexpected. And if there is anything I have learned about this universe, it's to expect the unexpected."

Steve grinned at Tibs. "Amen".

Tibs' wrist display chimed. He opened a message and read it. "Ah! I have gained permission from your council to take you with us when we go, assuming you would care to join in this venture."

"Of course, Tibs" Steve responded. "I wouldn't want to miss a chance to grab Harden."

The conversation lapsed into silence for a moment, so Steve changed the subject again. "Chief Engineer Mackenzie is working on my gunship, now that the refit of the *Jade Temple* is complete. Hopefully, it will be ready when we return. And by the way, Tibs, how long will we be gone?" He wanted to talk with Mary before they departed.

"Steve I have absolutely no idea how long we might be away. It all depends on what we find on the other side. To be honest I really don't want to leave right now. Opening that invisible spacecraft you found might mark the most significant discovery in the last hundred years. Possibly more significant than identifying the Boson particle. It is incomprehensible that we have not met an alien race at any of the fourteen worlds we inhabit. Each of them has their own native species, both plant and animal, but it seems unreal to not also possess native intelligent life. That stealth ship might offer some answers, and indeed it seems likely that it will. I am impatient to have it open so we can learn more."

Steve's mouth dropped open in surprise. He could not believe Tibs already knew about what they had found. But if he had learned anything about Tibs, it was that he constantly surprises.

"I think I need a visit to your Barber, Tibs."

Tibs grinned wider.

Chapter 27: Untested

Leaving Tibs to his martini Steve sent Kyle a message about going on temporary duty aboard the *Jade Temple* and would be out of comm range for a while. Kyle was full of questions and expressed doubts about passing through the anomaly. Other than the *Pyotr Velikiyer,* no spacecraft had ever survived an attempt to transit an anomaly. The new technology that Tibs hoped would work for the *Jade Temple* wasn't even tested. Steve noted there simply wasn't time to build a test ship for the experiment. Kyle protested that Steve's new gunship could serve as a test vehicle with a little modification. Steve, although concerned for his gunship, had to admit Kyle had a good point. Steve sent Tibs and Chief Mackenzie a note about the idea. Mack responded it would require drastic compromises in the gunboat's hull integrity, but given adequate time was feasible. He began talking about careful calculations to ensure the hull could afterward endure the rigors of combat maneuvers under inertial dampening conditions and expressed his opinion that the size of the gunship argues against using it for this test. Then Tibs responded that there simply wasn't time. He was convinced that the modulinium fins would work.

Steve took the time to head down to Mary's store. He found the store open and saw Mary was busy with another customer. She waved a little wave at him with a smile and continued their transaction. Steve checked the prices on her refrigerated fresh vegetables and frozen meats. The prices were expensive, but not terribly so. She was clearly doing well on the Station.

He began checking out a burr grinder for whole coffee beans when Mary appeared at his side. "Hi, Mary." He greeted her.

"Hi, Steve. Are you ready to get started on your kitchen?"

"I've been ready, but the council keeps me hopping. I'm going to have to leave the Station for awhile and wanted to let you know. We'll have to reschedule I'm afraid."

Mary looked disappointed, but brightened at the thought that he had come by to tell her instead of just sending a text message. "How long will you be gone, Steve?"

"Unfortunately I don't really know, but hopefully it won't be very long. But I wanted to be sure you knew I'm not avoiding the job of fixing up my kitchen."

"Forget the kitchen, Steve. More importantly is this going to be a dangerous mission?"

Steve was taken aback. Forget the kitchen?

"Well, everything is dangerous..."

"Don't give me that line for once in your life. I want you to be safe, Steve. Every time I turn around you're on the news risking your life for people who take you for granted. I want you to promise me you'll come back safe." she insisted.

"You know I'll do my best to stay safe, Mary."

"You'd better do better than try, Steven Holbrook."

"Yes Ma'am. I will."

She smiled then, and on tip toe kissed him lightly on the lips. He was speechless. She turned to another customer who had been clearing his throat at the counter to get her attention.

After leaving the shop and feeling... well, he didn't know what he was feeling but it felt good... Steve headed toward the Administrative offices to verify his assignment with the council. Then he returned to his quarters to get his ready bag for the trip. He posted a message to Pat that he would be on assignment of unknown duration, but assured her he would try to respond to any email. He then used his terminal to clear his flight plan to the *Jade Temple*, advised his crew chief of imminent departure, and gave his tech crew an hour to prep the ship for launch, configured for light fighter duty, and then grab their gear and head over to the *Temple*. In the meantime he went back to the *Cog and Sprocket* for some coffee. And maybe a bowl of their fresh salsa mix fresh from hydroponics and those good imported crackers they serve.

As Steve sat munching on the last of the crackers and watching the news he received word from his crew chief that his ship was ready. Steve finished his salsa using the last savory cracker that gave such a satisfying crunch, and headed for the *Jade Temple*.

After seeing the ship's bursar, checking in with his crew chief and locating his quarters aboard the Aldebari cruiser Steve unpacked his kit and settled in with a reader to access the ship's library. He wanted to learn more about the Aldebari version of Earth's history. It was intriguing and held his attention for quite awhile.

Then he wondered about the Legion, and skimmed some research on them. He found that, following the expulsion of the Aldebari survivors from their adopted world, the paramilitary Legion had refused to return to Earth and commandeered all the corporate assets they could find.

Of further interest was an article revealing the Aldebar's belief that the Legion enforced their ideological hold on their populace by emphasizing duty and discipline. They eliminated unemployment problems by inducting almost everyone into their armed forces.

Using a network of moduli, the Legion 'liberated' several star systems from Earth. The last system they conquered was Eridanus, controlling all egress and ingress to the rest of the Legion systems. The area in space around the modulus at Eridanus was now protected with heavily fortified weapons platforms and interceptor flotillas.

When he grew tired of reading he noticed it was time, even a little late, to hit the mess hall for supper. Thinking fondly about the puzzle named Mary he patiently made his way in the orderly line of Aldebari diners, each with their eating utensils and napkins, waiting to reach the counter without jostling or even conversation. In his turn he reached the food counter and picked up a waiting tray of odd Aldebari foods that he couldn't name and a pint of their beer, which in the past turned out to be pretty good. He looked for a place to sit. Finding a spot, Steve sat and slowly began to eat, remembering when he had first done so aboard the *Jade Temple*, shortly after the destruction of his planet.

Soon Bobby arrived with his tray and sat down across from him. Bobby had a husk of fresh bread that he broke apart and offered half to Steve, just as Steve had done when Bobby was hungry and alone in the Station.

"So how have you been, Bobby?" Steve asked, dunking his bread in the thick hot soup made of some kind of greenish bean, or maybe it was a nut. The soup was pretty good, reminding Steve of potato chowder and his stomach growled hungrily. He thought the soup could use some carrots.

"I've been fine, but very busy since coming aboard. Did you know that they have some actual paper books here? I don't even understand how to read the date written in the inside of the cover. It seems to be backwards from our dating systems. I'm not even sure it counts from the same date as ours." he replied.

"Been reading much have you? How is your math?"

"Oh, the math is the easy part. Once you let go of what you think you know, it isn't all that difficult. The hardest thing is letting go of what I want the answer to be. Thinking what the answer is before I calculate it just gets in the way. I wish the rest of what I have to learn were as neat as math is. I especially like algebra, because you can almost program computers using decision operators and conditionals. But my big victory was discovering how calculus figures irregular areas. Sometimes when I find and prove my solutions I feel wonderful."

It was the most Steve had ever heard Bobby say at one time. The boy seemed in a talkative mood, so he decided to ask a question that had troubled him. "So you are... 'free'... to study whatever you wish?" Steve asked.

"Free?" Bobby frowned, making his delicate eyebrows approach each other. Then his brow cleared. "Well I don't know about that, but what the instructor presents does keep me busy." Bobby chewed thoughtfully. Steve chewed thoughtfully right back at him.

"You know," Bobby said, swallowing, "Tibs sometimes asks me about free things and it is really puzzling that you should bring that up."

"How is it puzzling, Bobby?"

"Well, I had never heard that word used like that before I came here. Where I'm from, 'free' means something is being given to you without charge. Sometimes you have to do something else, like agree to read advertisements. But here it's sometimes used in talk about the Aldebar religion. And just now you used that word in a double way even though you aren't in their religion. You just used that word like it was a real way of choosing." Bobby was looking into Steve's eyes intently, like he was trying to see some clue he had been seeking. "What do you mean when you say it, Steve?"

Steve looked down into his half eaten soup and bought some time with a bite before he looked back up. Double way? "Well Bobby, I think freedom is real, even if it is rare. There are all sorts of problems that arise without it. Responsibility, for example. How could we hold anyone responsible for something they did if they weren't free to not do it in the first place?"

"But sir, talking about what might happen if freedom didn't exist isn't telling me what it is. Or is it? I want to know what it is in itself.

"I understand cause and effect," he continued, "It seems to me that everything I decide is a consequence of what happened previously. If that were strictly true, then maybe I would never make a mistake. Yet sometimes I do. Maybe I forget, or choose without considering all the information. But every time I look at my mistakes I can find causes for them. When I look at choices I make that are right, I think there wasn't a useful alternative that would have worked as well. So is freedom the ability to have happy accidents?"

Steve took a bite of something like meat that had a pretty good meat-like flavor. Fortunately it was chewy and he couldn't reply with his mouth full. The kid was a real thinker. Steve decided he shouldn't try to oversimplify.

"Well, Bobby, here's how I look at it. At some point in a person's life all causal forces and all foreseeable consequences balance each other when you are presented with a big choice. You may feel like you don't know what to do, and it can be confusing. Perhaps you could model such a condition using algebraic variables, but while the equation would remain in stasis, you would be unable to decide. We, on the other hand, *can* decide. When all else is equal, then what you choose to do defines your freedom."

"That sounds like an awfully rare condition Mister Steven."

Steve munched on a piece of fruit that was sweet and a little tart, but really juicy, and he nodded, looking calmly at Bobby.

"Yes, I suppose that when a big decision really stands out, and you feel like you have the freedom to choose, it is pretty rare. But it happens. And even when life is just cruising along between big decisions we're always making choices even if we don't notice them.

"But when we find an occasion to make a decision our choice helps define who we really are. And to a lesser degree those many points in life where we make choices, those for the most part are certainly attributable to the sum of the preceding causes, but some small part of them is our preference for what we value.

"For example: You chose to share that bread you shared with me today. Part of the reason you chose it was from cause, but I think part of it was because you thought it would express your personal values to share it with me. I'd like to think part of it was sentiment. There are things that don't equate with the sum of preceding causes. In a completely mechanical world you might have only considered either your hunger, or how useful I might be if I didn't starve. But I am not starving and you know it. It was the part of your choice that was sentimental that made what might have been totally mechanical into an expression of free will."

Bobby looked like he was very busy doubting what Steve had said, but he was at least thinking about it. "I might have shared the bread so you might like me better, Steve."

Steve was unsure how to proceed then. Freedom is a fairly hefty concept. "It is probably more important to ask good questions than it is to think we know something we don't, I guess. Just like math, we have to really know the problem, whether by calculation to solve in math or by evaluation of probabilities, facts and values to make a decision, before we can confidently answer a good question. But sharing your bread with me won't make me like you better than I already do, because I already like you a lot, son. That tells me you probably honor values similar to mine. But other people don't always have the same values we do. It is safe to say Harden has quite different values, for example.

"Our values are what we decide *for*, Bob. You may not notice it because you are always you, but someone really different will choose differently in those moments of real decision because they weight their values differently. But you would notice if someone required you to decide based on their values and not your own. Then that decision would not be yours, and you would not have expressed your freedom."

Bobby looked thoughtful.

"Bob, I'm going to go hit the sack, but give it some thought and let me know if you think I'm just a religious nut, okay? People have been arguing over these things for several thousand years.

Bobby stopped chewing long enough to smile a crooked grin. Then he went back to his meal and Steve retired to his quarters.

Chapter 28: The Hunt

Kyle, Graham, and Delaney also arranged to join Steve on the *Jade Temple* to hunt for Harden. Somehow word leaked out about the mission and they refused to be left behind. Steve learned ten pilots requested permission to come along, but Tibs limited the space available to only three more, with their fighters and tech teams, so Steve would have to make the selections and arrange to get them and their teams aboard ship.

As the cruiser left dock at the base Tibs appeared on the ship-wide comm. The Aldebari from the research station were still clearing the mines from around the anomaly to let the ship pass, and patrolling in strength as those defenses were disarmed and recovered one by one.

On the monitors Tibs announced, "When we arrive at the anomaly, in just about forty minutes, we will deploy our energy rods to draw on the power of the anomaly itself. We will feed that energy into our shield generator which has been modified to allow us to accurately modulate and rebroadcast it to form a bubble of safety for our transit to wherever the anomaly leads. And wherever that is, we'll seek a trail to follow. The trail of the criminal who destroyed a beautiful world. A trail that will lead us to serve justice in the galaxy."

"The math works. Our finest engineers have checked the calculations exhaustively. There is no flaw in our numbers against the theoretical requirements to gate through the anomaly. Of course, I must confess that we have never actually tried this."

"On the other hand we know it has been done."

"I therefore ask you to complete your every task in preparation for this magnificent test of our science, and of our courage. In the available time frame we have no other option to prove what we must prove. We must do this now."

"You each know why we do this: To serve justice upon an interstellar criminal and mass murderer, and hopefully to extract some of our brethren scientists from a betrayal of their profession, knowledge and talent."

"With us go four men whose home planet was destroyed here in the Al Najid system. You all know them. Their loss is our loss, and justice for them will be justice for all."

"As I offered before, so do I offer now, If anyone aboard does not wish to see this mission through, you may still remain on the research station. There will be no loss of face. Let there be no shame in acknowledging your internal truth. I ask you, please: If you do not wish to participate in this with us, or have second thoughts, let us arrange for your passage to safety. You each know my personal email address, just send me a note. That's all it will take."

"For the rest of us I celebrate your courage and determination. It is my profound honor to serve with you."

Just listening to him gave Steve butterflies, aware of the risks but determined to see it through.

Steve viewed the progress on a large monitor as the *Jade Temple* neared the objective. The anomaly's power seemed to radiate right through the ship's shields, hull and bulkheads. He could feel a deep vibration in his bones as the *Jade Temple* drew even closer. All around the ship flew formations of fighters from the nearby research lab, patrolling for danger.

Tibs extended the energy absorption rods, port and starboard. The rods were equipped with thermal vanes that looked like wings. They appeared to be composed more of ceramic than steel, possibly some sort of laminated fiber. There were eight rods altogether, spanning the length of the ship. Each was as long as the cruiser was wide. The disks that capped them pushed through the faintly visible energy shield, their modulinium faces exposed to naked space.

As the bow eased into the seething energies of the anomaly, the ship's shields began to flare and visibly weaken. This was a maelstrom of energies ranging across the spectrum from heat through ultraviolet and beyond, produced where a fold in space causes points far distant from each other to overlap, causing an energy storm that to all appearances is a sphere, but in fact was unimaginably different.

Transiting between these overlapped but very distant areas of space would be a simple matter except for the awesome destructive forces that the phenomenon generated.

Steve felt himself growing nervous as the anomaly's energy wore away at the ship's shields. Tibs was eased the ship into it far too slowly for Steve's comfort: If the shields eroded before the energy sinks could feed power back into them, the shields might collapse too soon.

After an agonizing few seconds Steve could see the first of the rods begin pulling in a torrent of power. The shields visibly brightened from a weakening opalescent gray color, then started to grow stronger and regain a strong cobalt blue tint as more rods gained position within the anomaly and pulled in yet more power.

In the monitor, as the sensors feeding it became enveloped by the shimmering blue of the shield, Steve saw dim, alien stars in positions they shouldn't have had in that region of space, indicating that the distance between the two sides of the anomaly was enormous. There was no way to guess where the other side would take them, other than Tibs' guess of the Trondheim system. But Steve knew the Aldebari astrogation teams were already taking readings and plotting their translated position.

Then, like a dancer through a beaded doorway, the *Jade Temple* emerged into normal space.

Chapter 29: The Hunted

With the shield capacitors almost at capacity from the transition, the Aldebari cruiser's engineers fed some of the excess back into the modulinium disks at frequencies that would slowly bleed off outside the shield envelope. All hands hurried to their assigned tasks as the astrogation team worked at their terminals to plot their location, comparing star positions with projections derived from all fourteen human worlds.

All indications confirmed it was indeed the Trondheim system. Tibs greeted the news with a raised clenched fist like he had just won a rare prize. Then he signaled Elder Kinkaid, who began dispatching orders to the *Jade Temple*'s ready room and the pilots already gathered there.

Kinkaid revealed plans for two scouting flights, each composed of six modified light fighters. Each flight would begin a coordinated search pattern expanding from the *Jade Temple*'s position. The cruiser would remain dark, all running lights off, engines at idle but warm. Sensors would be set passive with only one signal emitter broadcasting a frequency of otherwise meaningless, almost undetectable electronic static into the spectrum of white background noise found all over the universe. The scouts would use that signal to acquire the *Jade Temple*'s location when they transmitted their reports over a tight binary laser signal that was unlikely to be intercepted.

According to the Aldebari cartographers, the scouts' initial leg in the search would take them through a dense asteroid field within the nearby Trondheim planetary system.

The light fighters had been modified to reduce the weight of armaments and provide improved electronic sensors and electronic intelligence countermeasures. The mass of a heavier reactor and increased fuel condensate was compensated with a reduction in armor. The fuel was enriched to enable greater range, increase thrust potential, and produce a less noticeable contrail while at cruising speeds. These measures would shorten the practical life of the engines, but that was not an immediate concern. The heavy standard communications array was replaced by a lighter, directed coherent beam system that would rely on a line-of-sight (LOS) laser translating a pilot's audiovisual information into binary transmissions that would not give away the location of the transmitter. If a scout's

LOS was blocked by an intervening body, then it would repeat the signal sequence when the *Jade Temple*'s white noise transponder was reacquired.

~

Once the scouts gained some distance, the *Jade Temple* launched a flight of medium fighters to secure the distant modulus. They hoped to prevent any warning to the Board of Corporations forces beyond the sector that anything unusual was happening.

Kyle, Delaney, Graham and Steve were notified to prepare for flight orders that could come at any time if either the scouts or the modulus interdiction team found any threat. Additionally a strike team of Aldebari commandos suited up in case Harden, the science team, or other high value human objectives were located. Technical crews were preparing an assault shuttle for this potential mission. The commandos' powered 'Crawlers', powered metal and ceramic exoskeletons bearing forward armor and heavy weapons were loaded onto the assault shuttle. Crawlers are well-suited for combat within the constricted corridors of a ship. They could climb ladders and turn abrupt corners, though it took considerable skill and practice to maneuver them quickly in confined areas.

All other Aldebari pilots readied themselves to respond quickly if need arose. Throughout the *Jade Temple*, the atmosphere was alert and active.

The primary mission was to locate and arrest Harden or, failing that, gain information that would provide a good lead. If it turned out that they would have to transit the modulus to continue their search deep in Corporate space then the odds against a successful mission climbed unacceptably. In that scenario Tibs resolved to cut his losses and return through the anomaly empty-handed to let the Aldebar and the *Perry Station* council know that the technology to transit an anomaly worked. Once that knowledge was shared, the council leadership and Aldebari leadership could confer and make further evaluation. If it was determined that securing Harden and his science team was sufficiently important to risk an open war with the Board of Corporations, then a task force could be fitted with the anomaly-traversing technology to conduct reconnaissance-in-force. Corporate Earth would take any military incursion into their space as provocative, to say the least, regardless of the purpose.

Hopefully the *Jade Temple*'s less belligerent tack would prove productive, and they could slip back through the anomaly and conclude her mission without being positively identified. Tibs and Steve were reasonably certain that the Board of Corporations did not yet have Harden's technical advantages. The psychological profile that they developed suggested he would never share a trump card with his business competitors. Harden would consider patriotism a fine sentiment for 'the little people' but, when it came to business interests, possessing an advantage far outweighed ideology.

The secondary mission objective was to secure the scientists who had originally discovered the solution to anomaly transit and planet-busting weaponry used to destroy Perry. Hopefully *Perry Station* and the Aldebari could remove them from Harden's asset ledger and gain their talent and technology.

The *Jade Temple* silently coasted further in toward the Trondheim planetary system.

~

The scouts approached the dense asteroid belt between the orbits of the system's fifth and sixth planets and began picking up electronic signals from something about ten degrees off their plotted course. If the signal came from among the asteroids they might find it time-consuming to locate. So they signaled their intent to investigate.

Slowing his speed for careful maneuvering among the relatively stationary but densely clustered stones, one scout noticed that the signal strength of the electronic emissions varied with his position, indicating the asteroids were dense with iron. Behind him the maze of asteroids he had already passed completely blocked his communications to the *Jade Temple*.

A few small automated mining installations operated nearby, but their electronics would not have produced the signal he detected. Their floodlights, which illuminated when the platforms detected his ship, were distracting and threatened to compromise his position. Tethered to the automated mining equipment were great nets holding refined ingots ready for towing.

Then, as the scout maneuvered around one large asteroid, he spotted a large industrial installation, bright with harsh exterior lighting. He tensed as his eyes scanned the side of the installation, exposed to open space clear of asteroids, where a tremendous shipyard housed a warship much larger than the *Jade Temple*.

Bringing his craft to a relative stop, he carefully observed the warship and the installation. Several docking bays in the structure bore large stenciled letters. On high magnification he could read the word '*Lab*' next to one of them.

The scout started backing away the way he came, weaving carefully through the asteroids until his thrusters could no longer be seen from the installation, then pivoted his ship and flew clear of obstructing asteroids to report what he had found.

~

Aboard the *Jade Temple* the scout's transmission triggered orders to Steve and his flight to escort the commandos in the assault shuttle to the industrial base. The mission for the commandos was to extract any scientific assets at the facility and seek information on Harden.

Simultaneously Aldebari fighters would attempt to disable the capital ship before it could get underway and attack the *Jade Temple*. Other Aldebar fighters would be launched to provide cover and close support for the commando assault and escorts.

Tibs hoped the commandos could reach the docked ship before it raised shields and cleared the dock. It was imperative that the *Jade Temple* remain unidentified, recover needed information and assets from Trondheim, and escape back through the anomaly before her intrusion into corporate space became undeniable. Now was not a good time for the Aldebar to renew open hostilities with Earth.

Steve, Kyle, Graham, and Delaney launched one by one and formed up near the cruiser to await the assault shuttle.

"Steven:" Tibs commed using LOS (line-of-sight) binary transmission, "Our scout was heading back in to identify the class and condition of their docked capital ship. Had I tried to order him back I would have had to broadcast and it would have given us away. Our situation is already in a crisis, especially if that corporate warship manages to fight free of our efforts to disable her. I don't know yet whether it is a heavy cruiser or worse: the scout only said it was bigger than the Jade Temple. If it is a battle cruiser or larger we won't get away unscathed unless we can disable her. We still have people scouting and securing the modulus. If we fail to disable that ship I cannot abandon any of my pilots here and we would just have to fight. I'd rather not. Once you have successfully escorted the commandos to their entry point on the installation, try to locate that scout and send him back at top speed."

"I'll find him, Tibs," Steve responded.

"I hope so, Steve. Elder Kinkaid has informed me that the scout is our boy, Bobby."

"WHAT? Bobby's too young…"

"He was ready for this, Steve. He has great observation skills and superior potential as a pilot. He needed to be entrusted with this mission."

"Tibs he intends to take out Harden by himself and exact revenge for forcing his parents into the act that got them killed. This may lead him to take chances he would otherwise avoid."

Tibs sighed audibly. "Just find him, Steve, and bring him back."

"Understood," Steve fumed.

The commando team launched in their shuttle and Steve's escort formed up around them, heading toward the point outside the asteroid belt that was Bobby's last known location. Steve thought about the kid piloting a light scout fighter through those asteroids near a hostile installation. He was much too young and inexperienced for that mission. Steve felt Tibs' rationalization that it isn't age that matters was hogwash. Steve recognized the point Tibs made, but disagreed that capability was the only salient factor in the argument.

"Tibs:" he said into the mike, "I wish we hadn't let Bobby do this."

"I know, my friend," Tibs responded quietly, "and personally I also wish we hadn't allowed it. But Bobby's obsessed with making a difference against the evil in this galaxy. I think he had to do it to quiet the ghosts of his parents."

Steve was grim when he replied "He will not be inexperienced long, one way or the other."

~

Aboard the Trondheim industrial installation the watch commander was alerted by a warning strobe over one of the perimeter consoles. "What is the alarm, Specialist?" he asked the woman seated there.

"Impending low velocity collision detected, sir: looks like a small asteroid is drifting too close."

"Scramble a maintenance shuttle to haul it back away from the facility and make it quick: I don't want to have to send you out there on a repair team."

The specialist opened a channel to maintenance and relayed the order.

Down in facilities section, maintenance specialist Mike Hecker just sat down to lunch when the order came in for a maintenance sortie. His supervisor told him to just take care of it. In disgust Mike glowered back at the maintenance chief and said "Okay, but you owe me for this one. I'm on my lunch break." He grabbed his sandwich, stuffed it into his tool pouch and headed for his locker to put on his EVA suit. He left his open drink on the lunchroom table.

Bobby's scout ship hung quietly suspended in the void near the hostile station. He identified the docked capital ship's class as an older corporate battleship, and would try to get closer to see whether it was space-worthy. Hopefully it was in dock for some heavy refitting and couldn't deploy for battle.

Suddenly a warning strobe blinked on his console. He quickly looked through his canopy to see a small maintenance shuttle emerge from the installation and head directly toward him.

Inside the maintenance shuttle Mike had just taken a big bite of his sandwich when in total disbelief he identified the asteroid he expected to see as an Aldebari scout. As the maintenance shuttle drew closer he could see the scout's pilot looking back at him, and Mike frantically tried to decide what action to take. His hand started to activate the comm, but when he tried to swallow his overly large bite of sandwich, it would not go down. Mike began to choke. It was too dry, too big, and he could not swallow. He couldn't breathe, and he couldn't spit it out. All other thoughts fled as he panicked, trying repeatedly to choke the sandwich down. His brain started to go into a primal mode where the only priority is to survive, to get the blockage out, to swallow and simultaneously take a breath. Instead of hitting the alarm or opening comm his hands went to his throat and his stomach spasmed.

Bobby could see exactly what was happening in the maintenance shuttle although, of course, he didn't know why. In the maintenance worker's thrashing he might hit an alarm, warning the facility and leading to disaster for Bobby and the *Jade Temple*. He bumped his controls to position his aft hatch toward that of the shuttle and left his flight couch, setting his automated shipboard functions to maintain attitude relative to the shuttle. He then disconnected from the pilot's interface, unstrapped himself from his flight couch, and moved into the airlock smoothly and quickly. Thinking twice, he stopped and reached up to the netting, pulled out his kit, and pulled his old fletchette pistol. He slipped the weapon into the large thigh pocket of his suit. He entered the airlock and started its cycle. The airlock evacuated and he opened the airlock's outer door. A slight puff of residual atmosphere swept him off his feet and out, into the void.

He hadn't been centered in the doorway and he was moving out into space uncontrolled, causing his stomach to flip-flop in panic. Bobby had failed to tether himself. He muttered harshly, but his self-advice was a little late.

The closed maintenance shuttle hatch was growing closer, but his trajectory was a bit to the side. All around him nothing but empty space and bare stones the size of mountains fell away forever toward unknown stars. If Bobby missed a grab for a handhold on the maintenance shuttle he would spin slowly forever, off into space. He would orbit the star called Trondheim like a tiny living asteroid until his air ran out or his suit ran out of power, and then a frozen carcass named Bobby would fall forever.

He knew the natural impulse to try and swim would not help in space because there was nothing, not even air, to push against. The motion might start him spinning around his center of gravity. Bobby desperately tried to think. His legs were longer than his arms, but his cumbersome boots couldn't grab hold the way his hand could. His mind raced to find a solution, but time for any action was rapidly slipping past.

Bobby remembered the fletchette pistol in his thigh pocket. It had mass... maybe sufficient mass that throwing it opposite the direction he needed to go would shift his body closer to the shuttle. With desperate regret he tried to retrieve it, but the clumsy glove wouldn't fit into his thigh pocket. Bobby's alarm grew desperate. He tried squeezing the pistol up out of the pocket by pressing on the bottom from the outside, and gratefully he felt it move against his thigh, closer to where he could grab it. Finally he got the fletchette pistol into his gloved hand, but he judged it was too late to try changing his trajectory by throwing it. The shuttle was already was too close. It was now or never.

Holding the long barrel he reached out with the pistol and hooked the grip over the shuttle's rung and pulled. His momentum was carrying him past, but the hooked pistol grip gave him a fulcrum that swung his body into the side of the shuttle. Pulling on the pistol reduced his arc and increased his angular momentum. Bobby realized that when he hit, his body would bounce off the hull. He might lose his grip on the pistol and spin off into space again. He focused most on holding his grip on the pistol, keeping it hooked, and prepared for impact. His body hit hard, nearly knocking the breath out of him. Concentrating all his will and strength, he ignored the pain and pulled steadily on the pistol to keep it hooked as his body bounced off the hull and swung out once more into the void.

Pulling constantly on the pistol that was now his life-line, he reached for the rung with his left hand and finally got a grip on it, and pulled himself to the hatch.

After his ordeal Bobby was sloshing in his suit, drenched in sweat. His heart beat like a trip hammer as he struggled to slow his panting, to regulate his oxygen. It would be fatal to hyperventilate. Gradually his self-discipline exerted itself and his breathing slowed to a tolerable pace. He turned the exterior airlock handle to initiate an evacuation cycle. The whole event had taken place in mere seconds. Somehow the thought floated up that his had been a lesson in freedom.

When the airlock LED turned green, indicating the pressure inside the airlock balanced the vacuum of space, he twisted the batten and pressed the hatch inward and to the side. He stepped into the induced gravity inside. Turning, he closed the hatch and resealed it with the batten. He activated a recessed squeeze grip labeled 'pressure' and the airlock began filling with air. He waited till the inner lock telltale turned green and opened the door.

The maintenance worker was now unconscious, floating free in the cabin, probably dead. Bobby removed his helmet. Someone with a harsh voice aboard the facility was on the comm demanding to know what was happening. Bobby removed his glove and felt for the worker's pulse. He was surprised to feel it hammering away, trying to get oxygen to the brain. The guy didn't have long before he went into cardiac arrest at this rate. It was surprising he hadn't already, as out of shape as he looked.

Bobby pressed the man's unresisting body against the bulkhead and grabbed an overhead bar. He swung both feet up to deliver a heavy kick to the man's upper belly, and sure enough, the glob of sandwich popped out of the worker's throat. The man coughed and started heaving great breaths of air while Bobby silently cursed himself for complicating his predicament. Spotting a tether line, he tied the maintenance worker to the bulkhead's structural beams to prevent his reaching the restraining knots. Then Bobby turned his attention to the shuttle itself.

The maintenance chief on the comm sounded like a real piece of work, threatening to dock Mike's pay for the cost of dispatching a second team. Bobby had no idea what the reviving worker sounded like, but answered the comm saying 'it's okay, I'm alright' in a wheezy voice he hoped sounded out of breath.

This started the man cussing on the other end, demanding an answer as to what happened and how the hell could he have failed to answer the first time, then threatened to both fire him and appropriate his pay for the next six months just for the aggravation he'd caused. Bobby imagined six month's pay from the man he just fired would not amount to much.

"I choked.' Bobby wheezed. The response ignited a new tirade, filled with even more extreme invective. Bobby turned down the volume and studied the shuttle controls. In the sudden quiet he heard the maintenance guy breathing raggedly behind him. Bobby turned and looked into the man's bloodshot eyes.

"Who are you?" rasped Mike, sounding remarkably like Bobby's imitation. "What were you doing out there? And why in hell did you tie me up?"

Bobby just smiled a sly little grin and turned back to the controls.

Mike raised his voice threateningly: "Look at me when I'm talking to you, you little punk!" Bobby looked up, out upon the stars and asteroids. He pulled his fletchette pistol from its pocket and turned to aim it directly at the man's left eye, still smiling. Mike shut his mouth with a snap. Bobby turned back to the controls. 'Piece of cake,' he thought.

"Or sandwich" he said to himself.

~

Steve held position above and slightly aft of the assault shuttle. As they approached the asteroid belt the Aldebari fighters swept past en route to ensure the corporate capital ship would not interfere. Over the comm he heard a report that the modulus flight successfully secured the Trondheim side of the modulus without casualties, having scored two kills on the patrol stationed there. Two corporate pods sped back toward the asteroid field and the industrial facility it concealed. The only problem the modulus flight reported was an approaching outbound freighter. Tibs ordered them to disable the freighter's drives and communications boom but not destroy the ship if possible. Tibs was clearly weighing political consequences. If they minimized damage, then eventually diplomacy might more easily assuage the impact and allow the incursion to be explained more successfully.

Steve flew ahead, with Kyle slightly below and to port. An Aldebari fighter approaching the objective identified the target as a battleship. A chill went down Steve's spine. If the battleship made way before it could be disabled there would be hell to pay. Electronic activity was heavy up ahead, but it was clear Trondheim had been caught flat-footed. That fact raised Steve's hope that Bobby was okay. Had Bobby been caught, Trondheim would have been on alert and would be manning it's defenses. Had Bobby's light fighter been destroyed, then his lifepod should have returned to the *Jade Temple*... unless, like his dad, he just hadn't punched out.

The gigantic stone asteroids drew closer, and the pilot of the assault shuttle eased up on the throttle, forcing his escorts to do the same.

Steve's graphic display showed four blue blips closing fast. Kyle warned the shuttle, and the four Perry escorts nosed over and hit their thrusters. The assault shuttle held steady toward the shelter of the asteroids.

"Delaney, cut to starboard and let's see if we can split them up."

Delaney, with Graham on his wing, cut to starboard. After a moment all four of the Corporates veered after them.

"Rabbit, Rabbit!" called Graham, trying to draw the Corporates after him and Delaney, running all out. The maneuver was intended to allow Steve and Kyle to get behind their pursuers. Delaney split off from Graham but two followed. "Rabbit!" called Delaney as he went evasive to deny them a decent shot. Kyle and Steve held to the two still on Graham and began burning the nearest pilot with their beams. The targets maneuvered too much to invest hard-ball ammo. Any ballistic rounds that missed their target would keep going, and might accidentally hit Graham. Laser fire is immediate, so as long as

Graham was out of the way he wouldn't take friendly fire.

The shots Kyle and Steve fired hammered their target. With its shields depleted the fighter began shedding puffs of vaporized armor. The defender and his wingman bellied over to target Steve, leaving Graham on their six but going away. Immediately Graham bellied over, his thrust on max and opened up on the fighter himself. Kyle and Steve split to make the two opponents either split up or choose one of them, freeing the other. As long as Delaney kept leading the other two fighters without buying the farm Steve felt the good guys were going to win this one.

Suddenly all four Corporate fighters broke off and fled at high speed toward the industrial installation and battleship. Although Steve wanted to give chase he had a mission to complete, and finding Bobby to get him back to safety took priority.

"I think the battleship is worried about the Aldebari fighters and needed help from those guys" said Kyle.

"I bet your guess is on the money as usual."

~

Four flights of four Aldebari medium fighters and a flight of four gunboats from the *Jade Temple* swept in on the stern of the battleship *Ariel*. The *Ariel*, built two decades earlier at the Foster shipyard orbiting Paradiso IV, had already survived two corporate retirement reviews. For all her age, unless disabled, she remained a formidable threat to the *Jade Temple*.

The gunboats maneuvered for a missile run at the *Ariel's* massive engines before she could clear the dock and raise shields. Like all the last generation capital ships she was heavily invested in point defenses. Her main armament consisted of four turret batteries of prodigious rail guns complimented by a formidable array of medium range launching tubes. For now, the gunboat pilots were most wary of the point defenses.

Their escorts were successfully defending the attack from defending interceptors when the great ship's engines lit up, having taken that much time to warm up and prime. The *Ariel's* two aft railgun turrets flung metal slugs almost half the size of the gunboats. But the range was still so great that those slugs were predictable to the threat analysis computers, and reasonably easy to dodge by an alert pilot, but there wouldn't be time to predict and dodge as the gunboats, with their lethal missiles, drew closer.

The real danger was mid-range, and increased with proximity to the battleship's point defenses. Pulse laser beams, which no one can dodge, and small anti-fighter rail guns, which fire projectiles that can seldom be detected before they either hit or miss. The rounds thrown by these electromagnetic weapons measure thirty millimeters in diameter and five centimeters in length, but the velocity is so great they could punch right through any unshielded armor a small starship can carry. So far, the beams weren't hurting the Aldebari much due to the range, but that would change as they approached their weapons' release point. The point defense rail guns were a threat at any range.

Red flight's gunboats were each carrying two 'Valkyrie' armor-piercing high yield conventional missiles. If the battleship shields were still down, the Valkyries could survive the active exhaust of the *Ariel*'s engines. Their warheads would survive long enough to reach the engine interior and disable the magnetic bottles that control the detonation of antimatter with hydrogen. The *Ariel* then could not use her own fuel without risking catastrophic destruction. If the gunboats could take out at least two of the three main thrusters it would assure the *Jade Temple's* survival.

If they took out only one thruster the *Jade Temple* might still be able to recover the fighters and retreat to the anomaly before the *Ariel* could find her.

For the attacking gunboats, flying straight into live fire was extremely dangerous. It made the gunboats essentially sitting ducks unless they flew a corkscrew trajectory to try and confuse the enemy's targeting computers. Red 2's poorly timed corkscrew created the most perilous path possible. A gunnery sergeant down on the *Ariel's* fantail spewed a steady stream of ballistic rounds without concern for the targeting computer's confusion, and Red 2 skewered himself on the stream of hyper velocity slugs, shields going down in one moment and his armor was ripped from him the next. Behind the three remaining gunboats his two Valkyrie warheads exploded, completing his destruction so thoroughly that his lifepod was just a memory.

Steve heard three Aldebari pilots call "Missiles away!" just as the assault shuttle arrived at what they believed was the science lab dock. The installation's heavy shields blocked external communications.

Delaney spotted Bobby's scout down at one of the maintenance docks. It just hovered there, like a dog awaiting his master. Kyle and Steve swept near and saw it nose out, hatch open and empty a few meters away from a maintenance shuttle parked just inside the atmospheric shield on the bay deck. Normally that shuttle should have been parked toward the back, leaving the maintenance bay entry clear. Steve asked Kyle to wait in close support and slid his fighter to rest on the deck alongside the maintenance shuttle. Steve set his controls to keep the anti-matter bottle hot but idle, told his security mod to ignore any command without his vocal password, and prepared to disembark.

Despite emergency klaxons sounding and yellow strobes spinning all over the shield-pressurized hanger, Steve could hear muffled cursing somewhere nearby. It seemed to come from inside the maintenance shuttle. It didn't sound like Bobby. Pulling his sidearm Steve peered into the cabin from the viewport and saw a large man struggling against his restraints.

Over in the dock's bulkhead, a pressure door lay wide open, a sure sign of unusual activity. Steve moved quickly next to the door and risked a look inside. He saw the bloody body of another man sprawled face up near another open door. A young woman cowered in a corner unharmed, and apparently unarmed. He raced to the second door and looked. An empty hallway led to still another door open.

As he entered the hallway Steve saw a lean silhouette enter from the other end. Steve almost squeezed the trigger but at the last moment saw it was Bobby. "He isn't here." Bobby said.

"Who isn't here?"

"Harden."

"Okay, come on, we have to get back to the *Jade Temple* ASAP," Steve warned. "There may be some serious trouble about to hit."

"Let's get it done then, Steve."

Both pilots boarded their respective boats and launched from the facility, openly speeding back toward the *Jade Temple*. Steve felt a growing sense of liberation hoping Bobby would soon be safely back aboard, but now Steve found himself worrying over Graham, Kyle and Delaney as they flew in support of the assault shuttle.

~

Lieutenant Matsuo, leading the marine detachment assigned to the *Jade Temple*, had not expected it would be all that difficult to locate their objective, but the warren of passageways in the facility had no posted signs or floor-plan directories, physical or digital. They had met only light resistance and there had been no casualties among his troops, but he knew the advantages of surprise and speed were rapidly dwindling. He didn't want to split his force but he desperately needed reconnaissance. He ordered his two Crawler squads to start searching while he remained at the ready with the heavy weapons/support squad in the docking bay to provide reinforcement.

Their Crawlers, the exoskeletal assault vehicles, led the way. They were specifically designed to navigate the confines of a spaceship or orbital installation. In order to pass beyond bulkheads at doorways their four treads could be lifted and moved like legs, but normally they rolled forward faster and more quietly than most men could walk. Their bows were armored and targeting sensors fed view screens above the controls. The sides and back of the vehicles were open, flanks protected by heavily armed infantry walking or trotting behind or, when possible, alongside. Generally speaking, the opposition was composed of non-professional installation staff who barely knew how to point and shoot, but some Corporate ex-military among them organized into more tactically effective pockets of resistance.

~

The facility's security chief received an incoming transmission from Anton Kruczewski, the captain of the inbound Corporate cruiser *Viksholm* and commander of the escort flotilla intended to protect the now crippled battleship *Ariel*. The escorts raced in from the rings of a gas giant in the system where they had been collecting antimatter. The *Ariel* launched her few remaining fighters, but was barely maneuverable unaided. Nevertheless she was making way, if barely, to try and clear the asteroids. She was attempting to reach a position where her big rail guns might be useful.

Chief Glass briefed the captain on the situation as he understood it, adding that they thought the attackers were probably mercenaries in the employ of a competing corporation or corporate alliance, probably brought by the freighter than had just left filled with a load of nickel-iron ingots just hours before.

Captain Kruczewski checked quickly and saw on his system chart that the suspect freighter now sat motionless in space near the modulus. The ship might be awaiting a signal from the mercenaries for pickup. Kruczewski ordered one of the destroyers in the flotilla to interdict the freighter and capture her. "If you encounter resistance, then blow it out of space."

He returned his gaze to rest on Chief Glass in the viewer and issued his instructions.

Glass acknowledged his orders and prepared to notify the assigned security officer in the Science section. Kruczewski gave the ETA for the escort flotilla. The ships wanted to coordinate with the facility and requested all surviving human assets should locate and neutralize the attackers. To remove the attackers' most likely objective, and to follow prescribed security protocols, Kruczewski ordered the neutralization of the research lab, its scientists, and the data. The data had already been transmitted and what remained in the lab was now redundant. The scientists could be replaced, and if the security of the lab was breached their knowledge would become a liability. Captain Kruczewski transmitted his order on digital letterhead with his secure signature. He ordered Glass to place a copy in a small Remote Autonomous Transport (RAT) vehicle. The RAT would be dispatched to the security chief ASAP. Officer Glass acknowledged, downloaded the orders to his own PDA for lack of another handy device, put the PDA in the RAT, and set the destination for the RAT to the lab.

Captain Kruczewski remained troubled by one thing: Mercenaries from a freighter seeking tech did not explain what had happened to the *Ariel*, especially given multiple reports identifying the attacking fighters as Aldebar.

But how could that be? There were no reports of an Aldebar incursion into corporate space. If they had, the news would be all over .Mil net. The *Ariel* would never have been caught sitting in dock with her engines cold, and her escorts would have been at the ready to defend her instead of off gathering antimatter. His mind thought back, and his fingers raced over his computer terminal's input interface. His research indicated the installation had once been part of Harden's holdings, recently awarded to the Rodriguez Trust after Harden was stripped of his assets.

According to the logs, Harden had been here only days before the events that destroyed a planet. Strangely, the Al Najid system was too distant to have been reached in the time Harden needed to get there from Trondheim.

Kruczewski pulled up the eyewitness broadcast that had so infuriated the Corporations when it caused a mass exodus of skilled labor. In an intelligence report an agent repeated hearsay that a cruiser emerged from an Al Najid anomaly. At the time the report was discredited as impossible. Yet this Trondheim sector claimed just such an anomaly.

"Ready a courier boat for a top priority hardcopy communication to the home office, ASAP." he commanded into his comm link.

~

Lieutenant Matsuo's force in the science lab dock used some quick laser fire to capture a speedy little RAT they spotted headed for the lab itself. Matsuo was relieved to find a digital map of the ship displayed on the RAT's control surface. He opened its small access door and retrieved an electronic notepad. At his touch the screen revealed a message written on official Corporate letterhead. The message was digitally signed. Matsuo quickly read the message and called over one of his support team. He downloaded a copy of the document into a tiny mass storage device and ordered that the contents were to be flashed by narrow beam comm back to the *Jade Temple*. That meant either the shuttle or one of the fighters guarding it would have to clear the asteroid field to transmit it. He emphasized it was vital to get it to Tibs: There were more corporate warships incoming.

Pocketing the original notepad in one of his zippered pockets, Matsuo then called over another team member to discuss an idea that had just occurred to him.

~

Security Officer Leeds settled into his new defensive position near the Science Lab access way and directed his men to coordinate their fields of fire. Suddenly a RAT whizzed into the Lab and stopped. Risking exposure to enemy fire, Leeds hustled out, scooped up the RAT, and brought it back to cover. The body of the RAT was heavily scored with laser fire. His men squatted nearby as Leeds opened the RAT's access hatch, triggering Matsuo's fragmentation grenade.

~

Captain Kruczewski looked into the admiral's eyes on the comm screen. He had just recounted his theory that the Aldebar had discovered a way to transit the anomaly, pointing out the account by the eyewitness agent, the log entries and the impossible distance Harden would have to travel to be at Al Najid system for the destruction of Perry. Kruczewski also noted Aldebari fighters disabled the *Ariel* when there had been no word of any Aldebar entering the sector through the modulus. He thought his argument pretty convincing.

The admiral thought otherwise. "Kruczewski, you just told me you dispatched a fifty-billion-credit, state-of-the-art destroyer to intercept an ore freighter. That ore freighter is, according to your own report, doing what no ore freighter would ever do. He's sitting motionless, out in the middle of space near a perfectly good modulus, while the money he used to buy his cargo would have accrued interest in a savings account faster than he's moving. What's wrong with that picture, Captain? Did it never occur to you that it might just *look* like a freighter? What if it were modified to carry Aldebari fighters instead of ore? Sure, okay, he took on a full cargo of ingots at the facility. But he's probably jettisoning that load right now, and preparing to recover his fighters and pick up the information assets they went to great expense to steal from the Corporation! What's the ETA for that rendezvous?"

"That's the *Ocean City*, sir. She's a Hawkins class destroyer, sir, a missile boat. They should be in active scanning range within minutes, sir."

Kruczewski was ashen faced to have missed the admiral's analysis while proposing his fantasy. Of course they hadn't come through the anomaly. How many men and ships had died trying to prove it could be done?

A message was incoming from the destroyer "...four Aldebar fighters. Repeat: The freighter appears to have four medium Aldebari fighters with him, sir. Permission to engage? Sir, the fighters have seen us and are running on bearing 1462.88 at high speed. Shall we attempt to intercept and destroy, sir?"

Captain Kruczewski looked at the Admiral, who barked his orders "Negative! They are trying to draw you away from that freighter. I want you to blow that freighter to hell, do you hear me mister?"

"Aye-aye, sir!"

"How far out are you now, Captain Kruczewski?" asked the Admiral.

"Maybe ten minutes, sir."

"Come alongside the *Ariel*. I'm assuming command."

"Aye-aye, Admiral." Kruczewski gave a smart salute to the monitor.

~

"We must hurry, sir." Lieutenant Matsuo urged the unimpressive looking lead researcher.

"We need not hurry at all." We are Corporate scientists, will always be Corporate scientists, and we will never abandon the Corporation for such as you. We are not traitors; we are patriots! We will not yield to your demands!" The lead scientist was suddenly developing a patriotic fervor he had previously never experienced.

"Sir, certainly I respect your sentiments." Matsuo said. "They are admirable and honorable traits. Please, just read this official corporate document we intercepted a few minutes ago. It concerns you and your colleagues." Matsuo handed the RAT's notepad to the lead scientist. The man peered through his lenses at the tiny font displayed in the miniature screen. He looked up at Matsuo for a moment, a light sweat beading his parchment-like forehead, then reread the words and closely examined the letterhead and signature.

"They were going to kill us," he protested. "We uploaded our findings so they no longer had any use for us. Rather than risk our disclosing information to another company, they were going to neutralize us!" he exclaimed in a disbelief. "Look at this!" The rest of the scientists gathered around to read it.

"I think we successfully duplicated some of your work to get here. Through the anomaly." Matsuo explained.

"You did?" asked the scientist. "And it worked? Well, obviously you wouldn't have come through a Corporate modulus." The scientist was at first incredulous, then impatient with himself. "We hadn't completed our studies. How did you find out about our work? Harden would never have shared our findings with anyone outside the company." Patriotism seemed a very transitory, easily misplaced sentiment.

"Oh, he shared them in a very real way," Matsuo replied. "But as a consequence he demonstrated that your theories were true, and we witnessed the effects. Knowing then that traversing an anomaly was indeed possible, and after examining your original installation, our engineers reproduced the tech. Based on what they learned we traversed the Trondheim-Al Najid anomaly today. It is how we got here."

"Our scientists would very much like to meet you, to compare notes," Matsuo confided.

The scientist looked thoughtful. "Compare notes? That would be refreshing." He moved over to confer with his team. Despite the pressure to extract the scientists and return to the ship Matsuo and his men gave the science team some time. After a brief discussion the lead scientist returned and asked, "Do you think we could see how you applied our theory? What the housing was made of? How did your people articulate the modulinium conduits?"

"Sir, if you will come with us you can examine and test the materials yourselves. We have a sophisticated lab aboard the ship: I think you'll be pleased."

The scientist appeared tempted, but then grew stubborn. "I'm sorry, we cannot leave our work! You will have to help us get the memory cores and our workstations packed before we can leave with you. There is too much that would be lost."

Matsuo's team moved to comply, believing it easier and faster to have willing members working with them than hostile prisoners resisting at every turn. The scientists carefully packed everything they could on a null-gravity maintenance sled and moved to the shuttle at the agonizingly slow pace of conversational scientists.

~

Aboard the Corporate destroyer *Ocean City* the commander was dismayed. "Permission to deploy navigational beacons, sir?" he requested of Captain Kruczewski.

"For what purpose, Commander?"

"Sir, there is now an expanding sphere of iron ingots surrounding the freighter's wreckage, sir. It is in a direct path to the Trondheim dock, and if a ship strikes it unaware, well, it could cause serious damage, sir."

"Were the ingots free before you attacked, Commander?"

"No sir. The area around the freighter was clear, sir."

"I see: and the fighters that fled upon your arrival: What was their bearing?"

After a few moments the *Ocean City* commander reported "1462.88, sir."

"Thank you commander. Affirmative your request to deploy navigational beacons," replied Kruczewski. He pulled up his navcomp display and input the location of the new navigation beacons and projected a straight line through bearing 1462.88. It intersected the anomaly. Leaving his navcomp display up, he rose deep in thought, straightened his uniform and left to receive the Admiral.

On his way, he took his executive officer aside for a moment and spoke quietly. First was to dispatch the courier with the datacube the Captain pressed into the palm of his exec. Second, he issued orders for the *Ocean City*, the destroyer at the modulus.

~

Lieutenant Matsuo finally got the scientists and their equipment squared away on the assault shuttle and launched from the science lab docking bay. The virus in the industrial installation's computer systems and network would probably buy them extra time for their escape.

Graham, Kyle, and Delaney were waiting to escort the shuttle back to the *Jade Temple*, growing increasingly nervous as the corporate escort force approached. But in short order they maneuvered with the shuttle into the asteroid field and cautiously made for the loitering *Jade Temple*. On their sensors they saw the corporate fighters already beginning to arrive, swarming like angry hornets around the Mining and Research facility and especially the *Ariel*, but quickly the dense asteroid field with its iron blocked their sensors.

~

"ATTTENN-HUT!" the Corporate marine honor detail snapped crisply to attention as the hatch opened and the admiral stepped into the cruiser to the salutes of assembled staff aboard the *Viksholm*. "Welcome aboard, admiral." the captain said. "Recommend we get underway immediately, sir."

"And just where do you think we are going, captain? What's the rush?"

"Sir, we must seek out the Aldebar before they can withdraw. The *Ocean City* reports the freighter at the modulus was indeed fully laden with nickel-iron ingots when she was destroyed, sir. The four fighters that accompanied her must have stopped her to prevent word of their presence escaping the system. If the freighter wasn't the origin of the Aldebari fighters that attacked the *Ariel*, sir, then they must have a capital ship in Trondheim system. I recommend that we find and destroy it, sir."

The admiral appeared confused, but quickly his eyes focused. "Then we should join the *Ocean City* at the modulus and await reinforcements."

Captain Kruczewski kept his eyes level and straight ahead, still in a crisp salute that waited for the admiral to acknowledge it. "With respect, sir, I believe they didn't arrive through the modulus and won't leave that way either. They would only be 'escaping' deeper into corporate space. Admiral we must interdict them before they can escape back through the anomaly."

"You are fixated on that anomaly, captain! I shouldn't have to tell you no one can survive the transit of an anomaly. No one ever has, no matter how strong their armor and shields. It simply cannot be done! There is a more logical explanation, but we haven't explored it because of your impossible hunch. It's a delusion, captain! Get it out of your head this moment, or so help me you'll find yourself in the gutters of Paradiso begging for credits."

Captain Kruczewski realized it was time for his decision. He had prepared for it. He snapped his salute to completion, looked the Admiral in the eyes, and barked his orders to the sergeant major of the honor guard: "Sergeant Major Anderson!".

The sergeant major stepped forward and saluted, "Sir! Yes, sir!"

"Kindly escort the admiral to the brig."

"Aye-aye, Captain!" The sergeant major faced the admiral and with great civility requested that the admiral accompany him.

"I'll be damned if I will!" the admiral raged, his face red with a towering anger.

Immediately two Corporate marines appeared at his elbows and 'escorted' him to the brig behind the sergeant major.

"Helmsman you have your orders: Let's get moving," ordered the captain into his comm link.

~

Delaney had point and Kyle held to starboard, with Graham hanging back as rearguard. Just as they were about to emerge from the asteroid field, Delaney flashed his running lights and used his lateral thrusters to snug up close to the last large asteroid. Matsuo and Kyle took their cue and flew as close as they could, twisting their attitude to minimize profile with the wide, but flat, shuttle. Graham took position aft of the shuttle. Against the starry void they saw a formation of corporate fighters pass first, and then the immense side of the cruiser *Viksholm* appeared, sliding massively past them on a heading toward the anomaly. The great ship's primary thrusters appeared to be at maximum, but it takes tremendous thrust to propel that much mass. Farther out two corvettes and a destroyer passed, with a sprinkling of fighters on picket, in pairs and quads. Then, just above their sheltering asteroid, a quad of corporate gunboats passed parallel with the cruiser, like outriders alert for ambush. Matsuo searched the spectrum for the *Jade Temple*'s beacon, and after finding it, sent a binary laser signal detailing the number and type of ships heading toward the anomaly.

The *Jade Temple* acknowledged to their exact position using binary laser transmission, ending with a 'standby' sequence. After about two minutes orders were received to make best undetected speed to rendezvous away from the anomaly. The *Jade Temple* would pick them up. The signalman added that another destroyer had been detected, approaching from the direction of the modulus.

Steve and Bobby had only just reached the *Jade Temple*'s bridge. Tibs looked grim. The *Jade Temple* came about, to run from the destroyer toward the anomaly.

Tibs explained, "We cannot afford the time it would take to dismantle that destroyer in battle. She has her sensors on us, and transmitted our position and bearing to the rest of their flotilla. If we stand to fight the others would surely catch up, and we would be in quite a bind. With the energy absorption advantage of our improved shield capacitors give we could probably take the cruiser, but add in the two destroyers and two corvettes and we would be dangerously outgunned. We have only a limited number of missiles, and our new heavy beam can only focus fire on one target at a time. So we will improvise and use whatever advantage we can create." Tibs winked at Bobby.

"Bobby," asked Tibs, "I read the reports that you and Steve transmitted while returning. I am curious: Why didn't you let the man in the maintenance shuttle die? For that matter, why did you save his life?"

"Do we really want to talk philosophy now?" Bobby was incredulous. "Here we are getting ready for a naval engagement and you want to know why I ..."

"Yes, Bobby, if you would please humor an old man. You see, it was illogical to save his life. You created more trouble for yourself and put yourself in greater danger than necessary. You could have let him die on that shuttle and just flown into the docking bay. That would have been much simpler. Do you get my point?"

"Yes, Tibs," Bob sighed. "You want me to confirm that free will exists, right?"

Tibs nodded.

"Well, I don't really know," Bobby observed. "It seemed the right thing to do, so I did it. It doesn't seem like it should matter whether it was free will if it were good."

Tibs looked delighted, clapping his hands and rocking backward in a good humored chuckle. "You see Steven? That's why Bobby is qualified to fly as an Aldebar! His mind and his spirit are as Aldebari as I am. Despite his birth in Corporate space."

Bobby was puzzled, and looked thoughtfully at Tibs.

Steve objected, "But Tibs you were pressing Bobby to admit that free will exists. His answer tells us the jury is still out, but you seem delighted. I confess I don't understand."

"Steven," Tibs began to reply, then looked down at his hands. He looked up at the ceiling, then back at Steve. " I was indeed pressuring him. Although it would have been easier for him to agree, he chose to question the question itself, rather than obediently accept my authoritative assertion." Tibs looked back at his hands. "But that is not the whole of it, Steve. Bobby identified that in the face of the good, freedom is a lesser issue, even irrelevant. That insight is so much like me that I cannot help but be delighted."

Then, Tibs looked away and became serious once more. "So now we turn to lesser matters. Difficult matters, but lesser. I feel better knowing that at least something important was accomplished this day, despite all this combat."

"Kinkaid?" he asked the air.

"Yes Tibs?" Kinkaid replied.

"Is the destroyer in position?"

"Yes, Tibs, she is hot on our stern, nearly within missile range."

"Very good. Do you recall our session in the simulator when I took out your frigate?"

Kinkaid paused. "Yes Tibs I recall the trick. Most unfair, I might add."

"You are quite right. Otherwise you certainly would have won, I confess. But do you see a current application that might be useful?"

"On it, One."

Tibs looked very pleased with himself.

~

Captain Kruczewski pondered his charts as a report came in over the comm from the destroyer *Ocean City*. "Aldebari cruiser has come to a bearing that will take her to the anomaly. She's accelerating smartly. Will come in range in roughly two minutes. Permission to engage?"

"If you see a good shot, go ahead and take it, but I doubt you'll distract her enough to slow her down. Otherwise, just maintain contact no matter what she does and keep us advised so we can join you with more convincing muscle. Repeat: Weapons free, but your primary is to maintain contact and report, over" Kruczewski ordered. He directed the helmswoman to adjust course toward the anomaly and where he expected them to make contact. He glanced at the chronometer, thinking again that battle seems more about waiting than shooting.

The comm from the destroyer *Ocean City* reawakened to an open mike, with sounds of alarm and chaos. In the background someone warned, 'Mines! Mines!'.

The *Ocean City's* commander clearly wasn't worried about his live mike as he ordered his helm hard to port. But it was too late for the *Ocean City* to avoid mines the Aldebari had unexpectedly lain in her path. No matter how he tried to turn: the powerful inertia compensator could not quickly overcome the *Ocean City's* forward momentum.

The *Ocean City's* comms shut off and Kruczewski labored mightily to control his dismay for the sake of his command. He waited tensely for a report. Assuming the ship survived he knew the *Ocean City* would be bedlam running damage control. Mines pose a nasty surprise, since they aren't moving fast enough to be stopped by the warship's shields, nor were they directed energy that could be absorbed. Mines just sit there at whatever velocity they were lain, waiting for something to trigger them. Yet anti-ship mines are so powerful that anything less than a capital ship had little chance of surviving the encounter.

Mentally Kruczewski invoked damnation on the Adebari captain for the tactics' perfidy.

"*Viksholm* do you read?" asked the commander of the *Ocean City*.

"Affirmative *Ocean City*. What's your status?"

"Sir, we have major damage in our fore-starboard quarter. Forward magazine was not compromised. We have casualties but I don't know yet how many. To maintain atmosphere we hardened and reduced our shields to the skin. Sir, we are no longer battleworthy. I request permission to retire from the fight."

"*Ocean City* can you make it to the Mining Facility on your own?"

"Affirmative Captain. We can still make way. Maneuvering thrusters are undamaged even if engineering determines the main engines are unstable. We need to get the *Ocean City* out of the fight, there's no real question about it. I'm just glad she held together. I still have the Aldebari cruiser on scope but she is reaching my outer band. Captain, just nail the bastard's hide to the bulkhead for us, sir, for my crew's sake."

"I'll do my damnedest, *Ocean City*. Return to port and have a tall one for me. *Viksholm* out."

~

The Corporate cruiser and her escorts moved beyond sensor range. Delaney judged it was safe to move from the shelter of the asteroid and led the shuttle and Graham out of hiding from among the asteroids toward the rendezvous coordinates designated by Tibs. The designated location was literally in the middle of nowhere. It was highly unlikely that an enemy search algorithm would ever suggest it.

Behind them, a corporate scout rose from behind a smaller asteroid, noting their classes and course. The scout transmitted the information to the cruiser *Viksholm* by laser.

Unaware of the stealthy scout shadowing them, Delaney kept their speed down to reduce visible emissions and held a course on tangent until they were well out of sensor range of the asteroid field, then once he felt sure they weren't being observed corrected course. Arriving at the rendezvous he scanned for the Jade Temple's beacon hidden in the background noise and was gratified to see she was there waiting for them. At first just a tiny jewel among the stars,

Delaney gradually gained sight of her distinctive shape dimly lit by the distant local sun. The *Jade Temple* had diverted as soon as the crippled *Ocean City* was left behind out of sensor range. The rendezvous would delay their access to the anomaly, but that was unavoidable.

Just as the fighters and assault shuttle were about to enter the *Jade Temple*'s docking bay, long range sensors detected the corporate scout. "I think we've been made, Tibs" reported Graham.

"We see him, Graham: we will be gone soon." Tibs set their course once more for the anomaly. He pondered the presence of the scout and what it meant. He did not want to underestimate the opposition. Once the scout was out of sensor range Tibs ordered another course change, anticipating that the enemy might lay mines along his last known course. He also dispatched a picket of fighters in pairs and quads to detect any further shadowing.

~

Captain Kruczewski had something different in mind to surprise the Aldebari. He knew that before the Aldebar could deceptively traverse to the modulus, instead of the anomaly, there would be warships on-station there to cut off his quarry's other possible escape route. Around the anomaly Kruczewski's corvettes sowed a minefield capable of shredding the Aldebar into confetti. The captain was pleased with the irony of trapping the Aldebar captain with mines after what he had done to the *Ocean City*. The only other escape option would be to strike out across space itself, leaving her out of the picture altogether for the foreseeable future. Cruisers can go fast, but not fast enough to transit interstellar space without a modulus. Kruczewski watched his viewscreen as the corvettes worked to complete the spherical pattern of proximity mines around the warp in space. In every direction, at the edge of the *Viksholm*'s sensors, he deployed fighters to effectively double his detection range.

~

Aboard the *Jade Temple* the newly arrived corporate scientists were shown their spartan quarters, but what they most wanted was to engage their Aldebari colleagues in conversation and to set up their various instruments. In particular, they wanted to work on the extendable energy-absorbing modulinium vanes and their interfaces with the shields, as well as the shield generation plant itself. Their requests were driving security up the wall until Tibs issued specific clearances for them. A small element of their team was already in the lab testing the modulinium-inlaid steel and ceramic housing of the vanes to discover their properties and calibrate the rest of their instruments. In the lab these people were a marvel of inspiration and efficiency. Elsewhere they seemed as clumsy as large birds walking on the ground with nowhere to put their wings. In the lab it was as if they could soar again, inspired by what they were doing, completely adept.

The *Jade Temple*'s leading pickets detected the corporate perimeter ahead, and battle stations sounded. The scientists raced to squeeze in one more measurement before finally being herded back into the stations in the lab. There they sat buckled in, rapt before their readouts and screens, running mathematical models and checking to ensure they had ample storage in their memory banks to integrate their models.

The Aldebari fighters started to tangle with the outermost corporate fighters, so Tibs called for them to disengage as soon as possible and return to the ship. He hoped to get through the defenders and into the anomaly in one pass. One by one the fighters disengaged and docked, parking their ships in orderly ranks. The automated systems secured the fighters against becoming dislodged in the event the *Jade Temple* sustained a severe hit. The pilots remained at the ready in their cockpits with engines warm, just in case they were once again ordered to defend the ship.

The *Viksholm* launched the first salvo with four of her long range Archangel missiles. The powerful high-velocity standoff missiles screamed toward the *Jade Temple* long before the Aldebari could effectively strike back. Kinkaid responded with eight mid-range Shrike anti-missiles and keyed in weapons' release for his coherent beam, short range point defenses. The Archangels displayed surprisingly effective countermeasures. Only one Archangel exploded early, hit by a Shrike. The remaining three flared out, going ballistic at very high velocity. Each looked like a sure hit until the Aldebar's defensive beams lanced out at each, pocking their surfaces with small craters in a staccato dance of deadly bright energies. Two Archangels detonated safely beyond the *Jade Temple*'s shields but the fourth struck the shield, unloading tremendous explosive force. The metal remnants of its casing sprayed viciously into the hull, punching the armor plating with enough force to make the ship reverberate like a bell.

"Tibs", said Kinkaid, "Imaging has detected reduced luminosity at the anomaly. Normally the luminosity is constant. Imaging suggests the reduction isn't consistent with what would be expected from a warship moving in front of it. They think it could be a result from several small asteroids, maybe fighters, or possibly anti-shipping mines deployed, blocking some of the radiance. We are still too far away for our optics to resolve the images."

"I don't recall any asteroids nearby when we emerged, do you?" Tibs asked, his fingers stroking his chin. "Clearly we need to fly closer without committing to a headlong rush for the anomaly, but I don't want to stop within their firing range. Have the helm veer outside of the destroyer and we'll give them something to think about. We will make a high speed pass. Direct imaging and the other sensor sections to prepare to gather all the information we need in this one pass."

Kinkaid paused a second. "Their cruiser just launched another salvo, probably more Archangels judging from the thrust and acceleration. The rearming cycle appears to be just over a minute."

"Kinkaid: who is our helmsman?"

"Helmswoman, sir, and Kira's our best," Kinkaid responded.

"Right. Ask Kira whether she can keep our forward aspect toward the enemy when we pass by on our firing run."

The helmswoman responded directly using Tibs' formal honorific, "One, the *Jade Temple* cannot generate enough side-thrust to spin like a fighter, and even if we could the stresses might destroy her. I'm sorry, sir."

The ship's armor rang again, like a great bell.

"Two Archangels reached the shield that time," reported Kinkaid. "Tibs, we are now close enough for them to maintain thrust all the way in."

"The shields are holding up, I trust?"

"The shields are fine. I am using more Shrikes than I like at this range, and they aren't very effective against these upgraded Archangels," said Kinkaid.

"We may need them later more than we need them now. For all the Archangels advances they don't seem to have effective warheads," Tibs observed.

"I believe that is only because of our capacity to absorb their energy, Tibs. My metrics indicate our old shields would be in serious trouble by now, but the new capacitor is still holding them firm."

~

Captain Kruczewski shook his head at the last report. "Their shields should have flickered by now. Change the pattern to fire one Archangel at a time. I want to see sixty second reloads, and a launch every fifteen seconds."

"Aye-aye, captain," acknowledged Master Chief Singh as he turned from his console to give the order.

"And chief, ready the mid-range missiles. Badgers, aren't they?"

"No, captain, we have Scimitars in the magazine, sir. Badgers have been unavailable since last year because of Resistance sabotage."

"Very well, Scimitars it is. But we don't have much time, chief".

"We'll be ready, sir"

Kruczewski returned to his command chart. The ship shuddered noticeably as another Archangel left the launcher.

"The Aldebari cruiser has changed her bearing and is accelerating, sir" reported Tracking from Navigation. "Ten degrees or so, sir. On her current heading she'll pass just off the *Jason*'s port."

The captain's eyes narrowed. Another Archangel left the rails. A flickering finger on the buttons and his view changed from a plotting chart to a viewer trained on the incoming Aldebari cruiser. Even at maximum resolution it was hard to see her lines clearly, but she was rapidly closing.

"*Jason* did you see the course change?"

"We did indeed, *Viksholm*. We are ready to lay into her."

"Ready torpedoes aft as well to run up her exhaust when she shows you her fantail, *Jason*."

"We will be ready"

"Sir." It was an ensign at his elbow, a pretty girl young enough to be his daughter. "We have positively identified the Aldebari cruiser as the *Jade Temple*, sir. She has had some modifications that threw us off for a while but we are certain of the ID, sir."

The captain sat forward, a furrow creasing his brow. "Thank you, ensign. Wait: What modifications?"

"She has a new weapons mount forward, sir. Energy we believe. Also some new apertures on her sidewalls, but we haven't been able to identify them. Possibly new missile tubes."

The captain sat back in his chair once more. "Well, well: the *Jade Temple*." Kruczewski steepled his fingers. "Let us see how well you earned your reputation, Tibs."

~

As the *Jade Temple* closed the range she launched her own anti-ship missiles, all targeting the destroyer, while the *Jason, Viksholm* and the two corvettes, *Garand* and *Springfield,* answered in kind.

The incoming hail of missiles and railgun projectiles continuously impacted the *Jade Temple*'s shields, and the casings and shrapnel from the ordnance occasionally struck against her hull plates. Kinkaid's Shrikes were well used to help fend off the incoming missiles, but the rail projectiles weren't targetable. Damage control teams ran constantly, trying to help the automated systems check for any hull breaches. Her shields, while flaring and fluctuating in opacity as energy washed through them, held firm. The excessive energy was channeled to the remarkable modulinium absorbers which were beginning to heat and radiate with the charge.

The destroyer *Jason* put up a valiant fight under the onslaught from the *Jade Temple*. The *Jason's* shields intermittently flickered and died, only to spring up again as the generators rejuvenated, yet anything that struck in the brief down cycle caused serious damage, breaching her hull in multiple hits.

As the *Jade Temple* passed broadside to the *Jason*, both ships unloaded on each other. The *Jason* reeled and began to slowly twist under internal explosions, losing control in the onslaught. Casualties ran high from explosions and loss of atmosphere. The hull was breached, and her superstructure was shredded askew, yet *Jason* continued to fight.

The *Jade Temple*'s new forward energy weapon, muzzle extending through her shield, ceased firing on the *Jason's* ravaged hull. Tibs diverted the new weapon to focus fire upon the nearest of the mines blocking access to the anomaly. The mine remained inert, moving only slightly away as its armor vaporized. The Corporate mines were clearly well-armored. The beam could have destroyed them, but given the speed of the Jade Temple's pass there wasn't enough time.

The Aldebari cruiser pulled aft of the *Jason,* heading off with maximum thrust to get out of range of the corporate weapons and come about. The Jason looked like a wreck, twisted metal drifting from her, burning gases and flickering sparks deep within her torn hull. But at her stern a surviving marine gunnery sergeant fired her battery of six heavy torpedoes at the retreating enemy.

Torpedoes travel faster than any warship, but not so fast that they will be stopped by shields. If their sensors can maintain acquisition their range is sufficient permit them to run down a target moving away at emergency speed. The *Jade Temple's* aft defenses were fully armed and at the ready, but until the torpedoes crept closer they could do little except take manual pot shots with ballistics and watch.

Kinkaid launched a flight of six fighters who would try and interdict the torpedoes. A minute later, he launched a second flight.

~

Captain Kruczewski was appalled to have gained nothing from the engagement but another broken destroyer. He watched dejectedly as the torpedoes chased the Aldebari without success. If he got nothing more out of this fight than his life and the secret to those damnable Aldebari shields he would consider it a victory.

"Corvette *Garand* on the comm, sir"

"Put him on."

"*Viksholm* this is *Garand.* Should we pursue the Aldebari, sir? We are just sitting ducks here while he has all the room in space to hide."

"*Garand*: Negative your recommendation. He can only escape through this anomaly, and if we move he can pick off the mines while leading us on a game of *Fox and Hounds*. We must remain here to prevent his escape."

"Sir, I didn't think anyone could transit an anomaly. Are you sure that is how he got into the sector?"

"Absolutely, commander. There is no other way for him to have reached this sector without passing through moduli we control. Besides, if he didn't want access to this anomaly he wouldn't be fighting so hard for it."

The *Garand* commander fell silent to digest the incredible information. "I am having trouble believing that he was able to take everything we threw at him and survived. His shields hardly fluctuated. We might as well have been taking pictures for all the damage we inflicted."

The response prompted Kruczewski to check with Imaging to see what could be learned about the Aldebar.

"I suspect whatever she did to her shields relates to how she survived the transit of the anomaly, *Garand*. I have sent a request for reinforcements. We must hold our position and defend the mines. The Aldebar will pay for the visit, and the longer she takes running around out there the better. We will have plenty of help here soon."

"Aye-aye, *Viksholm*. *Garand* out."

"Ensign, find out what naval intelligence has found from our imagery of the *Jade Temple*."

~

The *Jade Temple* survived the torpedoes through the skills of her fighter pilots and the accuracy of the ship's onboard point defenses. Tibs requested full assessments on damage and casualties, as well as inventory of their remaining ordnance. Then, Tibs called a meeting of the ship's leadership, inviting Steven as leader of his people, the chief engineer, and the leader of the corporate science team. Bobby snuck in with Steve, and everyone pretended to not notice the young man's presence. Also attending were Kinkaid, his three Master pilots, the ship's ordinance master, and Lieutenant Matsuo representing the commandos.

"We are confronted with a situation," Tibs began "In order to return to friendly space we must traverse the anomaly. I'm certain that by now the Board of Corporations have invested the modulus with even heavier defenses than we face here. In all likelihood we have only a little while before their reinforcements arrive.

"If we can enter the anomaly intact, I feel confident the technology that first permitted our entry into this sector will get us through again. I believe we can probably survive the combined fire of the assembled forces opposing our exit, due to the amazing energy absorption capabilities our experimental equipment. However, that equipment has its limitations. It can absorb tremendous amounts of energy, but we have no way to shed quickly what it has stored except by transiting the anomaly and feeding that energy back into our shields. Without something to draw off the power from the shields they would overload and catastrophically fail. It takes too long to bleed the energy back into our modulinium in the inertial and gravitic wavelengths to dissipate it that way. If the shields overload, we have no way to save ourselves except by ejecting the new modulinium wings away from us. And if we do that we cannot transit the anomaly. After the fight we just survived the wings are at approximately seventy percent estimated capacity. We cannot afford to make another firing run or we will fail our mission and be unable to return home.

"What's more, we cannot extend the vanes until we have entered the anomaly because anything we extend out beyond the shields will surely be destroyed in the firestorm we expect.

"There's also the matter of the mines. Corporate anti-shipping mines are much like our own. They are just as powerful, and more heavily armored. We cannot detonate them from afar with either missiles or energy weapons. If we had heavy rail launchers we could probably batter them into the anomaly but unfortunately we don't have those weapons on this ship. True, given time we could push them into the anomaly using multiple high-explosive warheads on our missiles, but the problem there is the guidance system. Mines don't emit an energy signal for the missiles to lock onto, and we don't carry any of the interferometric density guidance systems. We might try and rig visual guidance, but I don't believe we have enough parts aboard to adapt the required number of missiles.

"Frankly, I'm at a loss to suggest an acceptable action plan. So I turn to you. Does anyone have an idea that can help us?"

For a moment everyone remained quiet, deep in thought.

One of the master pilots, Monk Pradesh, speaking in a firm, almost defiant voice suggested "My pilots claim the honor of pushing the mines into the anomaly."

Immediately another flight leader, Williams, complemented the idea but argued that the honor should be for his pilots, by reason of seniority. A third master pilot, Fisk, volunteered it would be his pilots' honor to defend them all, since his group had the most kills while suffering the fewest casualties.

Tibs raised his hands: "Peace, for now. Your proposals have been heard and they have merit, but we need to solve a few more problems before making a decision. A small flotilla of warships will be taking shots at you while you attempt such a delicate operation. If your idea is chosen, Pradesh, we would still have to work out the timing of everything. Our ability to absorb energy is down to only thirty percent capacity. How are we going to withstand the punishment delivered by the cruiser and those corvettes? We have to stay in-system to pick you up before transiting the anomaly. I refuse to leave any of my pilots behind.

"Instead of leaping to the first solution let's think this through. Before we commit to anything, by discussing this in depth we may find a better way. But, Monk Pradesh, you have given us a good start."

The engineer was dubious and spoke up: "The nacelles on our fighters are rounded and, while they are sturdy with armor, I am not confident they can handle the stress of pushing those massive mines. Further they are round, and since the mines are also round it will be difficult to push them where you want them to go, and even that assumes they have been set to only trigger for masses greater than our fighters. They might not be."

The guest corporate scientist at the table timorously cleared his throat and raised his hand. Tibs nodded to him to continue and everyone else quieted to hear what he had to say.

"First a point of order, sir. I don't wish to offend our host but I hadn't heard your rank so I don't know how to address you. Are you the captain? Admiral?"

"Call me Tibs, Doctor. Everyone does. Talk to me as though I were your uncle and everything will be fine."

"My uncle?" The suggestion confused the doctor, but he quickly recovered from the distraction. "Well, this is in regard to the problem of overloaded shields. I noticed you have a large energy weapon on your ship."

Everyone nodded at him. "Well, uh, I presume that when you use it you actually extend it beyond the shield. Well, of course you do: you must. Well, there is no reason why, well maybe there is a reason if you don't have enough conductor I suppose..."

"No reason why... what?" Lieutenant Matsuo asked.

The scientist turned to him, the palms of his hands fluttering like white wings as he attempted to express himself.

"Well, you should be able to run a feed from the energy rods to the power supply of the weapon and bleed off the excess energy that way. I mean, you probably already thought of that, right? What was I thinking..."

"No doctor, none of us thought of that. It sounds a wonderful idea." Tibs turned to engineering "Will it work? Do we have enough conductive cabling aboard?"

The engineer had left his mouth partly open as he stared at the scientist, then caught himself. "I'll have to see, Tibs. The conductor can't present too much resistance over that distance or it will fuse. We can't approach the rods themselves for the heat... but maybe we could patch into their shield feeds. Still..."

~

Captain Kruczewski was read the messages from the *Abram's Solace* , the Vera & Rodriquez corporation's flagship, together with her escorts which had just transited the modulus. It had been several hours since the *Jade Temple*'s run and the destruction of the *Jason*. The flag battlegroup was making way at flank speed, and Kruczewski considered it was about time. Putting military matters in the hands of accountants had its benefits, but it came with a significant downside.

Imaging had only confirmed that there was some sort of aperture capped by what looked like protective disks punctuating the *Jade Temple's* sidewalls and the presence of a new energy weapon on her forward deck. In the fight that had cost him the *Jason*, the Aldebari hadn't launched any missiles from the oddly shaped apertures, so what they were and how they were to be used remained a mystery.

"Sir, we are sensing high energy discharge off our port beam."

"Can you identify the source?"

"I'd hazard a guess it's the Aldebari heavy beam weapon, sir. But if that's what it is, then it's strange that they would fire it continuously like this. I don't think we have any assets out there at which they'd be shooting. Yet sensor analysis says it's output appears to be more powerful than what the Jade Temple was using during the battle earlier. It is hard to judge without knowing how far away she is. Nevertheless, if you look at the graphic analysis on screen twelve, sir, you will see the signatures are very similar."

The Captain consulted screen twelve and had to agree the two looked quite similar but the depicted intensity indeed appeared significantly greater than it had when firing on the *Jason*. Tibs surely hadn't pulled his punches on his first pass, so this new data didn't make any sense, the captain reflected.

"Is it moving?"

"If it is, then it is either moving directly away or towards us, sir.

Same bearing. It is too far to tell, otherwise."

"Keep an eye on it then and let me know if there are any changes. Try and patch in with the Corvettes and send them wide. Perhaps we can triangulate and get a fix on them. Once we have an accurate measurement transmit their position and bearing continuously. The flagship's main rail guns have no practical maximum range. They might be able to plot their ordnance well enough to solve our problem even before they get here."

"Yes, sir" the intelligence officer acknowledged. Captain Kruczewski scanned once more his available assets: he was as ready as he could be except for the nagging headache he always got when running on too little sleep. He had an awful lot of fighter pilots without corresponding spacecraft. His inventory of space-ready fighters was deplorable, but there was nothing to be done about that now. Then again...

"Hanger deck"

"Sir?"

"Send a shuttle full of the pilots standing around with their hands in their pockets back to the mining facility to appropriate the *Ariel's* inventory. Issue them requisitions for the transfer to *Viksholm* so the bean counters don't run crying to command about it."

"Yes, sir!"

"Sir, the *Jade Temple* is off port incoming, sir!" it was Naval Intelligence again.

"Have you sent her position and bearing to the Flag as I asked?"

"Sir, Yes sir!"

"How about sharing that info with me then?"

"It should be on your screen two, sir"

"Very good."

"*Garand*" the captain sent to the lead Corvette.

"Ready, sir!"

"Commander, when the *Jade Temple* moves into range I want you and the *Springfield* to attack her flanks and stern where hopefully her armor is thin. We'll focus here on trying to get their shields down."

"Very good sir, *Garand* out."

Kruczewski scanned his assets once more, trying to think of anything that remained undone. Then he sighed and rubbed his eyes. "The only thing left is to wait." he muttered.

~

Aboard the *Jade Temple* the techs reluctantly finished attaching four metal prongs onto the nacelle of each of Monk Pradesh's fighters so they could reliably push the mines into the anomaly. The energy in the absorption rods or vanes was slowly bled off into the forward turret's beam weaponry in an inelegant sprawl of conductors whose only merit was that it appeared to work without overheating. Already the charged capacity of the rods had fallen to 60 percent.

The *Jade Temple* was moving in on the anomaly more slowly than on their first pass in order to arrive at the warp in space only after the fighters had done their job, and allowing sufficient time to recover all surviving fighters. The engineers' biggest concern was that the energy being bled off by the beam weapon exceeded the weapon circuitry's design tolerance, but there was little to be done about that except hope. There was some reassurance because engineers, by ancient tradition, always understate the allowable specs on everything, just to allow for the inevitable dumb human who always pushes beyond stated tolerances.

"Standby for launch. Pilots perform preflight inspections," came the flight-master's instructions over the comms. In the glare of the hanger lights the welding crews wrapped up their leads, gathered their welding stubs from the deck, and stowed everything away so that nothing would be out of place when Tibs arrived for inspection.

Steve commenced his walk-around, checking the structural integrity, external systems, and weapon systems on his fighter.

Everything appeared to be in perfect condition. The flight-master then issued the command to form up, and Delaney, Graham, Bobby, Kyle, and Steve formed their own flight along with the three Aldebari flights of six pilots each. Bob would fly a standard Aldebari light fighter. Kyle and the rest were in medium fighters but, like Steve, were irregular in their individualized munitions loadouts.

The pair of very large doors in the rear of the hanger opened. Tibs and Kinkaid walked out of the darkness into the brightly lit main hanger. Steve saw the silhouette of something big back in there as Tibs approached the pilots, but when his gaze rested on Tibs he had to stare: Tibs was in a pressure suit with a helmet under one arm and some sort of deep reddish enameled rod or stick at his side, attached to his utility belt. It might be some sort of fancy walking stick but it didn't really look like one. The Aldebari pilots were uncharacteristically buzzing with quiet crosstalk, sounding almost excited. Kinkaid looked distinctly uncomfortable. Something was up, and that's for sure.

"Pilots!" addressed Tibs.

"ONE!" the Aldebari shouted in unison, and as they did they snapped to attention as if on the parade ground. Steve and the *Perry Station* detail stood at attention. The shout rang on the hanger deck.

"Rest easy my friends." and the pilots stood at parade rest, looking toward Tibs.

"If the *Jade Temple* is to survive this we must succeed in our missions. We must not fail her. I cannot sit by while you are out fighting for her honor and glory. Nor will I allow myself to return to the ship until every one of you is back aboard. I will consider it my greatest honor and privilege to fly with you for this engagement."

Williams, Pradesh, and Fisk stepped forward. "It is we, your monks, who are honored," said Williams.

Tibs shook his head gently, and with a shy smile said "You do not fully realize that *you* are the *Jade Temple*. *You* are my heart, my arms, and the light of my mind. I vow I will not leave you here. I will not willingly quit the field to return to the *Temple* until every last one of you is aboard." As he said it he looked squarely at Bobby and Steve.

Steve could swear Tibs' eyes were shining.

"Some of you may have noticed I am wearing the sword of my ancestors." As he said it, he drew forth a length of gently curved bright steel from what Steve had mistaken for a stick. "Since ages before the Aldebari were Aldebar, before the Legion and Board of Corporations separated from our common heritage, this sword descended through the generations, parent to heir, for so many years we do not even really know when it originated. For all this time, however, it has been revered as the soul of my ancestors. Of *our* ancestors, for by now you should know you are my family.

"It is by this sword that I promise you: We will achieve our objective or die trying.

"Be at peace, my brothers and sisters, for you know I neither promise lightly, nor do I often die."

"Kinkaid!"

"One?"

"You have the helm."

A shadow flickered across Kinkaid's face. "Return to us, Tibs: Without you the *Temple* is empty." replied Kinkaid with a slight bow.

Then the lights turned on in the back hanger illuminating the oldest gunboat hull Steve had ever seen. Polished to a bright finish, the hull was apparently made of some kind of emerald-colored alloy. In her racks was an impressive loadout of ordnance.

As Tibs turned to his spacecraft, the rest of the pilots turned to theirs.

~

"Incoming fighters on scope, Sir"

Captain Kruczewski snapped awake, realizing he had momentarily drifted off while waiting for action. And now it had arrived. He quickly checked the position of his reinforcements and realized they were still traversing the sector and were now no closer than the Trondheim research and mining facility.

Examining his display he saw the Aldebari had fielded four full flights against him, but the *Jade Temple* was laying back, moving slowly. Looking closer he saw the tracking computer considered four of the fighters in one flight neutrals, since their symbols shone gray instead of the green he expected for the Aldebar.

"Do we have an ID for those neutrals?" he asked Sensors.

"Negative, sir. However we did get a report from a scout shortly after leaving Trondheim that identified unknown neutral fighter craft escorting an Aldebari assault shuttle leaving the asteroid belt."

"Ensure this information is recorded in the log. Those so-called *neutrals* are enemy combatants and shall be dealt with as such. As evidence we can later cite the assault on Trondheim and flying with the Aldebar in an overtly hostile attack on corporate assets."

"Aye aye, captain."

He scanned his roster of able fighters and came up a few short of matching the Aldebari numbers. However he would have one of his two corvettes to throw in with the *Viksholm*'s superior firepower when the *Jade Temple* was in range.

"Launch all fighters to counter them." *Springfield:* I want you to attack those fighters as well, to put the odds in our favor."

The *Springfield*'s commander acknowledged his orders.

Meanwhile the Aldebari fighters had drawn closer, and

Kruczewski felt curious about that oddball flight. He switched his display to digital optics and zoomed to maximum magnification. The supposed 'neutrals' looked like generic medium fighters, plus an Aldebari light fighter escorting an ancient-looking green Aldebari gunship. Kruczewski panned left to look at the other Aldebari craft and saw the usual mix of mediums and lights. Nothing remarkable there, except they were Aldebar, deep in corporate space. That green gunboat looked at least last generation, maybe earlier. Ah, Kruczewski thought, they were responding to the approaching corporate fighters. The neutrals seemed to be following rather than leading that flight. As they swept into new formations, adapting to the aggressive flying of the corporate pilots, the other flights also seemed to fly protectively around the old gunship.

"I wonder... Communications, patch me into our pilots' channel I'd like to listen to their chatter for a bit."

"Patching you in, sir"

"...snug it up there blue four..."

"One of them has a lock on me, I'm going evasive"

More of the pilots reported with alarm that the Aldebari had gained targeting locks on them. Kruczewski decreased his zoom slightly to gain a better view. In classic textbook fashion he expected the Aldebari to expend their missiles early, trying to improve their odds before the fight was joined. Kruczewski was alarmed over the number of missiles incoming on his fighters. He noticed that old gunship launched, acquired a new target and launched, and again acquired a target and launched in rapid sequence.

The captain could only watch. He gritted his teeth as his fighters twisted and turned trying to break lock. One by one the impressively fast Aldebar missiles found their targets. It seemed very few missed. Kruczewski counted his survivors engaged in the tangled action and kept losing track of those he had counted. In the middle of it all that damned green Aldebari gunboat and its escorts swept back and forth chewing up the corporate fighters.

"Springfield?" No answer. He turned up the volume to hear his pilots cursing their enemies.

"Springfield!"

"Sir!"

The corvette struggled to get clear shots.

"A week's R&R when this is over if you can take out that old green gunboat" the captain barked.

The Corvette seemed to lose its indecision and maneuvered toward the gunboat that swept along, firing hardballs from his magnetic rails and connecting. Its neutral escorts seemed to take turns covering his back, interposing their shields and armor between the *Springfield* and his prey, and all the while that green gunboat kept hammering corporate fighters.

"Sir!" Kruczewski looked up from the scene in his display. "The anomaly! Look at the mines!" It was naval intelligence who noticed what the Aldebar were up to. The captain panned his optic feed to the anomaly and watched as one of several Aldebari fighters nosed up to a mine and pushed it into the anomaly, then turned away and maneuvered for another. The captain panned back to the *Jade Temple*.

"Are you still feeding the Aldebari cruiser's bearing and speed to Flag?" the captain asked.

"Yes Sir: Flag has been firing but it is a very long shot"

Sure enough, even as he watched, a massive projectile from the battleship *'Abram's Solace'* hurtled through space toward the *Jade Temple*. The Aldebar clearly spotted it and was trying to get out of the way. The captain involuntarily cheered as the round shoved the Jade Temple aside as it passed through her shield, narrowly missing a direct hit. She was hurt, but accelerated and changed course.

But the integrity of the minefield was being compromised.

"*Garand*: Destroy those fighters around the anomaly NOW!"

"Aye, Captain."

~

Another hit by the corvette punched through and rang heavily off Steve's armor, making his boat dip and stagger.

"Tibs my armor is getting thin, even though we have been rotating your cover. I don't think you can pull him far enough without us, but if we keep this up we are going to start popping hulls" Steve advised.

"Steven, this old girl is still pretty nimble, and they don't make armor like this anymore. Recommend you boys back off and give me some maneuvering room: Besides, if he is getting shots at me he's more likely to not realize he is entering the killing field."

"What makes you think the corvette's after you, Tibs? Maybe she's after all of us," said Graham.

"No, they're after Tibs. Just you watch." said Kyle. "I think that's why he chose that old green relic of his: To divert their attention from the guys at the anomaly."

"Kyle's psychic, I keep telling you guys," Steve laughed.

So they gradually backed off from Tibs. He started his old ship dancing, rocking back and forth just long enough to set a pattern before he'd break it, rolling and swerving the other way but always moving closer to the approaching *Jade Temple.*

Kinkaid had interposed the anomaly between the *Jade Temple* and the still distant battleship. For all the *Abram's Solice'* mass and power, those long shots never re-emerged from the anomaly once they entered, at least not on this side of the galaxy. That didn't seem to faze whomever was directing the battleship's fire because the rounds kept hurtling in, only to disappear in the seething energies of the warp.

The *Springfield* scored hits on Tibs but his old gunship wasn't struck as often as his escorts riding cover had been. The Corvette seemed to be falling for Tibs' gambit, forging ahead eagerly, right up until the *Jade Temple* unloaded on the *Springfield* with a salvo of heavy missiles and deadly bright beams of focused energy.

Before the corvette *Springfield* could turn to escape another salvo lashed her and her shields went down. The fierce energy beam of the *Jade Temple's* forward weapon ripped into the corvette's armor. The Springfield turned to flee, trailing spinning scrap metal and venting a plume of smoke and gas as she accelerated.

"Pradesh: Report!" commed Tibs.

Pradesh, too busy to respond right away, responded as quickly as he could "We are nearly finished with the mines on the near side, Tibs, but the other corsair is hammering us now, and Master Fisk's flight is having trouble peeling her off our backs so we can finish."

"Well don't worry about the far side: we will never reach it. We're on our way over and will try to lend a hand."

Tibs smoothly pivoted his gunboat and letting his thrust counter his inertia to head him back toward the anomaly. The *Springfield* was just ahead, moving toward the anomaly, and it looked like she didn't have shields.

"At times like this I always wish I had saved a couple of missiles." Tibs observed wistfully.

"Exactly why I still have two on my racks, Tibs" said Steve as he bumped up his throttle to move close enough for a missile lock. The others surged right with him.

~

For Captain Kruczewski things seemed to be falling apart. The anomaly was almost completely exposed on one side, the *Springfield* was badly damaged, and reinforcements were still too far away to effectively counter the *Jade Temple's* escape.

He checked his remaining ordnance inventory and estimated he couldn't disable the Aldebari cruiser without bringing down her extraordinary shields.

The *Springfield* raced for the anomaly ahead of the *Jade Temple*. "*Springfield*: Take up a position in front of the anomaly to block the Aldebari." Kruczewski ordered.

"Straight away, Sir." came the response.

The captain reassessed the situation visually as two missiles leapt out from the lead fighter, supposedly a neutral. Both missiles struck heavily into the *Springfield's* stern.

"*Springfield*: Report!"

"Awaiting confirmation from damage control, sir, but I think we have lost our engines."

In frustration, Kruczewski pounded his fist on the console. The *Springfield* was now ballistic, with no way to stop her inexorable course toward the anomaly, and her doom.

"If your engineering team cannot quickly get your engines online, you need to abandon the *Springfield*, Commander." Kruczewski counseled.

"Engineering has not responded, sir, but I am ordering everyone else into lifepods."

Things had quickly changed from bad to worse for the captain, and he had never felt so frustrated. His anger threatened to overwhelm his self-control. He shook with rage, panning his view back to glare at the *Jade Temple*. To his amazement, the Aldebar cruiser changed course. Her new bearing would bring her out from behind the shielding anomaly and toward the *Viksholm*. More importantly she was exposing herself to the *Abram's Solace'* massive armament. "Helm, move to meet the Aldebari, flank speed. Looks like she wants to settle this, once and for all."

"Aye-aye, captain"

"Intelligence: ensure the *Abram's Solace* is aware of the target's new bearing"

"Verifying, sir"

"Singh: fire all our remaining Archangels and ready a full salvo of Scimitars as soon as she's in range"

"On it, sir"

The Aldebari fighters that had swarmed around the *Garand* started streaming toward the *Jade Temple*, except for the green gunboat and her escorts. "That has to be Tibs." Kruczewski muttered. The old gunboat appeared to be flying right toward him. He did a barrel roll and then veered back toward the docking bay of the Jade Temple, still out of Scimitar range, even as his last four Archangels erupted from their launchers.

~

Aboard the battleship *Abram's Solace*, the new telemetry solution fed into the targeting computer for the forward main rail caused a microscopic shift in its aim. The next round, a polished 400 kilogram pellet of ferrous nickel alloy was set into position and the powerful serial array of parallel electromagnets, exerting nearly 700 megajoules, pulled and released in exquisitely calibrated sequence to accelerate the projectile at more than 10,000 meters/second. Hurtling through the frictionless vacuum of space, the projectile would travel forever at that velocity until it hit something.

~

Kinkaid's feint toward the *Viksholm* was a carefully calculated gamble. He hadn't been certain the *Viksholm* would be drawn from its position until she started moving. If all went well and she didn't change speed or course the *Viksholm* would soon be occupying the same space as the next shot from the battleship. He glanced at the time: in five, four, three, two...

As the last four Archangels struck the shields of the *Jade Temple*, the shot of the far distant *Abram's Solace* punched through the *Viksholm*'s shields, armor, and hull astern. The massive projectile cracked her hull wide open, passed completely through the ship, and then hurtled out into empty space. Lifepods that had been streaming from the *Springfield* toward the *Viksholm* diverted to head back toward the incoming battlegroup of the *Abram's Solace*. Very few lifepods now trickled from the *Viksholm's* spinning wreckage.

The *Springfield,* helpless without thrust, launched all lifepods and coasted inevitably to her destruction in the anomaly.

The old green gunboat was the last to return to the *Jade Temple*, just as Tibs had pledged. When the old ship's engines powered down and the cockpit opened Tibs received a deafening cheer from his assembled pilots. Steve grinned from ear to ear, his heart exultant as the *Jade Temple* extended her remarkable modulinium-capped wings, and passed safely from corporate space.

The *Temple*'s chief engineer, observing their passage on screen, wondered if someday an array of modulinium absorbers might be suspended from a transmission platform into an anomaly, enabling the energy they absorbed to be beamed as a limitless energy source.

Chapter 30: The Hunter

As the *Jade Temple* emerged from the anomaly into normal space, communications reported wide-spectrum interference. When the sensor array cleared the effects of the anomaly, simultaneous trouble reports swept through Tibs' command console. On his visual array, chaotic transmission signals resolved into imagery of the Aldebari Station being battered by the onslaught of Paul Harden's great black heavy cruiser. This ship, which Harden called the *Black King,* did not have vanes that would enable her passage through an anomaly, so it had to have come through the modulus.

"Harden has chosen vengeance over survival," Tibs observed. A white hot lance of energy erupted from the *Black King*'s forward battery, punching through the research station's shields and deep into the hapless superstructure. The great black ship hung arrogantly in the void, blasting apart the living quarters with selective fire. Debris floated from the installation. Bent girders, still attached to sections of seared plating, spun slowly away from the wreckage. Obviously the station had irretrievably lost her battle with the mighty warship. Shuttles, transports, and life pods trailed away toward the fledgling *Perry Station.* Fighter craft wreckage littered nearby space.

Steve worried about Lian, the lithe Aldebari dancer engaged to Kyle, his best friend and wingman. Steve realized Kyle must be going crazy. Lian lived aboard the science installation, or at least she used to live there. Steve turned from watching the receding evacuation craft to try and find his buddy.

A signal from the *Black King* opened a comm channel to Tibs, and Harden's face resolved onscreen. Steve could not help turning to listen. There was more silver in Harden's hair, and new wrinkles in his forehead. "Tibs! So good of you to show up for our little party. Unfortunately you're too late, as usual. The appetizer has been served."

Tibs did not respond.

"I see you unlocked the secret to traversing the anomaly. Think of the possibilities this technology promises! Too bad it can't help you now. You are, as ever, too late with too little to defend those who believed in you. Your allies aren't here to save you, nor save that damnable scrap of metal you call the *Jade Temple.* Nevertheless, you're here. I would be bereft of satisfaction were I to deny myself the pleasure of exacting your complete destruction." Harden seemed to savor the resonance of his every word.

The heavy black cruiser, almost as powerful as a battleship, started to slowly move under the thrust of her three main engines. She began to come about, swinging her bow threateningly toward the *Jade Temple*. Steve wondered whether *Perry Station* had also fallen to Harden's attack.

On high magnification the visual display revealed the Aldebari fighters defending the research installation had left their marks on the black cruiser. The strategic hanger bay doors were damaged and possibly unable to close. The ship's atmosphere was held by their traversable atmospheric shield.

Tibs turned to Kinkaid. "We'll probably be unable to defeat him alone in open battle, but our enhanced shields and ability to absorb and use the energy of his weapons fire should enable our survival for quite a while. Considering all the wreckage out there, Harden's fighter inventory should be nearly depleted." Tibs considered thoughtfully, and made a decision.

"Direct Lieutenant Matsuo to ready his commandos and assault shuttle to board our enemy and secure the damaged hanger as our beachhead. The lieutenant will be my tactical commander once we are aboard. Launch every able fighter we have, after ensuring our pilots are issued infantry weapons. Relay my commands to the flight leaders. Once our fighters eliminate his mobile defenses send every pilot to follow Matsuo's boarding party onto his ship. We will take them out from within." Kinkaid turned to carry out his orders.

"Intel?" Tibs asked his comm, "Has there been any signal from the local defenders?"

"Affirmative, sir. *Perry Station* has not yet been hit, but they lost most of their fighters assisting in our research station's defense. They say their remaining pilots are en route to help us here."

Tibs looked solemnly at Steve. "As I thought, you are good neighbors."

Kinkaid stood at the ready once more. Tibs turned back to him. "My friend, will you again take the Temple's helm? Will you allow me to lead our boarding action?"

Kinkaid was clearly disappointed, but he quickly covered it. "I would fight at your side, Tibs, but as you wish I will do my duty here."

Tibs nodded to him. "Remember as you have him engaged he

cannot easily move to destroy *Perry Station*."

"Kinkaid," Tibs moved closer and gripped his executive officer's arms above the elbow. Kinkaid mirrored his friend's gesture. "I recognize and respect your disappointment. You are a brother to me. But I face two conflicting challenges at the same time. I need to lead my people as I send them into a most dangerous engagement. Once we board the enemy ship if they are hit there will be no life pod to preserve them. At the same time, I need the *Temple* in the hands of a capable, ingenious and trusted commander if she is to survive at all. Thank you for being my exec, Kinkaid, and thank you for being the kind of man our descendants will sing of when they need courage."

Kinkaid put on a brave face, but underneath it Steve could see his disappointment adopt just a hint of pride at Tibs' words. Then he turned to the command console as Tibs transferred the helm with a code and selection entered at the terminal.

Kinkaid asked Steve to prepare his flight to escort Matsuo's assault shuttle once more. Steve headed down to their quarters to brief the pilots. He found Kyle shaken, leaning against a bulkhead in the ready room. Kyle tried to put on his boot but it wouldn't fit. Steve knelt to help, and then began to fasten the buckles. He looked up into Kyle's eyes and saw a man wracked with worry.

"Kyle, she may be safe and staying with the rest of the evacuees. We don't know. There is nothing we can do for her now except to finish this battle and then try to find her."

"Jeeze, Steve! I knew I shouldn't have left her there. I had a strange feeling Harden would be back, but I let my head carry me away. My brain thought he would be over there in corporate space, beyond the anomaly."

"Kyle, if you hadn't gone with us I wouldn't have made it back. You know you're the one who kept me alive through all our fights. No one else had my back. The whole mission might have failed except for you, and Harden would still have shown up here. Had you been here you would have launched to fight Harden, whatever has happened to Lian would have happened anyway, only you would be either dead on that research station, podded, or floating out there among the wreckage." Steve pointed to the images in the wall screen, wreckage from perhaps a hundred corporate and Aldebari fighters floating around the remains of the research station. "They ran out of fighters. They podded back and there were no more replacements. You would have been caught in the ready room without a boat, and been killed by that bastard. Lian would have been evacuated with the rest of the non-combatants, only instead of reuniting with you when this is over, she would have been mourning you for a lifetime."

Kyle reflected on Steve's words and nodded. "She has to be on *Perry Station*." Kyle appeared to firm up and squared his shoulders. "Sorry I lost it, Steve. Let's go make sure we stop the bastard."

"It's okay to be human, buddy" Steve reassured him. Kyle managed a small smile. Steve slapped his shoulder solidly. "Come on, we have to get the guys together and fly cover for Matsuo's marines."

"Semper Fi," Kyle said absently.

"What?" Steve stopped, puzzled. He had never previously heard those words.

Kyle's eyes focused. "It's something Matsuo's men say. It's like a good luck thing, I think. They say it when the officers aren't around."

Delaney and Graham, already suited up, joined Kyle and Steve in the ready room. Steve outlined the plan to have the rest of the pilots follow behind Matsuo's marines once opposing fighters had been removed from the equation. Graham objected that they should try and take out the shield generators as they did on the *Pyotr Velikiyer*. Steve agreed with him, but he underscored their orders to the contrary. Then he texted Graham's suggestion to Kinkaid.

Kinkaid texted back "Her shield generators are embedded: heat sinks are targetable, but too many. No point."

Steve shared the info with his team. They just nodded and looked grim.

Matsuo's marines walked their two heavy Crawlers across the hanger deck followed by the riflemen in a column of twos and loaded into the assault shuttle. Steve and the others boarded their readied fighters. Matsuo walked behind his marines with some techs, fiddling with some sort of electronic device in a carrying case. Steve sealed his hatch, released the umbilical feeds, and rose off the deck in preparation to follow. The Aldebari fighters were launched from their quick-deploy tubes. Beyond the atmosphere bubble at the hanger bay door, Steve could see them already engaging the enemy. He hoped Tibs had been right to think the corporate fighter reserves were nearly depleted.

Waiting for the launch signal in the glow of his ready lights Steve also saw the old green gunship launch.

Matsuo boarded the assault shuttle last and waited until the Aldebari fighters had finished deploying. The gunnery sergeant was checking the heavy laser turret's controls from inside his weapons station. The shuttle's thrusters glowed active as they powered up, and at last the she lifted off in the artificial gravity of the hanger and slowly moved toward egress.

Steve's flight maintained position behind the shuttle, watching for any corporate fighter outside the shuttle bay. His flight would be hardly maneuverable in the confines of the hanger, unprotected if anyone passed through the ship's main shield and attacked the open hanger. Tension ran high.

The *Black King* remained distant, but as far as Steve could tell appeared hardly damaged from the preceding engagement. It was moving closer.

Fighter resistance was light, as Tibs predicted, and Steve gained comfort that their gamble would pay off. Boarding actions in space combat are rare, and always risky... a last ditch tactic every commander preferred to avoid. Combatants were unshielded, lightly armored and without a lifepod to return them to their base.

The *Black King* and *Jade Temple* opened fire almost simultaneously with heavy ship-to-ship coherent beam weapons. The *Jade Temple*'s shields absorbed the hit, but the *Black King*'s shields also held firm.

Evidently Harden was out of missiles, and Kinkaid elected to hold his in reserve in case his opponent's shields failed before the boarding party secured their landing. The swarming Aldebari fighters filled the void between the two ships. As the corporate fighters grew even more rare, Steve could see the Aldebari sweeping in to attack the cruiser's point defenses and anything else that their weapons had a hope of destroying.

On his sensor display Steve saw reinforcements approaching from *Perry Station*, but the number of surviving fighters was pitifully small.

Matsuo headed for the *Black King*'s hanger bay and the escorts took station on each of his quarters, scanning space for danger.

Through all this the two great ships exchanged fire, and each flash of bright fury lit up Steve's cockpit with stark white incandescence. Then Steve noticed the *Black King*'s firing stopped. He increased magnification on his screen to take a closer look, and saw the main weapon pointing right at the assault shuttle. The traverse between the cruisers had been too regular, too predictable.

"Assault group: Evade!" Steve commanded, moments too late. The four escorts reacted promptly, but the shuttle was clumsy. Delaney used his fighter to block the terrible beam of the heavy cruiser's main armament from evaporating the shuttle. There wasn't time for his automated systems to react and shunt his pod. Steve looked toward where Delaney's fighter should have been and saw only glowing fragments.

"No!" screamed Graham. All Steve could say was "Oh, No!" blaming himself for flying too casually. They provided predictable, tempting targets for the cruiser's main gun. Only Delaney's choice of direction had saved their mission, although it cost his life.

The *Black King* continued firing at the shuttle as the group approached, but now they were in evasive mode, maneuvering as unpredictably as possible. This slowed their progress considerably, but helped assure their landing. The cruiser kept trying, clearly recognizing the threat, but her traverse was too slow and couldn't track them well. The shuttle's flight path was too erratic for the cruiser's main armament to reacquire them. The remaining point defenses, vastly more agile, easily acquired them and lit up their shields and armor as they bored toward the hanger bay. Gradually, one by one, the avenging Aldebari fighters silenced even these defenses.

The corporate fighters grew very scarce, eliminated by the Aldebari in the battle to control intervening space.

Graham circled back to mark the location where Delaney had been lost. Dodging salvos from the cruiser, Graham ejected an electronic marker buoy where pieces of Delaney's ship still spun in frictionless space. If Graham survived, he intended to return to leave Delaney's few remaining mementos there with him, especially the holo of his wife and kids who had been lost, with so many others, when the planet was destroyed. It was the only way he could think of to bury his friend in the void.

The Aldebar began assembling their fighters near the *Black*

King's hanger bay like a swarm of angry wasps, awaiting the marine assault to secure the hanger and environs. Once a beachhead was established the fighters could dock, and the pilots could bolster the marines in the boarding assault.

The heavily-armored defenses of the cruiser's secondary weapons would have taken more gunboat-mountable AP missiles than the *Jade Temple* carried, even in stores. The ship-to-ship variants were plentiful, but those could not penetrate the intact and powerful shields: Gunboats would have had to fly the Aldebari armor-piercing missiles inside the shield envelope for them to score. The cruiser's secondary weapons were certainly more nimble than the main armament. Fortunately for the assault shuttle, the very armor that preserved those weapons from neutralization by the Aldebari fighters also slowed their reaction time. Apparently these weapons were universally automated, so the shuttle wouldn't be destroyed by either some human gunner's sheer luck, or by a fire control team's bracketing fire, using predictable projectiles to 'herd' a target into a heavy beam weapon's kill zone.

It quickly became a more harrowing ride than the marines preferred but they kept up their light banter, teasing their pilot as the flat, heavily armored shuttle bobbed and weaved to throw off the predictive fire control of the powerful beams and projectiles.

Tibs came on the comm: "Kinkaid reports *Black King* is accelerating and changing course: We need that hanger secured before she moves too fast for our fighters to board her." Harden recognized his danger, and was eager to avoid any chance at defeat and possible capture.

"Understood, sir", Matsuo acknowledged, and the shuttle put on a burst of speed, reducing evasive maneuvering to try and land the marines there in time. If they could secure the hanger the Aldebar might win this fight, but if they failed Steve believed Harden would return until he satisfied his vendetta. He would certainly never present this opportunity again.

On the other hand, Steve thought, if Harden reached flank speed before the hanger could be secured, then Matsuo and his marines would be trapped, severely outnumbered, and eliminated.

Steve ran some calculations on his onboard systems and came up with an eight minute window to secure the hanger and permit most of the fighters to board. He transmitted his calculations to

Matsuo, who responded with his own estimate. The timeline didn't differ, except it included a set of timed tactical objectives to accomplish the mission.

Sweeping toward the open hanger, the assault shuttle left the cruiser's main armament's line of fire. The closer it came to the cruiser's broad hull, the fewer secondary emplacements could acquire the shuttle as a target. Their speed increased and their course straightened. A couple of Aldebari fighters hovered outside the damaged hanger doors looking for targets inside the hanger but, except for one Aldebari light fighter that appeared to have become stuck somehow between the bay doors, the fighters pulled back as the assault shuttle approached. The wide-bodied assault shuttle was flat enough to fit into the aperture left by the damaged doors, but the fighters were too tall. Steve could only watch as the shuttle's turret pivoted, acquired a target just inside the hanger, and fired. Then it acquired a new target and fired again as the shuttle settled to the deck. The aft hatch opened downward to form a ramp and the marines rolled out in their exoskeletal assault machines. The cruiser dropped the atmospheric shield and the hanger was opened to hard space, but the wheels of the heavy exoskeletons gripped the deck preventing them from being dislodged by the sudden evacuation of atmosphere into space.

Designed for boarding actions, a heavily armored crawler essentially fills a corridor as it moves. The marines mount them prone, feet back, resting on belly and chest to leave their arms and shoulders free to control movement and fire the heavy weapons. Infantry move along behind them, shielded by their armor. When the assault Crawlers came to a hatch or bulkhead door they could fold back their armor plating enough to fit through most doors, and step the wheels through like feet. They could even scale stairs.

The most effective counter to the Crawler is emplaced explosives. But aboard ship it is challenging to find places to set that sort of trap.

Lt. Matsuo directed his squad leaders to take up three defensive positions around the hanger. Then he moved over to an array of electronic panels and conduits with a case of electronics. He was joined by two lightly armed technicians. The marines were taking light small arms fire, but the weapons arrayed against them were not plentiful.

Five minutes passed, and Matsuo appeared stumped by

something in his electronics.

~

That fighter wedged in the hanger bay's blast doors was Bobby's. He was no longer in it.

Bobby had seen the hanger bay's flashing amber warning lights turn red through the atmospheric shield, and the damaged doors begin to slowly move shut. He impulsively edged his light fighter between them, to stop the doors. There was no guarantee they would stop. They might slice through his little ship like scissors through plastic. He reassured himself that there would be a safety override, believing no corporation would leave itself open to a wrongful death and dismemberment lawsuit over the accidental closing of the hanger doors. In truth, of course, he acted on instinct, before thinking.

Bobby recognized the foolhardiness of his action, but for him the prospect of death seemed unreal. He could not quite accept death as a simple biological cessation, a permanent winking out of self-awareness. Even the laws of physics could be construed to mean his parents could somehow have continued on, and that he could continue on with them. Maybe his 'energy' would somehow be conserved as a coherent, self-aware being. He mentally chastised himself for holding such an absurd sentiment. It was imbecilic, he thought to himself, to imagine that consciousness continues beyond the death of his organism. And yet his belief persisted. But every time an opportunity arose to leap into the hungry jaws of danger, Bobby invariably jumped. He shook his head in disbelief.

It turned out that Bobby was right about the safety features built into corporate industrial machines. As the doors met the resistance of the fighter's armored hull the safety solenoids were triggered, shut down the hydraulics, and brought the massive doors to a stop.

Not that the scout would ever fly again. The pressure from the heavy doors sprung the little ship's small emergency hatch, breaking its seal but preventing any possibility of opening. The massive doors also broke the canopy from its seals, allowing Bobby to escape quickly into the hanger by crawling out in his environmental suit. In the artificial gravity he dropped lightly to the deck.

His comm relay with the rest of the Aldebari network had lost signal.

Out in the open, he quickly slipped behind some nearby conduits and metallic housings. He crept farther in, taking shelter behind some rocket motors on magnetically secured pallets. His previous experience trying to fish out the fletchette pistol from his utility pocket had led him to slip a strap around its handle, making it readily accessible. It was only now that he realized he couldn't fire it without removing his glove. The atmosphere might soon be pumped out of the hanger, as the flashing amber warning lights had already turned red in warning.

"Well I've done it to myself again," he muttered under his breath inside his helmet and decided moving forward would be better than just hiding. "An exercise of freedom" he muttered. He furtively scanned the hanger for some kind of exit, noting the lighted windows in back, where the silhouettes of people moved about without the encumbrance of a pressure suit. There had to be a way in, he reasoned, but it would only be through an airlock. There were so many red warning lights scattered about the darkened hanger, about to be exposed to the hard vacuum of space. It was difficult, but not impossible, to see. He looked for a door. The door would have to be an airlock for it to open.

Nearby the tell-tale light of an airlock door turned green. Bobby ducked behind the rocket motors just as a two-man security detail in pressure suits entered the hanger and headed for the wreck of his fighter. They stopped suddenly, clearly startled by something outside the bay doors. One pointed in alarm and they scrambled for cover behind some crates stacked between where Bobby hid and his mangled fighter.

Bobby used their distraction to move quickly from his cover into the airlock. He tried to stay low and keep his movement smooth to reduce attention. Once inside he hit the large airlock cycle button, and only then turned to see Matsuo's assault shuttle enter the hanger.

The airlock's outer door closed on his view as the shuttle turret began firing on the men behind the crates.

~

The marines set up defensive positions in the depressurized bay at the three hanger deck airlocks. Their tactical deployment problem was simplified, since the airlocks were only large enough to let a few people through at a time.

Matsuo was feeling his own kind of pressure trying to use his portable ELINT (Electronic Intelligence) unit to hack into the corporate ship's data network. He wanted to try and fully open the bay doors, and possibly even shut down the engines. There was just too much data traffic to get a good sense of logical orientation. If he did the wrong thing, he could suffocate everyone aboard who was unprepared with a respirator. While that would be an efficient way to eliminate the threat of the *Black King*, it would not be Aldebar to commit indiscriminate murder, even if his enemy might not hesitate to do it were their roles reversed. He did not want to win by becoming his own enemy.

While waiting for an inspiration he uploaded a virus into the ship's network that would specifically degrade the ship's digital communications, first the least defended channels and then those more secure.

One of the two tech sergeants with Matsuo walked over to a large, plainly labeled emergency override switch next to the blocked hanger bay door. He looked it over, looked at the crumpled Aldebari fighter next to it, then back at the Lieutenant hunched over his console. The other tech noticed and nudged Matsuo, who looked up, saw the switch, and nodded in the affirmative. The sergeant threw the switch and the doors began to ponderously open. Bobby's crumpled scout ship was caught on the upper door and rose with it. Pulled by the hanger's artificial gravity, the wreck came free and fell to the deck.

Tibs was among the first in, his old gunboat sweeping into the hanger to settle farthest in. Quickly the rest of the waiting Aldebari followed suit before the acceleration of the cruiser could make access problematic.

Steve's fighter settled into the grip of the magnetic moorings on the cruiser's hanger deck. He powered down his systems to standby, unbuckled, disconnected, and pulled the powerful Aldebar coherent beam pulse rifle from its rack. Checking the integrity of his suit systems and establishing his suit's interface with the weapon took just a moment. Then he passed through the fighter's airlock to join the rest of the pilots.

Matsuo double-timed past Steve toward where Tibs was organizing his pilots into squads under each of his flight leaders. The lieutenant reported what he had learned about the ship systems and layout and, after affirmation by Tibs, assumed tactical leadership of the operation. Once he was clear with Tibs on the mission objective Matsuo explained why he didn't take extreme measures against the ship's life support system. Tibs concurred with Matsuo's decision with an approving smile.

"Lieutenant, you have the command decision. My suggestion is that we try and take the bridge to capture or kill Harden and end this threat to the settlement of the people who survived the destruction of the planet."

"I have tactical command, sir. Whichever way we go, these corridors are too narrow for us to bring more than a fraction of our firepower to bear. I'm going to take a chance and divide our forces. I'll leave our heavy weapons squad here to defend the hanger bay and our boats, and take the rest of my Marines and the two crawlers aft to seize engineering. Once he knows we have split our forces I anticipate he will counterattack here to divide us and sever our communications. The heavy weapons team and the assault shuttle turret should provide a very strong defense. As soon as I can secure engineering we will shut down the ship's engines, bring down her shields and neutralize her weaponry. Hopefully we can stop the ship before it gets within range of *Perry Station*. Meanwhile, sir, lead the pilots forward to seize the bridge and take Harden. Between us we should manage to neutralize him one way or another."

Tibs nodded, and turned to his pilots. He motioned to his squad leaders with a gesture to let the rank and file know the plan.

One of the pilots pointed out that the crushed scout ship was empty. Tibs looked at Steve. Both recognized the ship's identification number and knew the missing pilot was Bobby. Steve wondered with dread where his young friend had gone.

Monk Williams' squad was picked to be the first team through the airlock, and they moved out. The rest of the pilots followed.

Lt. Matsuo's first and second squads briefly shook hands with the heavy weapons support squad and turned toward the aft airlock, one exoskeletal unit leading the way and the other to bring up the rear. The defending Heavy squad took up sheltered positions to cover the three airlocks. They paid special attention to the airlock amidships, since those fore and aft should be cleared as the mobile forces advanced.

The marines striking aft toward engineering didn't have enough troops to leave anyone guarding side passages as they progressed, but one of the crawlers moved with them in reverse to cover their back. It slowed their progress, but provided a strong rearguard.

There were enough Aldebari pilots with Tibs to secure his route and flanks on his way to the bridge. Tibs assigned a young Aldebar pilot to complete Steve's squad.

~

Once Bobby emerged from the airlock into the pressurized ship he made swift, reasonably stealthy progress as he sought his way forward. He stashed his flight helmet and pressure suit in an empty locker and memorized its number.

Apparently everyone aboard was either manning a duty station or assembling into a defensive formation to repel the attackers, but there seemed to be confusion among the defenders he successfully bypassed. They tried to use the comms but got no response. They took to assigning people to run messages since communications were down. Bobby would have to be increasingly alert for messengers racing through the corridors with hardcopy orders and situation relays.

As he ran down the long passageway toward the bow of the ship he heard the pounding footsteps of a runner getting close. He tried ducking into a side door but the door was locked. The surprised runner saw him and skidded to a halt. The messenger reached for his sidearm so Bobby raised his weapon and riddled the man with a dozen fletchettes. The weapon's rate of fire made overkill almost unavoidable. Bobby looked at the blood-soaked tatters of the uniform and felt horror, as if he were a spectator and someone else had just pulled the trigger. He had just killed a person, and the gruesome remains that slumped lifeless before him had been someone hardly different from himself.

There was nobody nearby, and in the silence of the hallway his heartbeat was loud, accompanied by the rushing sound of his bloodstream through his veins. He felt fear. There was no spark of life remaining in the young messenger, and Bobby's faith in his own immortality terrifyingly disappeared. He felt like he was going to vomit. His former self-assurance, his wishful immortality construct, construed from the first law of thermodynamics, the preservation of energy, mocked him. Dead is dead.

Bobby shook himself, trying to think clearly. He took stock of what he must do. Alone like this he faced almost certain death, but he was committed and far from his friends. He felt very alone. Bobby chided himself to get a grip. It would be as dangerous now to run back to the security of the Aldebari in the hanger as it would be to go forward on his self-assigned mission. Probably more dangerous since the defenders would be gathering near the boarding party. He hurriedly evaluated his options and decided that if it came down to it, he would rather kill than be killed. But he felt very frightened.

With a sigh Bobby squared his shoulders like he had seen Steve do, and straightened his posture.

There was nowhere close to drag the body, and the pool of blood left by the kill would raise an alarm the first time it was seen. The secret of his presence had been his ally, but it could not last now, and there was nothing he could do about it. He raced ahead with resolve, looking for a side corridor to disappear into, when behind him, much too soon, came a shout of alarm as someone came across the messenger's body.

He broke into a run, trying to keep his footsteps quiet. As he ran, he tried to think of a way to gain an enemy uniform. He felt he might be able to reach Harden if he looked like he was on their side. Of course, Bobby wasn't exactly clear what he would do when he reached Harden. He steadied his breathing and eased his run into a lope and thought of infiltrating through the air vents. The size of the vent grills he saw suggested they were too narrow to use. He had nowhere else to go, so he pushed forward. Whenever he reached a door he would close it behind him.

Bobby stopped a moment to check a side room and heard a heavy cadence of footsteps nearby. Several men were trotting in unison, presumably to catch up to him. He pushed a door open next to him onto a room bracketed by elevators to different decks of the ship. A young man in a clean uniform and no apparent weapon stood near one of the elevators, his mouth open and his were eyes wide in surprise at the muzzle of Bobby's fletchette pistol.

"Take off your jacket, quickly and quietly, and I will let you live" Bobby commanded.

The young man started to object, then thought better of it and began removing the uniform jacket. Bobby made him get into the first elevator that arrived and sent it to the deck below as his own elevator arrived. As he took up the uniform jacket his eyes and hands were steady. He entered the opened elevator and pressed the fifth deck button. He noted that he was on the second deck. So when he was finished, if he could he would need to reach second deck to get back to the hanger, even though his fighter wasn't spaceworthy. The elevator door closed. Bobby pressed the stop button, pausing the elevator's ascent between floors, and quickly removed his flight suit. He donned the corporate uniform jacket, which was not a bad fit. His pants weren't terribly different, and he hoped no one would notice them. Without his flight suit there wasn't a good place to put his weapon except to stick it in his waistband under the jacket. It was uncomfortable, but it wouldn't be obvious and he wasn't going to leave it behind. Then he was unsure what he should do with his bundled flight suit. So he pulled the pistol from his waistband again and wrapped the flight suit around it in his right hand. If needed, he could still shoot. Then he pressed the fifth floor button again and held the bundle as if he were carrying it as part of his messenger duties.

The elevator arrived at the fifth deck and the door slid open onto an empty landing. Bobby released his breath and took a quick look left and right. He no longer had a notion of which direction was forward, and which was aft. He assumed the longer corridors went the length of the ship, so the shorter ones should be port and starboard. There was a sentry down the long corridor to his right. Reasoning the bridge would be guarded more heavily, he turned toward the guard and broke into a trot, as if he intended to deliver important information and knew where to go. As he approached the guard, however, he observed the man suddenly snapped to attention, eyes level. Bobby slowed down warily.

~

It wasn't as fast as simply running, but the well-trained marines executed the over-watch maneuver with their forward crawler making rapid and fairly secure progress. Matsuo found it suspicious that the airlock had been so poorly defended. Only two sentries in pressure suits, and they still had their sidearms holstered when the crawler nailed them. The suspicion nagged at him that their progress had been too easy.

Since leaving the hanger the only fire they had taken was from troops who fought like they were embarrassed to shoot.

Suspicious or not, he had a mission and wasn't going to waste time outsmarting himself. It was always possible that these amateurs simply did not have a clue how to defend. What mattered was getting in, doing the job and getting out. That possibility didn't assuage his feeling that they were about to discover the wrong end of a trap.

Matsuo and his men had to reach the engineering section to shut down the engines as quickly as possible. The ship was accelerating toward *Perry Station*. While *Perry Station* enjoyed reasonably strong defenses they were no match for a heavy cruiser, even with the *Jade Temple* alongside. If he could gain control of the helm he could move the cruiser away from the Station and lessen the danger.

~

Meanwhile, Tibs and the pilots made their way to an elevator lobby almost unopposed. He had reduced the number of pilots in the forward group as they moved, positioning defenders at key intersections along the way.

Steve's group remained with Tibs. Steve figured they still had enough men to get the job done, even if the corporates started to fight back. The question now was whether to pull back the pilots that they had left behind into the main group before assaulting what they thought should be the command deck.

Tibs decided to double the team left defending the elevator on the hanger deck and pull in his flanks and rearguard.

Steve's squad would perform as point team and ascend to the bridge deck while the hanger deck forces assembled. Steve's team would stay together and hold the fifth deck lobby until the rest of the force was up there. It sounded like a sensible plan.

The elevator arrived and the pilots of Perry entered.

~

The sentry was standing at attention under the gaze of an officer who had been out of Bobby's sight. The officer emerged and immediately noticed the arrival of someone who looked like an intern in a regulation jacket but wearing civilian trousers. The intern's shirt also wasn't regulation. His name tag read *Smith*, but this intern's face did not look like his security photo. The officer's eyes narrowed. The boy had not saluted. "Who are you, intern?"

Bobby had no idea what his name tag read. Belatedly he saluted, as he replied "Intern Evans, sir."

The officer nodded, and turned his eyes to the sentry. "Take this intern into custody and bring him with me. Check him for weapons."

Bobby fired, shredding the officer who flung up his arms trying to protect himself. The sentry unlimbered his heavy laser rifle and Bobby fired his fletchette pistol into him. The sentry sagged against the other wall and slumped to the ground. There was blood everywhere. The officer lay still and quiet. Then Bobby pulled what was left of his shredded flight suit away from his pistol, used it to wipe the blood from his face and arms and tossed it aside against the bulkhead. Two growing pools of blood soaked the hallway carpet dark, and wet. For a moment Bobby felt dizzy, and he put a bloody hand to the wall to support himself. He refused to think about those he had just killed, and grimly pushed himself to keep going. He was amazed that the two men had died silently.

Then he opened the door that the sentry had been guarding.

Inside the room Paul Harden faced a bank of monitors on which Bobby could see the Aldebari marines moving smartly with their assault exoskeletal vehicles. When they came to a junction in the hallway the lead would quickly enter it, leaving the one behind to take over point. The articulated chassis and 360 degree rotation on the treads allowed astonishing maneuverability in tight quarters.

In another monitor Bobby saw Steven and his team on foot in an elevator looking nervous. A terrible sense of foreboding gripped Bobby as Harden turned to gaze on him. Harden smirked, looked back to an antique plastic keyboard on his desk, and keyed a command into his console. A beautifully modulated feminine voice announced, "Initiating Hull Breach protocol test in five ... four... three... two... one... Mark."

In the monitors Bobby saw air-tight bulwarks slide down from the ceiling sealing the corridors into sections. The partitions effectively stopped the assault in its tracks and divided the boarding party from one another. In the monitor he also saw Steve look up toward the ceiling as his elevator stopped suddenly.

Harden turned his eyes to Bobby like a predator upon his prey. "Robert Morrison, son of the late Gavin and Elaine Morrison of Paradiso, in Hell's Gate, Board of Corporations space. Your parents worked for me. Through them *my* money paid for your birth and childhood. That makes you *mine*."

Strong arms gripped Bobby from the back and disarmed him. Bobby chastised himself for hesitating. Waiting for crucial information is a liability for anyone who must make an instantaneous decision. He should have determined his decision beforehand and acted upon it at first opportunity.

Harden smiled like a wolf. "In fact, you were raised in my old neighborhood, Robert. That makes us related in a way. You and I are more alike than you probably realize." Bobby thought of those he had killed and felt guilt.

~

The Corporate defenders arrived in force and had Tibs' group pinned down in a savage crossfire at the elevator landing. The pilots took scant shelter in the corners of the room. They were taking fire from the corridors on all three sides, and the situation looked very grim. More than a quarter of his men were down already, caught in an open room without real cover. The floor was slick with blood and the cries of his wounded were an agony. Then the Corporates ceased fire and one of their officers called out, warning they would use explosives unless the Aldebari surrendered.

Tibs knew they wouldn't need to use very many grenades to wipe his remaining force out. He recognized the grenades would not be powerful enough to compromise the hull this deep inside the ship, so the threat was no bluff. He regretfully told his men to throw their weapons into the middle of the room and called out his surrender.

~

Bobby remained silent, not daring to glance away from Harden's gaze and look at what was happening in the monitors. Harden would have noticed, and might have turned to see the Aldebari marines escaping his trap. There was a tapping at the door. The officer who had disarmed Bobby opened the door a crack and briefly conferred with someone outside. "What is it?" Harden asked, clearly unhappy at the interruption of his soliloquy.

"Sir, we have their leader."

Harden brightened. "Ah! Show him in, Michael. Gather up the rest and keep them under guard in case we need them later. Do it efficiently and simply. Don't get fancy. We don't need complications."

While Harden's eyes were diverted, Bobby quickly checked the monitors. The marines were nowhere to be seen, but the bulwark that had stopped them was gone and the hallway where they had been was filled with haze and debris. Steven and his team were still trapped in the elevator probing the ceiling, trying to find an exit. Bobby kept his face neutral but gazed back at Harden in time to meet his returning attention. The door opened and Harden watched his security team bring in Tibs.

"You have disarmed him?" Harden asked. One of the security men showed Harden the heavy pulse rifle Tibs had been carrying. Bobby noticed Tibs still bore his sheathed sword, which vaguely looked like a highly polished, slightly curved walking stick. The Corporates had no idea it was a weapon.

Harden palmed and cocked an expensive looking antique pistol from his desk and motioned the security team out, leaving only the two captives and the officer in the room. Harden glared suspiciously at Bobby, holding his weapon casually on the young man.

Tibs gave no sign that he was armed, but he didn't look intimidated either. Harden kept his weapon on Bobby. Any wrong move would probably have meant the young man's death.

"As I was saying, Robert, we have more in common than you think. We come from the same culture. We share the knowledge that, unlike the mythologies of these poets and priests who have been mesmerizing you... the mythologies woven for you by this charlatan," Harden motioned with the pistol toward Tibs, "the universe is ruled by those who hold power. We have the will and foresight to keep and use power effectively. If you joined with me, then that kind of power could be yours.

"I've read your dossier. They want you for the same reason I want you: your genetic heritage is that impressive. You have potential that should not be wasted, Robert.

"Humanity isn't guided and shaped by a romanticized, anthropomorphic illusion. Those tales are misleading, low-tech distractions aimed at the weak minded. Those myths are for the animals that think they are men, the stinking masses of ignorant people who are little more than tools for those with the vision and talent to use them.

"The religious ideas Tibs has fed you are in fact no more meaningful than the video games and commercialized events we use to entertain and control the ignorant on Paradiso, on Earth, and on every other planet we own. The laws that bind them to our purposes are an adaptation of their own cultural conventions. Those laws were invented long ago, before the real powers of our world reworked the popular conscience. We used our understanding to slip the leash they once thought could control us.

"Their systems of control were insidious, and many remain fooled by them. But wolves like us, Robert, have no tolerance for any such leash. Governance by sheep is artificial, alien to the natural order. It is the predator, and not the prey, who is designed by nature to rule. And rule we now do. It is our evolutionary imperative," he said with a grim smile.

Harden looked keenly at Bobby. "My agents tell me that you somehow blame me for the deaths of your parents, even though it was actually that Perry sheriff who murdered them." He gestured at a monitor that was now empty, but he didn't look at it, and didn't skip a beat. "You helped Tibs persecute me because of what that sheriff did, and enabled Tibs to manipulate the corporations into confiscating my property and doling out my assets to my competitors. But Robert, I am innocent. Your parent's blood is not on my hands. In fact I am the one who has been wronged."

Bobby found Harden's account incongruous and found his voice. "How can you imagine yourself innocent when you murdered an entire planet filled with people who never even knew you existed?"

Harden looked pained. "That wasn't murder, Robert. It wasn't personal, but necessary and unavoidable. Those half million lives did not outweigh the billions of people that will be lost if we don't act now to save them, and that modulinite out there is key to their survival."

"What do you mean?"

"You have no idea the challenge humanity faces. Earth's overpopulation has to be relieved. It's a problem we must solve quickly. I had the solution, but nobody else had the courage to act. I sacrificed those people to save humanity itself. There was no time to waste on negotiation. There wasn't time to figure out how the modulinite could be safely mined. I had to make a life or *extinction* decision, and I chose to save the lives of billions, even at the cost of that one planet.

"It's time consuming to lift great mineral wealth from a planetary gravity well, and we are extremely short on time. So I decided to use my very real power to... redistribute... the mass of that planet. I applied inertia dampening on a grand scale, stopping a quarter of the planet for a moment and allowed the rest of it to disintegrate against that mass. It was fast, relatively cheap, and effective. Those people did not have time to suffer.

"Unfortunately the one planet I had to have, the only planet we could not be without, was inhabited. Their deaths were collateral damage. There was nothing I could do about that. Those people chose to live there. Had I warned them they would probably have mounted a real defense to stop me. And I knew they weren't going to leave voluntarily; they weren't going to abandon all they had worked for no matter how long I negotiated or how much I offered."

Tibs finally spoke up. "They were people, Harden. Each of them had a right to live life every bit as valid as your own. Civilization has advanced because we work together in common cause, for the good of all. Those laws you think so little of are articulations of a social contract. We each give to our governments key personal powers for the sake of the common good."

Harden's eyes grew hard and bright. "I never signed any such contract, Tibs, and real wealth is anything but *common*. Priests like you have manufactured and marketed the myths that kept you in power for thousands of years. Don't preach to me in that sanctimonious tone about your preconceptions of right and wrong. Your myths have caused more death and destruction than any other cause in the history of humanity. Business, in contrast, is efficient and clean. Business is clear sighted, unimpressed by your shamanic mysticism. This design was to save many more lives than were lost on Perry."

"Myths?" Tibs replied. "People need to be able to think freely, to think for themselves, in order that they might explore all options and choose well. To do that they need to be liberated from distractions and learn to question what is told them. That is why we uphold as examples of enlightened education such things as the classic liberal arts. These are not illusions, they are ideas evolved for countless generations. They are the survival tools of civilization. These are more important to humanity than your short-sighted profit margin. They are necessary to ensure our thinking has enough diversity to solve any problem. If all we have are your solutions, Harden, then we will be doomed to failure."

"You haven't the first clue how necessary what I did was, *old man*," Harden sneered, "and free thinking is a stupid frivolity at this point. It wasn't profit that motivated me, no matter what your pitiful free thinking might suggest. Within ten years Earth *must* either kill outright or transport half of our nineteen billion people to other planets or we face global death." Harden took a step toward Tibs, eyes growing fierce. "Imagine starvation, famine, and cannibalism among nineteen billion human beings, Tibs, and you might understand the decision I made."

"There was simply not enough modulinium left to build the ships it would take to carry even one billion people away from Earth to resettle in the time we have left, except for what lay so long unknown, deep in the crust of Perry. Modulinite cannot be mined in atmosphere. It cannot be lifted safely or in sufficient quantity out of the gravity well of the planet. We had to get it into the vacuum of space, Tibs, and we had to do it fast. Your reaction was to pass judgment in abject ignorance, not a '*free thinking*' decision at all.

"I had to do what I did." Harden drew himself up. "There was absolutely no alternative. Now you may think it is inexcusable to destroy a planet on which half million people lived, but I tell you that was nothing! *Nothing!* Compared to watching humanity fall into an extinction-level event in which we might lose nineteen *billion* people in less than ten years' time, a half million is regrettable, but hardly more than that. For every single person who died on Perry I would save almost four hundred thousand people. But you wish to stop me. Earth can no longer grow, harvest, manufacture, or import enough food to feed them all, and the stupid unthinking animals will *still* not stop breeding. Earth. Cradle of *mankind*, will die, Tibs."

"The corporations, and the World Government before them, did all they could to sustain humanity thus far, but we have exhausted all solutions. Already millions riot and starve in Asia, South America, and Africa. Humanity is at our own throats. We cannot wait for your environmental studies. We cannot wait for everyone to negotiate and agree. We must to get enough people off the Earth as soon as possible or we will lose them all." Harden shook his finger at Tibs. "And don't think the unrest would not spread to your people, Tibs. You know you would not escape the repercussions.

"Would you prefer the mass murder of nineteen billion individuals, and lose all their genetic heritage, or an instantaneous and unexpected loss of five hundred thousand? Those are your only choices, Tibs: which do you choose?"

Sensing that Harden really believed what he said, Tibs remained quiet. Harden's pistol was still pointed at Bobby.

Harden continued "Corporate Earth discarded your so-called 'liberal' arts for being completely impractical. They are not only a total waste of time and money, but they are dangerous to our ability to feed and clothe humanity. 'Liberal Arts' should be removed from existence and expunged from history. They cause too much trouble: your mind-tricks, you illusory freedoms, pretending to empower those who should never in a million years be empowered."

Harden seemed to grow more comfortable dealing with intellectual controversy. The redness of his face returned to a more natural hue and his expression looked less stricken. He held the power here, and that fact soothed him. It seemed almost sexual.

"The common people, with their abysmal intelligence, should never be shown truth beyond whatever psychological illusions we must use to guide them into safe behavior. Such tools give power to the corporations, so that the correct decisions are made timely and well. To think about illusory and impossible promises like *freedom* and *democracy* only causes problems they cannot imagine well enough to solve.

"How could any thoughtful person think democracy could ever work well at all? People are stupid, Tibs, and they make stupid decisions all the time! The very word *Liberal* is laughable. Exactly what do your liberals think they are liberating themselves into? Chaos? Bad idea, Tibs. Wasteful ideas lead to inefficiency and bad decisions. People are too easily manipulated. They would cast their votes based on inaccurate information.

"Business rightly rules. Business does not tolerate lies. Business is brutally honest, and business shall rule the galaxy."

Tibs observed, "What is not an abstract idea, Harden, is that you have been killing people. Many people. Whether you think it justified or not, it is neither yours nor ours to decide."

"Today, old man, it is *mine* to decide, and *today* is what matters." Harden looked down in satisfaction to his beautiful antique keyboard to input a command.

~

When the elevator suddenly stopped Steve noticed the ceiling was composed of fiber panels that held the lighting but hid the structural roof of the elevator compartment. He had Graham and Kyle boost him up, steadied by the Aldebar pilot.

Kyle complained that Steve really needed to go on a diet.

The ceiling tile lifted easily. Steve shifted it to the side and found a maintenance hatch he could open. He pulled himself up and motioned for the Aldebar to come up similarly, helping to pull the slender man onto the top of the elevator. They both then reached down to grasp the forearms of the other two and helped Kyle and Graham up.

Steve told Kyle he really should increase his workout schedule to get a little more upper body strength.

On the side of the elevator shaft were the rungs of a maintenance ladder. Steve told his squad that if the elevator started up again they should get onto the top of it as it reached them, and they all began climbing. As Steve passed the fourth deck elevator door he saw that there was a hand wheel that could be used to manually open the inner door. He kept climbing.

Reaching the fifth deck Steve did not immediately open the elevator door, but waited for Kyle to get up and situated for defensive fire. They did not know whether there would be sentries present when the door was cranked open. Steve's shoulders and forearms recovered from his exertion quickly and he began turning the stiff hand wheel.

The hallway inside was deserted at the elevator portal. Steve looked in quickly and pulled his head back quickly, then looked again more slowly. There were bloodstains just past a hatchway down the hall and what looked like a pile of rags against the wall. He entered the corridor quietly. The carpeting helped muffle his footsteps. Kyle, Graham, and the Aldebar followed.

The rags were a heavily damaged Aldebari flight suit, but showed little sign of blood. The carpet and part of a wall were drenched and sticky with blood. It looked like two men had gone down here but their bodies were gone.

Then Steve heard voices behind a nearby door, and motioned his companions to ready themselves.

With everyone in place he kicked open the door. Kyle was in position and moved in quickly, weapon ready and in a crouch. He aimed his weapon and was about to say something when he was shot by someone hiding behind the opened door. Steve threw his shoulder into the door and sent a corporate officer sprawling. Steve fired into him three times with the heavy pulse rifle, then turned to cover the rest of the room. Graham and the Aldebar had Harden in their sights. Tibs and Bobby looked unsurprised, but Bobby moved with no wasted motion to Kyle's side, checking his wounds and pulling his fanny pack medical kit.

Steve commanded "Paul Harden! Drop your weapon. You are under arrest for the murder of the population and destruction of the planet Perry. You have the right to remain silent. Anything you say or do may be held against you in a court of law."

Harden seemed surprisingly calm, even amused. "Well that would be unusual, where I remain silent, Sheriff. But there may be a few impediments to your cute little declaration. Two of them are small and the other is a bit bigger, if a little worse for wear."

"In the first place I am not the one who should be arrested: you are. I am not a criminal, but a hero. I am the one who will save the Earth, and you are the one who will be infamous for standing in my way. I can do what must be done, but you keep getting in the way of my work with your misguided efforts."

"I don't really care what you believe, Harden. You are under arrest and will stand trial before the Law." replied Steve. "Drop the weapon and put your hands behind your head."

"Drop this?" His eyebrows arched. The antique weapon was pointed resolutely at Tibs. "This is the last known M1911 Colt .45 caliber automatic pistol. It's over a thousand years old. The ammunition alone costs me more to manufacture than you make in a year. This pistol is far more valuable than you or your children will ever be."

"Speaking of whom," Harden confided with a smile, "you have very little time left."

Harden briefly looked down at his keyboard and tapped a function key with his left hand, changing the image in the monitor. In that moment Tibs snaked out his long, gently curved sword of utterly sharp steel from its polished burl wood scabbard, and reached out with it.

Taking his cue from Tibs' movement, Steve fired three powerful pulses from his rifle to Harden's center torso, but the shots dissipated in flares of light on a bubble of energy that only became visible when each laser pulse struck it. Harden was wearing a personal shield.

The shield did not recognize Tibs' blade as a weapon, however. As fast as Tibs struck, it was not as fast as a bullet, and it was not coherent energy.

The pistol fell to the desk, cracking its glass surface, and Harden watched the Colt fall in disbelief. His hand was cut deeply by the tip of Tibs' sword, severing a metacarpal and several tendons. Blood surged from Harden's hand and began spilling wetly onto the pistol and desktop. The handsome man howled when he saw it and he gripped his wound tightly to staunch the bleeding. "You sanctimonious bastard!" he snarled at Tibs. Then Harden stamped his foot on the floor.

Immediately the floor beneath him snapped open and he dropped from view.

In the monitor above and behind the desk Steve saw an image revealed by Harden's last keypress. Pat and his children were huddled together in a spartan metal room, but they were in trouble. Kathlyn, Stevie, and Pat were panicking, trying to breathe. They could not get enough oxygen. Pat's eyes looked heavily bruised, as if she had been beaten. Pat was holding Kathlyn and Stevie protectively, looking grimly determined to hold onto consciousness.

"The brig!" barked Tibs. "It will be on the lowest deck!"

Steve burst from the room, at once unbelieving but horrifically desperate. He looked left and right for a way down. There was no time to think of anything but finding the kids and getting them oxygen.

Tibs leaped to the desk to get the keyboard, reaching over Harden's escape shaft. He hit the alt and tab keys, switching applications from the monitors and began searching for environmental controls for the ship. Fortunately Harden had already been logged in. Unfortunately when Tibs found the application to access the ship controls he was challenged for a password he did not have. He did gain access to communications. He broadcast a text message he knew Kinkaid would pick up aboard the *Jade Temple*. "Kinkaid: capture or neutralize that launch immediately!". Tibs knew in his heart that escape tube did not lead to any mere lifepod, but to the captain's yacht.

Unfortunately the virus Matsuo had uploaded into the ship had at long last broken through the Corporate anti-virus defenses and done its job too well. The message failed to transmit. Tibs scowled at the error message.

"Graham, lets get Kyle down to the hanger he needs medical attention. Barnes:" Tibs turned to the Aldebar "Find Matsuo and make sure he is tending to the wounded while securing the rest of the ship."

~

Steve ran back the way he had come, swung into the elevator shaft and began descending the rungs faster than was safe. Holding the handrails loosely he jumped down five rungs at a time until his hands became too abraded by the friction. Then, disregarding the pain of his blistered palms, he descended to the elevator and beyond one rung at a time. He passed the open doors of the hanger deck and finally reached first deck, dropping the last meter completely out of breath.

Driving himself beyond normal endurance limits, he wrenched the hand wheel as fast as he could and squeezed himself into a gap still too narrow. He forced himself through with a great groan and fell onto an uncarpeted hallway floor. He faced a metal hatch battened tightly shut, but it could be opened using another hand wheel. This wheel spun easily, and he quickly opened the hatch. He spotted the brig, but a warning red LED glowed bright next to the door. The door refused to open, locked because of a detected atmospheric pressure differential.

"NO-o-o-o!" he cried in despair, trying to open the door. "NOO-o-o! He cried against the immovable steel door, the gray metal bulkhead, and the glaring red light. Steve pulled his sidearm and fired five pulses into the door trying to make holes for some ventilation but the holes immediately filled with a meteorite sealant sandwiched between its layers. Uselessly he threw his shoulder into the door until it hurt too much to do again, and then, beyond exhausted, leaned against it, sagging, unwilling to give up but having no other option present. "No..." he weakly moaned, his cheek skidding down the smooth metal. He despaired, but refused to give up. In fury he rejected impossibility and looked with wet unfocused eyes toward the ceiling.

"Jesus, Mary, and Joseph help me!" he called fiercely. "Lord God, help me *Now!*" In frustration he cried, and beat upon the door with both fists.

The malevolently red LED turned a beautiful green with the sound of a welcome chime. He gasped, amazed, and said in a whisper 'Thank you!' as he threw open the door.

~

In engineering Lieutenant Matsuo had meticulously slowed and then reversed the cruiser's engines to bring it to a stop, but maintained gravitics and life support. He sighed with relief, because it had looked for a few minutes they might collide with *Perry Station*. He then noticed an odd discrepancy on Engineering's large graphical display. The floor plan of the brig section on deck one was blinking red. Life support there had been cut off. Considering anyone in the brig might be a friend, he restored their air.

~

Pat and the children were huddled together, unconscious but breathing. Pat held Kathlyn, and Kathlyn had her arms protectively around her little brother. Pat had swollen discoloration around her eyes, evidence that she was recovering from a recent concussion.

As Steve checked pulses, Pat stirred and opened her blackened eyes, recognizing his face. "Steve?"

"Are you able to walk, Pat? We have to get you and the kids to safety, and you should be examined by a doctor as soon as possible."

Pat started trying to put her hair in place. "I look that bad, do I?"

"No, I..."

"Kidding Steve: I was at Sandy's on Oberon. Two men knocked me out. I woke up here with the children." Pat told him. "They are great kids, Steve."

"Yeah, I know. Thank you. Where's Sandy?"

"I don't know, Steve. I was talking with her on the porch viewscreen when the two men jumped me. That's all I know, Steve, I'm sorry."

"Can you help me get the children out of here?" Steve checked his daughter, who seemed to be coming around. His son was also beginning to stir.

Kathlyn's eyes fluttered and focused on him. She wondered aloud "Daddy?" She weakly reached her slender little arms up toward him.

"Oh, Daddy!"

Steve smiled down on her with calm, thankful eyes. "Hi, little one: How's my darling?" he said to her quietly, and she opened her arms wide, flowed into his caring embrace, and held onto him as if she would never let go.

~

Paul Harden immediately accelerated away from the cruiser the

Aldebari had captured, keeping the ship between his personal yacht and the Aldebar attacker.

His right hand hurt badly, and he feared the loss of blood might hamper his ability to maneuver and deploy decoys against the inevitable missiles that would soon target him. He did not want to leave his fate to the yacht's autopilot, so he remained at the helm. It would take a miracle to survive this day, and he hoped he might help make that miracle happen.

To his growing amazement the Aldebar ship showed no awareness of his escape. His small craft was now rapidly approaching the probable edge of their detection range.

Harden, never one to question luck, could only assume that somehow the *Jade Temple* failed to receive warning of his escape.

Immediately after the two ships receded out of his sensor range, he set course for a point far outside Al Najid system that was already logged into the astrogation suite of his yacht's main computer.

Harden painfully removed the restraints on his acceleration couch and rose unsteadily, barely avoiding a lapse in consciousness from blood loss. He recovered his balance and some clarity and released the back of the acceleration couch to stagger toward the yacht's living quarters. He steadied himself against a bulkhead to unseal the hatch and enter, not bothering to close it behind him. To his immediate left was the sterile emergency medical station. He tried to open the plastic seal that kept impurities out, but to open it normally required the use of his right hand. Exasperated, he held the plastic sheeting in his teeth and with his left hand pulled away at the sealed seam until it finally parted. By then he was breathing heavily and could feel his blood-soaked bandage seeping again. Uncaring and very weary he collapsed onto the treatment couch, automatically triggering the medical station's active circuitry. The artificial medical intelligence system immediately powered on its sensors and began diagnosing it's patient's condition. He felt the pressure of something cold on his arm and the pain receded along with his consciousness.

It would be six days before reached his first way point.

Epilogue

Liam was in a good mood as he keyed in the path pattern for the floor polisher, then set out ahead of it to remove any stray litter missed overnight by the automated sweeper. More people were showing up, fresh from their morning ablutions, skin flushed with the traditional high-gravity morning exercise. It was a good morning, and Liam' eyes twinkled as he greeted the early risers cordially, some of them clearly still asleep, others bright and alert.

Liam was pleased by his new contract with the Station administration for his nascent janitorial business. The command interface for his new floor polisher worked as it should, and his floor sweepers operated flawlessly through the artificial nights to sweep away wrappers and other light trash, only to deposit their gleanings and park themselves for their daily maintenance cycle. His sons' technical jobs were providing them and their families respectable incomes and had a plan to move their families into new quarters, and over breakfast his daughter shared the news that her social forum on the Station net had attracted more advertising revenue from two Corporate firms and a Legion political lobby.

So it was no wonder he was whistling an old favorite as he walked down the well-lit hallway. Everything appeared to be going right.

He stopped at a locked door, looked back toward the now-distant floor polisher working its way toward him, and reached for his communicator. He scanned the door's address plate and checked for the keycode in memory, then transmitted the keycode into the receiver. The door popped ajar and a light illuminated the small room. Liam entered looking for anything out of place on the floor. It was a small office with another door on the back wall: he opened that door to a small closet. On a shelf were battery packs, recordable holodiscs and other portable data storage media, and a bottle half full of a California brandy. Everything looked in order so he left the doors open for the floor cleaner, and moved further down the hall to the next locked door.

It had been a gamble, he knew, selling his old business on Earth while it was still profitable, and then moving his extended family on his personal dime out into the farthest reaches of space to Perry Station, suspended above the remains of a destroyed planet. A big risk, but it looked like it would pay off nicely, and he still had almost half his profits from the original sale earning a modest dividend in a diverse portfolio of stocks and rare metal futures on Earth's Central Market.

So it was with a light heart that Liam entered the apparently empty dry dock, nodding to a grumpy Chief Mackenzie. He noted a few tools were unaligned with McKenzie's customary sense of organization and needed cleaning. He pulled a soft cloth from the hip pocket of his coverall and began polishing the tools one by one and putting them back where they belonged.

By agreement with the council and more importantly, Chief Mackenzie, this is where Liam would complete any necessary repairs on his equipment.

Mackenzie stood in frustration, his face slightly flushed and blood pressure slightly elevated. The strange object Steven had found among the asteroids baffled him. It was so effectively concealed Mackenzie found himself doubting it was even there. The thing didn't emit any radiation and made no noise. It could not be felt other than as an adamant resistance to penetration. If he measured the volume and density of the atmosphere in the dry dock before the object was there he could measure its displacement, but that small victory was scant compensation for the complete denial to understanding how the thing worked or what in heavens it even was. He rubbed his face with two clean meaty hands wearily, trying to tame his sense of frustration.

Behind him Liam was whistling an old tune called '*Red River Valley*', appreciating the acoustics in the hanger as he polished the already impeccably clean tools one at a time and replaced them into their assigned places. Mackenzie's universe was symmetric and perfectly organized. Everything in its place... except this one alien object. Stifling a yawn and yearning to stretch, Mackenzie stopped rubbing his face with his palms. When he took his hands away from his eyes and his vision cleared he realized he was looking at a silvery gray spacecraft of obviously alien design. Her lines were clean and elegant. He noticed little wings or maybe fins standing out from it fore and aft. Heat dissipation was his first intuition.

Liam, behind him kept whistling, busy with the tools. He hadn't yet noticed the revelation, as neither it nor Mackenzie had yet made a noise. Then, just as unexpectedly, the slender silver spacecraft vanished once more, and Mackenzie began cursing mightily, stamping around in a small circle with his fists bunched. Liam stopped what he was doing to look around in surprise, whistle trailing off. Mackenzie stared hard where the silvery craft had been... and still was, really. His brow furrowed, and he slowly turned back to gaze at Liam.

Mackenzie calmly stepped over to a monitor and entered a few commands. First he saved the imagery to storage, then played back the scene. On the screen appeared a two dimensional image of the hanger interior, with him rubbing his face. Liam appeared in the background turned away, facing the tool bench. Liam stepped up behind the Chief to watch the screen just as the silvery spacecraft appeared on the monitor, and Mackenzie stopped the recording to hold the image there. Liam gave a low whistle of amazement. Mackenzie cycled through non-visible spectra images, then back to visible. With a finger on the controller wheel he increased magnification, centering on the most visible fin, trying to imagine what it might be intended to do. It wasn't an airfoil for descent into atmosphere. Mackenzie resumed the video at half speed until the ship turned invisible once more. When the image of the ship vanished there was no demarcation for where the edge of the shield actually extended, but Mackenzie had a hunch the surface exactly matched the outer edge of the fin.

"What do you think, Liam?" Mackenzie asked.

Liam was quiet for a moment. "I don't know what to make of it, chief."

Mackenzie nodded. "I think Steve was right: we need to get those scientists in here." He was fully convinced he needed to follow up on the recommendation for the council to call in leading scientists to investigate the spacecraft, but after so many hours of frustration trying to open it his curiosity was overwhelming. He knew intuitively that somehow the tune Liam had been whistling had triggered the shields to power down and open the access hatch. He estimated the hatch had been about four feet off the deck when it opened, so he went to the side of the hanger and picked up a step ladder, then asked Liam to whistle 'Red River Valley" once more.

Liam was a bit anxious and began whistling in a slightly elevated key. His mouth was dry with anticipation. His whistling was different, and the shields remained in place unresponsive. Mack wasn't tone deaf but he also wasn't a musician, so he didn't immediately recognize what was wrong. Despite his rising ire, a rebirth of his frustration, he decided to replay the whistling as recorded on the surveillance system. He reversed the recording and then played the sounds of Liam' original rendition through the speakers and it did the trick: the shields vanished once more. The hatch was still open. Mack stopped the playback before the whistle could reactivate the shield.

"Grab me that torch from the workbench hook, Liam." he asked, meaning a flashlight. He opened the step ladder under the hatch and stood on the first step examining the metal and machining of the hatchway itself while Liam complied.

Liam was quick to go grab the powerful flashlight from the workbench. This was exciting stuff to him, as it would be to anyone. This discovery was going to make the headlines across the galaxy when the news broke. Humanity had been baffled for centuries that, despite the presence of the moduli, there had never been any other sign of intelligent non-human life anywhere. This was a monumental event, but there were no other witnesses for the historical record yet. The monitoring record that was always running was inadequate to the occasion.

"Mack, I think we should at least let the council know what's happened before we do this." he advised.

The Chief replied in a distant voice that told Liam he wasn't listening "Uh huh. Yeah, you're right." as he took the next careful step up the ladder, flashlight in hand and an eager look on his face. His head and shoulders disappeared into the hatchway. "Hey. There's a ladder up here that wasn't extended. I think your whistle didn't..." Suddenly the Chief made a little barking noise and the toes of his shoes slipped from the step to barely catch their tips on the three ladder rungs below to the floor as he swore "JESUS H. CHRIST!" as he came down, his face white as a sheet. He stamped his feet in a tight little circle, arms defensively rigid, his shoulders were hunched, and he was swearing like a sailor until he calmed himself.

"What was it, Chief? What did you see?" asked Liam with concern.

The Chief shook his head vigorously at him 'Not now!" and raised his wrist communicator, keying into its holographic keyboard the number he needed. It was a direct call to Councilor Lyman, despite the early hour.

Liam decided that since nothing had swarmed out of the hatch and Mackenzie wasn't running for his life, he should take a look for himself. He went over to the step ladder and set his foot on the first step, half expecting the Chief to tell him to stop, but the chief was already talking excitedly to a sleepy Councilor Lyman. Taller than the chief, his head was already fully inserted into the hatch, which shielded somewhat the sounds of Chief Mackenzie talking on his comm set and gave the atmosphere a hollow echo that rang of metal. The sound from above him was comparatively dull and silent.

As Liam looked up he saw there was some light up there. He saw the rungs of a ladder that had not extended when the hatch opened. He supposed that his whistle was misinterpreted somehow by the spacecraft, but his whistle had been incomplete since the ladder had not extended.

Liam took the next step up, and the cabin lights inside the craft came on, bright and strong, revealing what had startled the Chief so badly, but for which Liam was better prepared.

He had seen things like it in nature holos. It's eyes were sunken and closed in a head that looked man-sized, but the facial features were like those of a lizard. Delicate bronze-ivory scales on its face tapered into what appeared to be feathers on its head and down its back. It had a very long neck with broad, articulated scales on its throat, like the underbelly of a snake. The creature was as large as a man, though now it looked dry and shrunken, as if it had been dead a very, very long time and dried, instead of rotting. It had strong claws on its sandaled feet, but on the ends of its forelegs were a pair of delicately scaled hands with powerful claws on the thumb and fourth finger.

Liam backed down the ladder to the floor, still amazed. Chief Mackenzie was in heated discussion with the Council while all members hurried to see.

Made in the USA
Las Vegas, NV
30 January 2023

66474313R00144